THE CARE AND FEEDING OF ROGUES

A LADY'S GUIDE TO ROGUES
BOOK I

LAUREN SMITH

For Andrea Hamblin who graciously donated money to the Richardson Literacy program. Our daring, brave and intelligent heroine was named after Andrea's beloved niece Elise.

PROLOGUE

ENGLAND, 1870

Prospero Harrington hated the dawn. It brought too many regrets, too many thoughts of a life too short, a life he hadn't even had a chance to live. As he watched the purple velvet of what might be his final night alive fade, he wished *this* dawn would never come.

The field he stood on was quiet. Only a few songbirds dared to sing as the pink and red hues of the sky became striated with gold light and wisps of vaporous clouds. He drank in this sight and burned it into his mind, knowing that in just a few short minutes that mind might go dark forever.

The trail of darkened footprints behind him where he had disturbed the silver netting of dewdrops in the grass was the only evidence of his trespass. What else would be left of him as a legacy when this dawn had passed to sunny midday? Would he be buried in a lonely field far from a churchyard, or would his parents see his body laid to rest in the family tomb? The thought of being alone, resting in a quiet place where no one could find him, made his throat ache.

I wanted so much more from life than this, he thought bleakly. *I'd only begun to taste the joys and pleasures of this bright and beautiful world* . . .

"If we're caught participating in an illegal duel and Jackson dies, you'll be facing a murder charge... Are you sure about this?" Nicholas Hughes, the Earl of Durham and one of Prospero's closest friends, asked as they stood waiting for the pair of men coming toward them from the opposite end of the field.

"I'm not sure about anything anymore," Prospero muttered. The weight of his pistol felt as heavy in his hand.

Nicholas squared his shoulders and cleared his throat as the other two men reached them.

"Morning, gentlemen," Nicholas greeted solemnly.

Prospero said nothing. He simply stared at the one who had caused all this trouble.

"Mr. Jackson, your pistol please." Nicholas held out a hand to inspect the weapon.

Aaron Jackson handed his gun to Nicholas. John Gower, the man beside Jackson, held his hand out to Prospero.

"Your weapon, Harrington," Gower demanded, and Prospero handed his gun over to Jackson's second. The pistols were carefully examined and returned. Prospero wanted to toss his to the ground, tell the other man he never planned to fire, but he held silent. Jackson wouldn't let him off so easy, not when he believed in Prospero's guilt.

"Are we certain this matter cannot be settled in another way?" Nicholas asked. Jackson had been the one to initiate the challenge of the duel, and he could stop this at any point and consider his honor satisfied.

"No. Harrington compromised my beloved sister and will not marry her."

Prospero gritted his teeth. "If someone slipped into your sister's bed, it wasn't me. I know she's set her cap for a countess's coronet, but I'll be damned if I give it to her like this when I've done nothing to her."

He had nothing against the lady. She was pretty and had seemed like a nice enough lady when he'd danced with her. But Prospero was barely twenty-two. He didn't want to settle down and marry yet, so he'd been damned careful around any young lady who was on the hunt for a husband. As an earl's son, he was considered quite a catch. He had stolen some kisses since he'd been let loose upon London, but none of those kisses had been with Jackson's sister, and he'd *certainly* never gotten a woman with child. If it wasn't so embarrassing to admit, he would have told Jackson he was still a damned virgin.

"The bastard won't admit it, so I demand satisfaction for my family's honor." Jackson's tone was icy.

"Very well," Gower said. "You will stand back-to-back, take forty paces apart, and then you will turn and face each other. On the count of three, you will fire once."

Prospero turned his back on Jackson, and they each counted their paces. Then they turned. Despite the fact that three other men stood in the field with him, Prospero felt utterly, completely alone.

Prospero drew in a deep breath as he angled his body to make himself as slender a target as possible. He tried not to think about his parents, about how this was all a terrible mistake. Why couldn't the Jackson girl have told her

LAUREN SMITH

brother that someone else had taken her to bed? Why the devil had she said it was him? He had done nothing wrong, yet he might perish today for a man's pride. He did not raise his weapon, however. He wanted no death on his conscience or blood upon his hands.

"On the count of three, you will fire," Gower called out. "One . . . Two . . ."

Prospero once more filled his lungs with air and prepared himself to meet his end. He tried not to think of the regrets he had of things he'd never done, cities he'd never seen, women he'd never kissed.

"Three!"

Crack!

Pain lanced through Prospero's upper arm, but he didn't believe the wound to be fatal. He grimaced as Nicholas ran toward him.

"How badly are you hurt?" Nicholas asked.

"It hurts like a damned devil, but I believe I'll live." His shoulder felt numb, which must be the shock from the wound, but he was alive. It was over.

"You made it," Nicholas murmured. "You made it." His friend was grinning with relief as he touched Prospero's good shoulder with a shaky hand. "Thank Christ. I don't know what I would have done if you hadn't."

Good old Nicholas, he thought as his knees buckled a little. It was going to be a long walk back to the coach, but if his friend helped him, he'd make it.

Suddenly, Jackson cursed loudly at him. "Fire your weapon, Harrington!" he bellowed.

Breathing hard, Prospero simply tossed his pistol on the ground and turned his back on the other man. He was done. He wasn't going to stay here. Honor had been satis-

4

fied. Now he could go home and return to his life, to the future he'd so longed for.

"Blood has been drawn, my friend. Let him go," Gower counseled Jackson. "You had your chance."

"It's not enough!" The sudden rush of footfalls was Prospero's only warning as he spun to face the other man.

Jackson had picked up Prospero's pistol from the ground and had the barrel aimed at his own chest.

The relief he'd basked in so briefly was now drowned by a sudden wave of rage. How could this fool think to force him to fire when it wasn't *his* honor that had been damaged? He wasn't going to do anything to ruin his life, not when he just wanted to leave this damned field. Jackson's lip curled in a contemptuous sneer.

"You're a coward, Harrington. Face me and take your shot!"

Coward? He was no coward. Prospero slowly walked back toward Jackson and stopped when they were almost toe to toe.

"What the bloody hell do you want from me, Jackson? I'm bleeding and your honor has been satisfied," Prospero snarled as he clutched his wounded arm.

"Take your shot, Harrington," Jackson growled. "Or I will. Either way, you'll be damned."

"You're mad."

"Take it, or there will be consequences for everyone you love," Jackson warned.

"Are you threatening me?"

"I am. Now take your shot," Jackson said, his voice so cold it could have frosted the air between them.

Prospero pushed the pistol's handle, trying to turn the barrel away from both of them, and something happened in that instant he had not expected. The pistol fired, and birds shrieked in the distant woods. Jackson's face drained of color and blood bubbled between his lips as he coughed. Then he grunted and the pistol fell to the ground between them.

Jackson groaned and sank to his knees. "You've . . . killed me . . ."

"No, no, I didn't!" Prospero protested, but as his opponent fell onto his back, he saw a hint of a smile lingering on the dying man's lips.

This was a trap. Jackson had wanted this all along . . . but why? Why would he want to be killed? It didn't make any sense. How could he want to destroy someone bad enough to . . . to kill himself?

"We've got to go—" Nicholas grabbed his arm and pulled him back from Jackson. "Gower will tell everyone you killed him."

"But I didn't. You saw what happened."

"I did, but you were both struggling with the gun. It still looks bad. Even if you don't face charges for dueling, you will still be a pariah in society for participating." Nicholas dragged Prospero away from the field. "We must go, *now*."

Gower shouted after them, but they were running fast and they heard no sounds of pursuit behind them.

Dawn now bathed the trees in golden fire. A flock of starlings banked and turned in the air, and the sudden flutter of a thousand wings made an eerie sound in the previously serene landscape. As the birds flew toward the east, he had the sudden desperate urge to follow them, to be free of the storm that was coming his way.

ENGLAND, 1882 – TWELVE YEARS LATER

Elise Hamblin raised her skirts with one hand as she climbed the steps up to the townhouse at 223 Baker Street, her heart growing lighter with every step. Just beyond this door, a world of possibilities awaited. A brass plaque hung to the right of the door with the words "*Societas Rebellium Dominarum* – Established 1821" on it.

Every Monday afternoon, she came here to meet with the other members of the private society. The name was as close in Latin as they could get to "The Society of Rebellious Ladies." She rang the bell, and the butler in charge of the residence answered the door.

"Good afternoon, Miss Hamblin," Mr. Atkins greeted warmly.

"Hello, Atkins." She winked at the butler fondly as she stepped inside and removed her hat and gloves before passing them to a waiting footman. "How many do we have today?"

"Today? Just you, Lady Cinna, and Miss Tewksbury. The rest are still on assignment and will report back next week, I believe." Atkins, despite his appearance as a stodgy old man, was quite supportive of the society's efforts to spread intellectual studies among women. It certainly helped that his daughter, a woman who would have otherwise been bound for a life of service as a maid, was studying engineering and had far more career opportunities than a woman in her position would have had without such an education.

"Ah yes, that's right. Thank you, Atkins." Elise proceeded up the stairs to the drawing room, where Cinna and Edwina, her friends, would be waiting for her.

As the president of the society, she was tasked with keeping up with the assignments the members took, but this past week she had been busy with daughterly duties for her father and purchasing a fine new racehorse. Between hosting dinners for her father's business partners and researching the various breeding stallions and mares, she had been quite busy. At twenty-six, she had grown into the hostess role quite well, but it wasn't her preferred way to spend her time. She lived for the society's meetings, chances to explore the world around her and even attend horse races. She had a thousand exciting dreams that held her heart and none of those existed in the domestic sphere.

She traced the edges of a gold plaque that decorated the wall next to the drawing room with her finger. It read: *All those who seek to learn are welcome here.*

Inside, she found her two friends in a lively debate. Lady Cinna Belmont was showing off a design for a bridge, while Edwina Tewksbury argued about the bridge supports it would need.

"Yes, but if you add the height of the cables here—" Cinna's dark hair tumbled down her shoulder as she leaned in. "Then you can see how it could support the bridge."

Edwina peered over her shoulder at the paper, her lips pursed. "Well, I suppose it might work. We should test it with scaled models first, shouldn't we?"

"Nonsense. The math is sound. I'd stake my life on it." Cinna glanced up as Elise closed the door to the drawing room. "Elise, what do you think?" She turned the drawing on the table toward Elise so she could see it as she approached them.

It was a lovely cable-stayed bridge design. Elise was no skilled engineer like Cinna, but in her time at the society, she had learned far more about engineering than other ladies.

"I'm sure your calculations are correct, but one can never be too careful. Perhaps a model is the right place to start?" Elise said. "Just to test the strength before we send the proposal to Jacobs and Ellicott?" Jacobs and Ellicott was the engineering firm that Cinna secretly submitted her designs to under a male pseudonym.

"Oh, all right then," Cinna sighed. "Is it time for the meeting?"

"Yes." Elise collected the latest reports from their members from a nearby table. "Atkins will be up with tea and sandwiches soon. Shall we begin?"

Elise chose a seat on the couch beneath portraits of two of the society's founding members, Audrey Sheridan and Lysandra Russell. They, along with others, had founded the society in 1821 to give women a safe place to learn, share ideas, and advance themselves in academic, scientific, or artistic endeavors.

It was the only society of its kind that they knew of, and its membership was kept quite secret. Much like the gentlemen's clubs, they required prospective members to apply for membership, but not everyone was accepted. Those who were turned down were applicants more interested in the excitement of engaging in something they saw as novel or even forbidden, rather than growing their intellectual knowledge. The society had no other restrictions. The women who joined needed to crave knowledge of some kind.

Half of the society's members were married, and many had children, while the rest were single women or widows. Plenty had found it possible to continue to make time for the society despite having husbands or children. Elise, Cinna, and Edwina were single and spent far more time at the society's townhouse on Baker Street than the other members. It was rather fun to have their own place to hide from the world, just as the gentlemen had their clubs when they wanted to hide from their wives.

"I call to order this meeting of the Society of—" Elise's preamble was interrupted by the shrieking strains of a violin. It pierced the walls between the society's headquarters and the townhouse next door.

"Oh, good heavens," Elise muttered.

Cinna covered her mouth with her hand to stifle a laugh, and Edwina let out an unladylike curse that made the others giggle. The violin was so loud that it was quite impossible to continue their meeting.

"Whose turn is it this time?" Cinna asked as the violin continued to shriek like a cat with its tail stuck in a door.

"I can't remember," Elise sighed. "Shall we play stone, paper, and scissors?" They had recently discovered the Far Eastern game of hand gestures to settle their disputes. It was a tradition that had existed in Asia since the seventeenth century but had only just found its way to England. The three of them leaned forward into a huddle and balled their right hands into fists in their left palms.

"One, two, three," Elise counted as they tapped their fists into their palms, then each chose a hand gesture to represent a stone, a piece of paper, or scissors.

"Blast!" Elise said. She had stone, while Cinna and Edwina both had chosen paper.

"Good luck with our neighbor," Cinna called out cheekily as Elise stood and proceeded out of the society's headquarters and headed for the residence next door.

The woman who answered the door was a plain, middle-aged creature, but she had the most gentle and caring soul Elise had ever known. She had often shared afternoon tea with this woman and commiserated over the man she was about to confront.

"Hello, Elise dear," the woman greeted.

"I'm so sorry to bother you, Mrs. Hudson. Can I speak to *him*?" She nodded toward the stairs, where the loudest strains of the violin were now coming from.

"Yes, of course. He's in a mood, though, dear."

Elise was well-versed in their eccentric neighbor's mercurial moods. She marched upstairs and opened the man's study without bothering to knock. She'd learned long ago that the courtesy of knocking would only be ignored, and so she had taken to responding to this man's rudeness with her own.

The study was dimly lit, the curtains pulled tight across the windows. A red damask wallpaper filled the room with shadows. Books teetered precariously on poorly crafted shelves, and a large black bear rug dominated the floor, the beast's face aimed toward the door, its mouth open in a silent roar at anyone who dared enter the room and disturb its master. Little bottles with labels such as borax, copper sulfate, chloroform, and a dozen others were tucked in surprisingly neat rows beside a chemist's table that lay unused. Thankfully, it was empty of any current experiments. Usually, malodorous scents drifted up from several glowing glass beakers.

A man stood in the corner of the room by the fire, a violin upon his shoulder as he drew a bow over the taut strings of his instrument.

The slender dark-haired man abruptly ceased playing and turned toward her, revealing his aristocratic features that were both harsh and handsome.

"Miss Hamblin." He spoke in a clipped tone as he greeted her. "To what do I owe the pleasure of this visit?" His gaze roved over her, not with any masculine interest, but in simple curiosity. She knew it was one of his favorite parlor games, for him to prepare an impressive list of things to tell her about herself.

"If you're bothering to ask me that, Mr. Holmes, you are not the genius detective that the papers make you out to be."

"Ah yes. Society's *rebellious* ladies—quite a charming little club you have." His tone was completely condescending in an attempt to rankle her.

Elise didn't give the man the satisfaction of letting him see her bristle.

"And what is today's illustrious topic of discussion? The finding of husbands?"

She scoffed. "We study far more important matters than husband hunting, as you well know."

He abandoned his violin on a nearby sofa, which was covered with stacks of newspapers, and retrieved his cherrywood pipe. He stuffed it with tobacco and lit it, then puffed the smoke into his cheeks for a long moment as he watched her like she was a puzzle to be solved. She wasn't perturbed by this. They'd had this battle of wills before.

"Let's see," he drawled in his famous tone as he began his favorite game. "You're not wearing your usual style of unadorned walking dress," he observed. "This one has a more elaborate skirt, a bigger bustle, and the silk appears to be expensive. That blue color does suit your fair skin and blonde hair, which no doubt is to your advantage when facing gentlemen. You have stains upon your fingers, so whatever occasion you wore the dress for ended with you signing papers a few hours ago." He walked over to her and leaned in slightly, breathing deeply near her shoulder. "There's the faintest hint of the stable yard about you, but it's *fresh* hay and not dung. That leads me to one conclusion. I must congratulate you, Miss Hamblin. I take it you purchased a new racing horse?"

Elise expected nothing less from the famous detective.

"I am quite aware that I've just purchased a horse. *You*, however, seem to be unable to read the clock and calendar."

"Yes, all right, I shall wait until your gossip session is

over before I resume my practice." He waved airily at her as if he was ready to dismiss her from the room.

"Gossip session?" Elise couldn't help but react to that comment.

"Yes." Holmes grinned as he seemed to realize he had struck a nerve at last.

"Mr. Holmes, you know absolutely nothing of women," Elise said flatly.

He quirked one dark brow. "Don't I?"

"You, like all men, believe you understand exactly what makes a woman tick. We are not pretty pocket watches to be carried about and tweaked or adjusted to suit your moods." She crossed her arms over her chest, glaring. "You know only about criminals and murderers. You know nothing of ordinary people, especially women."

"It's rather curious how spinsters end up so shrewish, isn't it? I suppose it's because no man wants to hear them complain," Holmes said as he puffed on his pipe again.

Elise ignored the bait about spinsters and countered with her own verbal attack. "Let's see . . . you are smoking your cherrywood pipe rather than your clay one. You only smoke the cherrywood when you're feeling particularly disruptive and have nothing better to do than be a nuisance. Judging by the state of this room, and how no chemicals are currently in use and the neatly folded news-papers are stacked rather than strewn about the room like an untidy child's nursery, *I deduce* that you must be between cases. Therefore, you are delighting in one of your many bad habits, which is disrupting *our* meetings."

Holmes's eyes narrowed on her and his cheeks hollowed out as he drew another puff of pipe smoke into his mouth. She knew he was impressed by her deductions but wasn't about to admit it.

"I wager," he began as he pointed the tip of his pipe at her, "that I know far more about women than you do about men."

Elise tutted. "Please, Mr. Holmes, do not speak untruths that will embarrass you."

A glint of devilish mischief lit up the detective's eyes.

"Shall we make it official, Miss Hamblin? As you have correctly deduced, I am between cases at the moment and am in need of a diversion."

"I have rather far more important things to do than make a study of men."

"Ah, but that is because you only understand gentlemen. Those are easy creatures to decipher. But what of the rogue, the scoundrel, the cad, the delicious bounder? What about those men who live their lives in a gray area between the black-and-white spheres of your ordered world?"

"I'm not sure I follow you," Elise reluctantly admitted.

"You claim to study creatures, to focus on the natural sciences. Men are creatures just like any other. But the gentlemen you've met, they live by human laws. Their borders are easy to discern, their roads easy to navigate. Don't you wish to study what a man is like when he is unmotivated by laws or if he chooses to live outside of them? What motivates such a man to be the way he is? Study his base nature, his natural instincts. Study him as you have learned other creatures. To truly understand what men are capable of, you cannot confine yourself to those who are so well behaved. There you are seeing them at their best, you are seeing what they wish you to see. You learn nothing of the baser animal that lies within all men. To know what a man truly is, you must find a man who has battled the world and yet is still standing. Find a person at his worst low, yet he still holds on to who he is. That is where the truth lies, not in those fine gentlemen who escort you to the park or meet you for ice cream or picnics.

Elise rarely accepted challenges unless she was genuinely intrigued by something. Holmes's words stirred a flash of intrigue in her as she considered the sort of men she'd grown up around. Polite, perfectly polished sons of the kings of industry who paid court to her with flowers and walks in Hyde Park. By their very nature, those men had failed to hold her interest, and therefore, none had held her heart. Struck with a sudden inspiration for a proper wager that would hammer a blow against Holmes in his war against her society, she grinned.

"If I study men and prove I understand them, you will give me your precious violin for winning the wager."

Holmes glared at the instrument, then turned that scowl upon her. "That is a Stradivarius. It has a value you cannot possibly comprehend."

"Oh, but I *do* know its value. That is exactly why you will surrender it when I win."

"And if I win?" He steepled his fingers as he took a seat in one of the overstuffed chairs. "You and your society will find accommodations elsewhere in London."

Elise's heart skipped a painful beat. It would be hard to find another home for the society, and it had already moved so many times over the years. Few property owners allowed women to do anything like what the society did. It was a miracle that the current owner had let Elise sign papers for the townhouse without requiring a man's signature. She had told the man that she and the other women ran a sewing society. What she hadn't said was they were sowing the seeds of knowledge rather than sewing clothing.

"You are a terrible human being," Elise replied to Holmes, though it was rude to speak a truth like that out loud.

Holmes chuckled smugly. "I have one more stipulation," Holmes said, unfolding the newspaper on his lap and idly flipping through the pages. "You can't study just *any* man. You must study *this* one. In order to win, you must share with me what makes him the man he is. Explain the truth of his nature." He turned the paper her way so she could see an article headline that read: *The New Earl of March Returns to England Twelve Years after Being Suspected of Murdering a Man in a Duel.*

"But he is a titled lord. I have no way to approach him, nor would he likely agree . . ." Elise stared at the headline. She couldn't believe Holmes wanted her to study a man who was suspected of killing someone in a duel, let alone a titled lord. There was no way he would agree to let her study him.

"Lure him to you. I'm sure you can find a way. Isn't that what feminine charms are for?" Holmes chuckled darkly. "Make him an offer he can't refuse." He handed her the newspaper with a smug look. "Do we have a wager, then?"

"I suppose so," she said slowly.

"You have two weeks, Miss Hamblin." Then the detective turned his attention to relighting his pipe, his way of telling her she was dismissed.

Elise left the townhouse with Holmes's newspaper tucked under her arm as her mind raced with the idea of studying a man like the Earl of March. She'd been fourteen when Prospero Harrington, the future Earl of March, had fled to France. At the time, she'd been aware of some scandal but had been too young to understand it. She would need to research her target carefully and dive deeply into his past. Then all she had to do was find a way to lure the earl to her door so she could beat Sherlock Holmes at his own game.

2

Prospero's lips formed a grim line as he surveyed the condition of his family's residence. In the twelve years he had been living in France, the once beautiful townhouse had fallen into disrepair. The curtains had been ravaged by moths, the furniture either so worn that the stuffing puffed out of the frayed fabric or the legs were on the verge of snapping. Silver had gone unpolished and rooms had been left undusted. It felt as though no one had lived here in years, yet his mother had been here with a handful of servants since his father's death three months ago.

Why hadn't she maintained the place better? He considered the matter with a deepening frown. Given the state of things, it was almost as though the moment he'd left England twelve years ago, his parents' home had started its descent into decay. His parents had been appalled at his involvement in an illegal, lethal duel, at his leaving the country, at all of it, but when they'd finished shouting at each other, his father had told him the only way he'd be welcome back into England was when his father was dead. Had that been the beginning of this? His heart ached as he stared around at a place he'd once called home that had held such sunny memories so long ago.

"It could be worse . . . ," his friend Viscount Guy De Courcy said from behind him.

Prospero shot Guy a glance. "Oh? How could it possibly be worse?"

Guy dragged his fingers through his dark-reddish hair and shrugged. "At least it didn't burn down or have a rat infestation like that first flat you had in Paris . . ."

Prospero's frown deepened. Twelve years living on very little money had hardened him, but the memory of that place he'd lived in upon arriving in France with barely a pound to his name stung deeper than it should have. The dingy suite of rooms had indeed been filled with rats, and he'd actually been grateful when the entire building was destroyed by a fire a few months later.

Prospero moved deeper into the home. "We'd best see how the rest of the house fares." So far, there had been no sign of any of the servants his mother claimed to have in her last letter.

"Mother?" He'd expected her to be home, though he hadn't expected her to be at the door to greet him like a loving mother. He had expected a butler...and there was no one there at all. The door was unlocked and unattended. In that moment, Prospero learned just how *little* he and his family estate were valued by his mother after his father had passed.

Silence greeted them as they stood staring around at the poor state of this once beautiful home.

"What's this?" Guy retrieved a letter that had been

tucked into the corner of the mirror in the entryway. He studied it before he passed it to Prospero. "It has your name on it."

Prospero opened the letter, a sense of dread building in him.

Prospero,
I let the servants go and have gone to the country to stay with my sister. Do what you will with the house. I no longer desire to live there.

IT WAS HIS MOTHER'S HANDWRITING, BUT THERE WAS NO date as to when it had been written. So she'd left London before he'd even returned, and given the state of the dust on the surfaces, it might have been weeks, possibly months ago since she'd let go of the servants and abandoned the house. The thought pinched his heart. To have not seen her in twelve years . . . and to have her leave him in a quiet, cold, dusty house. The iron inside his heart turned even harder.

"It seems my mother has gone to the country to stay with my aunt. She's let go of the staff."

Prospero set the note on the table by the mirror and sighed. She'd given him yet one more burden to cope with. He would have to convince decent staff to work for him, or suffer hiring those who weren't of the caliber this house required. The cloud of scandal that had shrouded his life over the past decade still had not cleared. London society had a long memory when it came to scandals, and even the downstairs staff had their pride when it came to who they worked for.

"Perhaps Nicholas's butler will know where to post position notices to attract the best servants?" Guy suggested. He, like Prospero, had spent the last twelve years in France, and much of London had changed upon their return.

Prospero didn't say so aloud, but he was glad his friend had wanted to accompany him back to England so he didn't have to make this journey alone. Nicholas had wanted to come with him to France, but of his two friends, they both knew Guy would fare better on the Continent as he had fewer responsibilities than Nicholas since he no longer had any living relatives. Nicholas, newly made the Earl of Durham at the time, had the responsibility for his mother and two sisters. So Nicholas had reluctantly agreed to remain in London and watch over things here. It was Nicholas who notified Prospero of his father's death.

"Did you have a chance to pay our dues to Berkeley's for this month?" Prospero asked.

"Yes, thank Christ they didn't have a problem with reinstating us. A man would die without his club, wouldn't he?" Guy chuckled. "Why don't we have a drink and meet up with Nicholas?" he offered. "He left word for us to send for him when we arrived."

"Good idea. I don't want to stand here another minute. It's giving me a headache." He left his travel cases just inside the door, then they left.

They hailed a hackney and headed for their club. Unlike most things in England, the private gentlemen's club of Berkeley's was remarkably unchanged, which both relieved Prospero and filled him with melancholy.

Once he and Guy settled into a pair of chairs in the reading room, he paid a young lad to send a message to Nicholas Hughes's residence to meet them at the club for drinks.

"So, what's to be your plan?" Guy asked as he poured two glasses of scotch and handed one to his friend.

"I honestly hadn't thought about it. Just the idea of coming home after so long . . . It's been the only thing to fill my mind for weeks." Prospero tasted the fine scotch and relished the gentle burn at the back of his throat. The whiskeys from the cheap taverns in France had lacked the quality and finesse of good whiskey from Scotland.

Prospero was silent a long moment. "Before I visited my solicitor this morning, I thought that Father would have left his estate—now mine—with some money in it."

"He didn't?" Guy asked, his brows knitting in concern as he stared at Prospero.

"Apparently, after I left England, my father's investments turned sour and he took up gambling to such an extent that he nearly bankrupted the estate. Our country house, Marchlands, was sold. All we have left is the townhouse, and you saw what condition it's in."

"Christ . . . I never thought your father would . . . That seems so unlike him," Guy admitted.

"Yes, well, it seems having a son like me broke his heart, and he did all he could to ruin his life and his estate because of it." Prospero hated that he sounded so bitter, but knowing that something he'd had no control over had caused such devastation to his family was almost too much to bear.

"Well, you have a couple of choices," Guy offered. "Find an heiress or go into business. I recommend an heiress. You've never had a problem seducing women. With all those million-dollar beauties coming from America every day, you will be tripping over rich, pretty women in no time."

Prospero didn't immediately dismiss the idea of an heiress, but marriage was such a *permanent* solution. Yes, a man could live apart from his wife and take his pleasures on the side, but Prospero, as infamous as he was for his sensual appetites, had no desire to have a mistress. He was a loyal lover when he was in a relationship, and that especially applied to matrimony. That loyalty had made him a favorite in Paris. Wealthy young widows, eager to have a faithful lover who had no expectations except to be quietly paid for his companionship, were quick to seek him out.

For twelve years, he had moved from one widow to the next, keeping a roof over his head and food in his belly by being loyal to them until they sent him on his way and he found the next widow looking for companionship. But selling himself like that was not something he wanted to do again, not unless he had to. When he married, he wanted it to be to a woman who would hold his heart, what was left of it, and he wanted to hold hers in return. He didn't want to resort to marrying for money and fearing that at any moment his wife would stray from their marriage bed because she saw him as valueless as his own parents had.

"I think I'd rather pursue business for the moment," he said.

"Without any capital to invest, you'll need to find a way in the door," Guy said. "And by the look of the grumpy old fellows when we walked into the club, you're not going to find anyone sympathetic here."

"True," Prospero admitted. His gaze rose and moved around the room, studying the men there. He recognized most of the older gentlemen who were around his father's age. Those men wouldn't have anything to do with him. Being involved in Aaron Jackson's death had cast a long shadow over him.

"Perhaps I could find someone more willing in a younger set of men. Those who don't remember Jackson."

Guy frowned a little. "It's possible, but most of the younger set don't have money, and the ones who do tend to throw it away on women, gambling tables, and other vices."

There were a handful of younger men he believed wouldn't be caught up in the self-indulgence, men either his age or a few years his junior. They would also seek to prove themselves in the world of business, but they might become competition rather than allies.

Was he destined to repeat his life from Paris here in London? The thought turned his stomach. Even if he wanted to pursue that route, he was far too well known— or rather, too infamous. His current status made it impossible. A common gentleman could have gotten away with being a kept companion, but an earl? Any rich Englishwoman would have too much sense to get involved with him. The scandal could be ruinous. No woman would want to take him even as a husband, especially not an heiress who could have her pick of eligible, titled men.

A finely dressed man in his early twenties was intently reading a paper one table over and nursing a glass of brandy. His thin mustache twitched as he suddenly chortled. When he glanced about to see if he'd disturbed anyone with his laughter, he noticed Prospero watching him. He smiled ruefully.

"Sorry, old boy. Just couldn't believe what they print in the papers these days. Look at this." The man leaned over in his chair and tossed his newspaper to Prospero.

"What is it?" Prospero asked as he caught the paper and examined the pages.

"That advertisement, in the left middle column. Can you believe that?" The man laughed again. "What nonsense. Someone wants to pay to study gentlemen? What are we? Animals?"

Curious now, Prospero examined the advertisement, and Guy peered over his shoulder to read as well.

MAN WANTED FOR SCIENTIFIC STUDY

A GENTLEMAN IS REQUIRED TO PARTICIPATE IN A TWO-WEEK OBSERVATION TO FURTHER THE STUDY OF NATURAL SCIENCES. THIS WILL INCLUDE THE MANNERS, HABITS, AND HAUNTS OF THE PARTICIPANT. PARTICIPANT MUST AGREE TO BE INTERVIEWED ON VARIOUS SUBJECTS AND MUST BE PREPARED TO ANSWER QUESTIONS OF A SENSITIVE OR INTIMATE NATURE. INTERESTED PARTIES MAY COME FOR INTERVIEWS AT 2:00 P.M. ON TUESDAY THE TWELFTH AT #223 BAKER STREET. THE SUCCESSFUL APPLICANT WILL BE PAID FOR HIS TIME AT THE RATE OF £50–75 PER WEEK. PLEASE SEND A MESSAGE TO THE ABOVE ADDRESS IF YOU WISH TO BE INTERVIEWED.

"Baker Street?" Guy murmured. "Why does that sound familiar?"

"You might be thinking of Sherlock Holmes. The one

written about in the papers?" While they had been in Paris, Prospero had kept abreast of news events in London including Sherlock Holmes's cases.

"You don't suppose it's *him*, do you?"

"Holmes is at 221, and this is 223 . . . This is next door," Prospero said.

"So someone wants to *pay* to study a man? How odd."

"Not just any man. It seems they're looking for a specific sort."

"Even odder." Guy laughed. "I wonder why?"

Prospero wasn't laughing, though. Given that he had no food at his home and no servants, he was desperate enough to investigate this.

"Wait, you're not considering applying, are you?" Guy exclaimed, his brows rising as Prospero.

"Why not? At least this way I'm not a paid companion, but a paid subject for the advancement of the natural sciences. Surely that sounds more noble."

"Perhaps . . . ," Guy agreed reluctantly. "But I have my doubts as to what it is they are truly after."

"Only one way to find out," Prospero said, then turned to the man who had given him the paper. "May I keep this?"

"Certainly, I'm done with it," the man replied, then patted his pockets as if looking for a cigar. "Pardon me, I'm off for a smoke." He rose and left the room.

"Really, Prospero, you need not succumb to such desperate acts. I'd offer you to stay with me, but since I haven't a decent flat at the moment, I know Nicholas offered to host you until you have your house in order again."

Prospero wished he could accept Nicholas's offer, but he feared Nicholas's family would be touched by the scandal.

"He has two younger sisters who debuted recently. I don't want my presence to ruin their prospects in husband hunting with my mere presence in their house."

"Nonsense," Guy declared. "Friendship comes first. If Nicholas made the offer, he clearly thinks his family can withstand the scandal."

"I'll be all right. The interviews are tomorrow. I'll go and see what I think of this . . . study and whether it really does pay that much."

It couldn't be that hard to answer some naturalist's questions, whatever they might be. Naturalists were bookish sorts by nature, but that didn't intimidate Prospero. He took the paper under his arm and tipped his glass of scotch back, letting the burn of whiskey take away his worries for a short time. He would think about his troubles tomorrow.

THE MAN WHO HAD GIVEN HIS NEWSPAPER TO LORD March paused in the smoking room and checked his pocket watch before closing the lid and tucking it back into his waistcoat pocket. He then made his way down the stairs to the front door of the club, where he retrieved his hat from a footman, who summoned a coach for him.

He nodded his thanks to the footman. Then he

climbed into the hackney and gave the driver his desired address.

It stopped in front of a townhouse on Baker Street. The man got out and walked up the steps, tapping the knocker when he got to the top. A butler answered and stared down at the man for a minute before rolling his eyes.

"You'd best come in before someone sees you," the butler, Mr. Atkins said.

The gentleman stepped inside, removed his hat, and gave it to a footman, who studied him with a raised brow but said nothing as he politely took the item.

"Miss Hamblin is in her study," Mr. Atkins said.

The gentleman nodded and proceeded to the room with a grin that made his mustache twitch.

ELISE ADJUSTED HER SPECTACLES, MOVING THE THIRD magnification lens in front of her right eye as she studied the antennae of the privet hawk moth, the *Sphinx ligustri*. Its large pink-and-black striped abdomen and hind wings were often mistaken for a hummingbird when it hovered over flowers to drink nectar. The moth twitched its wings as it crawled over the petals of a large pale cluster of pink peonies.

"You are a handsome fellow," Elise murmured as the moth dipped its tongue into the flower, exploring it.

"I know! Funny, isn't it?" a voice said from the door to

Elise's study. "But I do make for a deuced good-looking chap."

Elise glanced up and winced as her spectacles made the distant world far too out of focus. She quickly removed her spectacles and set them down. A gentleman stood in the doorway wearing a light-gray three-piece suit. He stroked his mustache and watched Elise with amusement.

Elise laughed and got to her feet. "Cinna! Good heavens, you actually *do* look quite dashing."

The gentleman, who was no man at all, peeled the mustache off her face and shrugged out of her coat. The cleverly cut and styled wig covered Cinna's dark-brown hair, which had been flattened with pins and a cap to her scalp to allow the wig to settle on her head. She removed the pins holding the wig and the underneath tight-fitting cap in place and then began the process of freeing her hair so that it fell in loose curls around her shoulders.

Elise perched on the edge of her desk as Cinna settled into a chair opposite her. "Did it work?"

"I think so. I caught his attention with my comment on the advertisement like we discussed, and when he seemed interested, I passed him the newspaper. He even asked if he could keep it. He and the man he was sitting with were discussing his dire straits, and his friend seemed quite convinced that March was considering coming for an interview with you."

Elise watched Cinna pull the remaining pins out of her hair.

"You had no trouble getting into Berkeley's, then? I always thought they'd be clever enough to catch females trying to sneak inside."

Cinna shook her head. "My elder brother is still in

Scotland, and we resemble each other enough that passing servants don't seem to notice the difference when I'm dressed like a man. I gave them my brother's name at the door and spoke with a lower voice from deep within my chest, and they just let me in." She loosened the ascot around her neck and drew in a deep breath. "Lord, I despise wearing these things. It feels like I'm being strangled. You'd better write that down for your research. Between the ascots and binding my breasts, I feel rather squished. It's as bad as wearing a corset."

"So, what exactly did you overhear March say?" Elise asked.

"Well, it's as you expected, given the dossier you prepared on March. He's practically penniless. He got by in Paris by bedding some widows who funded his existence. He seems interested in business, but you know how people can be. Being involved in an illegal duel with a man who dies under somewhat disputed circumstances and suddenly no one invites you to parties or wants to do business with you." Cinna's tone was light, almost teasing, but her words made Elise frown at Lord March's situation.

"It was never proven that he killed that man, only that there had been an altercation following the duel and that the gentleman who challenged Lord March died." Elise moved the vase with the peonies to the side of her desk so she could retrieve the paperwork she'd prepared on Prospero Harrington. The hawk moth fluttered his wings as he repositioned himself on the thickly petaled flowers, but he did not fly off. She scoured the notes she had made the day before.

"The only son of the late Earl of March. He's thirty-four years old, which means he was only twenty-two at the time of the duel. He left for France shortly after, and his father's business ventures went from bad to worse over the last decade. He died three months ago. His mother is alive but apparently no longer in London, according to my sources. At this point, the man has nothing much left to offer London society except the title of March for some young woman who's willing to risk her reputation by marriage to him."

Cinna toyed with the loose ends of her ascot. "He and his friend were discussing the possibility of an heiress. Are you in the market for a husband?" Cinna winked at Elise. "He'd be happy to take you on, I'm sure."

"Heavens no. I cannot think of anything more burdensome than a husband. Papa has his steel company and the railway investments to keep him busy, and I have the society to run and my academic papers to pursue."

"Yes, but your papers are penned under the name Elliott Hamblin," Cinna reminded her as she fixed Elise with a look. "No one is going to give a woman, even one as brilliant as you, the recognition you deserve in scientific journals. Even if you became the queen of England, they'd still put you in your place because you wear skirts. At best, they'd humor you if you had a nice title and money for their society, but they'd never let you participate as an equal member."

Elise continued to frown as she leafed through some of the articles she'd collected on Prospero Harrington.

"I love our society," Cinna said softly. "I love that we have a safe place to learn and teach each other about the things that matter. But what if we can never break the walls trapping us in? We're no better than butterflies pinned down in a box and covered with glass so that men might come along and admire us until our wings fade in color and the life within us shrivels from loss of food and freedom."

Cinna wasn't wrong, and that hurt Elise's heart more than anything else. Time and again women had doors shut in their faces, conversations stopped, and opportunities removed from their lives simply for the crime of being *female*. For indeed they were treated no better than prisoners, no matter what level of society they lived at. To be told, over and over, that their minds were smaller, incapable of comprehending mathematics or sciences, that to sit quietly, sew, look pretty and bear children was their only true value . . .

There was nothing wrong with wanting to marry and have children, but every woman was entitled to dream of *more*, to have dreams that went beyond what they could give men with their bodies. Women deserved the freedom to choose their own paths, their own destinies, whatever they might be.

"In nearly every species except humans, the females are stronger, braver, tougher," said Elise. "They live longer, have skills or natural advantages that allow them to thrive and carry on their species. They have colors that help conceal them from danger so they might survive. They are the dominant force over the males, so why do humans act so contrary to the laws of nature? We are animals too. We are beholden to the same conditions of this planet as the rest of the creatures on it."

"I blame male hubris," Cinna said. "Women have always been more connected to the earth than men. It's their presumption, not ours, that they believe themselves to be above nature and women. Perhaps it is a good thing for you to study Lord March. Women desperately need to know how men work, or else we should never learn how to defeat them."

Elise chuckled. "I think you mean beat them at their own game. We don't want to defeat them—we just want them to admit they need us as equals and not just as mothers for their children."

"Speak for yourself. I haven't the faintest desire to play their silly little games. Think of all the things women have accomplished in spite of men. What would happen if men stopped holding the doors of academia closed against us? Sabina Baldoncelli earned a university degree in pharmacy, yet men only allowed her to work in an orphanage. Mary Anning discovered a complete plesiosaurus skeleton. Jeanne Villepreux-Power invented a glass aquarium to study aquatic life."

Elise placed her hand on the top of one of her two glass aquariums on the shelf in her study. A snake lay sleeping peacefully in a patch of sunlight inside one of them.

"The Royal Astronomical Society did allow Mary Somerville and Caroline Herschel to join, and Ellen Smith Tupper was allowed to be the editor of an entomological journal," Elise added.

Cinna sighed. "Small victories, but victories none-theless," she agreed. "Women make up half the population, and yet less than 1 percent of us are allowed even the smallest bit of intellectual recognition. And we must struggle to achieve even that," Cinna sat up. "So, tomorrow you will conduct interviews. Do you suppose more than just Lord March will attend? If they do, you'll have to find a way to scare those men off."

Elise brushed a stray lock of blonde hair from her face.

"I don't know. I fear putting an exact amount of payment down in the advertisement might have *too* many people showing up. But March is all that matters. Hopefully, he will be intrigued enough to see me, and at that point I may be able to suss out an appropriate amount of money to keep him on the hook for a full two weeks."

"I admit, I'm quite jealous. Think of all the places you'll go disguised as a man. I wish I could go with you."

"You went to a gentlemen's club today, and you've infiltrated a few other places. That's more than most women have ever done." Elise thought of the few times she'd dressed up as a man and attempted to give presentations at naturalist societies as Elliot Hamblin.

"Well, we didn't know if it would work. But it did, and Lord, it was fun, pretending to read my paper and light a pipe. I wandered around the cardrooms a bit and took a peep at the betting book they keep there. You wouldn't believe what nonsense they bet on. But I find the clubs a bit boring, to be honest. I always imagined they must be having a great deal of fun, but all they do is smoke and talk or play cards and billiards. The older ones sleep in chairs by the fire. Dreadfully dull, to be honest. It makes one realize that if women were to laze about all day like that, nothing would ever get accomplished in this world."

"Well, you were excellent, Cinna. I shall need your help in preparing my own disguise this afternoon. I want to be ready to go at a moment's notice if March agrees to sneak me into the spheres of the male domain. Perhaps he could teach me how to walk and talk like a man as part of the study."

Cinna giggled. "Nonsense. You've already mastered it. Remember how you fooled those old pompous arses at the naturalist society last month? They were hanging on your every word, never once suspecting you weren't a man."

"Until my mustache fell off." Elise couldn't help but grin at the memory. The shouting and utter outrage of a group of grumpy old men was almost laughable. Until they'd tossed her out, they'd been listening to her theories on animal migration quite keenly. That had been a victory. Now she wanted a bigger one.

"Those men would be fooled by a dog dressed in men's clothing if it paraded in front of them. I want to be able to fool the *real* men, the ones in the dockside taverns or the gambling dens. The men with stronger instincts who have their wits about them, not silly old scholars who barely look up from their own research papers."

"Do you want me and Edwina to be present tomorrow for the interviews?" Cinna asked.

"No, I should be all right. Atkins is more than capable of tossing out any men who might misbehave."

"Except perhaps for Lord March," Cinna said. "You might just want a man like that to misbehave."

Elise blinked at her friend's words. "What?"

"Come now, don't pretend you haven't considered the idea . . . He's handsome. I know I don't wish to marry, but I would be tempted to let that man into my bed if he kisses as nicely as I suspect he does. Do you remember that time we saw him in the park before he left for France?"

"That was one time and very long ago. I wasn't looking at boys his age. I don't actually remember seeing him."

"No," Cinna said as she rolled her eyes. "You were too busy counting the stripes on a pair of caterpillars, and I was sketching them for you. I think I still have those sketches somewhere. But my point is, March is a man now, not a young lad. He's . . . well . . . I'm not quite sure I know the word to describe him. He has a *presence*, even while brooding over his glass of scotch. Spying on him gave me a few thoughts."

"What sort of thoughts?" Elise asked, her voice hitching with slight alarm.

"I admit, the female in me was interested in him, and even more interested in the man he was with. I don't think I've ever been that curious about men before. They've always seemed so tedious, so frustrating, even if they're exceedingly handsome. There have been exceptions, of course, but you must know what I mean. It's like when you walk upon the carpets in your stockings in the winter and touch a door latch or another bit of metal and you get a spark of electricity."

At this, Elise hid a grin. "Oh dear, that sounds quite serious, Cinna. Are you at risk of falling in love with Lord March?"

"No," Cinna answered, their gazes locking. "But if you aren't careful, *you* just might."

"Me? Fall for a man?" She laughed. "I can't imagine that happening at all. You know I have no interest in gentlemen, *especially* the troublesome kind."

"You might be surprised. Spend enough time around him and you might be tempted to see him the way other women do."

Elise had little interest in love, not enough to pursue it, and she certainly wouldn't fall in love with a dangerous— how did Mr. Holmes put it? *A man who lived in neither the black nor white areas of life.*

No, she wouldn't love a man like that because a man like that wasn't trustworthy. She needed to trust a man above all else, because if she married, her very existence would vanish in the eyes of the law and society as she became her husband's property. She didn't trust any man other than her father to see her as his equal.

She had resigned herself to a solitary life a long time ago. A man like Lord March would not be tempting to her in the least.

3

Prospero checked his pocket watch and eyed the 223 Baker Street residence with grim resignation. A man a short ways ahead of him had already walked up the steps and knocked before being allowed inside. No doubt it was someone he'd have to compete with in order to be chosen for the study.

It was imperative that he obtain this position. Nicholas had offered money and a roof over his head, but Prospero had declined his friend's generous offer. He would not accept charity, not when he was still capable of earning a living, albeit briefly, even if it was in a highly unusual manner.

Most men with bloodlines and titles as old as the Earl of March would not have deigned to lower themselves like this. But Prospero had never been like his father, which was why the older man had been so quick to abandon him when society had falsely spun tales of his seduction and impregnation of an innocent woman and then killing her brother in an illegal duel.

Now he was preparing to apply for a study in order to be paid, and he wasn't as ashamed of that fact. He wasn't about to boast about it to anyone on the street, however. He would maintain *some* dignity. There were worse things in the world than letting some bespectacled man with a notebook and pen follow him about London and ask silly questions.

As he walked up the steps, he noticed a brass sign beside the door that read: *Societas Rebellium Dominarum*. He roughly translated it as the Society of Rebellious Ladies. That had to be a mistake. He glanced around the street, but it was fairly empty save for the passing of a hackney or the occasional person strolling along the pavement.

He walked up the steps and rapped the knocker on the door.

A butler answered, and Prospero gave a bow of his head. "I'm Lord March. I'm here for a two o'clock interview." He'd written to the address in the paper that morning to confirm if he needed an appointment or not and had received a message to be here at two o'clock.

When the butler's dubious expression didn't change, Prospero held up the advertisement he'd cut from the paper. "I'm here to interview for the study posted in the *Morning Post* yesterday."

"Ah yes. This way, sir. You may wait with the others." He escorted Prospero to a sitting room where a dozen chairs had been placed along the free spaces against the walls. Every chair but one in the corner of the room was occupied. All eyes fixed on Prospero as he crossed the room and took the last empty seat. Some sat reading newspapers in their best suits, while others stared idly at the walls. A handful of men held newspapers that they pretended to read, but it was clear they were waiting for something to happen. Prospero discovered what it was a minute later. A door opened down the hall, and a man stormed past the sitting room.

"Bloody mad, the lot of them!" the man snapped as he snatched his hat from a coat hook just outside the sitting room and slapped it on his head as he disappeared from view.

"Have a good day, sir," the butler said, following the man to the door.

"Good day? I think not!" The man's shout practically echoed through the townhouse.

After the front door slammed, the butler appeared in the doorway of the sitting room. "Who would like to go next?" he politely inquired of the room at large. A nervous man with wide eyes raised a trembling hand.

"I'll . . . go. Better to get it over with," he said to the room in an apparent attempt to bolster his courage.

Prospero hadn't expected this much interest in the study, and he had nothing to entertain himself with while he waited other than to study the men around him. Most seemed to be of a middling class, though a few were on the poorer end with worn suits and scuffed shoes.

He felt bad for those men in particular. He'd been in their position when he'd first arrived in France. If he hadn't met Madame Beauchance when he did and agreed to be her companion . . . He shuddered to think what might have happened. Finding employment in France wouldn't have been easy, not for an Englishman with only a middling understanding of the language. The tensions that existed between titled people and the commoners in France made it even more unlikely he would have found a place to work.

Prospero was still ruminating on the past when the nervous man who'd gone in for his interview flew down the hall like a banshee was on his heels. He didn't even stop to take his hat from the stand. The butler chased after him down the street to return it. Prospero stood at the window watching the entire encounter and chuckled.

One of the other applicants joined Prospero at the window. "What do you suppose they keep saying that upsets everyone?"

The poor butler was now making his return to the townhouse, his face red as he huffed after his unexpected mad dash.

"Damned if I know. It is a study, so perhaps the person conducting the interviews lacks a certain sensitivity?" Prospero guessed.

They returned to their seats, and one by one the men in the sitting room were admitted into the next room, only to leave in either a rage or some other form of distemper. The fellow who had spoken to Prospero at the window had been the second-to-last to be interviewed, and while he was not in a rush to leave, he clearly had a shocked look on his face.

"Well? What did he say?" Prospero asked.

The man shook his head. "I have no words for what I've just gone through, old boy. Good luck. You're going to need it." Then the man left him alone.

Prospero shoved his hands into his trouser pockets and waited for the butler to summon him. He felt strangely nervous, though he had no logical reason to be. When the servant arrived, he peered around the sitting room, noticing the absence of any other men.

"Are you the last, sir?" the butler asked him.

"Afraid so," Prospero replied. His curiosity and nerves were so strong now that he almost couldn't wait for the man to wave for him to follow.

"Very well. Please go to the room at the end of the hall and knock."

"Thank you." Prospero left the sitting room and walked down the hall to the door. He leaned in against it, listening, but heard only some papers rustling. After a moment, he raised his hand and knocked on the door.

"Enter," someone called out, their tone brusque and businesslike.

He opened the door and stepped inside; his lips parted as he surveyed perhaps the most chaotic room he'd ever seen, and that included the abode of one of his mistresses, Madame Barbier, who everyone had agreed was quite mad for collecting thousands of snuffboxes.

A pair of large aquariums sat on a short, waist-high bookshelf beside him. The first had a snake coiled up, asleep in a sandy environment. The second had a layer of rocks on the bottom, filled with water and weeds. A large turtle was perched on one of the higher rocks, basking in an errant sunbeam. Small brightly colored minnows swam beneath the weeds as a frog croaked somewhere in the aquarium's watery wilderness. The walls were papered with green plant patterns, making the room resemble a jungle, and flowers burst in bright colors from vases that dotted the surfaces of the desks and tables not covered with papers.

Half a dozen jars sat on the shelves, and Prospero spotted butterflies, beetles, and even sticklike creatures moving about in them.

Fascinating.

His gaze came to rest on the wonderfully rounded bottom of a woman in a red bustle gown who was bent over the desk in front of him, digging through papers as she muttered to herself. How he'd missed her amidst everything else he'd seen when he walked in was a mystery, because her backside was . . . *spectacular*. He'd always admired the way women looked in the current fashions, and this woman was no exception. However, as much as he wanted to stare at this woman's bottom for the rest of the day, he knew his interview was paramount.

He cleared his throat politely.

The woman in the red bustle gown straightened and turned to him. His throat ran dry at the sight of the most remarkable brown eyes he'd ever seen, framed by a tumble of wispy strands of honey-gold hair that was nothing short of enchanting. She wore the most peculiar pair of spectacles that had multiple lens that could be slid up and down in front of one of her eyes to help her see things up close, almost like a magnifying glass.

He didn't move, nor did he blink. He simply stared at the woman as she stared back at him, perhaps just as struck. He wasn't sure *struck* was the right word, but something inside him was different . . . like he'd collided with a celestial comet and all he saw were brightly spinning fragments of stars.

"I'm . . . um . . . here for the . . . interview." His voice deepened, turned gruff as he struggled to remember his manners. "Is the gentleman conducting the interview ready to see me?" He trailed off when he realized there was no one else in the room other than this woman who would have shamed Helen of Troy with her beauty. He certainly would have launched a thousand ships in her name if he had them in his possession.

The woman recovered herself far quicker than he did and removed her spectacles, setting them on the desk. "Please have a seat, sir. The interview shall begin shortly." She waved at a chair. He moved toward it and was about to sit down when he saw the large, long-haired feline curled up in it. Its fur was light gray and so dense it made the cat appear almost rotund. Its ears were oddly rounded and set low on the sides of its head. Black dots covered its forehead, and two black lines of fur zigzagged from its eyes to the corners of its jaw joints. The yellow irises of its eyes took him in with the lazy, disgruntled movement only cats were capable of.

"Is that cat . . . all right?" Prospero asked as he studied the sturdy-looking creature on the chair.

"Pallas? Oh yes, just give him a little shove from behind and he'll hop off," the woman said as she rounded the edge of the desk and sat down in the large leather chair facing him.

"Right. Come on then, chap, move along." He gave the cat a nudge, and with a low, angry meow, Pallas vacated his chair and Prospero sat down in his place.

"He doesn't look like other cats," Prospero noted. He was quite intrigued with the little beast.

She collected a stack of papers and tapped them on the desk to tidy them up. "He isn't. Pallas is a Pallas cat. He's actually wild and not domesticated, although he pretends to be when we ask him to."

"What exactly is a Pallas cat? I confess I haven't heard of such a thing before."

"Pallas cats were first discovered in 1776 by Peter Pallas

when he was at Lake Baikal in Siberia. They live in high, cold elevations."

"Ah . . . so is this little chap your master's cat?" Prospero leaned back in his chair and watched the woman set out a fresh sheet of paper in front of her and write the date across the top.

"My *master?*" The woman chuckled, not even looking up at him from the paper she was writing on. "I'm afraid to disappoint you, but I have no master. Now, shall we begin?"

Prospero blinked. "I'm sorry, I don't quite . . . ," he started and then halted as the plaque on the outside of the townhouse flashed across his mind. *Societas Rebellium Dominarum* . . . "The Society of Rebellious Ladies" wasn't a mistake after all.

The woman's lovely brown eyes held his gaze as she examined him the way she likely did the creatures in the jars upon the shelves.

"You are quicker than the others. They had to be told, and most didn't take the news well, as I'm sure you witnessed while waiting to be called in. Once I started in on them with my questions . . . Well, it was just a matter of time before each gentleman stormed out of here."

Prospero's pulse quickened as he sensed the very subtle challenge this beautiful woman had issued him.

"You are the one conducting the study," he said.

"Yes. Will that be a problem for you?" she asked. Those gorgeous brown eyes feigned innocence, but he was much cleverer than the men who'd come before him, and he saw that she was enjoying this far more than she was aware. No wonder the other men had stormed out in a huff. She'd likely said something to each of them to prick their fickle male pride. Well, she wouldn't find him so easy to ruffle, now that he understood the game they were playing. He took his time in answering her question.

"Am I bothered that a woman wishes to study a man? No, that poses no problem for me. But I suppose I would need some clarity as to the nature of exactly *how* you plan to conduct your study."

His calm reply seemed to startle her. He was rather enjoying this. It had been a while since he'd been around a woman who liked to spar in conversation, and he had a sense this woman had gone unchallenged for some time.

"Of course. Here is the contract I've prepared, which outlines my plan for the study and your requirements for participation." She slid a piece of paper across the desk to him. He picked it up and noticed the number of pounds per week had been left blank. He wanted to confirm how much he would be paid, but he couldn't reveal the financial desperation he was feeling, not yet.

"Take your time in reviewing it," she said. She seemed in no particular hurry as he read the terms carefully.

"The duration is two weeks . . . ," he murmured to himself. "Observations will take place at various times of the day, both in public and in private. The observer will accompany the participant to locations such as clubs, restaurants, brothels—brothels?" He glanced up as he choked on the unexpected word.

"You don't plan to go to brothels?" she asked, those doe-brown eyes so cleverly *innocent* still as she watched him.

"No . . ." He reached for a pen on the desk. "May I make an adjustment?"

She nodded. He struck the word *brothels* out of the list and instead added *gambling dens* and *racetracks* before he showed her the additions. She studied them briefly and nodded.

"What about a high-end house of courtesans?"

He couldn't help the bemused grin he flashed her. "Are you quite determined to see a man take a woman to bed? Is that it?" Perhaps that was the real goal of her study, to see how a man beds a woman because she had no experience of her own to go by and wanted to learn about it in the way she felt most comfortable, as an observer. It made a certain bit of sense.

"I . . . no, it's not that I'm determined, it just seems to be something that men do often, and I can't understand the appeal. Is it simply the act of sex that draws you into those houses, or is it conversation with women who are being paid to treat you as if your opinions need no challenging and you are a king among men?"

Prospero understood at once what she was seeking to understand, and she'd in fact already answered her question. "It's quite a mix of both. Some men need to be seen as a king and have everyone listen to them when they speak and treat it as if it were a royal proclamation. Other men simply want sex, as you've said. But not all men are like either of those two cateogories—I certainly am not. I enjoy sex immensely, and I enjoy conversing with women on an equal ground and do not require them to sit and raptly listen to me ramble on."

When she made no reply to that, he resumed reading, but he soon halted once more. "Observer shall reside at participant's residence as required in order to study morning, evening, and sleeping rituals?" He was torn between shock and laughter, but his mirth died as he realized he could not host anyone at his house, let alone a woman.

"That is where many of the previous applicants chose to leave. Will this be a problem for you?" she asked. Her dark-gold brows arched, and Prospero caught himself staring at her mouth with an intensity that nearly erased all thoughts of why he'd come into this room in the first place.

"Well yes, actually. My living situation would be unsuitable for you."

"Because I'm a woman?"

"No . . . It's because I haven't had a single servant hired yet to look after anyone. The place is a mess of dust and neglect. It's not suitable for *anyone* at the moment." He repressed a shudder as he thought of how he'd tried in vain to sleep upon a sofa with a broken leg the previous night. It had kept tilting at odd angles whenever he restlessly shifted to get comfortable. The beds in the house were out of the question, between the dusty draperies and the rickety frames that threatened to collapse.

"Ah, I see . . ." She steepled her fingers and leaned forward, wisps of her golden hair brushing her cheeks as it escaped her elegant hairstyle. He had a sudden flash of her lying in bed beside him, their faces close upon a shared pillow as he tenderly brushed those strands with his fingers. *Christ* . . . One moment had done this to him? This woman had him in knots, and he didn't even know her name.

"If you are accepted, I would propose this . . . You will reside at my residence for the duration of the study."

Prospero's lips parted in shock. "You wish for me to live with you? But your husband wouldn't—"

"I have no husband." Her reply was a little clipped, and he wondered if the subject was tender for her. Had she loved a man and been rejected? If she had, that man was a fool.

"But that's worse," he added grimly. "You do see how that's worse, don't you?" He couldn't stay with an unmarried woman at her home—that would blacken his reputation even further.

"No, I don't. I live with my father, and he won't mind in the least."

"You and he might not, but I can't speak for the rest of society." Prospero tried to ignore the stab of guilt he felt. He knew all too well how unfounded rumors of impropriety could change someone's life forever.

The woman chuckled, and he flinched at the unexpected sound. It was rich and intimate in his ears, and he hadn't expected the flash of raw lust it created in him.

"Society can hang itself." She pinned him with a confidant gaze and a smile that, for a woman, was surprisingly devilish. "I am twenty-six. I care not about marriage, nor my reputation as a marriageable woman. The only reputation I *do* care about is the one I am denied on the basis of my gender, and that is to be considered equal to a man intellectually. You needn't trouble yourself on my account."

Prospero couldn't understand this woman. She truly had no issue with a scoundrel living under her roof while she was unmarried?

"Your advertisement requested a gentleman for your study, but in some circles, I am not considered a gentleman. Perhaps you should know more about my background before you make that decision, Miss . . . I'm sorry, I don't even know your name."

"Elise Hamblin," she said formally with a nod of acknowledgment.

"Miss Hamblin, my name is Prospero Harrington." He waited for a reaction of shock and dismay, but none came. Instead, she simply wrote his name down on the contract that he had left on the desk.

"Miss Hamblin . . . Perhaps you don't understand. I am the *Earl of March*." Again he waited for some flash of recognition.

Her eyes fixed on him patiently. "Yes, that's correct. Should I add your title to the contract?"

"What? No, what I mean is, does my name mean nothing to you?"

"What else does your title mean other than that you possess an earldom?" She leaned back in her chair, watching him with eyes that he could not fully read. He supposed his only choice now was to come right out and say it.

"Twelve years ago, I was involved in an illegal duel in which the other man died. That has left a black cloud over my life ever since. I've only just returned from Paris and am trying to rebuild my life here in London. Given the scandal I've caused, I may never be able to fix my situation."

A small wave of relief swept through him at this chance to be honest with her. It calmed and centered him as he gave her his warning. "Associating with me may have consequences, Miss Hamblin. That is what I wish to say." He waited for the inevitable reaction of horror that any decent woman would have at the thought of the dire social consequences that would come with being caught in public with a man like him. But she merely leaned back in her chair, silent, her expression one of deep consideration rather than concern.

"Are you saying you do not wish to be part of this study?" she asked.

Again, her reaction baffled him. "Did you not hear what I just said?"

"Tell me, did you kill the man in the duel, or did he die afterward?" She arched one elegant dark-gold brow as she asked her question. "I have heard two versions of the story."

Prospero swallowed hard. That out of everything he had just said was what she wished to discuss? He let out a slow breath.

"It was after. I had been wounded by his shot and he grew deranged, insisting that I take my shot. I refused, and he charged me. We struggled, and he turned his own weapon upon himself out of desperation. I didn't want him to die, even at his own hand. So I reached for the weapon. I can't be sure what happened next, only that the weapon went off." The honesty that spilled out of him was unexplained. He'd never shared any of this with another soul except for Nicholas Hughes and Guy De Courcy.

"I will be honest with you, Lord March. When you sent a notice that you would appear for this interview, I did some due diligence, as I did on the other men who came to interview today. I am aware of the cloud that hangs over your head. But my understanding is that no charges were ever filed against you," she noted. "That means they either didn't believe you killed him or they had no proof."

"The other man's second, John Gower, told Scotland Yard that I was attacked from behind, which was true. He said that it appeared I was acting partially out of self-defense, and the Yard decided to believe me that I didn't try to kill Jackson, although Gower could not state outright who pulled the trigger. As you're aware, titled men and their sons are given some deference in the court of law. Without tangible proof of my killing the other man they could not bring charges, but I still wasn't welcome in England because dueling is illegal, so my departure was necessary." His voice softened a little as memories of that night came back to him so clearly.

Gower had caught up with him before he'd boarded a ship for France. God knows how Gower had found him, but the man had said he believed what Jackson had done in those final moments was without honor. He'd had his chance to fire, had struck and drawn blood, and it should have been the end. Then to turn a pistol on himself and try to force Prospero to action was unthinkable. He'd wished Prospero luck in France and said he'd report to the authorities the truth of what he'd witnessed in hopes that it would prevent charges from being brought. Nicholas had written to him a few months later saying that Scotland Yard had decided to put the case aside and leave the fault of Jackson's death undecided.

"Thank you. That is all I need to know," Miss Hamblin said.

Prospero was astonished at the woman's sense of efficiency. He'd expected far more questions.

"Now, about the value for your services as a participant. I was thinking a hundred pounds per week?" She changed the subject so quickly it took him a moment to collect his thoughts and catch up.

"The advertisement said the pay would be between fifty and seventy-five pounds per week," Prospero reminded her. He wasn't about to take more than another man would receive.

"Yes, but seeing as how your townhouse is across the street from mine in Grosvenor Square, I should like to have you use the money to put your property to rights and to hire staff again."

He narrowed his eyes as a flash of unexpected anger surged through him. "I will not take charity."

"Good. Because this isn't charity. Your home and its condition affects the property values of the other houses in the square, which includes my home. This is entirely a selfish decision."

Prospero stared at her. "You aren't like any woman I've ever met before."

She suddenly laughed, and the sound was so sensual, so *real* that it made him feel dizzy with delight. It was a sound a man adored to hear from a woman, both in bed and out.

"I should hope not. You know, that is the first compliment I've had all day. The other men I interviewed had plenty of things to say about me, but none so kind as that."

Prospero would have swung a fist at any man who'd dared to say anything uncharitable to a lady, especially *this* lady. She was a clever creature, a strong creature, but that didn't mean she deserved to put up with the nonsense of men who couldn't face a woman like her.

"I've noticed that weak men are often frightened by strong women," he said truthfully. He, on the other hand, preferred them.

"How right you are," she said, her face betraying a hint of sadness before she hid herself beneath a mask of politeness. "So, one hundred pounds per week, and I shall pay you the first week upfront." She counted out several banknotes and passed them to him. "We shall start this evening, if you don't mind. Be at my home at eight o'clock, and we shall have dinner and begin." She signed her name at the bottom of the contract and slid it over to him, along with her pen.

"So I passed your interview?"

"Indeed, and you are the only man to do so. Please don't disappoint me."

Prospero had the strangest feeling that his life was about to be turned upside down by this woman. It might be a mistake to agree to this, but he wasn't afraid to gamble since he had so little to lose, and something told him that this—whatever *this* was—might be worth it.

He picked up the pen and scrawled his name above the line designating the *participant* on the contract. Then he stood and started for the door, only to have her catch up with him and grab his arm.

"Your check . . . You forgot it," she said, pressing the bit of paper into his hand.

They were so close that he could see the depth of her light-brown eyes, and it made him want to curl his arms around her waist and haul her against his chest so he could kiss her. But he had a feeling that kisses were not the study this woman had in mind.

Still, he couldn't stop the thought that *he* wanted to study her the way she was to study him. He'd never met a woman that he couldn't charm. Most men believed women were all the same, cut from the same cloth, but he knew better.

Women were as different as the varieties of flowers on the earth. Some had soft petals. Some grew thorns and thistles. Some bloomed every year, while others had one great bloom before they retreated into the soil. Each was perfect in her own way.

Though he had much to be jaded about in his life, he never felt that way toward women. Even the widows in Paris who paid for his companionship, had been good ladies. They had been lonely, and he'd needed the money, so he'd given them himself in whatever ways they required. He'd done his best to treat them as well as he could, and they'd all been content. But he'd grown weary of that life, of being a man "owned" by someone in a transactional way.

The irony was that he was now facing a similar situation, being paid to perform. Only it wasn't about sex this time, which was a pity, given the beauty of the woman standing so close to him. He would have taken her to bed if she'd dared to give him but a hint that she wanted him.

Miss Hamblin cleared her throat.

"Er, yes. Thank you," he said softly and pocketed the check. "I shall see you tonight at eight o'clock." His gaze lingered upon her lips, then returned to her eyes, and he saw it, a flash of heat in her cheeks and in her gaze as she realized she'd been caught staring at his mouth too.

Perhaps this fiery woman was interested in him in more than just a scientific way . . .

If Miss Hamblin wanted to study a man, he would teach her *everything* she could ever want to know, including the art of seduction. Because it would be a crime to let this fascinating creature go without stealing at least one kiss.

"Perhaps we will end up teaching each other things, Miss Hamblin," he murmured to himself.

He exited the study, passing by opening door to the drawing room which was now empty of gentleman. He grinned like a Cheshire cat as he collected his hat and left 223 Baker Street.

E lise smoothed her skirts and stared at her reflection for the first time in her life with open concern.

"Mary, do you think I should change into the sapphire-blue gown or . . ." She plucked the lace just above her breasts, all too aware of how low the neckline was. Her breasts might pop free after one deep breath if she wasn't careful. She hadn't ever noticed that this gown was supposed to settle *this* low, but her maid, Mary, had tugged the gown down when Elise had first put it on.

Her maid chuckled. "Stop fussing, milady. The persimmon suits your eyes and hair better than the blue." It amused her that her maid called her milady because when she'd been born her father had called her a perfect little lady and the butler and Mary had adored the pet name of milady for Elise.

"Are you sure? Mr. Holmes said the blue—"

"Ach!" Mary tutted. "That windbag doesn't know a thing about ladies, let alone ladies' fashion. You look fine in blue, but any colors in the red or pink family make your eyes shine and your skin glow. Trust me."

Mary adjusted the sleeves on Elise's shoulders and then wiggled the elaborate bustle of pale-green bows and ribbons at the back of her gown. She adjusted it properly and then tied the bustle into the hidden loops of the back of the overskirt to secure it in place.

"There. 'Tis all settled for you to go down and meet your guest." Her maid beamed at her like a proud mother hen. "Your mother would be glad to see you like this, milady."

"Do you think so?" Elise bit her lip and slid another pin into her hair to keep the tight and elaborately styled coiffure that Mary had made in place. She had so few memories of her mother, but the ones she did have were full of smiles. Her mother had been an exquisite beauty, but also clever and full of life. That pang of longing for a mother she barely remembered was surprisingly deep, the pain ancient, yet still as fresh as if she were a child all over again. Her hands trembled as she touched the lace on her bodice again.

"I do. She always wanted to see you happy and find a man worthy of you, just like she found your father. Now here you are, finally showing interest in a man. And not just *any* man, but a handsome earl. 'Tis about time you married and settled down. Your father could use a grand-baby or two to make him feel young again."

Elise gasped. "I couldn't *possibly* think about children right now. Besides, I don't know why a grandchild would make a difference to Papa."

Her maid rolled her eyes. "Because when *you* have a child, your parents have a chance to love *that* child as they once loved you. It will remind him of the happy days when you were little and your mother was still alive." Her maid collected a pair of stockings from the floor and Elise's walking boots.

"Besides, you deserve to have a fine man courting you. You work too hard, milady. You deserve a bit of fun now and then."

Elise sighed in exasperation. "I told you, Mary. Lord March isn't coming to court me. I am *studying* him for the advancement of natural science."

Mary raised a brow as she stared at Elise through the reflection of the mirror.

"That and to win a bet against Mr. Holmes," she added quickly.

Mary shook her head. "Call it what you like, but that man *will* be courting you tonight, especially when he sees you in this dress. You'd best remember to take notes on *that*. You ought to be studying romance. And never mind about that Mr. Holmes and his silly wagers." Her maid then bent to retrieve Elise's day gown from the floor to put it away.

"Romance," Elise muttered. "How silly." She was far too busy discovering things that would change humanity's understanding of the natural world to be worried about things like carriage rides, flowers, and kisses. What nonsense. She tucked a defiant strand of blonde hair back in place and went downstairs. Mr. Roberts, her father's butler, was waiting for her.

"Has Lord March arrived yet?" she asked. Roberts shook his head.

She checked the grandfather clock by the door and frowned. It was two minutes until eight. What if he didn't come? She walked over to the slender window next to the door and peered out across the square at the townhouse that she now knew was his. It had surprised her to realize that they lived so close and yet she'd never been aware of it. Of course, he'd left for Paris so long ago, and she had never been one to think about gossip or society . . . but still. His own house had been just there across the square all this time . . .

Beneath the glow of the streetlamps, she saw Lord March exit his townhouse and step down onto the street and come toward her house. His steps were sure and his shoulders rigid. She remained hidden beside the window, her eyes lingering on the fine figure he cut. Her stomach tumbled and she ducked out of sight as he started up the steps to her home. A hard knock upon the door brought her back to herself.

"Shall I answer it?" Roberts asked. No doubt he was wondering why she was acting so unlike herself. She had never worried about guests arriving before.

"No. Wait . . . yes, you answer it. But let me go back upstairs first. Then send for me when he's here."

Roberts took her odd order in stride, and she rushed upstairs to hide just out of sight. The door opened and she heard March speak.

"Prospero Harrington . . . er . . . Lord March, to see Miss Hamblin for dinner." He still wasn't used to calling himself *March*, it seemed.

Roberts sent a footman up the stairs to where she was hiding and he whispered, "Miss Hamblin, Lord March is here for dinner."

Elise thanked the footman with a nod and waited a brief moment, as if she'd heard the butler from down the corridor, then took a deep breath and stepped out of her hiding place. She halted midway down the stairs as her eyes locked with those of Lord March.

He was the finest specimen of a man she'd ever seen. Not that it mattered, but she didn't make a habit of gawking at attractive men. *Interesting.* She would be taking notes on her own responses to him later.

Seeing him now brought her back to that moment earlier this afternoon at the society headquarters when he'd come into her study for the interview. She'd been struck then by his looks, but also by something not quite as tangible that created a heightened awareness of his innate maleness. She'd been around many men in her life, many who sought to remind her of her place in society as a woman, that she was beneath them, that being a woman was somehow a crime.

But not with Prospero. When he'd stood close to her and they'd spoken, his gaze had moved over her, not with predatory lust, but with honest male interest that held none of the usual superiority she was used to when men looked at her. She'd felt . . . feminine, *truly* feminine, for the first time in her life. With him, feeling feminine seemed to be a strength, something to be proud of because it made her feel . . . powerful. She was not simply some object to be coveted. She felt a strange sense of mutual attraction and desire that put her and Prospero on the same footing.

Prospero was taller than most men, with broad shoulders. His dark-blue evening coat had been tailored so well that it fit him like a second skin. His dark hair was cut slightly longer than was fashionable, and he had no mustache, despite the current trend to hide one's face with a stylish beard. His features were so perfect that the ancient Greek sculptors would have wept with need, demanding to capture his beauty in marble. His eyes filled with heat as he looked up at her, his hat halfway removed from his head. Had she stopped him quite literally in his tracks? The thought sent a frisson of pleasure through her. She'd never cared if she'd affected a man like that before, but now she did. Why was that?

"Miss Hamblin." He seemed to recover quicker than she did as he handed his hat to the butler. "You look lovely tonight."

They were silly words, words that any man could say to a woman, yet they had her heart fluttering strangely in her chest.

Don't be a fool, she chided herself. *He's only being polite.*

"Good evening, Lord March." She came the rest of the way down the stairs, and he bowed over her hand when she offered it.

"Please call me Prospero. If we are to work together, it would be far more comfortable, and appropriate." He then pressed his lips to her knuckles before he straightened.

Her skin tingled where he had touched her with his mouth. She'd forgotten her gloves, which wasn't unusual for dinners at home, but tonight it made her all too aware of this gorgeous earl. She'd heard women murmur about a certain type of men being dangerous, and she honestly hadn't quite understood what they'd meant. Danger, to her, had been the idea of a man pulling out a knife or something else that would threaten her physically, but now in this single, seemingly innocent moment, she finally understood what they meant.

That single kiss had completely blanked her mind of

rational thoughts, though it had happened for only an instant. The naturalist in her examined the response, and the resulting concern was what would happen to her if he were to kiss her mouth . . . or other places far more . . . intimate than her hand? Might that same mind blanking occur again . . . and for far longer? Many animals had courtship rituals, but none like this. Did the lioness feel a mix of fear and excitement when a male lion nuzzled her neck? Or was she simply comfortable in her choice of mate and had no doubts? Was it only humans who added extra layers of concerns and worries when it came to such rituals?

She shivered a little, and Prospero seemed to notice. His eyes narrowed ever so slightly, focused on the movement of her body like a wolf spotting a wild hare dashing away in the underbrush. Yet he waited. He didn't chase her. Somehow that waiting only seemed to heighten *everything* about his effect on her.

"W—well, Prospero it is, then." She cleared her throat, her skin suddenly flushed. Was it too hot in here? Had the maids lit the fires in every room in the house? It certainly felt as though they had. "I suppose, given the circumstances, you must call me Elise."

"Elise." His soft, sensual voice made her feel even warmer.

"Well . . . dinner should be ready for us." She gestured toward the dining room and started walking but Prospero gently captured her arm and tucked it into his. She looked down at his arm entwined with hers, startled.

"Shall we begin your first lesson about men? Most of us prefer to have the honor of escorting a woman to dinner. I say *most* men because I sadly know that some men do not act with respect or chivalry toward the female sex these days."

She looked up at him, more curious than ever about him. "And if you remove all civility, remove all chivalry, how would you behave? I mean, if you were a man without civilized laws and customs to guide you?"

He seemed to ponder her question quite seriously as he escorted her to a seat at the end of the table.

His gaze danced quickly over the expensively furnished room with a vast table, cherrywood paneled walls, and dozens of paintings of men hunting or women lounging beneath swings in pastoral scenes. Her mother had decorated this room years before Elise had been born and it was still beautiful, unchanged, like a memory of her captured in a bottle. Prospero didn't know this, of course. He would simply see a lovely room like in any other home in Grosvenor Square.

"I suppose you want an honest answer, not a gentlemanly one?" Prospero's hands lingered on the back of Elise's chair as he pushed her in toward the table.

"Of course. Honesty is key for any study." She turned to look up at him. He leaned down in that same moment, and they were close enough that their lips almost brushed. His eyes were such a vibrant blue, like a summer sky free of clouds. Heat spread through her body like a growing fire as she stared into those eyes and forgot everything else around her until he spoke again.

"Well then, honestly, most men will do anything to have even a chance to be near an attractive woman." Elise's breath caught, but before she could protest or ask another question, Prospero continued. "We pretend we want business and power more than anything else, but when it comes down to it, women will always be our deepest desire."

Elise finally found her voice. "Women, in the plural?"

His smile broadened. "Men curate their fantasies based on the women, or the singular woman, they are interested in at the moment. It differs based on the man as to whether he fixates on one woman at a time, or more."

Elise's throat felt dry. "Do all men have these . . . fantasies?"

"Well, let us say I took a fancy to you. I would fantasize about how much I'd like to get you alone." His voice was like silk. "I would spend countless hours planning to lure you into a dark alcove for a stolen kiss or caress. All men create fantasies of the things we want to do to you when we get you women alone. In my case, escorting you to dinner, letting me touch you ever so innocently, allowing me to inhale the scent of rosewater in your hair or the aroma of the flowery perfume that clings to your skin. Those are the sorts of things that stimulate my senses." He closed his eyes briefly, and her heart skipped a beat as he inhaled slowly, deeply, as if breathing in her scent to the depths of his soul.

"That's all so silly, though," she protested, her mind whirling. "My perfume, the smell of my hair? Any acquaintance of mine would make note of it. Why would that appeal to you as a male in such a heightened fashion?"

Prospero's eyes opened, snaring her. "Because, my darling Elise, all of this adds to my knowledge of *you*, which creates the illusion of *possibility*. A sweet scent or a rosy hue to your skin makes a man think of where it might lead, and that always leads to thoughts of sex. The primal man in me —the one you asked about, and the one for whom I answer honestly—hungers to take what my body so desperately wants."

"And if this wasn't part of a scientific study, what would a man such as yourself be looking for right now if you were alone with a woman for dinner? Hypothetically speaking, of course . . . ?" She could barely speak the words, her breath was so shallow with a strange excitement. It was as though she'd discovered a new species of butterfly or noticed a pattern in the migration of doves. He lifted his hand to stroke the backs of his knuckles along her bare arm.

"Hypothetically speaking, I'd want to ravish you . . . to strip you of every bit of silk and satin, cover your body with kisses, and stroke you in all the secret places that make you gasp and writhe. Then, when you beg for me, I will introduce you to the greatest pleasures that our mortal bodies can experience. A real man, a *good* man, craves to take a woman to such heights of pleasure that she fears she might die from the intensity."

His voice was low, hypnotic, and she found herself staring at his mouth once again in fascination. His lips curved up in a rakish half smile, as if he was all too aware of that fascination. *The greatest pleasures that our mortal bodies can experience . . .* His words echoed in her mind until she could only imagine what he might mean.

"Does that *honest* answer suit you?" he inquired.

It took an embarrassingly long moment for her to collect her thoughts. She gave a jerky nod.

"Good." He took his seat opposite her. Two footmen entered the dining room and approached the table with the first course of carrot soup, which they ladled into Elise and Prospero's bowls before retreating to the far corner of the room along with the butler to give them some privacy.

Prospero waited for her to try her soup. "May I ask *you* a question?"

"Yes, please consider this an open discourse between us. You may ask me whatever you wish." Questions would be safe, assuming he stuck to matters of natural science.

His expression turned thoughtful. "I noticed your father isn't dining with us. And your mother, is she here this evening . . . ?"

"She died when I was a young child. Papa usually dines with me, but he had a business dinner at his club." It was a question she was used to answering. Whenever her father had business dinners at home, the gentlemen dining with them, if meeting her for the first time, always inquired after her mother, who would have been the expected hostess.

"Ah. Which club does he belong to?"

She was glad when he didn't ask about her mother. Sometimes she didn't mind talking about her, but so often, that old grief, so deep for a child who loses a parent too young, could overcome her. It was a subject better left undiscussed.

"White's. You aren't a member, are you?" She knew the answer, but she didn't want him to know she'd prepared a complete dossier on him. Not yet, anyway.

"No, I'm over at Berkeley's. My family has been there for more than half a century. I was invited to join White's as a young man, as well as a few of the other clubs, but I ended up at Berkeley's. Some things are in the blood, aren't they?"

"Quite true." She'd made a study of inheritable traits in

animals, and she believed that people could be the same. "One can see it most clearly in dogs. They can inherit traits like eye color, fur pattern, even fur texture, but I also believe that some traits, such as herding or preferring the company of humans to being alone in pastures on farms, can also be an inherited trait bred into them over time. I'd love to expand my research further . . ."

She halted when she heard him chuckle.

"What?" she said, a little flustered. Was he making light of what she'd said? She was used to men mocking her.

"You, my dear Elise, are quite . . ."

She waited to hear what he would say and predicted it would fall in one of two disappointing ways.

"Fascinating," he finally said.

That wasn't at all what she'd expected him to say.

"You . . . you don't think I'm mad for comparing dog traits to men and their choosing of club memberships?"

"Mad? No, not at all. I think you might be rather brilliant," he replied.

She nearly sagged in relief at the clear honesty in his voice.

"Please never hesitate in telling me your observations. I find them truly interesting."

"Really?"

"Really." He flashed her that charming smile that had an all too noticeable an effect on the temperature of her body.

"You're blushing again. I must endeavor to continue doing whatever it is that makes you flush like that," he mused.

"Was I? Oh . . ." She hastily tried to think of something to change the subject. "Did you know that in 1851 a

German physician named Carl Reinhold August Wunder-lich discovered that humans have an average body temperature?"

"No, I had no idea," Prospero replied, leaning forward. "Tell me more about this Carl fellow."

She happily dove into a discussion about temperatures and measurements, and then the question of whether the average temperature shifted given age, gender, and general health conditions. All through it, he asked questions or added his thoughts, and she found she was truly having a pleasant evening with him.

As they finished their soup course, the footmen brought out roasted pheasant. Elise was startled by how *easy* it was to talk to Prospero. She'd never before realized that she might *enjoy* talking with a man. Most men at dinners kept the focus on themselves and bragged about their money or connections or their own banal observations, and they expected her to hang on their every word while they asked nothing of her interests.

With Prospero, conversation was smooth and easy. He had made her laugh with tales of his adventures in Paris with his friend Guy, the Viscount De Courcy. However, she sensed deep beneath his tales and amusing anecdotes that he had suffered much. She heard the longing in his voice as he spoke of his home and his old friends.

"Has it been hard, coming home?" she asked.

"Yes," he admitted. "Everyone has changed, and yet nothing *feels* changed. It's like I've come to watch a play on the second night, only all the actors are different while the scenery is the same as ever. It makes me feel . . ."

"Out of place?" she guessed.

He chuckled dryly. "That's exactly it. Out of place in a

setting that should be familiar but with players that I don't recognize anymore. Everyone wants to avoid me, except the few good friends I've had since boyhood."

"If there is one thing I know about people, they do not handle discomfort well. And I mean discomfort of *any* kind. People who know of your past will either look beyond it to see you or they won't. I suggest wasting no time on the latter." She set her glass of wine down on the table firmly as she made her point.

"Wise advice," he replied with a smile, softer than his previous rakish grin. To her surprise, she found she liked both expressions equally, as they were part of a complex tapestry that made up his personality. She adored complexity in all things because it gave her a sense of wonder and awe to study it and learn everything she could. Which was exactly what she planned to do with this man.

He pushed his plate away and drank the last of his wine. "So tell me, how do we begin this study of yours?" Elise felt strangely like she was the one under a magnifying lens rather than him.

"I would like to learn about your average day from start to finish, explore your nightly and morning rituals, and then expand into deeper subjects like your personal philosophies, things you see as triumphs and failures in your life. Mostly, I'm interested to know what motivates you on an instinctual level from day to day. Do you, say, eat only when you feel hungry, or do you eat every day at the same time? Do you feel the need to prove your strength against other males in physical tests, such as boxing or fencing? Do you enjoy hunting, and if so, why? Is it the thrill of the ride or the need to end the life of another creature? These are the sorts of things I came up with to start."

"Not that I'm not happy to be the chosen fellow for this study, but why not choose a more typical man? A dock-worker or a factory laborer or even a clerk at a bank? My background isn't exactly average. Won't that affect your study in some way or skew the results in a particular direction?"

"Actually, your background is what I was most inter-ested in. You see, it's easy enough to study those other men from the laboring classes. They are motivated by food for themselves and their families and a need to keep a roof over their heads. They cannot afford to indulge in the unusual activities that upper-class gentlemen do. A man of your station, by freedom of your title or money, have more flexibility to do as you please, to let your instincts and desires guide you. I don't wish to study the average man—I wish to study a man who lives on a knife's edge, a man with your exact history."

Understanding lit his eyes. "You knew about my past, and that was part of the reason you chose me? Because I've done something most men haven't when I faced Jackson in that duel and then lived in Paris the way I did."

Elise feared for a moment he would be furious, that he would see all too clearly that she'd marked him as the target for her study long before the moment he'd stepped into the society's headquarters for his interview.

"I suppose . . . that I can understand that, although it does leave me feeling a bit . . . unsettled. I want to put that part of my life behind me."

"Of course. I have no desire to make you relive any of it. I just wish to study someone like you, someone *complex*."

"Fair enough. Very well, I give my consent to continue the study."

She waited for the footmen to clear away their plates before she addressed what she considered to be a sensitive subject.

"I also have a room prepared for you to sleep in tonight."

He stood and came over to her, offering her his arm once more. This time the gesture, which she'd always seen as one of politeness, carried a charged sensual energy to it because she knew what he was thinking. It was undeniably fascinating and unsettling to have an insight into the male realm of thought where she'd never been privy before.

"Hypothetically, what do *you* think of when a man offers you his arm?" Prospero asked as they exited the dining room.

"Me?" she asked, surprised by her own question being turned back on her.

"Yes, as a woman, not a naturalist."

She tilted her head as she considered it. "I suppose I see it as a sign of trust and a sign of respect. I appreciate the consideration that a man will adjust his length of stride when we walk side by side. I am not as short in stature as many women, but I still like not having to run to keep up with a man who is taller than me."

"Respect is all that comes to mind? Nothing else?" His eyes glinted with mischief.

"Yes, that is *all* I think of." She was lying, however, and she knew by the flash in his gaze that he was well aware of it. She remained silent until she showed him to a room on the floor above them.

"This will be your bedchamber for as long as you require during our study." She opened the door, and he examined the room without comment.

"I'm sorry that I don't have a valet for you. Would you like me to hire one?" she asked uncertainly.

"That won't be necessary. I'm quite used to dressing myself until I can find a man of my own."

"Speaking of which . . . do you need any help? My butler, Roberts, has quite a network of connections with other households in the city. I could task him with posting your position notices when you hire your new staff."

Prospero turned to her. "My pride demands that I ignore the help, but frankly, I could use it. My contacts upon returning to London are not what they once were."

Elise made a mental note of this choice, how he was aware of his own pride but pushed it aside for the rational logic of accepting help from her. Then she realized that her help being accepted by him gave her a flash of her own feminine pride. She thought of Cinna's comment about defeating men. This didn't feel like a victory over an enemy, however, but rather a *shared* moment between two people partnering together.

"Write something up tonight. I will tell Roberts to put notices up for you tomorrow." She started to pull her arm away from his, but he caught her gently by the elbow.

"You mentioned seeing a man's nightly rituals. Shall we begin this evening?" He raised a brow as he waited for her answer in the blend of candlelight and shadow just inside the doorway.

Was this how Persephone felt when she faced the choice of stepping into Hades's beautiful twilight realm? Would she taste the bittersweetness of a pomegranate?

Prospero was challenging her, testing whether she would go through with her plan to study him. Did he think she would be too afraid to watch him undress?

She lifted her chin. "Please give me a few minutes. If I am to observe you this evening, I shall need pen and paper. I should also like to change into a tea gown to be more comfortable."

He released her and stepped inside his newly appointed bedchamber. "I shall await your return."

She whirled away and went to her own room. Mary quickly helped her change out of her evening dress and corset before she changed into a more comfortable light-blue tea gown. She stepped into fur-lined slippers and collected a notebook and a pen from her writing desk before she returned to Prospero's room.

He stood by the bed, leaning back against it, his legs crossed at the ankles as he waited for her. He said nothing when he took in her change of clothing, but she saw surprise in his eyes. It was a bit unusual to wear a tea gown in front of a man while alone. Tea gowns were less formal, less restrictive on a woman's body, and he was no doubt aware of that fact. It didn't usually make her feel exposed, but she did now as his eyes lingered on her unrestricted breasts beneath the thin silk.

She settled into a chair and placed a book on her lap to support her notebook, then looked at him expectantly.

"You may begin. And please, explain things as you go along."

He pushed away from the bed. "Very well."

Why the act of him moving away from the bed and toward her with purpose made her heart suddenly flutter wildly, she wasn't sure. Men never affected her like this.

Prospero is a specimen to be studied, she reminded herself. *No different than a moth or a beetle.*

But no matter how hard she tried to convince herself,

the truth was that this man *did* affect her. He presented such an elegant picture in his dark-blue tailored evening suit and gold waistcoat. He removed his frock coat and reached for the buttons of the waistcoat.

"I prefer to remove my waistcoat first, normally by starting with my pocket watch," Prospero said.

"Do you have a pocket watch?" she asked when he didn't reach for one.

His blue eyes darkened. "Not at the moment. I had to sell it in order to buy passage back to England."

"Oh, I'm sorry, I shouldn't have asked."

"You need not apologize. You couldn't have known." Prospero's tone was gentle, but she heard the melancholy in his words.

She forced her gaze down to her paper and made a few notes about watches and waistcoats. When she looked back up, he was studying her, his hands holding the edges of his waistcoat slightly open. She swallowed as he peeled the garment off his body to reveal his crisp white shirt of thin linen. He reached up, removed his ascot, and tossed the tie onto the bed before undoing the buttons of his collar.

Heat blossomed in her cheeks as he unfastened his cuffs and pulled his shirt out of his trousers.

"I tend to remove my shirt next. I can keep it cleaner that way if I wash my face or shave in the evening, which I usually do."

"You shave in the evening? Why?"

He seemed to consider her question seriously. "I don't do it every evening, just on the evenings when I know I will be spending time with a lady."

"Oh? What does that have to do with you shaving at night?"

He chuckled and crooked a finger at her. "Shall I demonstrate?"

"You want me to . . . ?"

"Come here, yes." Prospero's grin was playful—and dangerous.

"Oh, I don't need to—"

"Come here, my little naturalist. *Study* me." He said it so seductively that Elise found herself moving toward him before she could consider how this likely wasn't a good idea.

She was alone in a bedchamber with a notorious man, and here he was asking her to come closer. But he was a gentleman, and she needed to be close to him in order to properly study him, didn't she? What harm could it do to be just a little closer?

❧ 5 ❧

E lise was driving him mad. Prospero beckoned her with a crook of his finger, needing her to come to him. If she sat in that chair a moment longer, taking prim little notes about the art of a man undressing, he would go utterly wild with the need to strip her clothes off and teach her about a man's instincts.

"Come here, little naturalist, and *study* me," he commanded when she looked at him with those wide, innocent brown eyes. He knew she was vastly intelligent, it was quite clear from their conversation at dinner, but she was an innocent when it came to men. In that moment, he knew truly what his mission was. He would teach her everything about men and instruct her in the ways that a man could please a woman. He was well-versed in seduction and lovemaking, and for once he wanted to indulge himself in pleasure by seducing this clever, beautiful creature. He wanted to do this because she needed him to show her that learning about the opposite sex couldn't be done at a distance and kept completely scientific.

She needed to feel what he felt, the raw lust, the potent desire that wove spells over a person's body, heart, and soul that made the eventual lovemaking all that more intense. He knew she wouldn't fall in love with him, he wasn't a fool, but if he could show her what she truly needed to know about passion, it would be a gift between them, not simply a repayment for her providing him a means of income for a short time. No, he wanted to do this because he genuinely liked her and deeply desired for her to know what pleasures a woman deserved to experience with a man. There was more to love than logic and science could ever explain. He would show her the magic that lay in twilight kisses and soft, sliding bodies in the dark.

Elise moved at his command to come to him, and when she was close enough to touch, he grasped her right hand and raised her palm to his smooth, shaven cheek. He'd shaved before coming over this evening out of his usual habit. None of his Parisian widows had liked a beard or mustache.

"Feel that?" he whispered. She nodded, eyes wide and luminous. "Smooth skin is often preferred by ladies when they wish to be kissed. A man starts to grow a beard or stubble toward the evening if he shaves early in the morning, and some women do not like to feel that scratching their lips, cheeks . . . or other places."

"What happens when it is rough?" she asked.

She truly was innocent. Had this woman ever been kissed? If she had, it must have been some pathetically chaste peck; otherwise, she would know what he meant about roughness. They really *should* educate women more, because exploring things like this made it difficult for a man to behave.

Her fingers remained on his cheek as she continued to study him critically. Her touch burned him in the best way. It had been such a long time since he'd felt this deeply maddening desire for a woman.

"Well?" she prompted, and he struggled to remember what they had been discussing.

"Yes, well, when a woman is kissed by a man who hasn't shaved recently, she can get rubbed a little too vigorously and her skin can become sensitive to it."

"Is that why you have no mustache?" she asked. She blushed a soft color of persimmon. "To avoid irritating a lady's skin?"

He was aware mustaches were a fashion of the day in London, but he had no interest in them.

"In part, yes, but trimming and maintaining a mustache takes time and effort."

She squinted a little, as if trying to guess how he might look with one.

"Would you be interested in seeing me grow a mustache?" he teased, but she took the question seriously.

"Perhaps in the second week of our study?" She still had her palm up on his cheek, and traced his cheekbones, then the line of his jaw with her fingers. "So, you've already shaved?" she asked.

"Yes, just before I came here."

"Oh . . ." She looked disappointed. "I would like to see you shave in the morning to see how it's done."

"You've never seen a man shave?" he asked, more curious about Elise than she could possibly guess. It was clear she'd never been kissed, or at least, kissed properly, and it was unlikely she'd had any close encounters with men and their lives. Perhaps that was the true reason for her study, to fill this gap in her worldly understanding.

"No. I live with my father, but I've never had an occasion to see him perform his morning or nightly rituals such as shaving."

"I suppose that makes sense. It is a rather intimate thing. Likely only his valet or your mother would have seen him do it. When I was younger, my valet used to shave me, but it's been years since I've had a servant for such tasks."

She lowered her hand from his cheek, but he caught her wrist in both of his hands, warming her chilly fingers by rubbing them between his palms. It was something he did without thinking. He'd grown used to taking care of women in the smallest of ways. It was why he'd been so popular in France. He knew what a woman needed, not just what she wanted.

Women were strong creatures, so strong that they often went entire lifetimes without their needs fulfilled, however big or small. He'd found joy in being a man who gave women what they needed, from hours of exquisite lovemaking, making them a cup of tea, or setting up a picnic in the sunshine with their favorite books and treats ready for them.

He studied her brown eyes, enjoying the insatiable curiosity that shone in their depths. What did Elise need? She craved knowledge. She wanted to understand him. She sought the keys to unlock his mind, perhaps his very soul. To his surprise, he found that he wanted to give them to her.

"Shall I continue undressing for you?" he asked, his voice softer, deeper.

She nodded as he released her wrist, and then he pulled the shirt off before he tossed it to the floor.

A little gasp escaped her, and she covered her mouth with one hand.

She'd probably never seen a man's bare chest before. He was aware that his muscled form was quite attractive to most women, even those who buried their adorable noses in books. The only thing that marred his skin was a dark knot of scar tissue where Aaron Jackson's bullet had torn through him. But her eyes didn't linger there—as if she was too overwhelmed by the rest of him.

"I assume you've studied the musculature of humans?" He allowed himself to flex a little as he reached for the buttons at the front of his trousers. Her throat worked, and she swallowed hard as he undid a single button. Very good. She was as affected as he was by the intimacy of this moment.

"I . . . yes. I've studied the human form and anatomy." Her gaze lowered to his chest as he moved cautiously toward her. "I've seen statues in museums, of course, and I once visited a mortuary and was able to witness an autopsy, but this is . . . different," she admitted as though baffled.

"You may touch me, Elise. I am no marble statue in a museum behind a velvet rope. Explore me, study me however you *desire*."

Heat flashed in her brown eyes as he said *desire*, and he saw the effect it had on her. She intoxicated him on a level he didn't fully understand, but wanted to. He planned to study her just as she studied him until he discovered why *she* affected him like this. The only way he had ever learned about a woman was by taking one to bed. Of course, this woman was not going to fall into his arms like the others because—

In a blur of movement, Elise stumbled. Prospero lunged, catching her an instant before she would have struck the edge of the nearby dresser. Her body became tense in his arms for a moment before she sighed with relief.

"Oh heavens, I'm never clumsy like that," she muttered.

Prospero stabilized her and made sure she could stand before he loosened his hold on her.

"I think your slipper caught on the edge of the rug." He nodded at the evidence of her single slipper overturned by the corner of the Oriental rug. She glanced over her shoulder, and Prospero was stuck by the singular beauty of her swanlike neck. He had heard men describe a woman's neck that way before, but he'd never understood until this moment what they meant. Her ivory skin had a hint of blush, and the column of her throat trailed down into an elegant shoulder, slightly exposed when her tea gown fell off it. He wanted to bury his face in her neck, kiss and nibble it until he left faint love marks upon her skin. Prospero wanted other men to see his love marks upon her body, the marks of him loving her and giving her pleasure, but he didn't say that. Not yet.

She turned to look up at him, as if finally realizing that she was leaning against him, her body pressed to his tight enough that he could feel the beaded points of her nipples rubbing against his chest. His rebellious little beauty wasn't wearing a corset. This woman was going to be the death of him, and he had known her for less than a day.

He cleared his throat, stepped back, and let her put her gown to rights and tuck up a few coils of hair that had come undone in her tumble. "So . . . ," he began awkwardly. "Trousers." He had never been shy around a woman. He wasn't exactly shy now, but damned if he didn't feel odd removing his trousers before her and being studied like a breeding stud at Tattersall's.

"Trousers," she echoed as uncertainly as he had spoken. Their gazes met again, and he suddenly laughed at the absurdity of the situation.

"What?" she asked, confused.

"Usually when I'm stripping off my clothing, it's under rather different circumstances. Usually, the woman I'm with is undressing as well. I've never realized until now that there was a certain comfort in the act of *mutual* disrobing."

Again her cheeks flushed that perfect pink. "Oh . . ."

"Perhaps you ought to take notes?" Prospero reminded her. He bit his lip to hide a grin as she dove for her notebook. She made a show of sitting and taking notes. He was undoubtedly curious as to what she was writing about him, but he didn't dare ask her to share.

He removed his shoes and trousers until he was bare except for his smallclothes. He sat on the edge of the bed and waited. She glanced up, swallowed again, and then hastily scribbled more notes.

"I wish Cinna was here. She does better sketches than I do," Elise muttered to herself. But the room was quiet enough that he heard her.

"Cinna?" he prompted.

"Lady Cinna Belmont. My friend and fellow member of the society."

"I meant to ask during dinner, what exactly *is* this society of yours? Are you all naturalists, or . . . ?"

"No. We are a society for women to learn about

anything that interests them. The arts, mathematics, sciences, economics, politics. We have but one goal: to learn and share our knowledge with other women and to buck society's unfair restrictions on women."

"That's two goals," Prospero pointed out.

"In this society, they go hand in hand."

"Ah, that explains the *rebellious* part of your society's name."

Her eyes sharpened. "Do you disapprove?"

"Of women or of rebels?" he replied.

"Both."

He folded his arms over his bare chest. "I think, given my presence here, I rather approve of both."

"Perhaps you simply approve of my money?"

"Those other men who ran out of the interview suggest otherwise. With the amount you are offering, they should have stayed, but their own foolish sense of superiority prevented them from putting faith in your work as a naturalist."

"Most titled men don't approve of anything that challenges their social standing or their power."

"Those men fear that which is out of their control. It is a weakness, not a strength. Twelve years ago, I might have become a man like that, had fate not intervened. We shall never know." He honestly *didn't* know what his younger self would have become. He only knew that boy was gone and the man he was now, the man with blood and death upon his hands, had walked away from trying to control his life or the lives of others.

Her eyes softened a little. "Is it true you lived with widows as a companion to . . . to . . ."

His lips twitched. "To get by? Yes, how did you know

about that?" It was oddly amusing to see that his situation did fluster her a little. There was a woman beneath the naturalist, and he was fascinated by both elements of her.

"I confess, before your interview, I did ask around a bit, and was aware of the duel and its outcome. I pretended I was not aware of it during our meeting since I wanted to see how you would explain it to me. But as I said the incident doesn't matter to me, but I do prefer to be prepared with information."

"I can't fault you for doing your research. I would've done the same in your place." He didn't say anything more about the widows, however. He didn't want her to realize that he was no different from the ladies of the night in Whitechapel.

They fell into a moment of silence as she wrote a few more notes and looked up again.

"So, do you have any nightly rituals other than to shave?"

"Rituals?" He rolled the word around on his tongue for a moment. "I read a little, if I have access to something good. Otherwise, I suppose I just go to bed." He pulled back the bedclothes and climbed in. "Do you plan to stay here and watch me sleep?"

"Yes, I would like to observe you for a few hours." She made a show of settling into the chair once more.

"As you wish." He fluffed up the pillow and lay back on the bed, folding his arms behind his head. A single lamp lit in the room, and he would have no trouble sleeping despite the small bit of light.

The silence of night stretched on, marred only by the sound of her pen scratching against paper while she continued to write. At first he found it distracting, and he thought it would be impossible to fall asleep to it. But after a while, he felt a gentle calmness descend on him. He blinked once, twice, and as it sometimes happened, he fell into a dream almost instantly.

He was dancing at a ball, one years ago, before he'd fled to France, when he had still been twenty-two. Golden light bathed the doors around him, and he found himself grinning as he spotted the faces of old friends in the crowd.

"Nicholas!" he called, but his friend did not turn his way. More people failed to respond to him when he called their names. They swirled around and danced as his shouts continued to go unheard. Suddenly, a young woman slipped through the crowd and approached him.

Miss Jackson?

"Hello, Prospero," she purred and batted her lashes. "I'm so glad you came back." She leaned against his arm, her body strikingly cold against his own. "I've been waiting for you."

He turned to look more deeply into her eyes and saw a glint of darkness in their depths. She hissed like a viper. "Never forget that I own you . . ."

He bolted upright in bed with a gasp, specters of his past fading into the shadows of the room. For a moment, he didn't remember where he was. The bed was too lush, the room too warm to be his chilly flat in Paris.

He dragged his hands over his face, rubbing at his eyes as his body felt bone-weary. The remnants of his dream— no, *nightmare*—still lingered at the edges of his vision like vaporous ghosts. He hadn't had that dream in years, but being back in England had unearthed all sorts of old pains and fears.

Prospero glanced about and saw someone fast asleep in a chair close to the bed.

Elise Hamblin, the little naturalist. Of course. It all came rushing back: the interview, the dinner, the undressing. He needed a glass of scotch to drown his embarrassment as well as his desire for this woman. Prospero's gaze roved over her. Her notebook had fallen to the floor, and her pen dangled from her limp fingers as she lay sleeping in what had to be a most uncomfortable position.

Prospero quietly slipped out of bed. He removed her pen and set it down on the table, then carefully lifted Elise into his arms and laid her on the bed. He then removed her slippers and tucked the blankets up to her chin. She murmured something too quiet for him to hear and then rolled onto her side to face him, but she didn't wake.

Filled with an unexpected well of tenderness, he brushed her hair back and bent, pressed his lips to her forehead in a gentle kiss. She moved a little, her hand suddenly catching his fingers as he started to pull away. He froze for a moment, startled by the simple yet powerful connection as she clung to him. He held on to her hand, feeling a thread of some invisible spell binding him to this woman. Her grip finally loosened, and her hand dropped back to the bed.

He almost reached down to reclaim her hand but pulled back at the last second. Instead, he tucked the sheets around that hand to keep it warm. Then he turned to retrieve her notebook from the floor. With a careful glance over his shoulder to make sure she had not woken up, he studied the notes she had made.

This noble rogue has many qualities that lend to his natural likability. Naturally, attrac-

*tiveness matters, but good looks without some-
thing more to offer would fail to attract quality
females. No, this smarter rogue has developed
skills like listening aptly to a female whilst in
discussion and acting respectably when around
females, at least outside the bedroom. More
study is required as to a rogue's behavior once
he is in private with a female.*

Beneath these words was a sketch of a pair of piercing clear eyes and a slant of dark brows. *His* eyes. She thought she couldn't sketch? Her skill was quite evident because it felt like he was looking in a mirror.

Under the drawing of his eyes, she had written the words *"thrilling, captivating, bewitching."* Then she'd added the hasty comment: *"Windows to one's soul?"* She had underlined her own question as though debating with herself about the matter. His lips twitched as he considered the existential question of whether one's eyes were, in fact, the window to one's soul. He believed they were. He wished he possessed the same natural talent to draw, because he would have sketched her eyes beneath his own.

Eyes were indeed the most important feature in a person. Eyes did not age. Perhaps that was what he loved most, to know that if he was ever blessed to fall in love, he would have the gift of growing old and gazing into the unchanging eyes of the woman he loved. The face around the eyes might become painted with lines from living, but the eyes themselves would never age.

He turned his attention back to the woman asleep in

the bed. The thread connecting him to this puzzling, fascinating creature only deepened.

"Good night, my rebellious little naturalist." He closed the cover of her notebook and smiled before he settled in the chair to sleep.

CELINE PERKINS STUDIED THE CARDS IN HER HANDS, AND with a sweet smile of victory, she placed them down on the green baize gambling table. The man she played against groaned in defeat.

"Mrs. Perkins wins again," one man muttered.

Celine leaned forward and collected her winnings with glee. She was tucking the much-needed money into her purse when she spotted her elder brother, Adam Jackson, entering the gambling den. He spotted her, storm clouds brewing on his face. That didn't bode well for her. Ever since she'd married Charles Perkins, a man twenty years her senior, she'd done her level best to avoid her eldest brother and his cruelty. When her husband had died from a weak heart, she found herself once more under her brother's power. She bid her partners a good night and quickly tried to move past her brother. He caught her arm and dragged her into an alcove.

"Adam, what—?"

His eyes were as dark and burning as hot coals. "You'll never guess who is back in London."

"Who?" she asked in trepidation.

"Harrington. Of course, now he's the damned Earl of March."

Celine's lips parted in shock. "Prospero's returned?"

"Yes, and I mean to have my revenge upon him," her elder brother growled. "Harrington won't walk away from *me*, not after what he did to Aaron."

"Oh please, let it go, Adam, let him be," Celine pleaded. "He is not worth it. Besides, I've been married for years now."

"And now widowed. Don't forget, he killed our brother, Celine. You may not care, but *I* do."

Between her two brothers, Aaron had been her favorite, but he was gone. Adam, the eldest of the three, had a frightening temper. It was one of the reasons she'd been so quick to marry and escape a household where he could hurt her whenever an ill mood took him. Now he had forced himself back into her life, and all those old fears had returned.

"*Please*, Adam." She tugged on his arm again. "Let it be. I want to forget, to move on from the hurts of the past."

Her brother sneered down at her. "You made a mess by chasing Harrington after he got you with child, and Aaron got himself killed over it. So *you* will help me by bringing Harrington down, or I swear to God I shall not give you a moment's peace. Not one."

She didn't dare tell him the truth, that the child wasn't Prospero's. It could have been a dozen other men. She'd been so desperate to get away from her family, and being with child was the only way she felt she could manage it.

Prospero had never done more than steal a kiss once when she had been a debutante. She'd pointed the finger at him as the father in the hopes he would be kind enough to come to her rescue and marry her. But he'd refused because he didn't love her, and he'd vowed to marry only for love. Aaron hadn't believed him and had challenged him to a duel.

"What do you want me to do?"

"Find his weakness. I want to *hurt* him, to wound him so deeply he'll feel he can't breathe. Once he's dying inside, I'll put a bullet through his heart."

Celine shuddered. Prospero didn't deserve any of this. Her actions had gotten her brother killed and nearly killed Prospero as well. Now it was happening again, and she feared Prospero wouldn't survive her family's wrath a second time.

6

Prospero woke early, his body's natural rhythm pulling him from sleep as the room lightened. He was stiff as he sat up in the chair and stretched. He yawned and glanced at the bed nearby. Sometime during the night, he had stolen a blanket from the bed to keep himself warm, but there had been plenty of blankets to keep Elise comfortable. At the moment she was burrowed deep beneath the covers, only her face peeping out as well as one dainty foot that had somehow become untucked from the blankets.

He stared at that slender, feminine foot and found himself grinning. He *should* wake her, but he believed in always letting a woman sleep. If there was one thing he knew, it was that a well-rested woman was a happy one. He stood and retrieved his clothes from the night before and donned them again.

They were somewhat wrinkled by now and not at all suitable for wearing the rest of the day. He would have to retrieve his travel case from his townhouse across the street and change. He would also need to visit a tailor to acquire a new wardrobe. He had but a handful of outfits at the moment and would need more if he intended to meet with others about business investments. He had the money Elise had given him after his interview, and he would use part of that to purchase a few outfits.

Prospero quietly slipped from the room and went down the hall to the grand stairs. As he reached the entryway on the floor below, he ran into the butler, Roberts.

"Good morning, my lord." Roberts emerged from the doorway that Prospero assumed led down to the kitchens below.

"Ah, Mr. Roberts, would it be possible to have some breakfast?"

"Certainly, my lord. The dining room is prepared. Please break your fast at your leisure. The morning papers have been pressed and are laid out if you choose to read anything."

"Thank you." He nodded at the butler as the man turned to go, then stopped him. "Er. Mr. Roberts, Miss Hamblin mentioned you might post notices for household positions in my home. The one across the street?"

"Yes, my lord. I've seen to it already."

"You have?"

"Yes, my lord. I sent them off to the papers last evening. They should be in the appropriate places today and tomorrow. Applicants will send their responses here for you, and I will be happy to weed out any unsuitable candidates, if you'd like."

Prospero considered the matter. "Thank you. Leave any

qualified applications for me to review. I need staff who will be loyal to my house, given my . . . unusual circumstances."

"Of course, I completely agree," said Roberts. "I will notify you the moment responses to the postings begin to arrive."

Prospero entered the dining room and halted at the realization that he was not alone. A tall, strongly built man in his early sixties with graying dark hair sat at the far end of the table, a paper unfolded in front of him. He had a slice of toast raised halfway to his mouth as he stared back at Prospero, equally stunned. Why hadn't the butler warned him he was not to dine alone?

"Who the devil are you?" The man's dark mustache twitched as he seemed to hold back a more direct response to someone disturbing his breakfast.

"I am Prospero Harrington. I am participating in a scientific study for Miss Hamblin." There was probably a better way to introduce himself, but that was all he could think of in the moment. He was quite certain this was Elise's father.

The formidable man narrowed his eyes. "Harrington . . . Harrington. Hold on, you're the Earl of March's son."

Ah. There it was. Prospero waited for Mr. Hamblin to denounce him and demand he vacate the house. But instead, Hamblin only stared at Prospero with a mix of interest and a calculated gleam in his eyes.

"My father died a few months ago," Prospero said, filling the dead air.

"That makes *you* Lord March, then," Elise's father mused. "You have my condolences on your father."

"Thank you. I presume you are the Hamblin patriarch?" Prospero could see Elise's eyes in the man's face and the stubborn tilt of his chin.

"I am. You may call me John."

He stood and held out a hand to Prospero. Startled by the gesture, Prospero shook his hand.

"Then I must insist you call me Prospero."

"Now then, what's all this about my daughter and some study? What's she gotten herself into this time?" His gaze missed nothing as it swept over Prospero's wrinkled evening suit.

"She is studying gentlemen and has hired me to be the subject of her study. You were not aware of this?"

John's brows lowered dangerously. "That my daughter was inviting strange men into my home to study them? No, I was certainly not aware of that."

"Oh . . ." Prospero began to wonder if his initial concern of being tossed out of the house might yet come to pass.

"So you've only just arrived this morning, then?" John was once more studying him. Between Elise and her father, Prospero was beginning to feel like one of those insects in a jar at the Society of Rebellious Ladies' headquarters.

"I arrived last evening. We had dinner."

"You dined with my daughter? *Alone?*" John growled.

"Yes, I was not aware that you would not be present for dinner. She only informed me you had a business dinner at your club after I arrived."

John stroked his mustache thoughtfully. "And you stayed the night here?"

Prospero heard the unspoken question. In a strange

way, he felt far more in danger in this moment with this man than when he'd faced Jackson in that blasted duel.

"At her request, as part of the study. You have my word that nothing occurred that would require any kind of announcement between us. Your daughter's interest in me is *entirely* scientific."

At this, John sighed in disappointment. "Sadly, I believe you. I might be the only man in England who prays his daughter would notice men. Instead of wanting to marry one, she wants to study them. Christ, what's next? We have more skeletons, creatures in jars, and stuffed animals in this house than the new natural history museum that opened last year. Where would I store all the men if she begins collecting *you* lot next?" Elise's father gave a wry chuckle.

Prospero chuckled as well and took a seat when John motioned for him to sit. A footman brought toast as well as a pot of orange marmalade and set them close to Prospero on the table.

"So, a study of men? What could she possibly want to know? She lives with one. What else could she seek to learn that she cannot ask me?"

Prospero cracked an egg with his spoon. "As I understand it, she wants to know men on an instinctive level. What drives our daily actions, what motivates us, and so forth." He glanced John's way, curious to see how her father would react to that. The older man seemed unruffled by his daughter's odd choice in study.

"She's wasting her time, then, seeking deeper answers. There are only three things that drive men: the love of money, power, and women. I could have told her that," Elise's father snorted.

"I almost said as much last evening, but she still intends to go through with her study."

"I blame that bloody society of hers," John sighed.

"You don't approve?" Prospero asked as he ate his breakfast.

John let out a weary sigh. "I approve of it, but sometimes I wonder if she buries herself in studying to avoid living. Or perhaps it's because her mother was so involved in the society that Elise wants to feel connected to her through it. She was only a wee babe when I lost my Eloise."

"Her mother was named Eloise?"

John's hard face softened. "Yes, when my daughter was born, she looked so much like my darling wife that we named her Elise. Now she's grown up, and damned if she isn't the spitting image of her mother. I suppose I'm grateful at times that she hasn't married. To lose her now would break my heart." John's honesty made Prospero's throat tighten.

"Except for her eyes. I dare say she has *your* eyes, John," Prospero remarked.

"You think so, eh?" John's brown eyes fixed on Prospero with open curiosity. It was a look so much like Elise's that Prospero could only nod. Yes, Elise had just as much of her father in her as her mother.

"So, Prospero, if my memory serves, your parents used to live in this square." He nodded his head toward the tall dining room windows that faced the street.

"Yes, my mother retired to the country to be with her sister, and now that I've returned from Paris, I plan to update the furnishings and make any needed repairs."

John nodded in approval. "Good man. Property values in the square will benefit from that, of course."

Prospero marveled at how alike Elise and her father were. It made him smile.

"I understand you are in the railroad business?" Prospero asked after they had both eaten in silence for a few minutes.

"I am. Don't tell me you are as well?" John replied. "I admit, I don't follow much of the activities of your lot. Most of them are rotten at business."

Prospero knew what he meant. *The titled lot.* Often, titled lords did not engage in business unless they absolutely had to—at least not the older set—but as farmlands were giving way to buildings and sales of ancestral homes were frequent, the titled lot were forced to look to alternative ways to support their families and those grand estates that remained.

"I am not involved yet, but I would be interested to know if you believe it's worth investing in. For a man new to the industry, such as me."

"It would take a bit of coin to get you in unless you have connections. Most of the decent railways are tightly held by small but powerful groups of investors. But I suppose I can ask around. Do you know anything about steel production or railways?"

Prospero felt a quickening of excitement at the thought of doing something of value. But he had to temper that excitement with the reality that he had little to offer in the way of knowledge or experience. "Very little, but I am a quick study."

"You will need to be, if you expect to keep any investments not only afloat but profitable. The technology changes every day, it seems."

Taking a chance, Prospero leaned toward John a little.

"Would you be willing to point me in the direction of how best to learn about it?"

John paused. "Are you serious?"

"Absolutely. I mean to rebuild my family's fortunes, and I have no intention of sitting back on my title. If work is required, I am as able-bodied and able-minded as any man. I'd like to be of use to myself and to others. Getting into a growing business seems the smart thing." Prospero hoped John would never hear about the means by which he'd gotten by in Paris. It wasn't easy to see the difference between a disgraced *son* of an earl and a disgraced earl. The former had little to trade except his own body; the latter had a title and prestige to barter with. The unfortunate truth was that his father's death had opened up a few doors that had been shut for the last twelve years.

John studied him for a moment with the same cool, calculating, but not unkind sort of look that his daughter had given him during the initial interview at the society. Prospero saw that the other man's gaze held no judgment for his past, only what his future might be. John pushed back his chair and stood.

"Wait here," he said, and left the dining room. When he returned, John handed Prospero a thick volume entitled *A History of the English Railway* and a second slimmer edition titled *Propulsion Systems and Railway Engineering*.

"If you can still stomach the business after reading these, I can take you to a meeting with me."

Prospero was stunned at the man's willingness to help. "Thank you, truly."

John shrugged. "I can respect a man who won't let the past hold power over him. You are here now, demanding to be given a fair shot in life, not lording over a dead title and looking for things to be handed to you. Only a fool would stand in your way, and a good man would lend a hand. Someone once did the same for me, and I believe in paying forward such acts of goodness."

Something tightened in Prospero's chest at the man's generosity. Elise might share her father's kindness too. All because she had compassion, not pity, for his circumstances. He was grateful and wise enough to recognize the difference.

ELISE ROLLED OVER AND STRETCHED, ENJOYING THE warmth of the blankets a long moment before she bolted upright. This wasn't *her* bedchamber. It was the guest room she'd had prepared for Prospero Harrington last evening. Only he wasn't here with her. She was completely alone. And in the bed. She distinctly remembered being in the chair, not the bed. Had he moved her in the night? He must have. Her brows drew together. Why would he do that? Give up a cozy bed for her? Was it something the laws of gentlemen demanded, or was it something more . . . primal, more ancient in the way a male could care for a female? She needed to make a note to ask him about that later.

Her notebook and pen were neatly sitting on a table, and Prospero's clothing that had been strewn about the floor last night was gone. For a moment she considered the possibility that she had dreamed everything that happened last night. But no, it hadn't been some fantasy. She had watched the infamous Earl of March undress for her—for scientific purposes, of course—and the act had seemed to charge the room with an electricity she didn't know how to explain.

She felt like the sixth-century Greek philosopher Thales of Miletus as he rubbed amber rods together to demonstrate what was now called the triboelectric effect. When she'd stumbled and fallen into Prospero's arms, that electric charge had pulled her into him, keeping her attached to him. When his face had been close to hers in a near kiss, she'd half expected their bodies to generate sparks.

That was certainly worth studying. Was this electric connection of a male to a female limited to looks alone, or could this attraction occur between any man and any woman at any time under the right circumstances? It would explain quite a bit about human nature if she could find out.

It would explain why so many women allowed themselves to be compromised by men and why rakes and rogues in particular proved so fatal to a woman's reputation. For the first time, she felt she could understand why women sometimes acted so silly around certain men. She'd always looked down her nose at those silly, giggling creatures, but after what she'd experienced last night, she wasn't quite sure there were words to describe how she felt, only that she'd been close to giggling herself at how he'd made her feel.

Prospero's body had been firm, rigid, and strong, yet she had enjoyed leaning into him, feeling the warmth of his bare skin and his natural male scent that held a hint of musk. It made her think of amber and evergreen trees.

Being held by him had felt like she was straying into a dark, quiet wood where the trees spoke a language of soft cracks and pops as the roots moved beneath the rich soil and leaves above whispered secrets that mankind was still too young to understand.

The imagery was all so unscientific, and yet it made perfect sense. Her mother had read her fairy tales as a child, and she recalled a story of a girl wearing a red cloak fleeing a wolf, but she'd always wondered why any young woman would go into the deep, dark forest at all. Now she understood the allure. It was the mystery of the dark forest, not the wolf, that drew the girl into its depths.

Elise climbed out of the bed and shivered.

She hastily collected her notebook and rushed back to her own bedchamber. It was almost eight o'clock in the morning. She had slept later than she usually did, yet she felt incredibly rested.

Her maid was in a fine fury when Elise stepped inside her chamber.

"Just where have you been, milady? I was about to have Mr. Roberts tear the place apart looking for you!" Mary grasped Elise's hand and pulled her toward the changing screen. "We must get you dressed and ready for breakfast. Your father and Lord March are down there alone. Heavens knows what they're talking about without you there to explain yourself."

Elise nearly tore her tea gown off her shoulders trying to get it off. "Oh goodness, I forgot about Papa!"

Mary had a light-blue walking dress ready for her that had a slender bustle in the back and military frog braiding on the upper jacket that looked quite smart. She pulled her hair up into a loose coiffure and secured it with a mother-of-pearl clasp.

Mary sighed. "It will have to do. I expect you to be on time for dinner."

"It's possible we will be dining out."

Her maid frowned. "Either way, you will not leave this house unless I fix you up proper."

Elise bussed Mary's cheek in a light kiss and then dashed down the stairs in time to see her father and Prospero leaving the dining room together.

"Ah, there she is," her father chuckled, and shared a secretive smile with Prospero as though they were old friends. She was relieved, but also suspicious. She hadn't warned Papa of her intent to bring a man into the house, and certainly not one with Lord March's reputation. She couldn't blame him if he was upset with her for such a breach in propriety.

"May I have a word with you before you and Lord March begin your day?" Her father's voice was still calm, with no hint of displeasure.

"Yes, Papa." Elise shot Prospero a quick glance, who answered only with a shrug. She followed her father into his private study, where he closed the door, and sat down in his chair at his desk, facing her. She had a feeling she was about to be lectured. It didn't happen often, but when it did, she never enjoyed it.

"March seems like a decent fellow," her father said.

"Yes, he is."

"You could do worse."

That was a comment she didn't understand. He was rather perfect for her study, of course, not to mention that

Mr. Holmes had quite insisted she should conduct her research on Lord March.

"Financially, he is poor as a church mouse, but I imagine not for long. He seems like a capable man, willing to build his own future. I would not mind having him as a son-in-law."

Elise's lips parted in shock, but she didn't speak. Her father thought she and Prospero were *courting*?

When he saw her reaction, her father sighed. "He told me a little about this study of yours, about the study of *men*. I assume that's the only reason he's here?"

"Yes, of course. We've only just met. There isn't anything else—"

Her father raised a hand. "I ask very little of you these days," he said, "so please consider my next words carefully. That man would be a decent choice. I like him. More importantly, I don't think he has any issues with your studies at the society."

He was talking about *marriage* with Prospero.

"Papa, I have known him less than a day, and you know that I have no interest in marrying." It was a discussion they had from time to time. Marriage wouldn't work for her. She was busy, and she was not about to let a man rule her life by agreeing to marry him.

"I understand how you feel, my dear. But remember, your mother had me *and* a life full of adventure and freedom. Not every man would seek to rule you. The right one chooses to *partner* with you. I believe March is such a man."

She arched her brow, challenging her father. "You've learned all of this over breakfast, have you?"

He leaned back in his chair and smiled. "You'd be

simply amazed at what one can learn by *talking* to someone rather than peering at them through a magnifying lens."

She was tempted to say that seeing people through a lens was far safer than talking to them.

"Just tell me you will consider it. I'm not getting any younger, and someday, when I am nothing more than dust, I want to have left this life with the comfort of knowing you are safe."

"I *am* safe," Elise protested. "Don't you trust me to take care of myself?"

"I trust *you*," her father replied solemnly. "More than you'll ever know. But I don't trust the world we live in. Even the most capable people can be trapped by the evil in this world."

"I'm not some damsel in need of saving by a knight," she reminded him.

"No, you aren't. You've always been a Joan of Arc, your armor sparkling in the sun as you charge into the fray." Pride shone clearly in his eyes. "But I should like to see Saint Michael by your side, ready to slay the occasional dragon and guard your back if you need it."

Elise relaxed a little. "I will consider it, Papa."

He leaned forward, resting his elbows on his desk. "Now, what is *really* behind this study of yours? You've never shown an interest in men before now, not even academically."

"Oh, well . . . I may have gotten into a wager with Mr. Holmes."

Her father's brows rose. "That detective fellow? He always struck me as a bit of a loose cannon, that one. What on earth made you tangle with that man?"

"He was disrupting my meetings with that blasted

violin of his. So I demanded he stop, and he claimed our studies at the society were incomplete without first understanding the human condition. I pointed out that I understood it quite well and that men as a whole were quite boring. That led him to challenge me to understand men, and specifically Lord March because of his background being, well . . . not so black-and-white, but rather because he lives in a gray area. If I prove I understand men, he will surrender that blasted instrument over to me so we may have our meetings in peace."

Her father chuckled. "So it took London's most famous detective to get you interested in men? I may have to send Holmes my best bottle of Madeira."

"Oh, Papa," Ellie gasped in irritation. "It's *only* a scientific study."

Her father's eyes still twinkled. "Very well, my dear, off you go, then. I'm sure you have *much* to study. Just stay out of trouble. Well, on second thought, perhaps a *little* trouble would be good for you." Other men might have sounded patronizing when saying this, but Elise knew her father was teasing her.

"We won't get into any trouble. I thought we might tour the Natural History Museum for a few hours. I'm curious as to his thoughts on nature and history." The British Museum had grown over time, and just last year in 1881 they'd moved much of the original collection to a new museum built to house the natural history collections.

"Will you be home for dinner this evening?"

"I'm not entirely sure."

"Well, be careful and try to enjoy yourself, Elise. He seems like an intelligent and interesting fellow. I get the sense that he is unused to talking about himself, but when he does, the man is honest. You might be interested in what you learn about him."

Elise left her father's study, more than a little muddled over her father's request that she think of marriage to a man she'd only just met. He'd never done that before. It was so out of character for him to push her like that.

Prospero was waiting outside the dining room door. He escorted her inside, where he had prepared a plate of food for her, and then sat down to quietly go through a pair of books on the table.

"Since you were late for breakfast, I thought you might be hungry." He nodded at the plate.

"Thank you. That was quite thoughtful."

"You're most welcome." His soft blue eyes seemed to caress her before he turned his focus back to his texts.

"What are you studying?" she inquired.

He flashed her a bashful look and displayed the spines of the books. "*A History of the English Railway* and a book on train engineering and engine propulsion systems."

She giggled. "Oh dear. You *have* been talking to my father, haven't you?" It was just like her father to hand over textbooks on railways to someone. "You don't have to read them. I promise I won't tell him."

"Actually, I asked him about how to enter the railway business. He gave me some sound advice that I should study the history and science of the industry before I attempt to enter it."

That definitely sounded like her father. She ate her breakfast hastily as he read in silence, but it was a *nice* silence. She had so many thoughts that ran through her head on any given day that she dreaded being alone with a man when she knew they would expect sparkling conversation and wit.

Here she was, having a moment to just think, or even not to think, and it was *peaceful* in a way she'd never imagined. She caught herself stealing glances at Prospero as he read his books. She mentally traced the line of his jaw, his straight nose, the slightly fuller than average lips, and those impossibly long lashes that were currently downcast as he studied the texts before him. His dark hair fell into his eyes, and he would occasionally brush it away absentmindedly with his fingers.

Fascinating . . . Elise wanted to know every thought in his mind, peer deep into the well of this man's soul. But that was silly, wasn't it?

When she finished, he closed the books and watched her patiently.

"So, what would you like to see your male specimen do today?" He asked the question so seriously that she found herself remembering last night when he'd stripped his clothes off in that tantalizing way. The sudden sharp pang in her womb so utterly startled her that she wriggled in her chair. Elise clenched her thighs together.

"Well, I thought we might visit the Natural History Museum, and then perhaps you could tell me how you would normally spend your afternoons if I were not accompanying you?"

"I would probably visit my club for dinner, since I currently have no cook at home. After that, I might investigate the gaming tables. Not to gamble, but to see if I can renew any old acquaintances who could help me find a way into the railroad business. Many men can be more relaxed while playing games of chance, and be more willing to talk.

Unless they are losing great hordes of money, in which case they will want to talk to no one."

"Interesting . . . I shall look forward to learning more about that. I thought we could start with the Natural History Museum this morning. I could show you a part of my world and my interests so you will understand why I am called to be a naturalist."

"I would find that fascinating," Prospero said with honesty.

She called for a footman to bring her a pale-blue cloak, and then they headed for the door. It had been ages since she had seen the British Museum and she wanted to see the new Natural History Museum. She wanted to show Prospero some of her favorite exhibits.

JOHN HAMBLIN STOOD IN THE DOORWAY OF HIS STUDY and watched his daughter and Lord March speaking in the entryway. March put on his hat. It was a worn old thing that had seen better days. The earl's suit, while finely made, was a bit faded and had been discreetly patched in a few places. The man was in dire straits and no doubt desperate enough to escape the situation that he had agreed to play a specimen for his daughter to study. When his butler, Roberts, joined him to watch the young pair leave the house, John leaned toward his butler a little.

"What do you think of March?"

The butler kept his gaze on Elise and the earl until a footman closed the door behind them.

"I heard he was sent to France after he was connected to a man's death in a duel twelve years ago, but my sources tell me that he's kept out of trouble since then. He was shunned by most of Parisian society when it came to matters of business. He was able to get by through providing . . . companionship to wealthy widows."

John wondered if the young man had brought any complications back to England with him. He didn't want his daughter's heart or her fortune at risk, if that was the case.

"Blast. Did he marry any of those widows or father any children?"

"Not that I'm aware of. I could inquire further."

"Do so." John stroked his chin. "And keep your eye on him."

"You suspect he will be trouble?" Roberts asked, a hint of surprise in his voice. That alone betrayed that Roberts seemed to like the earl.

"Not exactly. I think he seems like a decent fellow. But there is only so much baggage one can tolerate. I wish to know if anyone will have a problem with him now that he's returned. I imagine the family of the man who died could make trouble for him if they felt he escaped justice. Best if we keep an eye on things. I don't want Elise drawn into a fight she doesn't belong in."

"I am currently assisting Lord March in posting notices for his staff and will be able to keep my eye on things, should he agree with the choices I offer him."

"Excellent." John returned to his study, and as he sat down, his chest tightened a little and he felt a flash of pain and then numbness go down his arm. He cursed softly. Pains like these were becoming more frequent, and he didn't like what his body was telling him. He called for Roberts and asked him to send for his solicitor saying that it was urgent. Then he leaned back in his chair and tried to relax.

Everything would be fine. He would make certain of it. He had to see Elise married to a good man soon. He prayed his instincts about March were right, because he was about to hang his hopes for his daughter's future upon a reputed rogue.

7

"I'm afraid you'll have to watch me undress *again*," Prospero said as they crossed the street toward his home.

"What?" Elise stumbled on a raised cobblestone, and Prospero reached out, catching her easily.

How does the man do that? It was as though he had the reflexes of a jungle cat. She had seen one of those large beasts once at the London Zoo. It had prowled about its enclosure with a slow and lethal grace, its yellow eyes glowing bright against its black fur. She had sketched its musculature for hours, marveling at the perfection of the creature and wishing she had Cinna's talent for capturing animals on paper. She thought of what the Reverend J. G. Wood wrote of the cat tribe upon his visit to the zoo:

"None of the Felidae can be ungraceful, whatever position they may assume, and whether they haunt the desert, the jungle, the tree, or the hearth, they display in every movement an unconscious grace that baffles the pencil of the most accomplished draftsman."

That was not only true of jungle cats, but also of this

darkly handsome man who now held her waist. He peered down at her, his eyes vibrant as he watched her.

"Are you all right?" he asked. "It seems you end up tripping whenever the matter of undressing comes up."

She knew the reason, of course. The man kept mentioning things that distracted her, and she found it hard to concentrate on walking.

"I got lost in my thoughts," she murmured.

"I'm sure you did."

She forced herself to refocus on the practicality of the situation. "You need to change clothes?"

"Yes, I can't exactly wear my evening suit to the museum. It's rather rumpled from last night's . . . study. I hope you don't mind if we make a quick stop at my house to allow me to change?"

"Not at all," she assured him.

He released her waist and tucked her arm in his to escort her to his home. The walls were thick with unkept ivy, but she liked that sort of *wild* look. As though it were a prince's home, but one you might find half-hidden in an enchanted wood.

"I apologize in advance for the condition of the house. It's well . . . You'll see." He unlocked the door and went in ahead of her to light a lamp and open a few curtains.

She followed him in and closed the door. Dust lingered on every surface in the meager patches of sunlight, and a mustiness hung in the air. It was not the welcome scent of old books from sunlight-illuminated tomes on shelves, but rather a dark, unpleasant smell of human absence and an intentional lack of care by those who'd lived here.

Through the grime and gloom however, she could see the house's bones, the sturdy walls, the fine oak staircase and ornately decorated ceilings. With some love and devotion, this could become a shining jewel of a home once again. She was glad that she had insisted on paying Lord March more than had been promised in her original advertisement.

It took her a moment to realize he was the one studying her now as she formed her first impressions of the house.

"It is in poor shape," he admitted. She could hear the regret and pain in his voice.

"True, but you can restore it. I have faith in you." Why she had said that, she wasn't sure, but she did mean it. She knew on an instinctive level that he was the kind of man who would care for the things and the people that mattered to him.

Perhaps her father was right—she could learn more from real, genuine conversations.

"Did you grow up in this home?" she asked.

He led her up the stairs and through a corridor to a bedchamber she guessed was his. "Yes, but my father also used to have a country estate. Marchlands." He sighed the word in a soft, sad way. "He sold it two years ago to an aging baron. Then the man died without an heir, and the property was all but abandoned. I adored Marchlands most. I hunted in those woods, fished in its lake, and skipped stones on the water. I climbed every tree and even built a little lodge once among the branches of one of the trees."

"You had a tree house?" She was enchanted by the idea. It sounded like one of the most wonderful things imaginable, both as a child and as an adult.

He grinned. "Oh yes. It had a little door, a thatched

roof that would have made any Cotswold native proud, and a pallet for me to nap. I had a collection of my favorite sticks and rocks, a few beetles in jars, and my pet squirrel."

"You had a pet squirrel? So did I!"

Prospero's eyes widened. "You did?"

She nodded eagerly. "Mine was a little beauty, one of those red squirrels with tufted ears. She used to sit on my lap while I read books in the garden." Elise followed him into a dusty old bedchamber and seated herself on the bed, although she coughed as a cloud of dust rose up around her. He waved his hand in the air to dispel some of the dust in front of his face before he set his travel case beside her.

"Squirrels can be delightful companions, can't they?" he said with a chuckle as he unpacked a few items of his clothing.

He set aside a light-gray wool suit and removed a pair of worn black shoes that he took a moment to buff with a cloth so that they regained some of their old shine. She observed these small male rituals, soaking in every detail.

And then he began to undress again.

She refused to look away. She took in the sight of him and the way the shadows played over the dip of his hips. Her eyes tracked the muscled lines of his arms as he pulled off the shirt he'd worn the night before. He ran a hand through the fall of his dark hair and turned to look at her, as if encouraging her to enjoy what she was seeing.

Elise found that she liked that . . . seeing him take pleasure in her watching him. There was an undeniable intimacy to it that she'd never imagined possible. That drive within her to seek knowledge in all its forms urged her to study this further, to learn everything she could about the feelings he created within her. The heat she felt low in her belly demanded some kind of relief. She wanted to under-stand everything about him, and she wanted to know how this man could make her feel so much when she'd been so determined to stay aloof during her study.

"I was thinking," Prospero began as he pulled out a fresh shirt. "My philosophies and motivations are all well and good, but I think there is a significant part of your study that is missing."

"Oh? What part is that?"

"You are operating under the knowledge that men are to be studied like animals, correct?"

"Yes, as I would do with women were I not already quite familiar with them." She watched his fingers button up the waistcoat that matched his suit.

Those fingers were long and elegant, though not too slender. She suddenly imagined them loosening the stays of her corset and how very deft they would be in removing *all* of her clothing. Her corset seemed to tighten as she inhaled sharply, imagining him doing just that . . . peeling her clothing off and studying her bare body.

Oh dear . . . She'd never had that sort of daydream before.

"Well, you realize being an animal means that part of one's instincts are about attraction."

"Attraction," she echoed.

The look he was giving her could melt butter and was certainly melting *her.*

"Oh yes. The laws of attraction, and I mean primal *animal* attraction, predate any laws that mankind has created. You haven't asked me about that yet. After all, a large part of any creature's life is the urge to mate and continue the species."

He finished slitting the last button on his waistcoat just as he said the word *mate*, and that juxtaposition of the man before her, the epitome of a gentleman, against his discussion of animal mating sent a wildfire through her body.

"W—well, yes of course. I had planned on having an interview with you on the subject. My research would be incomplete if I did not address the idea of . . . mating," The word felt suddenly dangerous and exciting in a way it never had before. Mating was so different than seduction. The latter was a performance, while the former was animalistic, raw, *wild*.

"Yes." He reached out and tilted her chin up so he could better see her face as he stepped closer. "Think of all that you can learn if you let me show you what it means to be courted by a male. Isn't that the most important part of your study? To know what males think about, what we dream about and hunger for?"

There were sudden flashes in her mind of male birds as they displayed their feathers and arched their wings in provocative ways in order to attract a female to mate. What did human males do to entice females into bed? She'd always thought that they talked of their money, their connections, or bragged about themselves in general, but Prospero suggested something quite different was at play. So far, he'd shown her none of the things she'd come to associate with men when they were around eligible women.

"You want to court me?" she asked.

"For the study, of course," he replied in a husky whisper, his warm breath fanning over her lips and cheeks. "Let me teach you about the lovers' language of kisses and caresses, of the pleasures that will enlighten you to the beautiful mystery of human desire."

The beautiful mystery of human desire . . . Had any other man spoken such words she would have scoffed, but when Prospero said them, those words held a dark, potent, and delicious power to affect her in ways she didn't understand. *But she could let him teach her* . . .

She wasn't a fool. She was no innocent young debutante just out of finishing school. Prospero's intentions were for a practical education, not theoretical discussions. He wished to seduce her, pure and simple. It would certainly gain her far more insight into the subject than any conversation, but it would mean ruination if anyone ever found out. Of course, she had no plans to marry, but the practical part of her had to at least acknowledge the consequences of what Prospero was proposing.

Still, she would have the answers she sought to the beautiful mystery of human desire.

"What's it to be, my little naturalist?" Prospero asked in a low, gruff voice that sent shivers through her. No one had ever talked to her with such a gentle yet possessive intimacy before. She liked it, perhaps a little too much.

"Yes . . . very well. Show me. But I must make one condition."

He waited patiently for her terms.

"I cannot bring a child into this world like this."

"We will take precautions. I am well-versed in them," Prospero promised.

She would have trusted no other man with something so important, but she did trust him. Yet something else niggled at the back of her mind, and she was too forthright in her nature not to bring it up.

"I don't want you to think of me as you did those

women in Paris. I don't want to use you, Prospero, not like that."

His beautiful blue eyes pierced her. "The fact that you said that is what makes it different. You wouldn't be using me, and I would not be selling myself. We share a mutual desire, and have much to teach each other. We would be sharing ourselves with each other as equals."

It was perhaps those last words that made her mind up for her. *Sharing themselves with each other as equals.* Yes, that was what she wanted if she was to agree to this.

Her tone turned breathless. "Then we are agreed that we can explore this attraction."

"We are agreed. And your first lesson starts now." Prospero bent his head, closing the distance between their mouths, and kissed her.

THAT FIRST TOUCH OF HIS LIPS TO HERS WAS LIKE A FIRE exploding to life for Prospero. The unexpected flash of thrill and anticipation was so strong that he reached for her, grasping her hips to hold her as tenderly but firmly as he could. The number of kisses he'd shared with other women was more numerous than the stars in the sky, but this one, so innocent, so new, so *pure*, was unlike anything he'd ever experienced. It flared like a newly born star in the sky, pure in its intention. There was no manipulation, no coercion, no inequality to the moment. It was a kiss between a woman seeking to know desire and a man who wanted to teach her all she might ever wish to learn. She gasped against his lips as he pulled her closer. Her hands fluttered hesitantly against his chest.

"Hold on to me. *Touch* me."

Bolstered by his encouragement, she settled her hands on his shoulders, her fingers digging in as she leaned close and held him tight. Her lips moved as hesitantly as her hands at first, but he showed her what to do and guided her mouth with his own. After a few long, delicious moments, she showed signs of mastering kisses in a way that any courtesan would envy. A quick study!

Prospero grew drunk on the sweet taste of her and dizzy from the faint floral scent that clung to her skin. Women often wore heavy perfumes, but Elise smelled like an English garden. She'd had dozens of flowers in her study at the society headquarters. He remembered how she'd studied that moth he'd seen clinging to the petals of a peony. Something about that filled him with quiet wonder, picturing her surrounded by flowers all day while studying a little creature, never aware that she was carrying the scent of those beautiful blooms about her. Evidence of her devotion to science.

The scent lingered even now, filling his head with visions of taking this woman to a bed of rose petals, or dancing with her beneath the starlight while moonflowers bloomed. He had the urge to learn all that he could about her, as though she were his own private museum to explore, and bask in the mysteries he had sworn to show her.

Elise's lips pulled away from his, and they stood, still clutching each other in the dim, dusty bedchamber. He'd actually forgotten they were in this old room and not among the flowers and trees outside. Elise's light-brown eyes, usually wide with curiosity, were soft and slumbrous now, and he saw a flicker of feminine knowing that came from discovering one's sensuality.

"Women are natural kissers," he said in a low voice. "It is often the men who must take lessons."

"Oh?" That single questioning syllable somehow heated his blood even more. Her lips, forming that O shape, gave him many wicked ideas about what he wanted her to use that mouth for.

"Indeed. Women are more in tune with their natures, though most men refuse to admit it."

"But you don't mind?" Her brown eyes traced the movement of his lips as he spoke. He had a feeling she was still thinking about kissing him, and he liked that. He wanted her to lose her scientific thoughts at moments like this, if only for her to experience passion without reason dulling its effects.

"I fully admit it. I adore women. You are a brave, beautiful, fierce set of creatures with mysteries that run deeper than the seas. And you have an inner light that, when given room to grow, can outshine the brightest of stars."

Pain flashed across her face. "In my experience, men often seek to dim or extinguish that light." She ducked her chin, looking away.

"More fools, they." He lifted her chin so their eyes met. "You know much of animals. Tell me, do the females in the wild allow males to dim their shine?"

When she shook her head, he smiled. "Then be like them. Defend your light with the ferocity of a lioness. Let no one take it from you, or diminish it. Protect it with all you have."

The light in her eyes brightened. "It isn't easy. It often

means being alone, working late into the night, resisting the crushing pressure of social expectations to conform to their standards."

"I can't begin to imagine how hard that is," said Prospero. "But there is one thing I know. Pearls, diamonds, mountains, and all manner of beautiful pieces of nature are made over time by resisting or reshaping themselves in the face of such pressure. Prove your strength by not succumbing. Instead, resist or reshape."

A single tear dropped onto her cheek. He brushed it away with his fingertip.

"How do you know so much about women and the pressures of life?"

The smile he gave her was a sad one. "I think you know why. When I left England, I was young. Twenty-two for a man isn't the same as it is for a woman. We take a little longer to understand the world, to see the ebbs and flows as well as the patterns of people, including ourselves. I didn't understand what agreeing to that duel would mean, that it would cost me far more than I could pay. It nearly claimed my soul. I should have refused to meet with Jackson that morning. It would have still cost me my reputation, but better that than a man's life and my own sense of self."

"What truly happened that day to Jackson? Why did he try to force you to kill him?" Elise asked, her hand still clutching his shoulder. Prospero was surprised that, for once, talking about it didn't hurt as much as it used to. Talking to Elise was strangely easy.

"I refused to fire my pistol after his shot struck me in the arm. He charged me, insisting I take my shot, there was a mad pain in the man's eyes that I couldn't understand. But when I continued to refuse him, he grabbed my gun and aimed it at himself. I tried to stop him, but my hands were bloodied from clutching my wound. Something slipped. I don't know if it was his hand or mine, but the gun fired. Jackson's friend and second, a man named John Gower, reported that he believed I acted seemingly out of self-defense. I still fled England, in case he decided to change his mind."

"Now you've come back, do you think Gower will turn you in?"

Prospero shrugged. "I've run from the past long enough. If he wishes to, I will face the consequences of that day. But I think he will not try to cause me trouble. He defended me that day, even though he didn't wish to since he was Jackson's friend, not mine."

"Jackson seemed intent on harming himself. Had you not interfered, he would have been dead. You were trying to prevent that. It would be unfair to charge you with a crime you didn't commit."

"Life is rarely fair," he mused.

Elise made a scoffing sound, and for some reason that made him chuckle. "It may be unfair, but that doesn't mean we have to accept such things."

He stroked her cheek affectionately. "*There* is that fierce fire I was looking for. Never let go of it."

She was quiet a long moment. He was content to hold her against him and watch her thoughts play across her face.

"I want you to teach me everything about human courtship."

"Gladly."

"But I still want to explore your world, the world of men," she insisted.

He stroked a fingertip down the bridge of her nose. "I would gladly sneak you into my club after the museum, but that would be difficult given your appearance."

"Oh, I might have a way to get around that." She grinned at him, and he had a suspicion that Elise was going to get him in trouble. But if she was, he was going to enjoy every second of it.

8

W ho knew that a museum of dusty old bones and fossils could be so stimulating and refreshing?

Prospero puzzled over this as Elise tugged him through the Natural History Museum that had been opened the previous year, housing the remains of animals both recent and prehistoric, along with other natural science discoveries. Elise's encyclopedic knowledge of the building and the exhibits was refreshingly interesting—or perhaps it was just that his companion made it so.

"Beautiful, isn't it?" Elise said as they wandered through the Romanesque interior.

His eyes followed hers to the vaulted ceilings made of arches of steel. It was a proud display of engineering technology. He'd remarked as such when they'd first arrived and he'd seen the outside of the newly built museum. The building resembled a cathedral, with towers topped by short spires. Dozens of round-topped Romanesque windows formed aisles that connected the towers. The buff-colored exterior had a mass of terracotta tiles and stucco terraces that were broken up by a series of blue tiles. The arched entrance to the museum was flanked by columns resembling a church entrance. Within this hallowed place of knowledge, he did indeed feel reverent.

"Surprisingly, it is," he murmured. "Not at all what I expected."

"Oh, of course, you wouldn't have seen it yet," she said with a frown. "As it only recently opened."

He nodded. "I heard of it, of course, but from the descriptions I expected something rather stark and bleak inside. I am happy to be proven wrong. Look at those . . ." He gestured to the painted ceiling panels that, rather than angels, were paintings of stylized plants.

"Scots pine, lemon trees, cacao plants," Elise recited. "Those are but a few of the many they've painted. I like the unique design." Her brown eyes shone in delight.

He nodded at a series of large fossils that appeared to be swimming along one wall, apparently of marine animals. "And what are those?"

"Ichthyosaurs and plesiosaurs. Several of them were uncovered by Mary Anning, a pioneer among the fossil collectors, and one of the very few women scientists in the first half of this century."

"Impressive woman."

"Indeed. She was incredible," Elise replied as they strolled through the museum, wandering past the other guests. He could tell by her manner how much she appreciated the scientists and adventurers who had come before her, especially the women.

When she spotted a row of tall cabinets, she suddenly tugged on his arm in renewed childlike wonder.

"Oh, come and see. These are some of my favorites!"

He quickened his pace to keep up with her, and they stopped before the cabinets. She opened one of the drawers, and he was startled to see dozens of butterflies. All of the little creatures had been carefully pinned through their thorax, something Elise had to explain to him, as he had no idea what a thorax was.

The wings of each butterfly were spread out to display the fore and aft pairs. Most shimmered with a stunning iridescence, as though they had been captured only moments ago deep in some Amazonian rainforest.

"Spectacular." He leaned in close at the same moment she did, and their cheeks brushed.

"My apologies," he whispered, but he didn't move. His gaze dropped to her lips.

"No apologies needed. It's quite breathtaking," she replied, her lashes fluttering. For such a strong woman who seemed a force of nature at times, he delighted at seeing this side of her, the girl full of wonder who had become the woman before him. This place was full of things that held magic for her, a magic that had made her the person she'd become, and for that, this place was sacred to him as well. It was a building designed to build dreamers. And as all good men knew, dreamers changed the world.

They marveled at the dozens of butterflies, with all their bewildering variety, before moving toward the larger exhibits.

A trio of stuffed giraffe specimens stood to one side of the main hall, and Elise stopped beneath them and pointed up eagerly. "Isn't it fascinating to think that they evolved long necks to eat from the topmost branches of trees? I wish we could study whether trees grew taller in Africa to avoid being eaten by herbivores."

Prospero joined her at the base of the exhibit and read the little plaque about the giraffes. Then he pointed at the black-and-brown bird that sat upon the midsize giraffe's back.

"Who's that little fellow?"

She looked to where he was pointing and grinned with joy. The beauty of her smile in that moment, so unguarded, so free, hit him like an expensive glass of scotch, warming his entire body deliciously.

"That's an oxpecker. Some naturalists put it in the Sturnidae family, along with starlings, but I think they actually belong to the Mimidae family with mockingbirds. It has been a fierce debate over the last few years."

"About what? The classification? Why is that?" He was genuinely curious, and he was strangely attracted to her when she slipped into her professorial tone. He couldn't help but picture her in nothing but a corset and those odd little spectacles with all those lenses as she straddled his lap and lectured him about, well . . . anything. His body hardened at just the thought.

"It has to do with how we see the animals and their behavior and whether behaviors and appearance are enough to classify 'like' species together or not."

He considered her point, secretly admitting to himself that he had not the knowledge of the natural world that he'd first thought. Of course, she was educated to the point of being a true naturalist, and he wouldn't begin to compare his knowledge to hers. But he liked that he could learn something from conversing with her. In fact, with her, he'd most likely learn something new every day.

"So what do these oxpeckers do with giraffes? I assume there is some connection if the animals are paired together in a display like this."

Elise nodded. "The birds gather around large herbivores like rhinos, oxen, and giraffes and eat insects that may be harmful to them." She turned her gaze back to the animals. "It is a beautiful symbiotic relationship."

Her quiet, energetic joy was so clear. In this place full of cold and dead things, she shone like a celestial sun, casting light in all directions making the exhibits glow. "You like that, don't you?"

"I do. To think that the entire fabric of life weaves together so perfectly that even species as vastly different as giraffes and oxpeckers can work and thrive by being *together*." Her voice softened a little, as though she were stepping reverently into a church and whispering a prayer. "It's beautiful. *Life* is beautiful."

Prospero continued to stare at her. "Yes, beautiful," he agreed, but he meant her. *She* was beautiful. Had he ever seen a woman so lovely? No, he didn't think he had.

"Come, let me show you the whale skeleton." She grasped his arm and tugged him through the crowd that moved past the arched doorways.

He could see the way she *fit* here in this place of relics and knowledge, a place she so clearly belonged, no matter what other men might say because she was a woman. She was a magnificent sight. She was pretty by the standards of men, but those standards were so limiting. By the standards of life, she was *exquisite*. She knew her place in the world and would not let the limitations imposed on her stand in her way. She knew her divine purpose.

Prospero envied her that. He was a man adrift, a man

without a true home or a sense of himself. He dwelled in the shadow of someone else's life. He wanted to be himself again, but the boy he'd been was gone. Who was he now?

He caught a glimpse of his reflection in a glass display case. It was the face of a stranger. Not an unkind face, nor was it the face lacking empathy or joy. In that reflection he saw for the first time in years the stirrings of someone he longed to know, longed to become.

Moved by the depth of that sudden feeling, Prospero clasped Elise's hand as they stopped before the massive skeleton of a whale that stretched outward from the center of the exhibit hall.

He wished this day would never end. He could here with her and look at old bones and speak of African birds for the rest of their lives. But it would eventually have to end, just as her study of men would come to an end and she would no longer need him. The thought of losing the light of her brilliance in his life left a hollow ache in his chest.

He listened intently as Elise spoke of whales, beetles and birds, until they next marveled together at a collection of nautilus shells.

"This one belonged to Sir Hans Sloane. It was carved by Johannes Belkien to enhance the shell's natural beauty. I think it is one of those times where nature and human art come together beautifully."

His gaze fixed longer on her fingers, tracing the shape on the glass, rather than the shell itself.

"We work better *with* nature than against it," Prospero agreed. "I heard someone once say that nautilus shells haven't changed much in design for hundreds of thousands of years?"

She peered at the exquisite etchings so finely executed

in the shell. "We think it may actually be *millions* of years now. And it's quite true. They are some of the oldest things discovered when digging in the earth. I think that's what's incredible about the natural world. If something works, it remains the same in design. If it doesn't, it changes until it does work. There's a beauty to that."

As they moved on to the next exhibit encased in glass, Elise's smile began to fade.

"What's the matter?" Prospero asked.

She nodded toward the black-and-white creature that resembled a penguin. "This one always breaks my heart." She placed her fingers on the glass in a faint touch and her eyes darkened. "This is a great auk. The last one the world ever saw was in 1852."

"What happened to them?" Prospero knew that with the passage of time species did die out and new ones took their place. He could understand how it might make her sad.

"The largest colony was found in Canada. Men slaughtered them when they came ashore to breed. Can you imagine?" Her face flushed with anger. "You and your mate swim to shore to lay your eggs and raise your young and are murdered the moment you step upon the sand? It seems the more of these birds that were killed, the more people desired their bodies for private collections. Hunters chased down the last breeding pair known to the world in Iceland simply because a merchant had requested a specimen, and the single egg the two auks laid was crushed beneath a careless hunter's boot." Her voice broke a little. "When we let greed and desire fuel our actions, those actions carry a great and terrible cost. Moments like these challenge my faith in the power of reason and logic. What good is it for the world to kill the last of a creature? It helps no one. I can tell you, no woman would ever have done that, killed the last of a species. It's heartless, it's *cruel*. Why must our world be run by such cruelty?"

Her words struck deeper, truer than she could ever know. As a young man, he'd loved a good hunt—he'd loved to chase foxes or hunt pheasants. He had never thought of the cost to them, only the thrill of the chase. Only of himself.

"Speaking as a man, I admit we have those urges that send us to hunt, to strike down creatures to prove that we are superior. It makes us feel as if we defeated that creature and are in control of our domain." She listened, as if memorizing every word, and he was careful and yet honest in how he chose to continue. "I cannot justify that urge, but it does make me see that there is a marked difference between men and women, at least in a general sense in this matter. Of course, I've met many women who enjoy the hunt and many men who do not. But women like you understand that nature needs balance. You see the laws that nature sets forth and respect them. Most men I know would trample them to satisfy their current desires."

"Why do you suppose that is?" she asked, her eyes alight with scientific curiosity.

He had no easy answer. "I know some will claim the right by simply being male. Others believe that God gave them providence to do as they pleased in this world. But I don't believe it's as clear as that. The idea that men stand apart from nature while women stand within it is not entirely accurate either. I think it's more complex than that. I believe there's a sense of aggressive need to control our environment because we equate control with survival.

We try to change the world to suit us, rather than change ourselves to suit the world."

"You're starting to see, aren't you?"

He tore his gaze away from the bird in the case and found she was watching him. Her soft brown eyes were so full of understanding that his heart stuttered painfully in his chest.

"Show me more," he said. "Show me *everything*."

BY THE TIME THEY LEFT THE MUSEUM LATE IN THE afternoon, Elise felt oddly drained. She had shown Prospero so much and, in the process, had run through dozens of emotions. All the ideas that had tumbled about in her head for years had come out that day.

This was the first time she'd had a real chance to think and speak with a man about these things instead of the other women of the society. Strange, she'd started out so focused on her study of men, but the moment they'd gotten inside the museum, she'd forgotten everything she'd wanted to ask him for her notes and instead had run about showing him all of her favorite things like a child in a toy shop. She'd had the most marvelous time, and couldn't remember ever having fun spending time with a man who wasn't her father.

They descended the steps as they excited the Natural History Museum. She halted abruptly and he turned, his bright-blue eyes alight with curiosity.

"I just had a thought . . . ," she said. "It's man, you see. I so often villainize them because it makes it simple to blame the wrongs of the world on them. But something you said adjusted my perspective on the matter."

He smiled wryly. "So we're not all villains, then?"

"It's what you said about urges. You spoke of your urges and the need to *win*, to claim, to conquer." She blushed at the thoughts such words conjured up, creating her own urges inside her. Urges that she was only just beginning to understand.

She cleared her throat and continued. "Those urges stem from elements that, in the natural world, are quite necessary. The aggressive need to control one's environment is not a negative trait in and of itself—it's rather how it's applied that matters. All species of life can be aggressive, even plants. Consider invasive species such as ivy, which grows so lovely on the front of your home. When rabbits were introduced to Australia in the eighteenth century, they weren't aggressive in terms of fighting, but without any natural predators they competed against native animals and threatened their existence.

"But when the aggression of any creature or plant is left unchecked, that is when imbalance occurs. Ancient man had diseases, the harsh elements, and other wild creatures to limit their behavior. You kill to eat, you kill to defend yourself and others from wild animals or other tribes of people."

Prospero seemed to understand her meaning. "But as our technology advanced, the laws of nature failed to keep us in check. Our aggressions, driven by our urges, have become limitless."

"Exactly." She stared at him in wonder. Before today, she had never considered the matter from that side. His words had given her a valuable insight. "If more people thought to look within themselves for answers rather than bury themselves in shallow concerns and desires, we might begin to affect real change. But I fear it would be a battle against the many who would not take the effort to try."

Prospero held out an arm to her, and she put her hand on his sleeve as they left the museum grounds. She'd always thought walking arm in arm with a man was a bit pointless. Yet with Prospero, she rather liked how he inclined his head toward her when speaking and how he helped her cut through the crowds as he ushered her along at his side. There was a symbiotic strength to them when they were together, not unlike the oxpecker and the giraffe. She couldn't help but wonder what else would be pleasurable to do with him? Just thinking of that sent a quiver of excitement through her.

When they reached the street, he hailed a hackney for them.

They were quiet and lost in their own thoughts on the ride back to her home. Elise stole a few glances at Prospero, trying to puzzle out how this man had been able to make her forget herself at times. She was learning quite a bit from him, though not all of those lessons were the kind she would have expected, given the parameters of her study. Only when they stopped at her home did she finally break the silence.

"Thank you," she said.

He raised his brows. "What for?"

"For reminding me that my assumptions can be *limited*." Her face heated at the embarrassing admission. "I let myself become too driven by my own preconceived notions of people in the world around me. I've been too harsh in my beliefs where men are concerned."

At this, he chuckled as he got out of the hackney. He circled around and opened her door, offering her his hand to assist her out of the vehicle. "Well, to be fair, we men are a wild lot. We have much to beg forgiveness for, but we do have our moments of usefulness, don't you agree?"

She thought of the wonders that filled the museums and libraries of London, the poetry that men had written, the paintings, the sculptures. Yes, men could be in tune with the world around them, if given a chance to stand apart from the darker side of their natures. She couldn't allow herself to forget that. Championing women's causes didn't have to come at the cost of looking down her nose at all men, even if they did choose to do so to women.

But still, the truth was that men controlled everything in a woman's life—her body, her property, her safety—and could do practically anything to her with few consequences.

She needed to understand why men believed the things they did and acted the way they did, so she might someday find a way to *convince* them that women were meant to be equals.

Women would have to be more cunning and clever about how they spoke to men if they were to convince them that they were not frail, insipid creatures with the brains of children.

Perhaps there was some validity to Cinna's point of defeating men after all. Certainly there were men who couldn't be reasoned with. The villainous cads, the abusers, and other truly bad men. Men like Prospero or her father listened, and it was possible they could change.

The complexity of her thoughts must have shown upon her face, because Prospero placed his hand gently upon her shoulder.

"Do you still wish to visit my club today?" he inquired. "We've had a long day and could always go on the morrow."

They walked up to her door, and Roberts let them inside.

"No, no. I still wish to go. I just need an hour or so to prepare."

"Prepare?" He removed his hat and handed it to Roberts before the butler left them alone in the hall.

"Yes, I need time to get into my disguise." She suddenly found herself grinning and feeling refreshed by the prospect of a new adventure.

"Your *disguise?*" he asked.

Elise laughed. "Of course. How else can I get into your club?"

"I honestly hadn't thought about it," he admitted. "But yes, you'd have to, wouldn't you? I don't suppose the clubs have scullery maids or some such thing you could pass for with the right garments."

"Hmm, yes, I'll be wearing some such thing to help me pass unnoticed," she echoed, pretending that was her intention. Wouldn't it be a surprise when he saw what she had planned to wear? She had to fight off a laugh. "Wait for me in the drawing room. I will be as quick as possible," she said as she dashed upstairs.

Mary helped her out of her clothing and into her masculine attire. She dressed in light buff trousers and wrapped her breasts tight before she put her shirt and waistcoat on. After that, she stepped into her brown leather lace-up boots.

"I believe I'm ready for the wig," Elise said. Mary, with a clearly disapproving frown, helped her pin her hair flat before placing a short blond wig upon her head. It was fashionably styled with a part to one side, and the hair swept up in a slight wave above the forehead in the way that made many men quite attractive. She added a small, slender, but sophisticated-looking mustache to her upper lip by using an adhesive Cinna had recommended. Then she looked about for the small hand mirror before Mary held it out to her.

Her maid's lips twisted down in clear disapproval. "This is *no* way to catch a man, milady. No way at all."

"I want to *study* them, not *catch* them," she reminded Mary. She nodded in satisfaction at her appearance and stood up, then slung her coat on. She was almost to the bedchamber door when Mary called out.

"You'll be needing this, I suppose." The maid held up a dark-brown wool top hat.

"Oh yes, thank you." She snatched the hat from Mary and put it on. She then rushed toward the stairs and halted. Overcome by a sudden feeling of playfulness, she was struck by an idea. She slowed her movements and added a little swagger to her steps as she started down the staircase. When she reached the drawing room, she casually opened the door and walked in. Prospero was sitting on the settee, *A History of the English Railway* open in his lap. He glanced up as she strode past him to the fireplace and opened her father's cigar box to casually retrieve a cigar.

Prospero was so focused on his reading that he didn't seem to noticed she'd even entered the room.

"I don't suppose you've seen John this evening? I was to

meet him for dinner," she asked smoothly, call attention to herself.

"Er, no, sorry, I haven't seen him this evening. I'm sure he'll be along shortly if he's to meet you. Are you a business associate of his?" Prospero glanced up at her as he spoke and then looked back down at his book, clearly engrossed in whatever he was reading and likely not paying attention to her at all.

"Something like that. The name is Elliot. Are you one of Hamblin's associates as well?"

He looked up at her, a calm expression on his face as though he was used to meeting complete strangers frequently. "I'm Prospero Harrington and no, I'm not yet in business with him, but I hope to be, assuming he finds me worthy of the investment."

"Ahh, I'm sure he will. Care if I join you? Hamblin doesn't mind if I pinch his cigars."

"Not at all," he replied and then he politely turned his focus back to his book.

She bit her lip to hide a grin and removed a cigar from the box. She turned back to the room and shot Prospero a look again, he was still not watching her. Apparently, he was quite engrossed in the book, which would give her father no end of delight.

Elise sat down in an armchair opposite him. "Nice night, isn't it?" she asked in that low, mannish voice she'd spent weeks practicing.

"Yes, it—" Prospero's head shot up and he stared at her, *really* stared at her this time. "Good God, it's you under all that, isn't it?"

She beamed in pride and triumph. "Do you think it will

fool the men at the club?" she asked with a devious chuckle as she stood up.

"I rather think it will. If I hadn't seen . . ." His words trailed off abruptly.

"If you hadn't seen what?"

"Er . . . it isn't polite of me to say."

"I'm not studying politeness," she reminded him.

"Well . . . Two things. I noticed your shapely bottom, but most men won't think much of it because they aren't looking for a woman's bottom in a man's trousers, so they won't expect it."

"And the other thing?"

His face colored a little more. "You're a little . . . flat." He nodded at her.

"Yes, I'm well aware. I had to bind my breasts." She patted her flat chest with pride, but her breath caught when his gaze dropped immediately to her chest as if studying where on earth her breasts had gone. Heat creeped across her face, and she forced herself to forget the fact that he was staring at her breasts, even hidden as they were.

This time he was the one chuckling. "Not your breasts. Your groin. You need to have *some* shape there. That is something some men might notice right away. They may not be able to put their finger on what it is at first glance, but if they start to really look at you, it will raise questions."

"Oh . . ." She blushed. "Is this something you men often do? Study each other's . . . groins?"

His face turned a ruddy color. "Not exactly. Well, I mean, there are always *some* men who obsess over their . . . size compared to others. But not me. I'm content with myself as I am. But many of us do . . . notice other men, from a comparative standpoint."

"What should I do, then?"

He stood and removed a handkerchief from his breast pocket and a second one from his trouser pocket, and he unfolded them and then loosely bundled them up together and handed them to her.

"Place that . . . here." He pointed at his own groin, and she swallowed hard as she looked at the outline of a bulge in his trousers. He was definitely *not* small, considering the other sizes she'd encountered between the Greek statues and the bodies she'd glimpsed at the mortuary during an autopsy.

"But your bulge is *so* large. This won't make me look that size . . ."

He winked at her. "Thank you for the compliment. But don't worry. Most men aren't terribly large. With this, you should do just fine." Then he turned his back to her, allowing her a moment of privacy to unfasten her trousers and tuck the wadded-up cloth into the right spot. She refastened her trousers and faced him again.

"Is this better?"

Prospero turned back around and stared at her groin openly.

"Much better." He swept his gaze over the rest of her with a critical eye. "Is that a wig?" She nodded. "Well, I must say you look like a very *pretty* man, but you do still manage to look like a man. Somehow. I hope that doesn't offend you."

"On the contrary, it pleases me greatly. I've spent a lot of time working on this costume. Thankfully, my taller figure and decent shoulders help fill out the coat. Shall we?"

"We might as well." He put the railway book aside but didn't offer her his arm. It took her a moment to realize why, but when she did she had to grin.

"What?" he asked, a suspicious look on his face.

"You didn't offer me your arm. You're thinking of me like a man already."

Understanding dawned in his eyes. "My God, you're right."

She clapped her hands and almost squealed in delight.

"Now, don't do that. That is *female* behavior, little naturalist. Try this instead." He clenched a fist and raised it in a gesture as though to cheer and exclaimed, "*Jolly good!* The key is learning our body language more." He waved at her. "Is that how you stand at ease?"

She glanced down at herself. "Well, yes."

"Try this instead."

He leaned casually against the doorjamb, one shoulder braced on the frame and his legs crossed at the ankles while he folded his arms over his chest in a very arrogant, relaxed, and utterly masculine look.

"So you lean against something, even though you have the strength to stand upright? I've always wondered why men do this. It's as though you are conveying a relaxed behavior while also being slightly dominating. Whatever you lean against, you own?" she suggested.

"You know . . . I never thought of it like that, but yes. Now you try it." He stepped back so she could take his place.

Elise leaned in the same manner and looked up at him for approval. Prospero studied her critically for a moment before he adjusted her arms and placed his hands on her waist, tilting her hips in toward the door more. The way he moved her body with such confidence sent a thrill through her that she didn't quite understood. She didn't like the idea of a man touching her like that, but whenever Prospero touched her, she seemed to, well . . . light up and glow from the inside out.

"Yes, there we are. You now look like a handsome fellow ready to break the hearts of women everywhere . . . perhaps even a few men." He winked at her.

"Even you?" she asked, half teasing, but his playful smile vanished and his eyes darkened. Then he ever so slowly leaned in and kissed her. She didn't even have time to react before it was over. He drew back a second later, laughing softly, but she felt her knees tremble traitorously.

"Christ, the mustache *does* tickle." He rubbed his upper lip, making Elise laugh. It was rather delightfully amusing.

Someone behind them gasped, and there was a loud clang as something hit the floor. They both turned to see a footman standing there gaping at them.

She pointed at her wig. "It's *me*, Thomas."

"Begging your pardon, miss. I didn't know." The young footman hastily collected the silver tray he'd been carrying and rushed away.

Elise was giggling again. "Poor Thomas."

"You'll have to stop that at the club as well. No adorable giggling," Prospero declared in a mock stern voice. He covered her mouth with his hand playfully, trying to stifle her giggles. She lost her breath as their eyes met, and he slowly lowered his hand, their mouths almost close enough for another kiss. It took quite a bit of control for her to speak.

"Your . . . er . . . advice is noted," Elise said. "I think I've giggled more with you around than I have in years. But I promise not to giggle at the club."

"Try snorting a laugh instead if you feel the need to . . . *giggle*." He suggested this with such mock seriousness that she immediately had to try the snort out. He appeared satisfied.

"I am ready. Let's conquer the world of the gentlemen's club."

Prospero looked heavenward, as if praying for divine intervention, but she caught a hint of a smile on him as they headed for the door.

What an adventure this will be, she thought. She was about to sneak into one of the most secretive male realms in England to research her subjects up close in their natural habitat, the way the very best naturalists would. This wager with Sherlock Holmes was going to be all too easy to win.

9

Berkeley's gentlemen's club was exactly what Elise had expected. It was a completely male sphere without a hint of a feminine influence to be seen. The décor was darker, the fabric choices lushly bold, and the satin wall coverings were either in bold or plain patterns, depending on the room. The furniture was beautifully carved, but heavy, large, and sturdy. It was a world built entirely for men. She marveled at thinking how Cinna had blended in so well when she'd set the bait for Prospero.

"Stay close," Prospero murmured. He led Elise to the front desk, where patrons of the club would check in for the evening. An attendant stood behind the chest-high desk, his gaze focused on a set of papers in front of him.

"Prospero Harrington...The Earl of March"

The man's head snapped up.

"I would like to bring a guest this evening. My cousin . . ."

"Elliot," she said, perhaps a tad too eagerly.

"Elliott Harrington," Prospero said, catching on smoothly with the lie.

"Yes, of course, my lord." The man lifted up the register toward Elise. "Mr. Harrington, if you could be so kind as to sign this as proof of your attendance as Lord March's guest."

Elise was grateful she'd had practice writing the name Elliot, since she signed all her publication contracts under the name Elliot Hamblin, but it was her first time writing the surname Harrington. There was a practiced ease expected when signing one's name, but if there was any uncertainty in her hand now, it did not show. She passed the register back when she was done.

"Thank you, Mr. Harrington. I hope you enjoy your evening with Lord March."

"Thank you." Elise kept her voice low, doing her best to sound more like Prospero.

"This way, Elliot." Prospero nodded to a curved stairway that led to an upper floor. A few men passed them by. None paid her any mind, but a few shied away from Prospero, though he didn't react. Elise's heart tugged at the thought that he might have grown accustomed to being avoided like that.

They entered a reading room first, which had dozens of round tables and servants pushing drink carts through the room. The servants paused by occupied tables to inquire if anyone wanted anything to drink. Prospero chose a table at the far back of the room and sat in a chair with his back purposely toward the wall. Elise slipped into a chair next to him.

"Excellent choice, Prospero. From here, I have a full

view of everyone's comings and goings, and I have the best chance to observe their behavior."

"Oh . . . yes, of course," Prospero said slowly, as if the thought had just occurred to him.

Elise realized in that moment his choice of table hadn't been for her benefit. "Wait, why did you choose this position, if it wasn't for the purposes of my research?" she asked in a low voice, so as not to be overheard by other men.

Prospero waved a finger at a young man pushing a drink cart in their direction.

"Oh well," he sighed heavily. "I learned early on that to have my back exposed is a bad thing. I try to avoid it whenever possible."

"Did something happen to you?" She sensed there was a story to this and couldn't deny her curiosity.

"I was in a tavern outside of Paris once. A man came into the taproom and attacked me from behind. Pulled me off my stool and started punching. Ever since then, I prefer to see my exits and know that my back is not exposed."

"Good heavens . . . Why did this man attack you?"

Prospero lowered his voice a little further. "After some of the other patrons subdued him, we learned that he was a painter, a starving artist. He seemed to be suffering some sort of fit or episode of instability in his mind. He was blind with rage when he flew into that tavern, and he attacked the first man he spotted." Prospero pointed to himself for effect. "There was a dark, bleak sort of madness in him that rose up on occasion, and he had no control over it. He later confessed to me that he didn't remember what he did during these spells of mania. Once everyone in the tavern was able to calm him down, we ended up sharing a drink, and he apologized. He told me that he put his heart and soul into his work, and that he feared he would lose his mind in the process someday."

"Did you become friends with him?" Elise asked. She wasn't sure why she asked, but she had a sense that Prospero was the sort of man who would offer forgiveness to others.

"Not exactly friends, but acquaintances. We did meet for drinks at the tavern quite a few times once he was feeling better. He even showed me some of his work. The way he uses color . . . it's like nothing I've ever seen before. He is incredibly talented, and wise. I told him how I had ended up in Paris, a broken man with empty pockets. It was hard to be so far from home and feel so lost."

Prospero was quiet a long moment, sorrow evident in his face as he seemed to fall back into his memories. "This fellow, Vincent, said to me there may be a great fire in our hearts, yet no one ever comes to warm himself at it, and the passersby see only a wisp of smoke. I understood what he meant. My life is nothing but a thin gray vapor to the rest of the world, but deep inside I'm burning with a desire to be my old self, or perhaps a better version of myself. After I heard that my father died, I considered not coming home, thinking only of the cloud that hung over me here. But Vincent told me that one must work and dare if one really wants to live in life. So here I am, wanting to finally live."

Elise was moved by the artist's words. She'd fought hard for what she had and what she had accomplished. There was a bittersweet validation to hearing from others that it was the right path to live, even if it became hard to hang on to her dreams and desires at times.

The young man with the drink cart stopped at their table.

"Two scotches, please." Prospero tossed the young man a few coins as the fellow poured glasses from a whiskey decanter and passed them to Prospero. Elise accepted a glass. She had never tried scotch before. Or any whiskey, for that matter. She tipped the glass back eagerly and took a big gulp. The alcohol hit her far harder than she'd expected. She sputtered wildly and gagged.

"Bloody hell!" she croaked.

Prospero leaned forward and gave her back a few surprisingly rough but effective whacks to clear her throat. "I should have warned you. That's a *sipping* whiskey." Prospero grinned as Elise managed to recover herself.

"Bloody hell," she repeated once she felt able to speak again.

Prospero was still grinning. The handsome bastard leaned back in his chair and sipped his own drink.

"So, what do men like about these clubs?" She wished she could have brought her notebook with her to sketch some of the men and jot down observations so she wouldn't forget anything. But it might have called too much attention to her activities. Prospero rolled his glass slowly between his palms, then lifted it up to the lamplight to study the liquid as he took his time answering.

"It's a place where we can be ourselves. We can sit in silence or chat with friends, we can forget the woes and worries of the world outside. We can go to the cardrooms and gain or lose fortunes, or we can challenge each other in the betting books. We can be men."

"*Interesting*," Elise muttered. "It's strange that women have no such place to escape to like that, other than retiring rooms. And that is not exactly a place we wish to be, except to see to our physical needs. The Society of Rebellious Ladies was created because women weren't allowed to meet except in homes, where, of course, men were allowed. Whenever men discover what we are up to in the society, we have to move our headquarters. The original society was located on Curzon Street about sixty years ago. We have had three additional locations since that original founding and the Baker Street address is our current home."

Prospero's gaze held hers. "You know, you're right. I hadn't thought of that. There are many places you are never allowed that we as men are always allowed to go. We can escape the world, but you cannot escape us."

They were silent for a while, and she could tell that Prospero's thoughts were miles away. She didn't know what he was thinking about, but she had more questions to ask and hoped he wouldn't mind if she continued her line of study.

"How do you tend to spend your evenings here? Are you a gambler, a billiards man, or do you sit in stoic silence and sip your whiskey?"

"I've been all those types over the years, but as I grew older, I've become more of a sip-my-whiskey-in-silence sort of fellow."

"You are only four and thirty. That is *not* old. I'm twenty-six, which, for women, apparently is ancient. But you are still in your prime as a man. I've seen you practically naked. You are a supreme specimen."

Prospero shot her a half smile. "I appreciate the compliment."

Elise fought off a blush that heated up her face.

"Do you still play cards or billiards at all?" she asked.

"I don't. Mainly because I have no money these days to gamble and lose. Thankfully, I don't have that compulsive urge the way some men and women do. I've seen it destroy lives."

"Oh . . ." She tried to hide her disappointment. She'd been hoping to see the cardrooms, perhaps play a hand or two.

"If we had money for the buy-ins, I could arrange something, but . . ." His voice trailed off.

She patted her trouser pocket where she carried a slim billfold. "I came prepared. We can use this, if you like."

He laughed. "Oh, all right. Finish your whiskey. Then we'll go to the cardroom."

She tried to down the rest of her whiskey as quickly as possible. It burned her throat and made her eyes water, but she had to admit it made her feel good too. Seemed to make everything glow in the most pleasant sort of way. It took far more glasses of sherry or wine to make her feel this way, but then again, whiskey was a stronger drink in most cases.

She slapped the empty glass down on the table and grinned. "I'm ready."

He chuckled at her enthusiasm. "Very well, then. This way, little naturalist." Prospero carried his glass with him, continuing to take small sips, as though savoring the smoky-flavored liquor and not wanting to rush his experience. That seemed to be something men did, savor a drink the way women savored flavored ices. She surmised this as a unique trait of self-control within the species, recognizing the finite amount of their preferred substance and resisting the urge to consume it too quickly. She could not think of any other animal that exhibited this behavior offhand. Of course, there were animals like squirrels and chipmunks who saved acorns and other nuts for later consumption, but it was prompted by the seasonal changes. With humans, that "in the moment" ability of restraint was different somehow. She needed to remember such details as these.

They left the reading room and descended one floor to the cardrooms. The first such room had a cloud of cigar smoke forming a hazy layer in the middle of the room where a majority of the men were smoking. It had a dozen tables where men were engaged in a variety of card games.

"What game is this?" Prospero asked a dealer who was setting up a new table.

"Draw poker, my lord," the young man replied.

"Excellent. Please deal me and my cousin in," Prospero said. He nodded at the other six men at the table who were also waiting to be dealt in. It put them at eight players, an ideal number for the game.

Elise had played this game before when the society members decided to learn the various popular card games as a challenge. The object was to get a hand of cards whose rank was higher than the other players' hands and to win more chips. Draw poker used a deck of fifty-two cards, and chips or other markers as stakes. She sat down next to Prospero and carefully mimicked his relaxed pose as the dealer shared the values of the white, red, and blue chips that they would use.

One of their fellow players looked at Prospero with smug arrogance. "Didn't think we'd ever see you back in London again, Harrington." It broke the pleasant silence of the men at the table.

Elise collected her cards and stole a glance at the man who'd spoken. He wasn't a large fellow, but he was muscular and stout. He had a square face and a heavyset jaw that enhanced the meanness in his eyes.

"Ah, well, life can be unexpected, can't it?" Prospero said coolly as he retrieved his own cards. "No doubt you've heard my father has passed. I'm *Lord* March, now." The way Prospero so coldly put the other man in his place by reminding him of his title shocked Elise. The other men at the table reacted with subtle nods of approval to Prospero's behavior. She realized she was witnessing a real-life challenge between two males. Prospero had just let out the equivalent of a lion's roar at the other man.

"Nothing like a title to keep your neck from the noose, eh?" the mean-spirited man asked as the card game began.

Interesting . . . He'd chosen to respond to Prospero's roar with one of his own. Elise scowled at the man. Why didn't he keep his mouth shut about things that had nothing to do with him? Was Prospero somehow a threat to him or his standing? Or was Prospero simply an easy target to make himself appear more powerful? There were no females here, or at least no man at the table knew Elise was one, so what were the men fighting for, if not for positions of power?

"I say," one of the other gentlemen gasped. "Really, Swinton. Have a care."

Swinton played his hand and shot a cool smile at Elise, as if she was supposed to somehow be in on his joke against Prospero.

If there was one thing Elise despised, it was bullies, whether they were in skirts or trousers. She decided at that moment she was going to wreck this man and take all of his money. The bastard deserved it. She shot him a wicked smile and began to play cards. The men at the table didn't know it yet, but she was a lioness and she was moving in for the kill.

HAVING HIS REPUTATION CHALLENGED WAS AN TIRING activity that bored Prospero. After twelve years, he'd quickly grown immune to the jabs and snide remarks people often made. He had to, or else he would have gone mad. He played a few cards and instead focused on the pile of chips that was growing on the table. If he could win them, it would mean a few more complete outfits and not just a handful of new shirts and trousers to get by. Perhaps he could purchase dinner for Elise and himself at a nice restaurant tonight once she tired of parading around in men's breeches. Not that those trousers didn't have some advantages, mind you. They showed off her legs rather nicely, and while he'd much prefer to see them bare of any clothing, he'd take her in trousers over skirts any day.

"Nothing like a title to keep your neck from the noose, eh?" Swinton sneered, and another man tried to hush him and shot Prospero an apologetic look.

"I say. Really, Swinton. Have a care." One of the other men came to Prospero's defense.

"It might," Prospero replied, leveling the other man with a cold look. "It might not. Either way it's not your business, is it? Now, are you going to provoke me into another duel, or do you want to play cards?" He kept his manner unaffected. He just wanted to be left alone and have everyone let his past go, but it seemed they wouldn't.

Swinton's brows lowered. He straightened in his chair, seemingly focused on the game. Over the next half hour and a series of hands played, the pile of chips grew to a staggering amount, and Prospero stared at the cards in his hand. He wasn't going to win. *Blast and hell* . . . He'd lose every penny of what Elise had paid him for this week's study to come up with the extra money he'd wagered, when his hand had started out well enough to win. When the final hands were played, Swinton cursed and slammed his balled fist on the table.

"You cheated!"

Prospero had expected some sort of accusation, but this wasn't directed at him. It was directed at *Elise*.

"I did *not*, sir!" Elise growled menacingly at Swinton. She was quite convincing in her persona, even now.

"You must have!" Swinton lurched to his feet. Before Prospero could stop him, the man swung a meaty fist at Elise's head, striking her so hard she toppled over the chair behind her and crashed to the floor with a grunt, the chair tangled with her legs.

A dull roar began in Prospero's ears, and his hands curled into fists.

"You all right?" he demanded as he bent over her, seeking out any sign of injury before he helped her stand.

"Y—yes," she stuttered and clutched a hand to her right eye. The dull roar in his head now turned to a piercing whistle. Prospero snarled and whirled toward Swinton, grabbing the man's collar.

"You lay a hand on my . . . *cousin* ever again and you will find yourself at the wrong end of a pistol at dawn."

When Swinton's face began to turn an alarming shade of red, Prospero realized he'd hoisted the man up in the air by his neck.

"I say, March, best to let him go. He seems to be running out of air," a familiar voice said from close by.

"I'm not sure a man like him needs air, De Courcy," Prospero replied.

"It may be true, but is he really worth killing?"

Guy De Courcy had a fair point. Swinton was nothing. He let go of the man, and Swinton stumbled back, coughing and gasping for air.

"Did you see that?" Swinton demanded of the other players at the game. "The bastard tried to kill me!"

"I saw nothing of the sort," one gentleman said.

"I only saw you strike a lad half your age," said another.

Guy stooped to pick something off the ground that had fluttered to Swinton's feet in the struggle. It was a card, one that would have won Swinton the game had it been played.

"I believe you dropped this." Guy smacked the card hard against Swinton's chest, giving him a pointed look. "I think it's best if you leave for the evening, Swinton," Guy said.

Swinton soon realized he had no allies and stormed from the cardroom.

"Sorry about that, March. This fellow deserves his winnings. Did I hear you say he's your cousin?" Guy asked.

"Yes, this is Elliott Harrington. Thank you for assisting us, De Courcy."

"Nonsense, men like Swinton are swine," his friend snorted. "So, introduce me to this cousin of yours." Guy slapped Elise good-naturedly on the back. She winced and nearly dropped the money that the other men had been busy handing her.

"Elliott, this is Guy De Courcy, a friend from my Eton days. He kept me out of trouble in Paris . . . mostly." Prospero chuckled at Guy's reaction. They both knew Guy had gotten him into more trouble than out of it.

"It's nice to meet you," Elise said. "I'd shake your hand, but—"

"You've got your hands full." Guy winked. "Nicely done. How did you beat Swinton?"

"Oh, I simply counted the cards—"

Prospero coughed hard, trying to cover her words before anyone nearby could hear. Card-counting wasn't exactly against club rules, but it wasn't gentlemanly behavior either. He gave her a very subtle shake of his head to encourage her silence.

"Ah," Guy said, clearing his throat. "Why don't we find somewhere *quiet* to talk?"

The three of them left the cardroom and stepped into one of the empty billiard rooms.

"Come with me." Prospero ushered Elise into the glow of a nearby gas lamp and lifted her chin up. Elise's right eye would be a nasty shade of purple within an hour or two. "How much does it hurt?" He couldn't help but gentle his voice as he spoke to her. He was also aware of Guy watching them closely.

"I'm all right." Elise licked her lips and looked away from him. A sweet liar. He knew it hurt, and he wanted to kill Swinton for causing this pain.

"Eh, Pross. Your cousin will be fine, he's a tough lad," Guy said.

"Elliott is a woman," Prospero whispered to his friend.

"And while she is certainly quite tough, I want to be sure she is all right."

"He's a *she* . . . ?" Guy leaned forward, studying Elise's disguise with fascination.

"Yes," Elise answered Guy. "I'm undercover, Lord De Courcy. I'm studying men."

"Studying men—" Guy burst out laughing. "Oh Lord, Pross, is this the study that you applied for? The one from the paper?"

"Yes, it isn't men who are studying men, but women. *This* woman, to be precise. Guy De Courcy, this is Elise Hamblin."

Guy's gaze roved over Elise, and he whistled softly. "Well now, that is quite something." Guy winked at her. "You make an attractive man, Miss Hamblin."

She smiled back at him. "I do, don't I?" she agreed proudly.

"So, what else do you need to study? How to kiss a man? Perhaps I could help you there—"

Elise's smile took on a touch of frost. Prospero jabbed an elbow into his friend's stomach.

"Oof," Guy grunted, a hand held over his stomach. "No kissing. My mistake. No need to learn about that sort of thing."

Prospero sent his friend a warning look. "No indeed. She is learning far more important things than kissing. She's a naturalist with advanced knowledge in a number of scientific fields. She doesn't need the likes of you getting in her way while she conducts her study."

"The likes of me? Ah yes . . . I understand, old boy. Touch her and die, eh? Very well, she is all yours, Pross."

"As always, you miss the point," Prospero growled. He

wanted Elise to have the freedom to be left alone to conduct her study without a seduction by Guy . . . but Guy was also right. Prospero wanted no man teaching her anything about kissing . . . except for him.

Elise noted this exchange with an adorable fascination. As an only child, she'd never seen men act like this. He and Guy had tussled more than once as young boys and as grown men. The instincts were still there.

"Elise, I should take you home and see to your eye."

"Oh, but I want to stay," Elise protested, her voice more feminine now that they were alone.

"I think you've tasted enough excitement for tonight. Once your father sees your face tomorrow, I'll be lucky if he doesn't murder me."

"If she wants to stay, I can keep watch over her," Guy volunteered, a little too eagerly.

Prospero shot his friend a look. "Elise is a lady, no matter how she is currently dressed, and I will *not* leave her in your company, old friend. I know you too well."

Guy sighed dramatically. "That you do, I suppose." Guy turned to Elise. "It was absolutely fascinating to meet you."

"Likewise, Lord De Courcy." Elise's grin had returned, holding a mixture of delight and mischief as she peeped at Prospero. He knew then that Guy and Elise should definitely not be allowed to be alone together. They would get into far too much trouble.

"All right, off you go, Guy. Have a good evening." Prospero nudged Guy toward the cardroom door so that his friend would leave them alone.

"Very well. I can take a hint, old boy." Guy bowed over Elise's hand, kissing her fingers, and then he took his leave.

"I like him," Elise said. "Now that I understand him

better. I thought for a moment he wouldn't take my study seriously, but now I see it was more about teasing you than seducing me. Quite a different thing, really."

Not sure how to respond to that, Prospero scowled a little. "I hope you don't like him too much. He's a bit of a libertine."

"As I thought. However, I thought *you* were a libertine," she said as he tipped her chin up more to the light so he could look at her eye again.

"Not me. I have been with a fair number of women, but I was always loyal to one at a time. Guy makes no promises to the women he is with. They know they have him for about a night or two before he moves on to his next conquest."

"That is quite a difference," she observed.

He hummed in agreement as he examined the swelling over her eye. "Yes, we best go home and put something cold on it, if you have an icebox."

"Oh all right. Oh, here." She dug into her pockets and pulled out the two hefty stacks of banknotes. "These are yours."

"No, you won them."

"I hardly require them. Besides, I got the impression from you and Guy that counting cards is not exactly gentlemanly behavior. Please, Prospero. Take them. Purchase a new suit or two, whatever you please."

"I don't want money out of pity, Elise," Prospero said quietly. He had some pride left, and this woman sure knew how to prick it, even though he knew she didn't mean to. The last thing he wanted was her treating him the way women in Paris had. Even well-intentioned pity was too much.

"There is an ocean of difference between pity and compassion," she said with gravity. "I never do anything out of pity. But this is not about compassion either. I require you to purchase a horse and a riding outfit. Riding in the park seems to feature heavily in a number of male rituals, particularly in the courtship of females. Consider this a research expense that I am paying you for."

With great reluctance, he took the money and tucked it into his pocket.

"It's time we left."

"Could we stop for a meat pie on the way? I'm rather famished." She followed him to the door, and Prospero couldn't help but laugh.

"Yes, all right. Meat pies it is. My treat, obviously." He patted the stack of money in his trouser pocket and hated himself just a bit. Tonight was the strangest night he'd ever had, and he had a feeling it was not over yet.

GUY DE COURCY WALKED UP TO THE MARBLE PEDESTAL that held the betting book in Berkeley's. He took up the pen that rested above the heavy tome. He opened the betting book using the black silk ribbon to find the newest page, and he bent over the pedestal to write a wager upon it. When he was done, he walked off with a smug grin.

A man sitting alone watching Guy waited for him to leave the room before he walked over to open the book and read the words in a whisper to himself.

The man scowled and slammed the betting book shut, then left the room in a hurry.

In the far corner of the room, a third man smoking a cherrywood pipe smiled as he puffed out a smoke circle in the air. Then he glanced at his companion, who was diligently reading a newspaper. His friend nudged his spectacles upon his nose and took a sip of his bourbon.

"I'll be damned if I lose my Stradivarius over this, Watson," the man with the cherrywood pipe said.

"Then perhaps you ought not to make foolish wagers against our Baker Street neighbors, Holmes," Watson replied. "I happen to think they are quite charming. There's a lovely young woman named Mary I would rather like to take to dinner some evening, if I can buck up the courage to ask her."

"Humbug," Holmes muttered. "What could be so fascinating about a woman, eh? You'd waste your considerable talents if you would content yourself with a tucking-in by a warm fire, allowing some woman to darn your socks."

Watson rolled his eyes. "I sometimes think you fail to realize that love is a grander puzzle than any you could ever solve, my friend and it certainly doesn't involve a woman darning anyone's socks."

Sherlock's eyes narrowed. He puffed out another ring of smoke, his gaze shifting.

"I wonder . . ." He stood and walked over to the betting book he'd seen De Courcy sign and another man read moments earlier. Holmes turned to the page and read the words to himself.

"Prospero Harrington, Earl of March, will be wed by Christmas of this year to Elise Hamblin. 100 pounds—Guy De Courcy, Viscount De Courcy."

"Wed to Hamblin . . . by God, I didn't expect that. But how did . . ." He replayed the cardroom fight he'd witnessed a few minutes ago and suddenly started to laugh, perhaps a little too loudly, given the stares the other gentlemen shot his way. He strolled back to where Watson sat, still engrossed in his newspaper.

"I've reason to believe a dangerous game is afoot, Watson."

"Oh? What was in the betting book?" Watson asked. Watson was quite clever at looking as if he wasn't inter-ested in the things going on around him, when in fact he was very much paying attention.

"A marriage wager."

"Sounds positively terrifying," Watson said with a hint of amused sarcasm. "Who's the poor devil?"

"Lord March."

"The man from your wager with Miss Hamblin?" Watson lowered his newspaper and fixed Holmes with a look that dared him not to meddle any further with the members of the Society of Rebellious Ladies.

"Yes, but it's not the marriage that's the danger. What worries me is that someone isn't pleased with March, and that wager may have given him a terrible idea."

Watson finished his drink with a sigh, stood up, and tucked his folded paper under one arm. "All right, you have my attention. What are we to do?"

"I'm not sure . . . Come, Watson. I have much to think about . . . and I wish to play my violin before that woman steals it from me."

❧ 10 ❧

Elise licked her fingers clean of the last bit of crumbs. Meat pies had never tasted so good before. She and Prospero had stopped at one of the pie stalls that were open late into the night and early into the morning to supply the working class with the means to get them through their long shifts.

As they ate and walked down the road, Prospero spoke more of his life in Paris and how glad he was to be back in England.

"It's strange, isn't it?" she observed. "That sometimes you must leave your home to realize how much you miss it."

"Strange, but quite true. If only the past weren't still so present here . . ." He paused, and she sensed he was thinking of what Swinton had said to him.

"You wish that people would let go of the past?" she guessed.

He nodded. "A man's club should be his sanctuary, but mine isn't. Not anymore. Swinton won't be the last."

Prospero was more like her than she'd realized, and if she'd been facing his situation, she'd have run straight to the society headquarters for refuge.

Before she could even think of why she did it, she reached out and caught his hand in hers. A flash of warmth blossomed at the connection between them, and he met her gaze, those deep, mercurial eyes so fascinating to her. He had a wealth of knowledge about things in the world that she didn't, and she wanted to question him endlessly to learn all that he knew about people and life. But right now, she could give him something . . .

"Perhaps you need to create your own sanctuary," Elise suggested. "Make someplace all your own. Like my society. We have our own private world."

He smiled a little, and that heated her right down to her toes. "What an intriguing idea."

By the time they returned to her townhouse, Elise had to admit that her eye was beginning to swell, and it ached fiercely.

Prospero noticed her gingerly touching the spot where she'd been hit. "Show me to the kitchens."

She led him to the servants' stairs, and they soon located the icebox in a wooden box insulated with tin in the kitchen. Prospero retrieved a small chisel and chipped away corners of ice from the block until he made a small handful of chunks. He retrieved a dishcloth and wrapped the broken bits in it before tying the ends together to make it a pouch.

"Now, hold this against your eye for a few minutes. It will bring the swelling down."

She placed the ice against her closed eye and winced, but the ache soon began to fade.

"You had quite the night," Prospero mused. "You gambled, fleeced a cheater at poker, had a good whiskey, and ate a meat pie. All in all, that's quite a good day for some men."

"Is it?"

"Well, some for sure."

She held the ice to her eye for a few minutes while she and Prospero lingered in the kitchen. It was unusually quiet as most of the servants had already gone to bed.

"So, what's it to be tomorrow?" Prospero gently took the melting ice and put it in the sink before he cupped her chin and studied her face. His warm breath fanned over her cheeks.

"Umm . . . I can't think . . ."

"Shall I take your mind off the pain?" he offered quietly. His eyes burned with a desire that scorched her very soul. She had but a moment to wonder that he still held such a fire in his veins after all the heartache he'd been through, before the beautiful devil was kissing her to make her feel better.

She moaned as his lips slanted over hers, soft at first, but growing rougher as she responded with her own eagerness. She wanted to slow down so she could catalog all the subtle ways he moved his lips and, oh Lord, how he moved his tongue! But soon he was overwhelming her enough that her scientific mind was silenced into submission.

"That's it, darling. Don't think. *Feel*. Feel me, feel this." He feathered his lips over hers in a teasing whisper before he dove back in with a sensual flick of his tongue in a raw, open-mouthed kiss that sent her axis spinning. She felt like that large painted globe at the society's headquarters. She was whirling, trapped in the beam of sunlight that was this man's kiss, and her entire world was spinning before her eyes.

Her foolish heart saw flashes of a future with Prospero, a life she couldn't have, not in a world that tried so hard to close every door to her." But here in the dark and quiet world of the kitchen, she could pretend to be someone else.

She imagined what a life with Prospero might be like. *Lazy mornings in bed, slow kisses and teasing whispers. Shared whiskeys by the fire and card games. Visits to the British Museum and rides in the park . . .* She even saw herself in a wedding gown, a bouquet in her hands, and then rocking a cradle in a sunny nursery. She saw it all. The life that she'd forsaken to be free of the control of men.

A stab of pain pierced her heart so swiftly, so fierce, that she cried out and pulled away from him. He let her push at him but didn't release her. He kept a gentle, comforting hold on her upper waist.

"Elise?" He breathed her name in a worried whisper.

"It's nothing," she lied. "It's the mustache. It caught on something." She frantically pulled the fake mustache off, glad to have a reason for tears to spring to her eyes.

"You should go to bed and rest." Prospero watched her closely, and she had a sense that he saw through her in a way no one, not even her father, ever had.

"We can tackle something new and grand tomorrow," he said, and gestured for her to exit the kitchen ahead of him.

She yearned to beg him to kiss her again, but she dared not, not when she felt so out of control. When had she ever felt so unmoored? It was as though she was a small ship left to beat against the rocks of this unknown land of desires and dreams for things she could never have. She could only watch them from a distance.

PROSPERO KNEW A FAIR BIT MORE ABOUT WOMEN AND their mercurial moods than most men. In his experience, women often had a flood of thoughts in their heads and a million worries. Women were creatures of vastness and depths to both their thoughts and feelings. Any man who said otherwise was a fool.

Right now, he could see quite clearly that Elise was shaken, but by what he wasn't sure. He also knew that whatever it was, she didn't want to talk about it. Not yet. He would let her keep her secrets, but not forever. He would just give her time for now.

Christ, he felt like he needed time as well. That kiss had changed something in him. It was as though his body and soul had been ripped apart and put back together. A kiss had never felt like that before, and he was damned if he knew why this one had. The women in his past had loved his planned seductions in gardens, alcoves, and ball-room corners, but those had been games. This was nothing like those perfectly planned moments. Neither of them had been looking or feeling particularly romantic, given her emerging black eye, and she was still wearing her masculine disguise.

Yet there had been something delightfully, wonderfully absurd about the moment. He wanted to laugh, to pull her close and kiss her again until she was laughing and smiling and they could simply discover what made this intangible thing between them cause such a deep glow in his soul.

Prospero caught Elise's arm as they left the kitchen and moved up the servants' stairs. He wanted to talk to her about that kiss, but he knew she didn't want to, and he was too much of a gentleman to press her on the matter to satisfy his own curiosity.

All he could think, all that made sense, was that this kiss had been *real*. More real to him than anything else in his life. It had grounded him like the ancient sequoia they'd seen at the museum earlier that day. He felt like he'd been planted deep into the well of Elise's soul and could grow for a thousand years beneath the light of her kiss. With a kiss like that, nothing could knock him flat or break him ever again. It was a kiss all good men could only dream of finding in a woman. It came from a woman who needed no man, who had her own mind and her own dreams. She had no place in her world for him.

It was then Prospero knew that falling in love with this woman would cost him not only his heart but his soul. To love her would be a game he was sure to lose. The question was, would he still find the will to put his cards upon the table and tell her everything, even knowing it would destroy him?

They walked up the main staircase now in silence. He paused as they reached his room.

"Do you need help undressing?" he asked. "I'm sure your maid must be asleep."

"No, I'm fine. She will be in bed, but I don't need her. It's more a matter of finding all the pins." She gestured to the wig she was wearing.

"I can help with that. I've had some practice."

She lifted her gaze to his, eyes wide, and bit her lip. "You don't talk much about the women in Paris," she said quietly, and he knew he couldn't avoid the subject any longer.

"Every woman I spent time with was a woman I liked, but nothing more. They were kind to me, but I never forgot when I was with them that I was being paid for my companionship. I was a kept dog. Not exactly leashed, but I was expected to come when called and to obey any command given."

"Then you know something of what it's like to be a woman," Elise said, her face hardening, but then she softened a little. "I suppose you must think me the same as those women who paid for your companionship?"

"No. Somehow this is different," he admitted. "I know you are paying me for your study, but during moments like these, where we are sharing ourselves like this, you aren't paying for that. It's not . . ." He struggled to find the words. "I feel more like myself when I'm with you than I have in many long years."

Her brows lifted. "You do?"

He smiled then, feeling the expression spread across his face. "Yes, I do, assuming I know what being myself even means anymore." He cleared his throat. "Now, shall we wrestle these pins free?"

She nodded, seeming to accept his avoidance of any further talk about a sensitive subject. For that, he was grateful.

"Very well. Between the two of us, I'm sure we can remove all these quickly," she agreed.

He led her into his room, where she removed the wig carefully and set it on the bed. Prospero was impressed with how tightly she'd coiled up her long blonde hair and managed to pin it so close to her scalp.

He motioned to the bed. "Please sit."

He realized too late how his request might be misconstrued. Before he could amend his words to asking her to sit on the armchair instead, she did as he bade, sitting down on the covers, her back straight, her chin tilted enough to see right through him with her warm brown eyes.

"I will just . . . er . . . sit behind you . . . to help remove the pins." He climbed up behind her on the bed, the scent of her teasing his nose. A flaw in her masquerade. She'd forgotten that men did not smell like roses. He'd have to teach her about cologne.

He straightening his legs out on either side of her hips as he shifted closer. She likely didn't realize why he'd suggested this position. Apparently, he had some secret desire to torture himself because he wanted to remain close to her, even without having the chance to take her to bed.

He breathed out slowly and began removing the pins. Her long straight hair, having been so tightly pinned in place for so long, had formed enchanting ringlets as each lock unspooled. He wound one around his finger, playing with the golden hair a moment. She didn't seem to notice as she made quick work of some of the pins within her reach. Soon nearly all the little coils were free, and she dug her hands into the ringlets, ruffling her hair, searching for more pins, totally unaware of the effect she was having on him.

"Allow me." Prospero heard how rough his voice sounded as he slid his fingers into her hair, but damned if he could control his reaction to her now. She let out a sigh, and he swore he heard a note of true relief beneath the pleasure.

"Who cares for you?" he found himself asking in a husky murmur.

"What?" she replied just as softly.

"You carry the weight of a vast world upon your shoulders. Who cares for you when the lamps burn low and the night grows dark?" He continued to massage the strands of her hair, finding two more pins and pulling them free.

"I take care of myself. Always have," she said with pride. "My father taught me to be self-sufficient so as to never need anyone."

This woman was breaking his heart, and damned if that wasn't the most surprising thing of all. He'd thought his heart had turned to stone years ago.

He had worked to harden himself against the world, yet she'd made fractures in the stone . . .

"It makes you weak to want or need someone . . . even just sometimes?" Prospero rubbed the tips of his fingers into her scalp, trying to ease the tension he felt there.

"I cannot afford to need anyone." She ducked her head a little, her eyes downcast, and Prospero moved one hand to her hip, holding her, letting her feel his support through his touch.

"Why not?" he asked as he moved one hand to the back of her neck, and he pressed his fingers into the knots of muscle there. She shuddered, as if between his touch and his words she was close to letting go, to unleashing the emotions knotted so deep inside her that they were weighing her down.

"I just can't. The moment I give up control, someone

will have power over me." Her voice hardened a little. "Trust a man, love a man, and he takes everything away, everything you have, even your freedom. I've seen it so many times. I can't be a victim. I *won't*."

Her bitter tone stunned him. She wasn't alone, was she? "What about your friends? Cinna and Edwina? You cannot trust them?"

The tears escaped her eyes, and she hastily dashed them away. "I can, but I feel it's wretched to ask that of them. Cinna carries so many burdens already, and Edwina's family has its own struggles. I cannot add my worries to them. Not when I should be fine."

Prospero continued to soothe this beautiful woman. "And why should you be fine?"

"Because I have money and some privilege afforded by my position." She said this in such a matter-of-fact tone it took him by surprise. "But it's all because of my father. Take him and his money away and I am no different than any woman paying for her own survival by living upon her back. Being born as my father's daughter was merely luck. You realize how horrible that is? A woman's fate is entirely up to birth, but a man . . . has a chance to better himself, to work, to find a way to make his life better through struggle. And he does it without the cost of his body or soul to the desires of others."

Prospero wanted to tell her that the idea of men bettering their station in life had far more to do with luck than she suspected. He had seen it both in London and Paris. But he held his tongue. She was right, after all. Women had the deck stacked against them far more than any man. There was no denying that unfortunate truth.

"There are men in the world who would give you a

chance, who would hold you up rather than pin you down."
Men like me.

"And *how* is a woman meant to determine which man is which without harm to herself or her reputation?" she countered.

"A fair point," he conceded, a smile tugging at the corners of his mouth. "Perhaps one could devise a scientific study on the habits and nature of men to determine which types would be satisfactorily supportive?"

He'd meant it in jest, mostly, but her small gasp and the way her skin turned pink alerted him to something deeper she'd heard in his words. She curled her shoulders in, just a little. She was retreating from him. She was on shaky ground, and she was running from him to protect herself. He needed to distract her.

"Kiss me," he said abruptly.

Startled, she looked up at him over her shoulder. He took advantage of the position and cupped her cheek, holding her face as he captured her mouth with his. He had so few answers to give her about life's inequalities and unfairness, but he could give her this—he could give her himself, whatever that might mean.

She opened her lips beneath his, and he drank in her taste. He fisted his hand in her hair, holding her captive for a deeper kiss, and then moved back, taking her with him until she lay atop his body, their mouths fused in a burning embrace.

Sometime later he broke the kiss. "Let me show you a secret, one that will give you the peace you need, at least for tonight." He rubbed his hand on her back over her bottom, lightly squeezing as he enjoyed the weight of her on top of him.

She arched a golden brow. "Are you trying to seduce me, Lord March?" she asked.

"I am *instructing* you, Miss Hamblin, my little naturalist. And this secret is only for you, not for me, although I will enjoy giving it to you."

"I am intrigued now," she admitted. "You may show me."

With years of practice, he swiftly rolled her beneath him on the bed. She gasped, eyes widening at the sudden change of their positions. He took some delight in shocking her, wedging himself between her thighs before she realized what he'd done. It was a far easier move to accomplish when she wore trousers instead of skirts.

"Put your hands above your head and do not move them," he commanded.

His little scientist seemed ready to protest.

"Trust me," he said as he kissed her. He took her wrists in one hand and lifted them up above her head to pin them down. "Leave them here." He pressed them down into the bedding before he let go, then slid down her body, unfastening the buttons of her waistcoat and tugging her shirt up from her trousers. He cursed to himself when he realized her breasts were still bound. He would have to come back to that inconvenience. He unfastened her trousers and began to tug them down, along with her smallclothes. She raised her hips to allow him to strip her lower half. Then she was bare to him from the waist down.

He grinned as he saw her startled, flushed face. She licked her lips, more excited, more *curious* than trepidatious. What a lesson he was going to teach his little naturalist.

ELISE WAS NAKED—WELL, *HALF-NAKED*—AND A MAN'S shoulders were between her thighs. Was this really happening? Prospero stroked his palms down the outsides of her thighs, and then he moved his hands to her inner thighs, his thumbs brushing over the delicate, sensitive skin of her folds. She sucked in a breath as fear and anticipation warred within her.

"Easy, love, easy." Prospero's voice was rough and dark. It reminded her of the whiskey they'd drunk at the club, and it made her feel a little dizzy.

"What are you going to do?" she asked. Her voice betrayed her nerves by holding a slight tremor.

"You have nothing to be worried about."

"Still . . ." Her breath was coming faster now. "If you wish to instruct me, p-perhaps it would be wise to walk me through what you're about to do?"

He looked at her, his wicked gaze softening a little.

"All right," he chuckled, but the rich sound didn't reassure her in the least. He licked his lips before he moved one hand down to the most sensitive part of her between her thighs.

"This little honeypot calls to me," he murmured.

"Honeypot? Why would you call it something so silly? It's—" Elise caught on the odd choice of words.

"Hush, little naturalist. Let me call it what I wish. And I call it that because I know you will taste as sweet as honey." Prospero drew his thumb along the groove between her thigh and her mound, sending a shudder through her.

"Any good lover will want to lick and suck and tease until you come apart with cries of pleasure."

He meant to put his mouth down there? "Is . . . is that normal?"

Prospero stroked his fingertips on the inner skin, just inches from her sex. Her lower belly heated with a languid feeling that excited and calmed her all at once.

"For any decent man, this is an important part of the mating ritual. A man who is too selfish and too foolish to enjoy this part of sex is not worth taking as your lover."

"Oh . . ." She was curious now that he'd told her it was part of a mating ritual. "Do women have a similar ritual with men?"

"Yes, but we need not discuss that tonight. Tonight is about *you*." He moved his teasing fingers over her until they touched the folds of her labia. She tensed instinctively. She had touched herself there before, of course, but someone else's hand felt like a clear invasion.

Yet she trusted Prospero. He would not hurt her, nor would he force anything upon her. No matter what Holmes or the newspapers said about him, Prospero had honor.

"Tell me how it feels—tell me what you *like*." He moved a fingertip along one side of her labia and downward, then up the other side until he reached the hooded sanctuary of her clitoris. He lightly pressed his finger down on the sensitive bud, then swirled around the sides of it.

A sudden burst of intense sensation made her hips jerk. She started to pull her hands down from above her head.

He tsked, leaning over her and pinning her wrists back

in place, holding them with one hand while his other continued the delicious torture between her legs.

"Use your words, Elise. Tell me how it feels to let me stroke you here . . ."

"It feels strange . . . um . . . a little frightening." She hated admitting any kind of fear.

"You should always be honest in moments of intimacy. A good lover will want that and respect it," Prospero said. He lowered his head, kissing her neck in a way that sent slow waves of heat through her body. "What do you feel now?" His voice was husky and low.

"It . . . it feels like you drugged me. Like chloroform moving through my limbs . . . I feel hot and unable to move, and there is a throbbing within me."

His hot breath fanned her skin before he resumed kissing her neck, and then he slid something inside her. A finger, perhaps? She was thinking too hard on that because he suddenly bit her, his teeth lightly pricking her skin at just the right spot, and suddenly she couldn't think at all.

A startled cry escaped her lips as he pumped that finger deep into her and curled it, striking some spot that she'd never known existed. No books on anatomy had ever covered *this* . . .

"There?" he growled in her ear. "Is that your sweet spot, love?" He rubbed it over and over as he continued to penetrate her. An embarrassing flood of wet heat rushed to meet his hand between her legs.

"Prospero . . . it's too much. It's . . ." She lost the ability to speak as he pinned her wrists tighter when she tried to raise them again.

"If I am your mate, Elise, then this is how I *claim* you. I prove my strength and my dedication to your pleasure, but

I control you here, like this. And you, my fierce lioness, must submit to me so that I might give you what you need."

She would have slapped him if she had been thinking clearly, but with his mouth at her ear, her hands trapped, and his fingers striking at that singularly glorious spot, she simply went up in flames.

Pure, overwhelming pleasure rippled through her, and she wavered like a tiny ship on a vast rolling sea, only able to go in the direction of each wave and drift where they might take her. This was something no book, no professorial lecturer, no scientist could explain. It was something that had to be *felt* to truly be understood.

This made so much sense for so many things that she'd never understood before. She had known the mechanics of mating, of course, but nothing about the pleasure one could feel, other than the fact it existed. No wonder people made fools of themselves for love and lust. If this was the goal they strove toward, she could now understand things that had previously eluded her comprehension.

A moment after these realizations came and went, she was overcome with a new flood of emotions. There was a man between her thighs, his hand between her legs, his fingers gently drawing out the little aftershocks of her climax, and he watched her face with unreadable eyes.

"How does it feel?" he asked in that dark, sinful voice. "You surrendered to me for just a few moments and the world did not end, did it?"

But she hadn't surrendered to just anyone. She had surrendered to *him*. For her, that seemed to make all the difference.

She chose her response carefully. "It was . . . unsettling.

I feel like I've drunk too much wine. Everything is glowing and I feel warm."

He smiled in approval. "Good. That was your first lesson. To trust me and receive pleasure."

She suddenly had a thousand questions. "Does it always feel like that? With any man? When you mate fully does it—?"

Prospero silenced her with a deep kiss, his tongue slipping between her parted lips to thrust in a slow, seductive tempo against her own.

"Save your burning curiosity for tomorrow. For tonight, just feel." He resumed kissing her, and his hand slid up to grasp her hip and hold her, his fingers digging into her skin in a possessive way that she liked far too much. She shouldn't want to feel possessed by a man, to feel claimed, yet . . . she did.

Just feel . . . She did feel. She felt so much of a great many things, and she knew it was only the beginning.

11

Elise woke up to the unsettling feeling of being watched. She blinked bleary-eyed and glanced around. She was alone in Prospero's bed, but she wasn't alone in the room. Her maid, Mary, stood at the foot of the bed, hands on her hips, her face red. She looked ready to burst. It was the epitome of Mary in a fine fury.

"*Milady!*" Mary hissed. "What on *earth* are you thinking? You're naked and in the wrong bed!"

"I'm not naked—" She sat up and gasped as the sheets fell away from her very bare skin. She frantically lifted the sheets up to her throat and realized she was quite naked after all. She hastily replayed the night's events. Had they . . . No, she was certain she would have remembered if she'd actually made love with Prospero, at least fully.

But what had happened to the wrapping around her breasts, her shirt, and her waistcoat? Prospero must have undone them last night after she'd fallen asleep.

"Well? What do you have to say for yourself?" Mary demanded hotly.

Elise was used to her maid acting like her mother, but she was far too old to be lectured like a child. Rather than primly remind her maid of her position, Elise simply said, "My research went quite well last night, Mary. You must congratulate me. I drank whiskey at a gentlemen's club, played cards, got into a fistfight, and I allowed Lord March to show me the finer points of what a man can do to bring a woman to pleasure. What do I have to say for myself? I say I had quite a *splendid* night."

Her maid stared at her as if she'd grown an extra limb. The color drained from Mary's face as she came closer and peered at Elise.

"Someone *hit* you? Was it March? I'll—" She was building to a fury again, her hands curling around an invisible neck in the air. Dear, sweet Mary could be so bloodthirsty when wanting to protect her.

"It wasn't March. It was a man who cheated at our card game. I turned the tables on him, and then the man called *me* a cheat and knocked me flat to the floor. Prospero nearly strangled him afterward. It was fascinating to watch men interact without the perceived presence of women around. I was able to watch them solve a territorial dispute amongst themselves. One minute this man was insulting Prospero, and the other men at the table clearly didn't approve of his comments. After the fight, the man then tried to paint Prospero in an ill light, but not one person in the room would side with him. When they discovered this man was the one who had actually cheated, he was all but thrown out." She realized she had just rambled excitedly the way she did when discovering something new like a subspecies of insect that she'd never seen before.

Mary cupped Elise's chin and studied her face, turning it this way and that, examining the bruise.

"Your eye is *purple*, milady. How will you explain *that* to your father?" She tsked and frowned while examining her for other injuries.

"I don't know," she admitted. "Have you seen Lord March this morning?" Now that the excitement over last night's events was fading, she became all too aware that she was still naked in his bed and he was not here. Where was he?

"He's dining with your father. Unlike *you*, he managed to get up at a reasonable hour."

Elise frowned. She never slept late. This was twice now that she'd failed to wake at an appropriate hour.

"Are they getting along?"

"Quite well," Mary said. "Apparently, your father plans to introduce Lord March to his business partners later this week." Mary had no qualms about eavesdropping when it served a purpose. And anything Mary could tell her about the goings-on in the house that she might not be privy to was information she needed.

Using the sheet as a wrap around her body, Elise left the bed and rushed to her own chamber to change, Mary at her heels.

She put on a pretty plum-colored day gown with one of the more elaborate bustles. There was a small part of her that was growing to enjoy dressing a tad more feminine, at least for part of the day. She always dressed with elegance and style, but now she found herself choosing gowns she usually reserved for more formal occasions. The silver and gold beading on the bodice formed small patterns of leaves, and the hem glittered in the sunlight when she finally entered the dining room.

Prospero's eyes lit up when he saw her enter. Her face flushed, flooded with memories of him touching her between her thighs.

Oh Lord . . . It was strange and wild to think that she had allowed him to do all that to her last night, and that he'd stripped her while she'd slept. She was going to have to speak to him about that, though not with her father in the room.

"Ah, Elise, I'm glad to see you up and about." Her father's voice called her attention to him. Both he and Prospero stood upon her entrance into the room.

"Good morning, Papa."

"What happened to your eye?" her father asked, a storm building in his voice as he got a better look at her face.

"I got into a fight last night," Elise quickly explained.

"With who? Not March!"

"No. March rescued me. We were drinking at Berkeley's club and playing cards. A man named Swinton started insulting March, and I decided to take the fellow for his entire pocketbook in the card game. He called me a cheat and hit me."

Her father turned to Prospero. "Is this true?"

"I fear it is. I never imagined a gentleman in my club would engage in such low behavior. I wouldn't have brought Elise there if I had known it would happen. Swinton was ejected from the club shortly after the incident."

"Prospero nearly strangled him," Elise added with pride. "The man's face was turning blue, and his feet were dangling in the air. That's when a card fell out of his sleeve, and it turned out *he'd* been the one cheating."

"You nearly strangled a man?" John asked Prospero.

"I . . . er . . . wasn't really aware of it. I simply grabbed him and was warning him not to touch Elise when someone pointed out that he was unable to breathe. I admit I was not so gentlemanly as I ought to have been."

"It has been my experience that one does not have to play the gentleman when around someone who doesn't deserve it. I don't dare to think what I might have done had it been me."

"I will cover the bruise with some powder," Elise assured her father. She probably should have done it before coming down to breakfast, but she'd forgotten in the midst of reliving Prospero's introduction to passion last night.

Her father's eyes softened as he looked at her, completely worried. "You must not get into any more dangerous situations like that. If anything had happened to you . . ."

"You would have less to worry about," she teased.

"*Never* joke about that." Her father's tone hardened a little. "I only survived losing your mother because I had you to live for."

Elise bit her lip. "All right. No more dangerous outings," she promised.

Her father cleared his throat and tried to resume his usual good humor. "Dare I ask what mischief you will be up to today?" he asked.

"Research," Elise corrected.

Prospero cut in. "Well, I thought we might interview staff this morning for my home, then go riding in Hyde

Park. I am under orders from your daughter to buy a horse."

Her father barked out a laugh. "She does love riding. Buy a good beast or you'll never keep up with her."

"I shall heed your advice," Prospero said solemnly, but Elise saw a hint of mischief behind his seriousness.

"Then I shall leave you both to your day. Elise, do not forget that we have a ball this evening at the Marquess of Rochester's home."

"A ball? Papa, you know I don't like to—"

"I have already informed our host we will both be there. I also requested permission to bring Lord March, and Rochester has agreed. It seems he and March know each other." Her father looked to Prospero for confirmation.

"Yes. We went to Eton together. I haven't seen him since my return, but I will be glad to renew the acquaintance."

"There you have it, Elise. You may continue your study of the male specimen at the ball this evening." Her father chuckled and kissed her cheek on the way out of the dining room. Prospero pulled out a chair for her so she could sit opposite him.

He nodded at the sideboard. "Shall I?"

"Oh, you don't have to—"

"Please, allow me." He gave her a look that set butterflies loose in her belly. He was most insistent about tending to her needs. Many men simply did what society expected them to do for women, but Prospero's actions seemed to come from a deeper need to care for others. She wasn't used to that. She had her father, and Mary, of course, but what Prospero did felt different. She'd never wanted to care for any man, save her father, but something about how Prospero treated her made her want to do the same for him.

"Here are the candidates your butler believes we should start with." Prospero placed a stack of letters in front of her, then began preparing a plate of food for her.

There were applications from a butler, a housekeeper, several upstairs maids, and some footmen as candidates. She read them all while she nibbled on her breakfast.

"These seem quite suitable, but we should conduct in-person interviews to be sure that you like them personally. It would be a terrible thing to hire someone that you find out later on you cannot stand." She finished her toast and licked the marmalade from her fingers before she realized he was watching her. She blushed.

Prospero crossed his arms and stared at her as she slid her fingertip out of her mouth.

She swallowed and cleared her throat. "Shall we send a request to meet with them soon?"

"It's already done. Roberts took care of it. They will start arriving at my townhouse in about ten minutes."

"Heavens!" She leapt from her chair and snatched up the letters. "Why didn't you tell me?"

"You needed rest and food," he said simply, as if that was a proper excuse for tardiness.

"I must powder my eye to hide that blasted bruise first. I shall join you in the entryway." She rushed upstairs to her bedchamber and quickly applied some face cream and powder to conceal the bruise. It was still tender to the touch, but icing it the night before had kept it from swelling.

When she returned to the entranceway, Prospero was

waiting, fingers tapping on the top of the black hat he held in his hands. He smiled in a soft way that made her chest ache. She'd never been looked at that way before.

"Shall we?" He put on his hat and offered her his arm. They stepped out into the morning sunlight together.

JOHN WATCHED THE YOUNG PAIR CROSS THE STREET ARM in arm from his room one floor above. He frowned as he considered his daughter and the Earl of March together. It seemed Prospero Harrington could be a dangerous man, given what he'd heard about last night's encounter with this Swinton fellow. But was that danger something that would harm his child, or protect her?

He saw something move out of the corner of his eye, and he turned, trying to catch sight of what he'd just seen. It had seemed so familiar . . .

"Eloise?" He moved away from the window and followed the figure that escaped his vision.

A soft, warm laugh filled the hall.

"Oh, John . . . stop worrying. She'll be fine . . ." His wife's voice echoed back to him. His arm ached with a dull pain, but he pushed it away.

"Eloise!" He called his wife's name again as he saw a flutter of skirts vanish around another corridor.

"Wait!" he called out. It had been too long since he'd heard her, and oh God, how he missed the sound. Feeling suddenly lightheaded, he stumbled and called her name again.

"Sir!" Roberts lunged to catch him before he fell. "What's the matter?"

"Roberts, my wife . . . She's . . ."

"She's what, sir?" the butler asked, eyes full of concern.

John knew what the man was going to say. *Gone.* She was gone. Been gone for years.

But he'd heard her voice, and he'd *seen* her, even if only for a brief instant.

"Sir, I believe it's time we summoned the doctor." Roberts took a more commanding tone, and for the first time, John let his servant tell him what to do.

"Yes, the doctor . . . of course. Roberts . . . I must talk with you. I must see that Elise is looked after . . . if . . . when . . ." He didn't have the breath to finish.

"Of course, sir. Of course," Roberts assured him as he helped John into the nearest sitting room and shouted for a footman to fetch a doctor immediately.

John put a hand on his chest, breathing slowly as he watched the sunlight cut wide beams into the room. The dust twirled and danced, and he thought for a moment, just a moment, that Eloise was there, watching him, made of half dust, half sunlight, existing in some world and place beyond his mortal imagining.

But he had *seen* her, he had . . .

ADAM JACKSON LEANED AGAINST THE LAMPPOST, watching March and some woman cross the street to another house. The house was March's townhouse—or rather, his late father's. The front garden was a mess, and the home had an empty, decayed feeling that came with places abandoned by people for long periods of time. That gave Adam a sense of justice, to know that March's once beautiful townhouse was in such a state that it would take quite a fortune to salvage.

March had no money, Adam had discovered that with discreet inquiries made around town to men he could trust. The rumors that the late earl had let the estate fall apart after March left for France were in fact true. March had nothing but the clothes upon his back, his father's debts looming over him, and that townhouse, which, no doubt, was a shambles inside. So what could make his enemy smile with such joy? It had to be that woman upon his arm. A rich heiress, perhaps? Someone who could erase all of March's debts? Adam's brows lowered at the thought that March could fix his problems so easily. The murderous bastard had the devil's own luck.

Adam removed his pocket watch and checked the time. It was still quite early for male callers to arrive at a woman's residence. Yet March was strutting about with that young woman with far too much familiarity. He'd worked quickly to find a rich woman to seduce in just a matter of days. If Adam hadn't wanted to see the man dead, he would have admitted to being impressed.

A chimney sweep and a young lad assisting him walked past, carrying their buckets in one hand and their brushes in the other.

He caught the man's arm to halt him. "Excuse me."

The man turned a weary, soot-stained face toward Adam. "Yes, guvnah?"

"Who lives in that house there." Adam pointed to the house March had just left.

"That'd be the Hamblin place."

"You don't say . . ." Adam tossed the man a coin, which he pocketed and continued on his way, the lad trundling after him.

Hamblin. That was the girl's name from the betting book at Berkley's. *Elise Hamblin*. The one De Courcy had wagered March would marry by Christmas. From what Adam had seen of her, the girl was pretty. Adam liked pretty women. They were even prettier when they cried after he'd slapped them around a bit. Women were only good for one thing. Even his little sister was a useless little bit of muslin. She'd traded her favors and destroyed his family's reputation in society, and now Adam had to clean up her mess. He'd thought he'd be done dealing with her once she'd married, but then her useless husband had gone and died, sending Adam's sister back under his control, much to his own frustration. With a low growl, he focused his thoughts back on March. He would deal with his sister later; for now he needed to focus on the man who'd killed his brother.

A slow smile spread across his lips at the thought of March's woman on her knees, tears in her eyes. So March had an Achilles' heel, it seemed. A plan began to emerge within Adam's mind. His smile widened so much that it stretched his face tight.

You will hurt, March. You will lose everything, and when it's done you'll hang.

🦑 12 🦑

"I believe that went rather well," Elise said once they were alone on the steps outside his home.

The morning sunlight illuminated her blonde hair, making her positively glow. She looked stunning, with the faintest breeze tugging errant wisps of gold hair against her cheeks and neck, her brown eyes bright and warm.

"What?" she asked after a moment.

He hastily recovered once he realized he'd been staring at her. "Er, nothing. I was just thinking the same thing. I was pleasantly surprised at how well it went. I admit, I expected more resistance once they learned who was interviewing them."

Thankfully, the staff seemed more than ready to help him put his townhouse back in order. The housekeeper he'd chosen, Mrs. Stanwick, seemed excited by the challenge rather than intimidated. Mr. Rueben, his new butler, had quite a few connections in the city and immediately sought permission to obtain estimates for wood rot repair, plumbing, and other things that desperately needed to be addressed before anyone could comfortably move in. Prospero had gratefully consented to Rueben's request.

Elise had handled the whole affair with ease and introduced herself to the staff as Mr. Roberts's employer, which seemed to smooth over any concerns about the impropriety of him bringing an unmarried woman with him to his house for interviews. She'd kept a cool appearance, offering only a polite, feminine interest in assisting her new neighbor.

Elise gave an elegant little shrug. "I suspect Roberts told them your name before he finalized their interview appointments so that we didn't have to bother with anyone who would have been uncomfortable with your reputation."

"Yes, I suspect you're right. That would explain it," he mused. "Either way, I'm grateful to him and to you. You thought of quite a number of things that I hadn't considered. I admit it's been years since I've had to manage a household."

Her gaze brightened. "Are you grateful enough that you truly won't mind buying a horse today?"

He couldn't help but roll his eyes. "Yes, all right. I will buy one. I suppose I do need to get about town on a horse until I can buy a coach."

"We have room in our stables until you have had a chance to assess the condition of your stables," Elise offered.

"Thank you."

"Now, if you don't mind, I need to change again. It's less fun buying horses dressed as a woman. Once we buy yours, we ride in Hyde Park. I wish to see it from a man's perspective."

"Very well. I will wait for you to change." They returned to Elise's home, and Prospero met with Roberts while Elise ran upstairs to change.

Roberts was delighted that Prospero had approved his selections. Once Elise bounded down the steps dressed as her male disguise Elliott, they set off for the Barnet Fair to look at horses.

Barnet had been primarily a meat market in the age of the Tudors, with butchers bringing their best meat to sell. Horses had started to be sold there in the late 1500s but often weren't pedigreed or registered on any of the Thoroughbred books, Prospero was aware of that. The men in his set always went to Tattersall's. Elise, however, seemed quite comfortable moving among the stalls, as though she visited such places frequently.

"Why Barnet?" Prospero inquired as they entered the market, which spread out on the green fields before them.

"Tattersall's is good," she admitted. "But you need an *exceptional* beast, Prospero. If there is one thing I know about horses, the Romani breed splendid mounts."

"*Gypsy* horses? Good God," Prospero exclaimed. "I heard they train them to escape their paddocks and return to the Gypsy caravans after they've been sold."

Elise shot him a quelling look, and he realized quite a few people had glanced their way at his outburst.

"I would think listening to such *rumors* would be beneath you," she said calmly. "And they prefer to be called Romani or Travellers. Now hush and follow me."

She led him past the paddocks loosely constructed into roped areas and toward a large tent with a striped tarpaulin top. Inside the tent, he found a smartly dressed man in black trousers and a black waistcoat, leading a range of horses through their paces. Dozens of men and even a few women watched the horses on display with keen interest.

The man in the black waistcoat had slightly olive skin and raven-black hair and was close to the same age as Prospero. The man gave a sharp whistle, and all the horses abruptly changed direction to go in a counterclockwise circle. It was clear he was in full command of these horses; he exuded a quiet confidence that the horses sensed and respected.

Elise watched the horse trainer with open admiration. "That is Anthony Ardelean, one of the best Romani horseman you'll ever meet. He studied at the Spanish Riding School with the Lipizzaners."

Prospero immediately fixed on the man. Any man or woman who loved horses knew about the Spanish Riding School and their beautiful Lipizzaner horses. They had coats as white as fresh snow and could perform incredible feats such as "airs above the ground," where a horse would balance on its hind legs with its front legs in the air, then it would make three or four jumps on just its hind legs. Then it would leap into the air and draw its forelegs under it and kick its hind legs out before landing on all four legs at the same time. The skill required for such a thing was nearly impossible to achieve without the most capable trainer and the most capable horse.

Prospero watched Anthony click his tongue, and the horses stopped their parade and waited patiently for the next direction. "He no longer rides at the school?"

"No. He wanted to use what he learned with horses of all sizes and breeding. He believes what matters is temperament more than the breed. Size and strength play a role, but a horse without breeding can still defeat the finest Thoroughbred in a race if it has the heart to win."

Prospero smiled at her. "Now I see why you like him," he said.

A blush darkened her cheeks, and he wondered if perhaps she was attracted to this good-looking Ardelean fellow. A flash of unexpected jealousy forced him to check his reactions, lest Elise notice.

"Anthony is indeed a fine man, but we are merely colleagues. We both believe that men often misjudge—not just women, but other creatures as well. It's refreshing to talk with someone who listens and doesn't dismiss my thoughts and observations."

Prospero wanted to point out that he did that too, but he feared it would make him sound petulant.

"Come, I'll introduce you." She led him closer to the paddock under the tent where Anthony could see them.

"Anthony!" Elise shouted, but then she remembered to lower her voice and called out again in a more masculine octave.

Anthony's gaze swept over Elise in momentary confusion before he burst into a grin.

"Well, this is a new look for you, Hamblin," he greeted as he came over.

She chuckled. "Today I'm Elliott Hamblin. Mr. Ardelean, this is my friend, Prospero Harrington, the Earl of March. He needs a good horse to ride. Something strong, dependable, and fast."

Anthony shot Prospero a meaningful look. "You mean one that will keep up with Honey."

"Yes, exactly."

Prospero felt another pang of envy. It was clear they

had a friendship that was built upon mutual trust and respect. He wanted that with her, and the desire was so strong it stunned him. He'd known this woman but a handful of days, yet he craved an intimacy not just of the body with her, but of the heart.

Anthony held out a hand to Prospero. "It is a pleasure to meet you, Lord March. If Hamblin likes you, you must be a solid fellow."

"Please, call me Prospero. I don't know if I am worthy of the praise you've just given me, but I will strive to be," he said.

Anthony's grip was firm and his gaze honest. "Let's find you a proper horse then, eh?"

Prospero ducked under the ropes with Elise as Anthony beckoned for them to follow. Other horsemen took charge of the beasts that Anthony had been leading around the paddock.

"You're a tall man, so you'll need a decent height. At least fifteen or sixteen hands," Anthony said. "No delicate Arabians for you."

Prospero nodded. If the horse was too short, his legs would come down too far and create discomfort for the horse.

"You'll need speed and stamina as well." Anthony eyed the horses in the paddock in front of him, then whistled to one of the grooms. "Renaldo, bring me the Palouse horse."

"Palouse?" Prospero had never heard of such a breed.

"He is only half Thoroughbred—the rest of him is a Palouse. We acquired him from the Americas. The Palouse is a breed raised by the Nez Percé Indians. They have mustang blood, descended from the Spanish horses brought to the Americas. Those horses were powerful, ready to carry the Spanish conquistadors in full armor. The call these horses Palouse because of the Palouse river that ran through Nez Percé lands."

The horse that was brought over was entirely black except for its flank, which was snow-white and flecked with black spots like a dalmatian. It was unusual looking, but not unattractive.

"This horse will not let you down, my friend. But you will face derision among the elite horsemen. They won't see this beast as we do. This stallion has heart, strength, and courage. He needs a man brave enough to ride him."

Prospero approached the horse, which cocked his ears forward curiously and flipped his lips up and down once or twice, making Anthony chuckle. Anthony reached into his pocket for a lump of sugar. The horse ate it happily and nudged Prospero's elbow.

"Sorry, old boy, no more sugar here. At least for the moment." Prospero stroked the horse's nose, and he leaned his face against his shoulder in encouragement.

"He's a beautiful horse," Prospero said. "How much are you asking for him?"

He had hoped to pay for the horse himself, but the truth was that the money in his pockets really belonged to Elise. She had told him to think of it as his own, but that still was a hard thing for him to accept. Running about London with her had been enjoyable, and he could not quite justify being paid for having such adventures with her.

Anthony considered the matter. "For a friend of Hamblin's? Seventy-five pounds."

He paid Anthony from the billfold in his coat pocket.

"Does he have a name?" Prospero asked.

Anthony patted the horse's shoulder. "I call him Raider."

"He sounds fierce indeed. What did he do to deserve such a name?" Prospero envisioned the horse charging across a battlefield, cannons firing around him as he gave no quarter to the enemy.

"He raided an apple orchard when he was a foal."

"So no fierce battles?" Prospero asked Anthony.

"Him? No, but he is a loyal beast and won't let you down. He just has a soft spot for treats." Anthony winked. "Shall I deliver him to you this afternoon?"

"Yes, that would be good," Elise answered for him. "He'll be staying at my stables while Prospero prepares his own."

Anthony smiled. "As you wish. It was good to meet you, Prospero. May Raider give you joy."

Prospero shook hands with Anthony once more. "I have no doubt that he will."

Elise led Prospero away from the tent. They spent the remainder of the afternoon visiting the other stalls and discussing horses before returning to her townhouse. Time seemed to pass so quickly whenever he was with Elise.

John met them in the hall as they entered the house. "Good Lord," her father muttered at the sight of Elise parading around in her masculine costume.

"Like my mustache, Papa?" She winked at Prospero, who bit his lip to hide a smile.

"Gracious, no. You'd better hope it comes off before tonight, or you'll have much to explain to your dance partners this evening."

Elise frowned at the mention of the ball.

John turned to Prospero. "And how was your ride?"

"We actually didn't have time after the staff interviews," Elise cut in, pulling her mustache off. "We went to the Barnet Fair and bought a beautiful horse from Anthony Ardelean."

"Well, I'm glad to hear that you found a good beast for him." John held a curious expression before he turned again to Prospero. "March, would you mind joining me in my study for a moment? I would like to discuss some business with you. It's about our meeting later this week with my investment partners."

"Do you mind?" Prospero asked Elise.

"Not at all. I suppose I ought to go bathe and change if we are to attend that *ball* in a few hours." Her nose wrinkled at the word, and Prospero almost laughed. She ran up the stairs two at a time, a feat easily managed in her trousers. John turned toward his study, and Prospero dutifully followed behind. John didn't sit down once they were inside, so Prospero remained on his feet as well.

John clasped his hands behind his back. "What do you think of my daughter?"

"Think of her? How do you mean?"

"I mean, do you *like* her as a woman . . . ? As a person? As a friend?" John's serious gaze calmed the strange flurry of nerves in Prospero's stomach.

"I . . . do." Prospero hesitated because he wasn't sure why Elise's father was asking him such an intimate question. Did the man know what he and Elise had done last night? He hadn't compromised Elise, per se, but he'd come damned close.

"I find myself facing an unfortunate situation." John glanced down at his trembling palms as he gripped the back of his chair.

"Situation?" Prospero was still confused by the direction of the conversation and more than a little concerned to see a strong man like John trembling.

"I am ill, my dear boy," John said. There was such a softness in his words that something in Prospero's heart shattered. This was a man Prospero would have gladly called *Father*, a man who treated him as a son despite having known him only briefly. John Hamblin was a good man through and through, and Prospero, more than most people, knew the value of that.

"Ill?" That single word held the power to destroy something precious to the both of them. *Elise.*

"Yes. It's my damned heart, you see." John tapped a finger against his chest with a rueful smile. "Never been quite right since Elise's mother died."

Prospero's lips parted, but he had no words that could comfort Elise's father.

John clapped his palms on the back of his chair. "So you see, I need to know my child is safe . . . that she is cared for, looked after, by a man who will love her and never try to change her. He must accept her running about in trousers, breeding racehorses, peering into microscopes, and collecting fossils. He must love every part of her for the perfection she is. For the *gift* she is." John held his gaze once more. "I'm asking you, March. Are you that man?"

Prospero did not answer right away. Was he? He needed time to reach into his soul and consider. He walked to the window that faced the garden of the townhouse and stared at the colorful blooms amidst the deep green. It was a stunning display of nature's beauty. He noticed the wild roses along the stone wall at the back of the garden. He feared that winter would strike early in their brief but brilliant lives and cover the petals with a velvety layer of frost.

How beautiful and short all life was; whether it was years or mere days that a creature had on this earth, it all ended too soon. When he'd been a younger man, the days had seemed endless, as though the summer skies above him would be blue forever. But now he was in the summer of life and smelling a hint of winter upon the air. Prospero had never felt that awareness so keenly until this moment. He turned back to John. Elise's father always seemed so in control, yet as he waited for Prospero to speak, as if unsure of himself.

"I'm afraid I have nothing to give your daughter, save myself. My estate is all but empty, and my ancestral home, Marchlands, is no longer in my family's hands. I possess nothing but that house across the street."

"I am aware of that, of course," John said. "What I want to know is what my daughter would mean to you."

"If she would have me, I would cherish her, and I dare say that I will love her." The words cut into his soul. Was it possible for his heart to bleed after being dead for so long? He hadn't thought love would be possible, yet as sure as the sun would rise, he *knew* that he would love Elise in time.

"She's a warrior, March. But she is still human. She can still bleed. My little Joan of Arc needs a knight by her side to slay those foes that may come at her back. Do you understand?"

Strangely, Prospero did understand. Elise was able to take care of herself, but it was her father's duty, and then her husband's, to watch over her in those moments when she could not.

"Even if you offer her nothing but yourself, that's all that she would want or need. Someday, when she comes to understand this arrangement—"

"What arrangement?" Prospero now realized this was more than just a heartfelt conversation.

"I've had everything prepared. I wish for you to marry while I am still well enough to walk her down the aisle. My solicitor has arranged for this house and half of my fortune to pass to Elise in a trust. The other half of my money, as well as my company and my business interests, will go to you as her husband. You may use it to settle any debts your father had and restore your home to its former glory. I do ask that you will not sell *this* house, though. Elise's mother is in every room. She decorated it with love, and I never want Elise to lose that part of her. To leave it, to sell it, it would break my child's heart, so I beg of you as a father not to do that to her."

"I wouldn't," Prospero whispered. He hadn't had loving parents like Elise, yet somehow that sad truth made him all the more fiercely protective of Elise's memories of her own parents.

"Tonight, after the ball, I will speak to her and tell her of my wishes. The archbishop of Canterbury granted me an immediate marriage license this morning. I have everything ready."

Prospero's throat worked as he struggled to process what John was saying.

"How . . . soon do you wish for this to happen?"

"Within the next few days, if we can convince Elise to agree. I shall rely on you for that. I can order her to marry, but she will not bend to my wishes simply because I demand it, no matter how much she loves me. I want her to marry you because *she* wishes it. I am giving you permission to do whatever you must do to convince her."

"You wish for me to manipulate her into marriage?" Prospero said, barely hiding the bitterness in his tone. He wouldn't do that.

"You and I both know what this world will do to her if she has no one to protect her. My daughter holds a light within her that many men would do anything to extinguish. I trust only you to protect that light, to protect *her*. So, yes, that is what I wish you to do."

Prospero rubbed a hand along his jaw and closed his eyes, letting out a sigh.

"She may come to hate me."

"She may come to love you. Isn't that worth fighting for, my boy?"

Christ, the man knew just what to say to slide a dagger into the heart of Prospero's resistance.

His chest felt strangely heavy. "All right," he agreed. He would do his best to convince her, but he damned well wouldn't manipulate her, no matter what John wanted. But he wasn't about to tell that to a dying man.

"Good. Now, you smell of the stables. You had better go bathe and change before this evening. I have an old evening suit that should fit you if you need one. I'll have it laid out for you."

"Thank you, I do need one. I had planned to see the tailors tomorrow."

"Then be sure to have them make a wedding suit for you as well."

Prospero nodded in assent and left John's study. His breathing was faint as he stared around the grand house, sunlight bathing the art and statues that decorated the space. Now he could see the woman's touch, an easy elegance to every room that was warm and welcoming.

I'm to be married . . . The thought still felt hollow and surreal to him.

What did he know of love and marriage? His parents' union was a transaction, just as his and Elise's would be. He wanted love, wanted passion, yet he'd given no real thought to having it because of his past. Yet how close he was to a future that held such a bright light. All he had to do was win Elise's trust. And let his own guard down so that he might allow himself to trust her in return.

But to do that, he had to convince a woman who wanted no husband into wanting him to be hers. Elise was no fool. She was one of the brightest women he'd ever met. He wanted no lies between them, no secrets, nothing that could tear apart the life they would share. So what then could he do to make her agree to her father's plan?

He ascended the stairs and passed by her chamber, hearing her singing softly and splashing lightly. She was bathing, and the thought of her wet and bare in a large tub of hot water, smoothing rose oil into her skin, made him burn with carnal hunger. If he could just convince her that they could make a go of a life together, perhaps they would find married life enjoyable. He would do everything he could to make her happy as a lover, as a partner, in any way that she wanted, if she would only trust him.

A voice whispered in his head, *I will dance with her.*

Yes. Dancing. He would show her that they would be a good fit, and it would all start with a waltz. After all, dancing was a metaphor for love and trust, wasn't it?

❧ 13 ❧

B *alls*. Elise shuddered at the word.

Was there any hell greater than being paraded about like a broodmare at a market to be examined and judged by one's simpering facade and pleasing submission to a man in a dance? No. There wasn't.

When she judged horses, she didn't just look at their teeth or think about the foals they could produce. She judged them for something deeper. Something more pure that went down to the animal's very soul. But the criteria of London's men could be boiled down to the three *B*'s that sealed every woman's fate: Would she be beautiful, biddable, and beddable?

She wanted to turn tail and run, but she was no coward. If her father wanted her to accompany him tonight, she would do her best to look pretty, smile, dance, and *repeat* until the night was over. She was under no obligation to do more than that.

Elise sighed as she stepped out of the coach, taking Prospero's hand as he and her father escorted her into the fashionable townhouse in Belgrave Square. Lord Rochester's servants greeted them at the door and took their hats and coats. Elise shrugged out of her red satin hooded cloak and passed it to a waiting servant.

"His lordship and the other guests are in the ballroom," the butler said as he escorted them toward the music. The ballroom was full of guests, and the dancing was well underway. To Elise's relief, she spotted her friends standing by one of the walls, half hidden by a tall potted plant. It was one of their strategies for avoiding the attention of men whenever possible.

"There are Cinna and Edwina." She pointed them out to Prospero. "Would you like an introduction?"

"Certainly. I've heard so much about them the last few days that I feel as though I already know them."

Her father nodded to them. "I shall leave you both to meet your friends. I'm afraid I have other matters to attend to this evening." Before he left to join a group of men who were clearly discussing business, Elise noticed the look her father shared with Prospero. Whatever they had discussed earlier seemed to have made them both more quiet than normal.

Prospero tucked her arm in his, pulling her a little closer. Had any other man done that, she would have pulled away, but when Prospero did it, she liked it. "What did you and my father discuss this afternoon? It seems to have left you both a bit morose."

"My future," Prospero said. "I believe he will be involving me in his business affairs more directly than I ever imagined."

"But that is good, is it not?" she asked. "I thought you would want to have some sense of stability."

"I was hoping to earn my own way, rather than be given as much as he means to. Does it upset you that he plans to give me something as valuable as his business? The man has only known me a few days."

"I suppose you would expect me to be upset . . . but I don't have much interest in locomotives or business. I am more my mother's daughter, with my head buried in books and my eyes trained to microscopes. It's not that I do not care about my father's business, but the idea of digging into that world and making a place for myself doesn't call to me. I think it calls to you, though, and that makes me not mind it as much as you would think."

The tension in Prospero's face eased a little. "You would trust a stranger with something like that?"

"I no longer see you as a stranger. Perhaps because we've been through so much in the last few days and I've asked you so many questions, I feel rather like I know you better than I know most people, except for my father and my friends."

This much was true. She'd questioned him endlessly about his life, about his past, about his hopes for the future, and all the things he'd longed for while he'd been in exile. This man was no stranger. He was kind, wryly amusing, a deep and thoughtful man. And he was passionate. Despite her own wish to stay clearheaded about the subject of her study, she had to admit, he'd awakened things in her she'd never imagined she'd feel.

But learning the exact nature of her father's plans for Prospero would have to wait, as they now joined her friends at their hiding place.

"Elise!" Edwina rushed forward and embraced her, which forced her to pull free of Prospero's arm.

"Edwina, Cinna, may I present to you Prospero Harrington, the Earl of March. Prospero, this is Miss Edwina Tewksbury and Lady Cinna Belmont."

Prospero stared at Cinna in intense puzzlement. "It is a pleasure to meet you both," he said as he bowed. "But . . . have we met before, Lady Cinna? I have the strangest sense of déjà vu."

A mischievous light shimmered in Cinna's brown eyes. "We haven't, my lord. But I am told I have a *very* familiar face."

"Oh, I suppose that's it. And how are you ladies this evening?" he inquired with the air of a perfect gentleman. Prospero touched the tall, arching leaves of the plant in front of them. "I see that this plant provides a measure of concealment from the tigers lurking nearby."

"It certainly does," Edwina agreed. "And they are tigers indeed, aren't they, Cinna?" Edwina giggled.

Cinna huffed, glaring at the dandies who preened like peacocks just a short distance away.

"And are you succeeding in avoiding those tigers?" Prospero asked them.

"I wouldn't mind a dance with you to escape them," Edwina confessed. "I'm trying to fill up my dance card before Lord Pavenly finds me. He's been pestering my father for a marriage agreement for months." Edwina's gold hair gleamed in the lamplight, accenting her angelic features. Prospero came to her aid without hesitation, claiming her last free dance.

"And you, Lady Cinna? Do you need to be rescued from a dance as well?" Prospero asked.

Cinna tossed her head, reminding Elise of the wild mares they'd seen in the paddocks that afternoon.

"Heavens no. I know it's impolite to refuse a man, but I have no such qualms about telling a buffoon off if he bothers me."

"I understand you've recently returned from France, Lord March?" Edwina asked.

He clasped his hands behind his back and stood proudly as he conversed with Elise's friends. "Yes, my father's death made it necessary to return."

Elise took a moment to study him. Prospero wore one of her father's evening suits, and with a bit of quick tailoring, it fit him well enough that anyone would have assumed it was his own. His presence acted as a deterrent to the other men in a way that Elise found fascinating and comforting. Several gentlemen had come toward the three women with purpose. No doubt they'd hoped to request a dance, but upon catching sight of Prospero, each of them turned about quite suddenly and acted as though they were needed elsewhere, some of them even waving at no one just to seem as though they'd been summoned away.

"How marvelous," Cinna murmured as she stepped close to Elise while Prospero and Edwina discussed the merits of Paris. "Did you see how every man who sees him positively flees in the opposite direction? That man is a society shield. We simply *must* take him everywhere with us from now on."

Elise chuckled, but something about Cinna's words stirred her memories. *A society shield.* Her father had said she needed someone to slay dragons for her, and here was a knight doing just that. Her mind flashed to that impossible future, a life that she could not have because it would mean giving up who she was. She gave herself a mental shake.

"Yes, he is something, isn't he?" Elise agreed. "You

wouldn't believe what happened when we went to his club last night."

Cinna's eyes widened. "What happened?"

"I was punched by a man during a card game. It was simply thrilling!"

"Truly? Now I wish I had snuck down to the cardrooms that day I showed him the advertisement about your study," Cinna whispered. "What was it like watching the men there? Was it full of smoke and blustering old fools wagering their fortunes?"

"It was, in a way. I had little interest in the gambling itself, but it was fascinating to see how men react to each other. They squared off like bucks in mating season, cracking their antlers together," Elise said. "I've taken some diligent notes, and soon I will be able to compose an article for Mr. Holmes that proves I quite thoroughly understand the male sex. There is no way he could argue otherwise."

"I cannot wait for him to turn over that wretched violin of his. I say we burn it in the fireplace," Cinna growled.

"It is not the instrument, but the man who plays so foully," Elise reminded her. "I rather think we should give it to Edwina. She could sell it for a bit of money. I know her father is struggling at the moment."

"Yes, we really should talk with her about that. I don't like thinking that her father might pressure her to marry some old codger just for the sake of their family."

"I agree. Perhaps my father could talk with hers. Maybe assist him in sorting out his situation." Elise stopped talking when she noticed two men coming toward their hiding spot, undaunted by their social shield. She recognized one as Prospero's charming friend from the gentlemen's club, Guy De Courcy. The other gentleman was familiar to her as well. She had met him once or twice at social engagements, but his name escaped her at the moment.

"Ah, Guy, Nicholas, may I present Miss Edwina Tewksbury and Lady Cinna Belmont. And this is Miss Elise Hamblin," Prospero said. "Ladies, these are my friends, Viscount De Courcy and the Earl of Durham."

"Miss Hamblin." Guy winked at Elise. "I'm delighted to see you again."

Nicholas looked at Guy with slight suspicion. "Dare I ask what you have been up to now, Guy?"

"Nothing you need to worry about, old boy." Guy nudged Prospero. "Right, Pross?"

"Guy has been a proper gentleman, and he will *continue* to be so," Prospero said.

Guy merely chuckled at the gentle warning before turning his attention to Elise's friends. He stepped up to Cinna, who raised her chin in defiance.

"Lady Cinna, please tell me you have a dance free."

"I do not dance," she said simply.

"Oh? Do you have two left feet? How unfortunate. I've met many gorgeous women who simply cannot dance due to the threat they pose to their partners' toes," Guy said offhandedly.

Cinna bristled. "I dance to *perfection*, my lord. I simply choose not to dance."

"I rather think I don't believe you." Guy tapped his chin thoughtfully, and Cinna's face reddened as she stepped closer to him, squaring off against him. "One cannot dance to *perfection* without actually having engaged in the act publicly as well as privately."

"Are you accusing me of lying?" Cinna replied icily.

"Not at all, but wouldn't it be *satisfying* to prove me wrong?" He held out a hand to Cinna, a playful, wicked gleam in his eyes. She had to dance with him to prove herself right, and Cinna, by the glare she shot the playful rogue, was apparently all too aware of her predicament.

Elise was certain Cinna would refuse, but instead she slapped her gloved hand into Guy's. He shot a victorious grin at Elise and Prospero before he led her friend to the dance floor.

"Oh dear," Edwina murmured.

"Should we be concerned, Miss Tewksbury?" Nicholas inquired.

"Well, I don't know. Cinna can be so . . ." Edwina trailed off and looked to Elise.

"She can be rather *prickly* when pushed," Elise clarified.

"Ah, I see," Nicholas mused. "Well, Guy has a hard head. It would take quite a few blows to his skull before he gets bruised."

"Nicholas is right," Prospero told Elise. "We shouldn't worry about them."

Nicholas focused on Elise's more gentle, soft-spoken friend. "Now, Miss Tewksbury, might I ask if *you* have any dances free?"

"Sadly, I do not," Edwina looked supremely disappointed, but Prospero stepped in.

"Miss Tewksbury, I would be honored if you would give my dance to Nicholas."

Edwina brightened. "You wouldn't mind?" she asked.

"Not at all," Prospero assured her. Nicholas escorted Edwina to the floor, leaving Elise and Prospero alone once more.

"I like your friends," Prospero said.

"And I yours." She was surprised that it was true. Neither Nicholas nor Guy was like most men she was forced to engage with at events such as these. She found she enjoyed Guy's teasing, and Nicholas had a gentle, steady patience that seemed to balance Guy's audacity and Prospero's burning intensity.

Prospero nodded at the refreshment table. "Shall I fetch you a drink?"

"Yes, thank you." She was rather thirsty, and a glass of punch would be welcome.

"I shall return in a moment."

Elise turned to watch her friends dance, but she was startled to see a tall, dark-haired man striding straight toward her. She glanced about, seeing no other women, and certainly none in her partially concealed position behind the large plant. What the devil did he want with her?

The man bowed when he reached her. "Miss Hamblin." He was fair in looks and just as intense as Prospero, but there was something about him that warned her away. Whereas Prospero's intensity lit a fire within her blood, this man's intensity was far more threatening. "My name is Adam Jackson. I apologize for the lack of a proper introduction." It was entirely against protocol for a man to introduce himself to her like this.

"Mr. Jackson?" she echoed.

"Yes, and I would like to request the next dance if you are free?"

She shot a glance at Prospero, who was talking to a woman by the refreshment table. He seemed quite focused on her and unlikely to come back right away. It would be bad form to refuse Mr. Jackson, and that would reflect poorly on her father. Elise would never shame her father by making a public spectacle.

"I . . . Very well." She placed her hand in Mr. Jackson's, and they walked to the dance floor just as the previous dance ended. Mr. Jackson pulled her toward him, but not so close as to be scandalous, as the musicians began the next tune.

"Mr. Jackson, may I ask why you risked scandal introducing yourself to me in such a way?"

"Because I am forward enough to say that I think you are the most beautiful woman here tonight, and I wished to be one of the lucky few who danced with you."

Elise saw a hint of something in the man's eyes that sent a prickle of unease through her. His eyes held no passion, no emotions of any kind. There was *nothing* there, save for a thin layer of ice beneath his clearly charming demeanor.

"I appreciate the compliment, Mr. Jackson, but we both know that I am not the prettiest woman in the room."

"Nonsense. We both know you are lovely. Were I a foolish man, I would risk asking you to accompany me into the garden, but I suspect you are far too sensible a lady and would decline."

"Indeed, I would," she replied. She wished he would speak no more for the remainder of the waltz, but alas, she was not that fortunate.

"Tell me, are you taken, Miss Hamblin? Everyone saw you arrive with Lord March. That was quite a statement to make, yet we hear no news of a wedding. Is there hope that you are still unattached?" Mr. Jackson offered her what would've been a winning smile on any other man. She thought of a hyena she'd seen in the London Zoo, how it had bared its teeth and made that terrible sound that was like an evil laugh.

"I am unattached, but I am *regrettably*"—she choked on the word—"never going to marry."

"More's the pity," Jackson said. "I believe you and I could have made an impressive couple."

"Mr. Jackson, would you mind if we continued this dance in silence?" she requested, aware of her tone hardening. She wasn't rude enough to refuse to dance, but she wasn't above demanding silence.

"Of course," Jackson said with the apparent amiability that one would expect, and Elise wondered if she imagined a glint of triumph in his eyes.

Elise pulled free of his arms the moment the waltz ended. But he insisted on escorting her back to Prospero, who stood on the edge of the floor holding two glasses of punch. His face was pale, and his eyes were as hard and cold as Jackson's when they reached him.

"Ah, March," Jackson greeted.

"Jackson." Prospero's tone could have turned the punch he carried into solid ice.

"Lovely partner you have this evening." Jackson bowed over at Elise's hand and kissed her gloved fingers. Then he strode away and vanished into the crowd.

"And *that* is exactly why I do not enjoy balls," Elise muttered once she and Prospero were alone. He didn't say a word but stared in the direction Jackson had gone.

Elise tried to pry one of the glasses of punch from his hands, and he finally released his grip on it.

"What did he say to you?" Prospero asked.

"Some nonsense about me being the prettiest girl here

and how all men wanted me and wondered if I was unattached. It was clear he had no genuine interest. I can see lies in a person's gaze quite easily." Elise sipped her punch, but there was a sour taste in her mouth from her time with Jackson. Something about him. The way Prospero had reacted . . . She had a violent flash of clarity.

"Jackson. Is he—?"

"He is." Prospero's voice was low. "He's Aaron's older brother."

No wonder he had waited until Prospero had left to approach her. Jackson had done it on purpose, the bastard. He'd wanted Prospero to see her dancing with him.

"Yes." Prospero drank his punch in one gulp and set the glass down on a platter as a footman walked by. Then he grasped Elise's hand and with his other hand removed her own glass of punch and set it on the tray beside his.

"Dance with me." It was a command, and quite unlike him, but Elise didn't protest. She led him lead her onto the dance floor.

"Thank you. I need a distraction. Something to keep me from doing something ill advised." Prospero's tone was cold as his gaze swept the ballroom before focusing on her.

Elise didn't ask what ill-advised thing he might do, so she simply tucked herself into Prospero's arms as another dance began. They didn't speak as she let Prospero lead her across the floor. She often had trouble letting men lead in dances, but it came second nature to her to put her trust in *this* man.

After a moment, the lines of tension on Prospero's face eased and he finally seemed to relax. And to Elise's surprise, she enjoyed the remainder of the dance, even laughing when she spun and danced beneath his arm with their fingers laced. The shadows in Prospero's eyes momentarily vanished in the light of her laughter. When the dance ended, she was hesitant to let go. She wanted to keep dancing, because something warned her that nothing would be the same once the music faded and they stopped twirling in each other's arms.

"Let's not stop," she whispered to Prospero.

"People will whisper about us," he warned.

"Let them," she replied. "Let them talk all they want." And so they danced again and again, until the lamps burned low and the guests began to depart for the evening. Yet they still spun in circles, talking about a thousand different things. For a precious few hours that night, she put off the sense of dread that hung over her with no explanation.

At last, the music ended and the musicians began to pack up their instruments. She and Prospero finally had to depart the dance floor. The Marquess of Rochester, Benedict Russell, met them and shook Prospero's hand.

"Glad to see you back in London, and with such intelligent company. A smart man surrounds himself with the brilliant minds of others, does he not?" Lord Rochester asked with a knowing look. He offered Elise a smile and bowed to kiss her hand. Rochester donated to many intellectual societies in London, and their paths had crossed often. He was one of the few men who was happy to talk about science and nature with her whenever they met at social functions.

"Thank you, Rochester. I am indeed blessed with Miss Hamblin's company. And thank you for extending me an invitation tonight."

"Of course." Rochester bowed and greeted her father, who now rejoined them.

"Wonderful ball, Rochester," her father said.

"Thank you, John. I'm delighted you could attend. Now, if you'll excuse me, I need to see to the musicians."

When their host was gone, Elise touched her father's arm. He looked exhausted, and she didn't like that.

"Papa, I think you've been working too hard. Let's get you home to rest."

John nodded, his gaze distant as they left Rochester's home and climbed into the waiting carriage.

They were halfway home when her father cleared his throat. "Elise, there's something important I must discuss with you."

Prospero shifted beside her. Suddenly her body grew tense like a coiled spring.

"Papa . . . is this about Prospero taking over part of your business interests?"

"Yes." Her father hesitated, then seemed to steel himself. "In fact, Prospero will be taking over *all* of my business interests soon."

"All?" She echoed the word. "But why? And why so soon?"

At first he said nothing, nor did Prospero. She looked between the two men. "Will *someone* please speak?" Her heart began to pound hard enough to bruise her ribs. That sense of dread she'd carried all night now grew heavier.

"I am unwell. I do not know how many more days I have. And so I've made preparations for my estate, as well as for your future."

Unwell. The word rang like a distant bell in the middle

of the night, a horrifying warning that all was not well. That terrible things were on the horizon.

"I'm dying, sweetheart." Her father's tone softened and he reached for her hand, giving it a squeeze. "But as a dying man, I have one thing I wish to ask of you."

His grip was strong and sure, betraying no sign of any illness. Elise swallowed hard, a lump caught in her throat.

"What . . . what do you wish me to do?"

"I want to walk you down the aisle at St. George's and give you away."

His words didn't make sense, not at first. "Marriage? To whom?"

Her father's gaze slid to Prospero.

"You mean for *us* to marry?"

"He is the only man I could trust with you. He knows you, Elise. He accepts you."

"Accepts me?" Her voice pitched up an octave with fury. "What about me needs to be *accepted?*"

"Nothing," Prospero broke in quietly. "You are *perfect* as you are. But other men would clip your wings and put you in a gilded cage. Your father knows I would let you remain free."

Betrayed. The word dug in her heart deeper than any dagger ever could. Her father had betrayed her, and Prospero had gone along with it.

She glared at her father. "How can you ask this of me?"

"Because I love you, and I know that an unwed heiress would be targeted by the worst sort of men."

"I wouldn't be silly enough to be *seduced,* and I certainly won't be compromised," Elise argued.

"But men have a way of breaking women, forcing them to do what they wish. When I was a younger man, it was common for heiresses to be abducted and forced to wed. That hasn't changed. Even your intelligence and determination would not save you if you were held at gunpoint. You'd be made to say your vows against your will, and the clergyman would be paid off. That would be just one of a dozen ways someone could catch you in an impossible situation that would force you to marry. It would be a terrible end for the child I love more than my own breath." Her father squeezed her hand again. "*Please,* Elise."

The coach stopped in front of their house, and her father climbed out and offered his hand. Elise didn't move. She couldn't.

"Elise?"

She made no move, no sound. It was as though the world around her was closing in, blackness creeping in at the corners of her mind.

"I'll stay with her, John. You go on inside." Prospero's voice sounded so very far away.

She was vaguely aware of the coach door shutting and darkness growing around her. Strangely, she felt like the coach was still moving, rocking even though she knew it had stopped.

Hands took hold of her gently, and she was lifted, settled onto someone's lap. The fog in her mind thickened and she struggled, striking his chest with balled fists until she choked on her own sobs and her tears blurred the glow of the carriage lamps around her and created striations of gold light across her eyes in the night. She heaved, her body drowning in pain. It felt as though her lungs burned with her own screams.

What seemed like hours later, she slipped into a quiet

state where only her small hiccupping breaths sustained her.

He cupped the back of her head, tucking her cheek against someone's chest. A steady heartbeat thudded strong and comforting in her ears.

"Hush now . . ." A hand rubbed up and down her back. Her eyelids drifted closed, and she woke later to discover that Prospero was carrying her up the stairs. She felt safe cradled in his arms in a way she'd never thought she would ever need to feel. He carried her to her room and laid her down on the bed.

She heard Mary's whisper from somewhere in the dimly lit bedchamber. "Thank you, my lord."

"Someone should stay with her tonight. I volunteer to do it so that you may get some sleep," Prospero murmured to Mary. "She'll need you come the morning."

"Oh, but—"

"Truly, Mary, it's all right. I don't mind," Prospero assured the servant.

Elise drifted to sleep again, only to wake as she felt her clothing being removed. She was tucked into a warm night-gown, and once more she felt herself slipping down that slope into the abyss of a dreamless sleep.

"Prospero," she murmured.

"Yes?" His reply came from nearby.

"You . . . you won't leave?" She wasn't sure if she meant tonight or someday after they tied their lives together in the marriage her father wanted. All she knew was that her life had been upended, and the only thing that kept her from drifting away was him.

"I will be here as long as you wish me to be," he said.

She rolled over in the direction of his voice and pulled

back her blankets in silent invitation. A moment later he joined her, still wearing his clothing but having removed his shoes and evening jacket. He pulled her into his arms, and at last the only real sense of peace she'd had tonight came over her.

JOHN STOOD OUTSIDE ELISE'S BEDCHAMBER DOOR, HIS heart breaking as Prospero held his only child in his arms before Mary joined John in the corridor and closed the door.

"The poor dear is exhausted. Cried herself to sleep."

"Yes." John's chest tightened. "Mary, she will need you more than ever once she marries Lord March and becomes mistress of this house. You will not leave her, will you?"

"No, sir. She is my child in all ways but blood."

"Good." John watched the maid walk toward the servants' stairs. A dull pain began in his temples and he blinked, watching a beam of moonlight dance and swirl before him. His wife's voice teased his ears.

"It's the only way . . ."

"The only way," he agreed. "I have so little time . . ."

He didn't want to leave Elise. His child was every bit her mother. "I've only lasted so long without you because she needed me, needed my love. But now I think she has someone who will be to her what I was to you."

"Yes . . ." That voice of starlight and half-remembered dreams came back to him. Tears fell down his face as he walked to his bedchamber and closed the door behind him.

The most beautiful things in life could be so brief, but love was something that lingered long after the source was gone. His heart had grown around his grief after losing his wife, but that pain, that loss, had never faded.

When Elise had been a child, shortly after her mother died, she had asked him why her heart hurt at losing her mama. He had but one answer. It hurt because it was real, because it was true. The pain she felt told her that the love she'd had for her mother hadn't gone away. It hurt because that love was trapped inside her and could no longer be given to her mother. The only way she would feel better was to find someone else to give that love to. And he'd told her he'd given that love to Elise. He had tapped her nose and wiped at her eyes with his handkerchief.

"But what happens if I lose you?" she'd asked in that wide-eyed way a child does when struggling to understand things she is far too young to know.

"You will love someone someday. Love them the way I loved your mother, with all your soul, with every breath inside you. And when you do, this pain you feel will blend into the love you give that new soul in your life, and the hurt will ease."

He'd made a promise that day he would make sure that Elise found a person to love, but his illness had come too soon. He only prayed that his daughter would forgive him for what he was forcing her to do.

❧ 14 ❧

Elise woke the morning following the ball with a pain somewhere deep in her chest. But that ache was lessened a little by something warm and hard pressed against her body. A heavy weight was settled over her waist, and when she explored it, she realized it was Prospero's arm draped over her body as he lay in bed beside her. All the pain buried deep in her chest from last night made it hard to breathe.

Her father was dying, and his last wish was to see her married to Prospero. It was hard to fully comprehend. She had never allowed herself to picture life without her father. He had been such a solid presence, like an old fortress bowing to neither invading armies nor the elements of nature. He was supposed to be here for a thousand years. She was not supposed to live one day without him. Thick tears pooled in the corners of her eyes, and her body trembled.

Prospero's arm tightened around her, and his head moved closer until he was pressing his lips into her hair.

Overcome with the need to be held, to be comforted, she rolled over and burrowed against his chest, seeking the warmth and shelter that he offered without words. She lay in his arms like this a long while before she spoke.

"Can we do this? Can we marry and survive whatever that means for us?"

Prospero stroked her cheek with the back of his hand. "Honestly, I had no idea what I would do once I returned to England. But from the moment I met you at your society, I felt as if I'd found a star to follow in the night sky." His words lifted the heaviness in her soul so much that she felt she could breathe again. "I would marry you, Elise. And I would do my damnedest to make you happy, just as your father hopes. I believe that we can weather this storm, so long as you believe in us as well."

The piercing blue of his eyes pinned her in place and held her steady. Prospero's words offered her the one thing she needed most: hope. As a woman who'd rebelled her entire life against a world that sought to drown her, hope was everything.

"Married . . ." She sighed the word, unable to hide her dread. "I don't even know what being married means . . . except that I would be your *property*." She couldn't hide the loathing in the last word.

"To many, marriage is simply a piece of paper," Prospero said. "What our union will mean is whatever you wish it to mean. I will not suddenly become a tyrannical lord over you. You will do as you please every day. Nothing has to change."

"And would we be . . . ?" She wasn't quite sure how to ask him what was on her mind. Her usual blunt honesty didn't make much sense in this delicate conversation.

"We would be intimate, if you wish. I would make no demands of you to satisfy my needs, but for the sake of honesty, I would like for us to be lovers, and to be loyal to each other, and maybe someday, if you desire, to have children."

Children. She'd never imagined she would be discussing future children, let alone with the Earl of March.

"I never thought I would have children. I don't want to be treated like a . . ." She swallowed the words that would've sounded course upon her tongue.

"A broodmare?" He quirked a brow, but his lips twitched with the hint of a smile. "I would never treat you as such, nor would I wish to be treated like a stud stallion. If we choose to have children, we can make that decision together."

She nodded. A dull throb began in her temples. She closed her eyes.

"You should have something to eat," he said. "I'll leave you to Mary's tender care, and I will see to myself, and I'll meet you in the dining room for breakfast. Then I suggest, if you are amenable to it, that we should discuss wedding plans later today. I believe it would be better to face the issue head-on rather than delay things."

"Oh, all right, damn you," she muttered, but she wasn't angry with him. She was glad one of them still had the good sense to think rationally.

He pressed a kiss to her forehead, and after a long searching look, he kissed her lips and she shifted closer, kissing him back. His mouth was warm and his lips soft and entreating. His kiss made something warm blossom in her chest and spread out until the coldness of her pain had completely faded away.

One of the things Prospero had taught her was that kisses could arouse and excite, but they could also heal. As hard as it was to imagine, she felt that if she trusted herself with this man, the pain of losing her father would heal in time. What was it her father had said about scars? No matter how hard or soft, old or new, a scar meant a wound was healing. Wounds of the heart, like the body, weren't meant to bleed forever. Blood clotted, skin knit itself back together stronger than before with the presence of the scar. Scars personified strength and were nothing to be ashamed of. They meant you had survived.

"Will you be all right?" Prospero asked, his voice low and husky as he continued to gaze at her. She still lay in his arms, lost in the swirl of her own melancholic thoughts. He hadn't abandoned her.

"I will be someday." She burrowed closer, taking in the heat of his body once again. Was this what it would be like as his wife? Would she always have the right to curl into his arms and warm herself at the fires of this man's heart?

Prospero rubbed his cheek on the top of her head, pulling her even closer as if he sensed she needed to feel his desire to keep her close too. Then after a long moment, he spoke.

"We should go riding in Hyde Park today."

Her heart leapt with a fleeting joy, but just as quickly her hopes of an enjoyable day were blown away like clouds during a westerly storm swept out to sea.

"Do you suppose we shall have to spend the entire day planning our wedding?"

"I had a thought . . . ," Prospero began. "Perhaps someone like Edwina could plan it for you. She seems like she might be up to the task. Unless, of course, you wish to be more involved in the decisions."

Elise wrinkled her nose. "I don't particularly wish to be involved. I really don't find weddings that interesting."

"I can't say I'm all that surprised," said Prospero.

"I suppose you wanted me to say something more feminine and romantic, but I'd rather look at species of beetles all day than plan a wedding. But Edwina does enjoy such things."

Prospero stroked a fingertip down her nose, and that feeling of wonderful warmth inside her grew. "Well, I'd rather look at beetles as well, fascinating little fellows. So many shapes and sizes and colors. Those iridescent-shelled ones you showed me at the museum were simply wonderful." He spoke about beetles for a time, and she felt herself drowning in his beautiful blue eyes. "But yes, back to Edwina. We ought to send her and Cinna a message to request their help. They are your dearest friends, and it would hurt them if you did not tell them."

"Why am I beginning to suspect that *you* will be the voice of reason in our marriage?" Oddly, when she thought of him as her husband now, the idea was a *little* less frightening than before.

"Because I'm the boring one. You will have to be our dreamer, our *visionary* in this marriage."

"Visionary. I like that."

"Good." He gave her one more soft, lingering kiss before he left the bed, his suit from last night rumpled and his hair mussed. He paused in the doorway and looked back at her.

"Everything will be all right," he said. "We must give it time."

She sighed and lay on her back on the bed and stared up at the ceiling. "Time . . ."

Her entire life had changed in a matter of days. She couldn't help but wonder what would have happened if she had never tried to stop Mr. Holmes from playing his damned violin. She never would have met Prospero. She might never have learned of her father's illness until it was too late. Strange how one poorly played violin could have made such a difference.

"How is she?" John asked as Prospero joined him in the dining room for breakfast.

Prospero examined Elise's father with concern. It was as though by sharing the news with his daughter last night, a great bit of John's life and vigor had deserted him. He looked drained, pale . . . older.

"She's hurting," Prospero said after a moment. "I suggested she let Cinna and Edwina assist in planning the wedding. I will take her riding today. I believe she needs a distraction after everything that happened last evening."

"That is very wise of you. I was also thinking that after you wed, you should take her on a honeymoon. She needs something not too far away but with plenty of diversions. Brighton or the Isle of Wight, perhaps? She's always wanted to dig for fossils on the beaches there. And another thing." He paused a moment, reflecting. "I've always detested those blasted rituals of mourning. I don't care what society expects—do not let her wear black for too long. Burn her black gowns in the fireplace if you must, but keep her in colors. I want my child to remember me by living in a world of light, not shadows."

Prospero nodded, feeling his throat tighten. "I will do as you wish, John." He turned away to prepare breakfast plates for himself and Elise.

"If I don't have a chance to thank you, you have my thanks now, March," John said.

Prospero faced John as he set the two plates down. "I've only done what any man would do."

"What any *good* man would do," John corrected. "You really are the only one I would trust with her." He left his chair and came around the dining table to place a hand on Prospero's shoulder. "Someday, when you have a daughter of your own, you'll know what this means to me." He squeezed Prospero's shoulder and then left the room.

Prospero sat down, staring at the food in front of him. His appetite, what little there had been, was gone. Knowing he had to take his own advice, he forced his breakfast down and was halfway done when Elise came into the room, wearing her wig and trousers, as well as her slender mustache. She looked every bit the handsome dandy she was pretending to be rather than a fine lady. A smile pulled at the corners of his mouth. Nothing would ever be dull with her, and he delighted in knowing that.

"Today we'll see how well my Gypsy pony performs," he said with a smirk.

She shot him a challenging look. "You mean your *Romani* horse," she corrected.

"Yes, of course," he chuckled. "But *Gypsy* has a rather romantic sound to it, don't you think?" He winked at her. "Supposedly, I have Gypsy heritage in my blood, many ancestors back, of course, but I suppose that does make me part Gypsy . . . er, Romani."

"Really? I wonder if that explains the dark gleam of your hair. It's so . . ." Elise swallowed a bit of food, her face reddening. "You and Anthony could be cousins."

Pleased that his method of distraction was working, he pushed on. "So, how did you and Anthony meet?"

"I met him a year ago when I started looking into racing fillies. He taught me so much about horses that I never would have learned on my own. I just recently bought a new racehorse from him," Elise said. "It was only a few days before I met you, actually."

"Oh?"

"She's young, but she should be excellent in some of the filly races. She is splendidly fast and utterly determined to win, no matter how fast her opponent is. I want to take her riding in the park today."

"You ride your racehorse in the park?" Most men who owned racehorses treated them better than their own wives and children. To ride a racer in the parks for simple recreation was unheard of.

Elise shot him a smug look. "And *that* is why she races so well. I've tested my theory on my previous horses over the last two years. When they get out in the various paths, they see all sorts of distractions and experience different terrains. It's good practice. And when you add in their need to be unbeaten, you can have a winning horse."

Prospero watched Elise eat as they talked, wanting to make sure she ate enough before they left. "I would've imagined you would be invested in bloodlines, such as the strongest Thoroughbreds, the horses that have history of winning in their blood. Wouldn't that be of more interest to you?"

"That is an easy thing to assume, but a horse's heart is always more telling than its breeding. I believe men and women are the same. I'm sure you've heard stories from wars where men encountered unthinkable odds and yet managed to survive."

He nodded thoughtfully. "Yes, that is true." He liked that he couldn't always predict what Elise would say or do next. She was incredibly original in her thoughts and observations, and it was endlessly fascinating to be around her.

"So, tell me about your new filly," he encouraged.

"Oh, she's positively beautiful. The color of champagne. I've named her Honey, and she's smart as a whip. She has a sweet temperament unless she senses an unfit rider sitting on top of her. Anthony told me that she watches the way a man wields his crop. If he acts impatient or temperamental, he doesn't stand a chance on her. But she's wonderful with women and children. When she hits an open path, she'll outrun lightning itself."

There was such love and adoration in her voice for Honey that Prospero was amused at the fact that he was jealous of a horse. He supposed some people might find it unusual for someone with an analytical and scientific mind to feel so deeply emotional for a creature, but to him it was logical. Elise loved everything about the natural world, and it only made sense for her to love the creatures in it.

By the time Prospero was satisfied she'd eaten enough, the grooms had prepared their horses and were waiting outside for them.

As Prospero studied his new horse, he realized he was excited to be back in the saddle. In Paris he'd had horses, but they'd always belonged to his paramours, and once he moved on the horses were always returned. Now he was to have his own horse again. Yes, it was a horse Elise's money had bought, but it was money he had earned from her. That was the only way he could accept it. To remind himself that he was showing her a part of life she wanted to study. He was stoutly refusing to think about what her father had offered him as part of the marriage contract, and how he hated feeling like he'd just been given money without having earned it honestly. He'd face that later, when he was ready to ruin his good mood.

He followed Elise to her lovely horse. "Do you need assistance?" The filly danced in excitement at Elise's approach, clearly recognizing her despite her masculine disguise.

"No, I'm quite capable." She pulled herself up in the saddle with an adorable, cocky grin. Lord, he loved seeing her beam with confidence. She rode astride like a man and seemed completely comfortable with it. He imagined that her trousers helped quite a bit in that regard.

"Excellent." He nodded to the groom who held Raider's reins and then mounted up.

They set off toward the park. Elise watched him closely as he nodded to the gentlemen as they passed, and she did the same in imitation. For having little practice pretending to be a gentleman, she was surprisingly good at it.

"Have you ever played this role before?" She seemed so at ease in her costume that it did make him wonder.

"I have. To attend meetings where ladies are not permitted. I presented a paper at an ornithological society about patterns of bird migration, but I was so nervous my mustache fell off. I later discovered that the adhesive I used was not resistant to perspiration." She casually reached up and touched her mustache, as though checking to make sure it was firmly affixed to her upper lip.

"I imagine the men were not amused."

"They certainly weren't. Thankfully, Lord Rochester was in attendance at the meeting. He applauded me, even after my mustache fell off, and not in a mocking way. He chided those around him who were crying for me to be pulled off the stage and thrown outside after my ruse was discovered."

"Ah, that explains his words last night. I believe he called you a brilliant mind. I quite agree with the statement. I would have done the same had I been there."

"You won't mind if I continue my pursuits once we're married? I know my father said you wouldn't, but . . ." She adjusted her hands on her reins as they entered Hyde Park.

"You need to hear it from me," he confirmed in understanding. "Yes, I want nothing of your life to change, except that I am to be a part of it. What about you? What do you wish for me to do once we are married?"

Prospero was getting accustomed to the idea that soon he and Elise would be wed. Elise's father could not force him to accept the situation, of course, but he *wanted* to. Yes, he'd only known her for a handful of days, but his instincts had never been wrong before. After more than a decade of feeling like he had no future, he saw quite clearly what this new path meant for him.

"What do I wish for you to do?" Elise asked, as if unsure of his question.

"What I mean is . . . Do you want me in all ways? As a husband? A man? A lover?" He kept his tone quiet. They were too far away from anyone to be overheard, but one couldn't be too careful, and this was a much-needed discussion.

"You meant what you said about giving me a choice?" Her surprise was so clear, but it wounded him. She honestly thought he wouldn't?

"Of course. I like you, Elise. I admire you. I daresay I will fall in love with you. But I respect you, and that respect has given me a clarity of thought that other men might not have. I don't want to force you to do anything. We can be married on paper only, or we can be married in truth."

She seemed to consider the matter for a long moment as they rode along the park's dirt paths, avoiding the more well-traveled routes.

"What do *you* want, Prospero? Forget for the moment any decision I might make. What is it you truly wish for?"

He stroked Raider's neck, and they slowed their horses to a stop on a grassy path that led to an open field. He'd mentioned before what he wished, but he could understand her need to hear it again, to reconfirm what he desired so that they were certain they understood each other.

"I would want *everything* with you. The passion, the contentment, the adventure. Children, if we are blessed with any. I would want it all with you."

"You wouldn't expect to have mistresses? Most men seem to think it a God-given right that they do as they please." The thought seemed to truly upset her.

"Even when I lived in Paris as a . . . companion, I never once strayed from the woman I was currently acting as a companion to. I am a loyal man. And I would be loyal to you." He didn't ask her to promise her loyalty in return. He didn't need to. Elise was the type of woman who was loyal by nature.

Her eyes suddenly brightened with tears. "Why?" she snapped, trying to ignore them. "*Why* are you content to marry me? Despite the scandal of your past, you could still have your choice of the finest ladies in England."

"Why?" Prospero's brows rose. "Do you truly not see yourself?" he asked, guiding his horse closer. Her filly playfully nudged the larger horse, and Raider accepted the filly's affections.

Her brows knitted together in confusion. "See myself?"

She truly had no idea? Lord, this woman had so much confidence, save in this. How could she not see why *any* decent man could fall madly in love with her? It was a damned travesty to witness, and he wouldn't let her suffer with such doubts a moment longer. She deserved to hear the truth.

"Oh, my little naturalist." He sighed and smiled. "You are *fierce*: fiercely beautiful, fiercely intelligent, fiercely passionate, fiercely amusing, and *real*. You are genuine in a way so many others are afraid to be. You make me feel the way I used to feel before Jackson's death."

They slowed their horses once more, this time leaving the path. She met his eyes again.

"Very well, we shall be in this mess together, and always." Then, with a sly look as his only warning, she added, "Now, shall we see what your new horse is capable of?"

Before he could fully process that she had just agreed to be his wife, she spurred her filly and took off at a mad gallop across the open field of the park.

"*Yah!*" he cried out and kicked his heels into Raider's sides.

The Romani stallion took off. Raider's head bobbed as he made up for lost ground behind the champagne-colored filly. Prospero laughed as they gave chase to their wild females. Honey truly could fly. Her hooves barely touched the ground. Elise kept her head bent low so she would not lose her hat.

The filly shot across paths and leapt over hedges. It was as though the horse had learned the falcon's secret to flight, and it was one of the most beautiful sights Prospero had ever seen—woman and horse so completely in tune with each other that they rode as one.

Raider took each leap in their wake and sprinted with ease after the filly. Elise was right—her filly was fast, too fast. Even Raider couldn't quite catch up. After a short while, Elise slowed Honey and with a lazy smile ran the horse in a small circle before slowing her down to an easy walk, coming toward them.

"Honey is like lightning," he told Elise. "I believe Raider enjoyed the challenge, even if he did lose." Prospero smacked the horse's neck lightly. "Didn't you, old boy?"

"I told you Anthony knows his horses." Elise chuckled.

"He does indeed. I bow before him, and you, in all future equine decisions." He removed his hat and gave a half bow from his saddle.

Elise nodded imperiously, as though she were Queen Victoria. "As you should."

"Shall we take a tour of the more well-traveled paths in order for you to observe gentlemen on horseback?" He gestured with his crop to a path up ahead where people were promenading on foot and horseback.

They had been on the path for only a few minutes when Lady Cinna and Miss Tewksbury appeared, riding ahead of them. Prospero glanced around and saw two familiar gentlemen farther back on the path, also riding.

"Go on. I've spotted Nicholas and Guy just behind us."

Elise nodded her agreement and urged her filly into a trot to catch up to her two companions. Prospero steered Raider around to return to his old friends.

"Ah, Pross, what are you up to?" Guy asked as Prospero turned Raider to walk alongside his horse.

"Just putting my new horse through his paces," he replied. "You aren't stalking those two young ladies, are you?" He nodded toward Cinna and Edwina.

Guy grinned. "Nick is. I am simply here to tease him." He pointed his crop toward Raider. "Beautiful beast, by the way. Where did you find him?"

"The Barnet Fair, if you can believe it," Prospero said.

Guy's brows rose. "You don't say. Gypsy horses, eh?"

"I am told they prefer to be called Romani," Prospero said without thinking.

His friend chuckled. "Really? That—"

"Hold on," Nicholas said, interrupting Guy. "Who the devil is *that* fellow?"

"Who is what fellow?" Guy asked.

"That man riding between Lady Cinna and Miss Tewksbury," Nicholas pointed out. "He was with you a moment ago, Pross. Who the devil is he?" Nicholas scowled at the trio ahead of them, unaware that he was looking at Elise in disguise.

Before Prospero could respond, Guy shot Prospero a sly grin and a knowing wink. "Oh, him? That's Elliott, Prospero's cousin."

"Cousin? Prospero, you don't have any cousins in London. I had better go see to Miss Tewksbury before . . ." Nicholas started forward, but Prospero caught his arm as he rode past.

"There's no need. It's just my fiancée."

Nicholas's face paled. "Did you just say Miss Tewksbury is your fiancée? When did this happen?"

Prospero couldn't help but laugh. "No, no, old friend, not her."

"Cinna, then?" Guy cut in, his eyes suddenly hard and cold.

Prospero choked on a chuckle. Lord, his friends were so clearly besotted with Elise's friends that neither could jump to the most obvious conclusion. "It's *Elise*. Elise and I are engaged. It is her that you see between Cinna and Edwina. She's dressed as a man in order to study male behavior in the park."

His friends relaxed, though confusion now replaced the concern on their faces.

"I will come back to the fact that she is dressed like a man," said Nicholas. "But first you must explain how you became engaged to Miss Hamblin in less than a week."

"'Tis not a short story," Prospero warned.

"'Tis not a small park," Nicholas countered.

And so Prospero told his friends how he ended up being engaged to the little naturalist. Guy crowed in triumph as he announced that he'd wagered this would happen in the betting book at Berkeley's, to which Prospero only laughed and Nicholas rolled his eyes. It was good to be with his two dearest friends again after all these years. He and Guy had missed Nicholas dearly while they'd been in Paris.

"OH, I DO LOVE WEDDINGS," EDWINA SAID. "AND YES, Cinna, before you chastise me, I am fully aware of how you hate them."

"I hate what they *represent*. They are barbaric rituals." Cinna looked toward Edwina, and her gaze turned serious. "Are you truly marrying this man because you want to?"

Elise nodded. "My father wishes it, but he knows better than to give orders, so he has made it his last request. In truth, I agreed because I like him."

"Of course you like your father." Cinna nodded in understanding. "But that's no reason to—"

"No, I mean because I like Prospero." Her face felt flushed, but she didn't want to lie to her friends about how she was falling under the spell of the infamous Earl of March.

"You do?" Cinna glanced over her shoulder at the three men following them at a polite, discreet distance.

"So you like him. But does he like you?" Edwina asked, hope shining in her eyes.

"Yes, he does. That is why he agreed to my father's request."

"Does this mean we get to help you plan your wedding?" Edwina asked. "Please say we can."

"I was hoping you would. It must be done in a few days. My father—" She halted as a lump formed in her throat. She'd tried so hard not to think about his condition over the last few hours. "We don't know how long he has."

"Then we will do whatever you need, won't we?" Cinna said, and she was met with a nod of agreement from Edwina.

"Thank you." Elise felt that knot of dread loosen a little. Prospero was right. She had two friends who wanted to help. It wouldn't be the end of the world if she leaned on them just a little.

Edwina took control like a general rallying her troops. "If we have only a few days to plan a wedding, we shouldn't be wasting time in the park. We need to organize. Cinna, you will help Elise find a gown and prepare her trousseau. I will handle the wedding breakfast preparations and the flowers at St. George's. We mustn't forget the invitations."

"You've made her very happy," Cinna whispered to Elise. "She'll be singing wedding marches for the rest of the year."

Elise sighed. "I know." Despite the lump of pain in her heart, she felt a stirring of quiet hope that she'd never felt before.

"Oh my . . . I've only just remembered your wager with our surly neighbor. What will you tell Mr. Holmes?" Cinna asked suddenly.

"Oh heavens," Elise gasped, startling all three horses. "What *will* I tell him?"

Edwina tapped her chin thoughtfully. "I rather think that when a woman agrees to marry a man, she must know him and understand him, so doesn't that mean you win?"

"Not all people know *or* understand each other when they marry," Cinna interjected. "Plenty of people marry strangers for money or other reasons. Or they do so in haste, fueled by their fleeting feelings of the moment. At least, I expect that is what Mr. Holmes would say."

"True, but women like us . . . we wouldn't do that," Edwina argued.

Elise frowned. "No, we wouldn't, but Cinna is right. Holmes might very well argue any of her points, so it is up to us to convince him otherwise. I shall present my case, offer him my scientific findings. I won't lose this wager without a fight. I think we had better send an invitation to Mr. Holmes and Mr. Watson and tell them to bring that blasted violin to the wedding breakfast."

❧ 15 ❧

TWO DAYS LATER

Elise held her breath as the coach rolled to a stop in front of St. George's. Her hands shook as she tried to calm her racing heart. She smoothed out the ivory wedding gown that flowed around her in a waterfall of silk. Her father reached across the coach and clasped her hands.

"Ready, my darling girl?" His gaze was solemn and intense as he waited for her reply.

"Were you nervous the day you married Mama?" Elise asked.

"Was I?" He smiled at some old memory. "I cut myself shaving. I didn't have a valet back then. My hands shook so much that I nicked a spot just here." Her father pointed to a faint scar partially hidden by his beard.

"But why were you nervous? Didn't you love her?"

"Oh, I did. *Fiercely*. But weddings can still terrify someone, even if they are in love. Perhaps especially so."

She nodded, somehow understanding that answer. "I just don't want everyone to look at me. You know I don't like this sort of attention." It was different when she was speaking about scientific matters to other naturalists, but to be paraded down an aisle as a woman about to be married? She'd never wanted that sort of attention.

Her father squeezed her hand. "Well, my dear, that's the price you pay for your loved ones. You must walk down that aisle with all eyes on you, but you won't be alone. You know that's why fathers walk their daughters down the aisle, don't you?"

"Is it? I thought it was a symbolic transferring of ownership to my husband because I am chattel?" She'd always hated the thought of weddings for that reason. She was more like Cinna in that way than the more romantic Edwina, who saw it as a joining of two souls.

Her father shook his head.

"Bah! Some man who never had a daughter made up that nonsense. The real reason a father escorts his daughter to the altar is so that she doesn't have to make that journey alone. It is our last chance to protect our daughters, to show you that we care so much for you that we want to be by your side until the *very* moment that honor and duty demand we let go."

His words cut straight to the very core of her soul, and her entire being filled with so much love that it hurt to breathe.

"That moment you step away will break my heart, because I must then share you with another. Everything changes once I let go of you in that church."

Hot, stinging tears blinded her, and she flung herself into her father's arms. She felt like she was a child again, facing a grave in a quiet churchyard and clinging to the only parent she had left. All her life, it had been her and her father against the world.

"Why does everything have to change?" she asked, her voice muffled by his waistcoat. He smelled of cigars, the rich kind that came from India, and it made her heart ache for those nights long ago when he read her stories in the study and she sat upon his lap, falling asleep as his voice followed her into her sweet dreams of magical beasts and beautiful kingdoms. If she'd known back then that some-day, sooner than she realized, there would be no more nights like that, she would have wept. Her father had surely known such a time would come. How much had that burden hurt him?

"You know better than most that all life must change," her father said. "It is a part of living on this tiny planet among the stars. We grow, change, and learn. This is but one more step on the path you are on to become the best version of yourself. You will live your own life now with a good man. Every bird must someday leave their parents' nest."

Live her own life? Leave the nest? Did he think she would abandon him?

"Prospero and I won't leave you, Papa. You know that, don't you?" She looked up into his brown eyes, so much like hers. She hadn't spoken to her future husband about it, but she knew he would never force her to leave her father.

"It won't be the same."

Never had so few words held the power to hurt while spoken with so much love. He tipped her chin up. "Now dry your eyes. Poor March will suffer if he sees you've been crying, and I like the fellow enough to want to spare him that."

"You truly like him?"

John nodded. "He's quiet. Respectful. But there is also an intensity to him, a fierceness that matches your own. You cannot love a man who would command you, nor could you love a man whom you must command. You can only love someone who is your equal. You and March fit each other."

"He called me fierce," she said thoughtfully. "He said he truly sees me."

Her father nodded. "That he does. And it is important that you see him too. He has had great sorrows in his life, as you have. He will guard his heart, and you mustn't let him." Her father held her gaze seriously. "You mustn't guard your heart either. Let love in when it comes for you."

But how could she even know what love was? What did it feel like? She lived in a world where theories were meant to be tested and proven. How could one prove love? Would there be some sign, like when a caterpillar crawled into a cocoon and began its transformation? Nature, as often as it was mysterious, still held many answers. Yet when it came to love, Elise had no studies, no books, no charts to analyze that could prepare her.

"How do you know he will come to love me?"

Her father's eyes brightened. "A woman like you? How could he not?"

He removed his handkerchief and gave it to her. She wiped her eyes.

"Feeling better?" He asked it in a way only a father could, with the same tone he'd used when she'd fallen from a tree or scraped her arm as a child. She nodded.

"Good, now let's face this together." He exited the coach and turned to assist her.

Once out of the coach, she accepted a bouquet of flowers from Cinna who stood with Edwina stood outside the church doors, waiting for her. They shared the same look of concern.

"You don't have to do this," Cinna said in a low voice. She curled her hand around Elise's arm. "I have a carriage waiting out back if you want to run."

"I love you for that," she told her dear friend, "but it will be all right. I want to do this. It's just a bit frightening. Remember the time we dove off those cliffs into that lake when we were seventeen?"

Cinna nodded. "It took a moment to build up the courage."

"And we still screamed all the way down to the water," Elise added.

"But damned if it wasn't glorious. We did it several more times that day."

"Exactly," Elise said with a small smile. "I'm taking another leap today, and it will be just as wonderful, I think, if I can but trust myself."

She then turned to Edwina. "I know you've worked so hard on the wedding plans. I can't thank you enough, my dearest friend."

Edwina wiped her eyes. "I know you don't believe in fairy tales or princes, but someone has to."

Cinna smiled in understanding as she put an arm around Edwina's shoulders. "And you believe in it enough for all three of us."

Music began to play inside, and two gentlemen opened

the church doors for them. Edwina went in first, followed by Cinna, both wearing lavender bustle gowns.

Elise tucked her arm in her father's and clenched her bouquet with her other hand. Then she and her father walked into the church together.

The guests stood and faced her as they walked past. Her father's presence kept her focused on the distant altar. Sunlight poured in through the windows, making everything in its path glow. Instead of looking at everyone around her, she watched the sunlight and the motes of dust that seemed to dance above her head. She'd never noticed that something as common as dust, when moving in sunlight, could be so beautiful.

I wish you could be here, Mama. She'd spent so much of her day trying not to think about the loss she'd suffered as a child. But today of all days, her mother seemed to quietly exist all around her, even in the dancing motes caught in sunbeams.

Prospero stood at the altar, and his friends Nicholas and Guy stood beside him. He neither smiled nor frowned when he saw her, but his eyes—Lord, his eyes— were like two brilliant sapphires. As she reached Prospero, Edwina stepped forward and took Elise's bouquet. Her father turned to Elise and leaned in to kiss her forehead.

"The hardest part is letting go," he whispered. "Holding on to love is infinitely easier." Then he gave a small nod to Prospero, who returned the gesture.

Her father held on to her just a moment longer. Then, with a soft sigh, he let go of her hands and stepped back. She walked up the two steps where Prospero and the clergyman stood.

Her future husband curled his hands around her trembling fingers.

"Ready?" he asked in a low whisper. So much meaning contained in such a small word.

"Yes." She was ready, even if she was also frightened. *I am ready to face this new change. Ready to take a chance. Ready to leap from this cliff and feel the joy of the water below.*

Prospero gave her hands a squeeze, and his sinfully attractive lips twitched into a ghost of a smile. He pretended to be calm and unaffected, but really, he was ready to smile or laugh. Unable to resist teasing him, she leaned in so only he could hear her.

"Now I shall observe a gentleman in his marriage ceremony and learn his secret rituals."

Prospero's eyes sparkled, and he suddenly barked out a laugh before he coughed and met the disproving glare of the clergyman.

"Man and wife," the clergyman pronounced, drawing the ceremony to a close.

"Er . . . *husband* and wife," Prospero corrected him. "If you don't mind, sir."

The clergyman raised a brow but cleared his throat. "*Husband* and wife."

Elise's brown eyes lit up.

"Thank you."

"We belong to each other now." He had never liked the idea of a woman being labeled *wife* while the man remained *man* in the pronouncement. He belonged to Elise just as fully as she belonged to him, and he wanted her to know it. He wanted her to believe it, starting now and for the rest of their lives. They were equals in nature, even if the laws of man didn't agree, and nature outlasted everything.

He leaned in and whispered, "We are mates," before he stole a kiss that was not nearly as chaste as it was supposed to be.

She tasted wonderfully sweet, and he couldn't wait to have her alone. The last two days had been busy for both of them as wedding preparations had eaten up many of the hours in the day. They'd met for breakfast and dinner, and not much else. He'd grown used to her going nearly everywhere with him, had grown used to her in bed beside him, even though it had been for just a handful of days. She'd become . . . indispensable. And he found he longed for her smile, her laugh, her lectures on science, her desire to explore the world, and even her tendency to get into trouble.

She had insisted on accompanying him to the tailor for a wedding suit, but she had been forced to visit the dressmaker for her wedding gown. Her maid had thrown a fit when Elise had dared to argue that she could simply wear one of her everyday gowns for the ceremony.

He and John had eaten a late lunch and listened to the two argue all the way downstairs. They'd cringed at the shouting, but in the end Mary had triumphed, and Prospero was glad because the lavish bustle gown made of pale ivory silk trimmed with lace looked exquisite on Elise. He hoped someday she would look back on this moment and remember it as a beautiful day and that she had been the most stunning bride.

Fear shone in her eyes, and he saw the vulnerable young woman that she'd fought so hard to hide from the world. She was trusting him with her body, her freedom, even her life. He was infinitely aware of that. He straightened a little, filled with an ancient pride. This was his duty, his honor, his destiny. To be her defender, her protector, her lover, her shield, so she could grow toward a brighter future like a young oak sapling stretching its branches toward the sky.

His wife was going to accomplish so many wonderful things, and his joy would be to witness them at her side.

"I'm here, darling," he whispered as he held her close a moment longer. Elise trembled but burrowed closer. His heart ached with an exquisite agony at knowing how much she trusted him at this moment. "You have only to reach for me and I will be here for you."

"Today?" she asked.

"Every day."

She murmured something that sounded like *thank you,* but the words were muffled against his chest. Then he let her go so they could face the crowd. His eyes sharpened on two men seated near the back. He hadn't seen them before while he'd waited for his bride to arrive.

"I say . . . Is that . . . ? No, it can't be."

Elise laced her fingers through his as they looked toward the back of the church. "Who?"

He nodded in their direction. "I believe that's the famous detective Mr. Holmes and his friend Dr. Watson."

A guilty look flashed over Elise's face, and a blush deepened her cheeks.

"Oh . . . They're my neighbors. Or rather, the society's

neighbors on Baker Street. We extended an invitation to them."

"By Jove, I'd love a chance to talk to Mr. Holmes. Could you introduce me?" Prospero asked, but his wife glanced away.

"Perhaps, if he has time," she hedged. "I don't think he'll be staying long."

She was avoiding discussing Mr. Holmes, but why? But this wasn't the time to question her further, so he planned to seduce the truth out of her tonight once they were in bed. Prospero led her down the steps and shook his new father-in-law's hand.

"Thank you," John said and stepped back as a crowd of friends swarmed them, mostly ladies, but quite a few others Prospero had known before he left for France.

"Damned glad to see you back in London, March," one man said. "May I offer my congratulations?"

On and on the well wishes came, and each one was genuine. It seemed his fear that he was being endlessly judged was not entirely true. He did have friends, more than he'd imagined. As he and Elise walked toward their waiting carriage, they shared a glance and his heart took flight when she smiled at him. She looked more at ease now than she had when the ceremony had ended.

He lifted her up into the open carriage by her waist and adjusted the elaborate silk train on her gown, tucking it around her. Petals had been strewn in and around the carriage, and flowers draped along the edges of the vehicle —even on the horses' harnesses.

Prospero saw Edwina standing in the crowd close by, watching him and Elise, discreetly wiping at her eyes with a handkerchief. The decorations would have been her doing. He gave her a nod of thanks for all the work she had done to make this day special.

The sun came out from behind the clouds to illuminate Elise's golden hair like a halo. Mary had pulled Elise's locks into a loose tumble of curled waves, and nestled in the crown of her hair was a jeweled beetle with bright blue wings.

"That must be your something blue," he said as he sat beside her in the carriage.

"Hmm?" she asked distractedly.

"The beetle in your hair. It's blue."

Elise beamed at him. "Oh yes. That was Cinna's doing. It was her gift to me. She wanted something less traditional, and this was perfect."

"'Tis a perfect gift," he agreed.

They waved to the crowd out on the church steps as they headed home for the wedding breakfast her father would be hosting. The ride gave Prospero time to enjoy this moment alone with his wife. *His wife.* The words made him smile so wide his face hurt.

"What about your something old, new, and borrowed?" he asked. Cinna would have seen to those as well, even if she insisted she was dead set against weddings.

Elise touched the necklace at her throat. "My borrowed." It was a single pearl drop hanging from a fine gold chain. "This belongs to Cinna's mother." She then discreetly reached into her cleavage, which immediately caught Prospero's undivided attention. She pulled out a circular shell that reminded him of the nautilus they had seen at the museum. She must have stashed it between her breasts, just out of sight. The shell was worn smooth and was of a creamy brown color with thin veins of dark purple that ran through it.

"It's an ammonite. I found this in a riverbed in Dorset when I was there on holiday." She placed it in his palm. "You cannot imagine how old it is."

"It's heavy." It had the weight of a perfect skipping stone that he would've thrown out onto the lake as a boy. It was also warm from being nestled in Elise's delectable cleavage.

"When something turns into a fossil, it essentially becomes stone. The organic material is replaced over time by minerals. It's called petrification. Fascinating, isn't it?"

"Yes. To think how something living and breathing can turn to stone over millions of years, that it could be permanently changed. It's incredible . . ." He put his arm around her waist and pulled her closer to him. Then with a rakish grin, he slipped the stone back into the soft spot between her breasts, which made her blush. Despite his smile, his inner thoughts had taken a more serious turn. His own heart, which had been stone for so long, had reversed course. It was beating stronger and stronger, and each beat belonged to this woman . . . his wife.

"And your something new?" He cleared his throat, trying to hold his emotions in check.

Red stained her cheeks. "That is something I must show you later." She giggled at his stunned look, then gave him a flirtatious wink.

"You're *wearing* it?" he guessed with a grin and glanced around. They were in an open carriage, but there was no one nearby who could see them clearly. Using her gown's train as a cover, he slid a hand up her skirts, tracing her calf with his palm.

"Prospero!" Elise gasped, clutching at his hand through the layers of her skirt. At any moment their driver could turn around and see them, let alone anyone else.

"*Hush*," he teased wickedly. "It is your *duty* to let me explore these beautiful legs." He knew his words would fluster her, but even if she railed against the institution of marriage, there was a part of her that liked it when he took control of their sensual encounters.

She looked torn between slapping him and kissing him. She would belong to no man as a piece of property, but she would belong to him as a lover just as he belonged to her, and a bit of teasing would do her good. Elise needed to understand that as husband and wife, they should have the right to tease each other, to feel comfortable enough to be playful.

She wriggled as he reached her inner knee and found the tie at the top of her stocking. He tugged at the tied bow of satin ribbon. Elise's lips parted, and she breathed faster. Nothing unusual about a stocking, so he continued on, feeling the silken skin of her inner thighs. She squirmed adorably when he found a scrap of lace that banded around her thigh. Ah . . . so that was it. A new garter. He made a note to remove it later tonight with his teeth.

He pretended not to notice the garter and slid his fingers up higher until he found her mound.

"Prosper—oh!" She jerked as he penetrated her with one index finger, and the last syllable of his name came out a delightful gasp.

"Is this the pretty present you've been hiding from me?" he asked, his voice deep and rough as he moved his finger in and around her sheath, spreading the wetness there.

She made a soft, strangled sound, her hands clenching her skirts, no longer trying to stop him.

"Now be a good girl, darling, and let your husband *play* with you," he purred and kissed her neck, not caring who saw them. She let out a sweet sigh, and her legs opened wider to let him do whatever he wished. Her surrender was beautiful, beautiful because it meant she not only desired him, she *trusted* him.

"That's it." He pushed a second finger in, gently fucking her as he murmured in her ear how excited he was for tonight, how he couldn't wait to get her alone, and she arched beneath his touch. He found the slightly rough spot inside her channel that would give her greater pleasure, and he curled his fingers on that singular spot over and over while she held back all the little sounds he couldn't wait to hear from her tonight. He was hard and desperate to have her right now, but this was about her pleasure, about showing her that he would always put her needs first, even in this.

"Oh!" She couldn't hold back her sounds any longer as she came. He chuckled as he drew out her climax, feeling her body clenched around his fingers.

Her face, flushed pink, turned shyly away, and he leaned in to kiss her cheek.

"You have no idea how much I adore you, wife. How much it pleases me to touch you like this. And someday, if you wish, I can show you how to tease me like this in return."

She looked back at him, eyes shimmering. She had needed to hear that, he realized, that she could still have some power in their relationship when it came to matters of desire.

"Oh yes, my little naturalist. I can show you all the ways you can bend me to *your* will," he promised, and her responding smile hit him hard behind the knees. Yes, this was going to work between them. He knew it would.

After he slowly withdrew his fingers from her, he used a handkerchief to wipe his hand. Again, his wife blushed madly.

"And do I get to have a pet name for you?" she asked, an impish glint in her eye. "My little earl, perhaps? My—"

He silenced her with a kiss and relished the moment she melted into him. He chuckled against her soft, warm lips and teased her with his tongue. She let out another delicious sigh as they broke apart.

He smirked playfully. "How about *my wonderfully large, well-endowed earl?*"

This time she silenced him as she kissed him back. He groaned in exquisite agony as his body tensed with a desire he could not fulfill for several hours still.

"Goodness gracious!" a woman shrieked.

Prospero jerked away from his wife. Another carriage had pulled up alongside theirs. A round-faced middle-aged woman in an expensive gown sat in an open carriage beside theirs, holding a ruffled parasol over her head. She gawked at them as if they were cavorting completely naked . . . and he secretly wished they had been.

"Pardon me, but I'm newly married and quite excited about it." He winked at the woman, who huffed and commanded her driver to drive on at once.

"Oh dear," Elise groaned. "She'll tell everyone—"

"That you and I were embracing after our nuptials? I

don't care who she is or what she says. Neither should you, *countess*."

"Countess?" Elise stared up at him with rounded eyes. "I suppose I *am* a countess, aren't I?"

"You hadn't realized that yet, had you?" He laughed.

"I hadn't considered it, no. I was a bit busy worrying about other things. Oh dear. This means I'll have to appear in society more frequently."

"Regrettably, yes." He still couldn't stop smiling. Most women would have been thrilled at the prospect. Not Elise.

"Perhaps we should run away." She clutched his arm desperately. "Let's run away to America and never come back."

"Easy there," he soothed and pulled her onto his lap. "We'll take it slow with society. I won't let them frighten you."

"I'm not afraid," she insisted. "I just don't want to be bothered with all of that."

"Then we will keep our social calendar limited."

"Promise?"

He touched his forehead to hers. "I promise."

A minute later, the carriage stopped. They climbed out, ready to face their wedding guests and partake in the wedding breakfast. He held her hand, giving it a squeeze, and she let out a breath.

"Together," he promised her.

The townhouse door opened, and they stepped inside as husband and wife.

❧ 16 ❧

"He's watching you again," Cinna murmured to Elise. They were gathered around the refreshment tables in the main dining room of Elise's home, along with Edwina.

"Who is?"

Cinna gave a low chuckle. "Mr. Holmes. I suppose he's furious you won, and now he's just come to glare at you."

"Actually, I believe he's watching Prospero, who is watching Elise," Edwina said.

"What?" Elise looked toward her husband, who was at the far end of the dining room with a group of men, including her father. They had formed a loose circle and were in a jovial discussion that had her father laughing and Prospero smiling.

But Prospero had positioned himself so he could still see Elise, and his eyes would flit to her every few seconds even though he spoke with the other gentlemen. Elise smiled back at him, and he gave her a sinful, *wicked* look before he raised his glass to her in a knowing way. Heat bloomed in her belly as she imagined what he might be thinking to cause such a smile. But before she let herself become distracted by her husband's sinful looks, she turned her attention back to Mr. Holmes.

Elise found him standing with Dr. Watson amongst several members of the Society of Rebellious Ladies. Holmes's gaze moved back and forth between Elise and Prospero in clear consternation. Dr. Watson, on the other hand, seemed to be enjoying the company of these outspoken women.

"I think it's time I acquired that blasted violin." Elise walked toward Mr. Holmes, eager to have this over with. Holmes separated from Dr. Watson and the crowd of guests he'd been with, and they moved far enough away from everyone to allow for the two to have a private conversation.

"I offer you my solicitations," Holmes said stiffly. His gaze swept over her figure as if looking for a critical thing to point out, but found nothing. She did look quite stunning in the gown that she was now glad Mary had forced her to have made for her wedding ceremony. The soft scent of oranges from the blossoms tucked in her hair permeated the room in a faint citrus scent that almost everyone found pleasing.

"Thank you," Elise replied primly. "And I trust you received my report on my findings as to the nature of men?"

He nodded, his eyes narrowing slightly. "We can discuss the value of your findings later. This hardly seems the time for it, don't you think?" He glanced around at the crowd. "Marriage was not part of our wager."

"No, it certainly wasn't," she agreed.

"That means something forced your hand. But what, I wonder?" Mr. Holmes said, his focus leaving her to dart about the room at the other guests as if trying to suss out a suspect. When his gaze settled on her father, his eyes softened ever so slightly. "My condolences on your father's health. If you wish, I could ask Dr. Watson to see to him. But I expect, knowing your father, he has already seen the best doctors in the city."

"You are right," she agreed. "My father requested the marriage. Given his illness, I could not refuse him such a request."

"Ah . . ." A brief flash of sympathy shone on the detective's usually cold face. "Pity. I find your father to be a fair and honest sort of fellow. The world needs more men like him, not less." It was as good a compliment as ever to be given by this famous detective, and Elise felt a lump form in her throat.

"Now," she said softly. "As you are aware, I am well-versed in understanding men, well enough to agree to marry one, even the one you chose for our bet."

His lips thinned. "If you believe marriage will tip the scales in your favor on the wager—"

Her palm connected with Holmes's cheek. She knew he was well trained in Baritsu martial arts and could have stopped her attack, but he didn't, because he knew as well as she did that he deserved the slap.

Fury sparked back to life in Elise as she leaned in close to Mr. Holmes, aware that the entire room was now watching them and their heated discussion.

"I gave up my life, my freedom, even my bodily autonomy to that man. Do you think I would've done that with *anyone* unless I trusted them and understood everything there was to know about them? I certainly didn't do that to win a wager."

Holmes stared at her for a long moment, weighing her words carefully. "No, I don't think you would. Other women might, but not you."

"Understanding a person goes beyond gender, Mr. Holmes. I can tell you all about how men behave, how to walk and talk and act like one, but to truly understand my husband, I had to love him." The words slipped out before she had time to think, but they were true, nonetheless. To know Prospero, his hopes, his dreams, his passions, even his fears, knowing all of that it was impossible *not* to love him. That realization would require more analysis later, but now was not the time.

"He left his entire world because a man forced him to. He lived a life that left him empty, and he returned to a crumbling home with no family. But he didn't do the easy thing. He didn't give up. Instead, he did whatever he could to make his own way. He studied, and rather than sit on his title and the past, he sought a way to adapt to this age of growing technological wonders. He honored my father's request to take care of me, knowing that others would gossip about him taking an heiress for a bride so soon. I know all of this about him, and it makes me adore him all the more. He has as much a rebel heart as I do. Is that proof enough that I understand him to your satisfaction?"

Holmes lifted his chin. "Yes. I suppose that proof is sufficient, Lady March."

Lady March.

It was the first time someone had called her that. She was Elise Hamblin no longer. She was someone's wife, someone's property and burden. Her stomach knotted and her heart clenched in protest. The woman she'd once been had slowly perished from one moment to the next, and she had to accept that that woman was gone. Elise Hamblin was truly dead. Now she was Lady March, and only time would tell what that might mean.

"I will see that the violin is delivered to you as soon as I return home, per our agreement." Mr. Holmes offered her a hand, and after a moment, she shook it. He turned to leave, only to stop and face her again. "Lady March, there is something that concerns me about your husband."

"And what is that?" She wondered what he might be playing at, but his tone wasn't accusatory. Rather, it was concerned.

"Yes, not of him, no, but I do believe he's attracting the wrong sort of attention." Holmes was uncharacteristically grave as he spoke next. "Please take care, Lady March. That is all I can say for now."

Before she could demand Mr. Holmes explain himself, he extracted Dr. Watson from the group of young ladies he'd been speaking to and left. Distracted by Holmes's warning, Elise turned away from the door and bumped into a hard body.

"Darling?" Prospero's deep voice was the comfort she hadn't known she needed just then. "What's the matter? What did he say to you?"

In mere seconds, her husband had seen her distress and rushed to her side, ready to defend her. And he'd called her *darling*. Why did that make her knees go weak? She'd always thought pet names were ridiculous, yet the way he'd said *darling*, as though she were something precious, yet also something deeper, something more lasting—it made her chest tight with a heady warmth.

"I . . ." She halted and tried again. "Could we speak about it later tonight?"

Her husband rubbed her back with his palm. "Of course," he assured her. "But you are all right?"

"Yes, quite fine. Thank you." She was grateful to have him thinking about her, worrying about her. She'd never imagined she would be thankful for that, but here she was, ready to weep over his kindness toward her.

The rest of the wedding breakfast went without further incident, and by the time the last guest left, Elise was dead on her feet. She entered her room to change into a tea gown and found several travel cases packed and sitting by the door of her bedchamber.

"Mary?" she called out in concern. Her lady's maid emerged from the dressing room with a pile of clothing in her arms.

"Ah, there you are, milady. I am almost ready to leave."

Elise gasped. "Leave? You're leaving?"

Mary chuckled and came over to her, patting her cheek in a motherly fashion. "*We* are leaving. Your husband has planned a surprise honeymoon to the Isle of Wight. We are taking a train to Southampton this afternoon, and he has booked passage to the island tonight."

Elise stared at her maid. "But he didn't tell me . . ."

Mary laughed. "I believe that is the point of a surprise. Now let's get you changed. I won't have this beautiful wedding gown anywhere near a train station."

Numb, Elise allowed Mary to change her out of her wedding gown and into a sky-blue and orange day gown, with a short train that wouldn't drag upon the floor. Normally she would have been delighted to wear such a burst of color, but at the moment, her heart wasn't in it.

"Why didn't he tell me?" Elise whispered. She sat down at her vanity table to have her hair arranged. "He can't just do things like that without asking me."

Her maid placed her hands on Elise's shoulders and met her gaze in the mirror.

"You are two people sharing a life now, my child. A good man, a good husband, will do things to surprise you. And if you love him, you should surprise him too. He wanted you to have time to enjoy being married before you came back and settled in."

"How do you know that?" she demanded, feeling rather childish and despising herself for it.

"Because he asked my thoughts if you would like a honeymoon, and he wondered if he should take you to the Isle of Wight after your father suggested it might be a good place to go. I said you'd certainly enjoy spending all day digging for those shells you love, and your husband simply smiled and said, '*Good. I want her to do what she loves most.*'"

Prospero had asked her maid her thoughts about what Elise would like? Well, that was intelligent as well as thoughtful. And he had seemed pleased about taking her to a place where she would be running about the cliffs looking for fossils. How could she be even remotely angry with him for that? She couldn't. Hadn't her father surprised her often enough with delightful adventures that she'd loved? The truth was, she was looking for a reason to be upset with him so that she could feel in control of something, and that was absolutely wretched of her.

"I admit, I was wary about that man at first, but he cares a great deal about you," Mary said softly. "He's putting you first. Do you know how rare that is?"

Elise swallowed hard. Yes, it was rare, and she had been

complaining like some spoiled child about it. Well, no more. She wasn't going to look for any more flaws in her husband. Mary was right. They were sharing a life, and he was a good man, and he'd done more for her in the last few days than any man had ever done for her, aside from her father. Edwina would have said he was a hero from one of her favorite fanciful novels. And as much as it seemed strange to admit, Elise thought Edwina was right.

"Now, let's get you dressed. We have a train to catch."

PROSPERO STUDIED THE VIOLIN IN FRONT OF HIM, STILL puzzled.

John stood beside Prospero in the drawing room, examining the gift. "Who is it from?"

The butler had brought a black case to them a few moments ago. When Prospero had opened it, he'd discovered a violin inside, with a note tucked between the strings. Prospero read it aloud again for John.

"*You win.* It's signed, *Sherlock.*"

"As in Mr. Sherlock Holmes?" John asked as he peered at the note. "He was at the wedding breakfast, but I didn't have a chance to speak with him."

"It must be. He and Elise were having a rather heated discussion at one point."

"I had wondered about what the fellow said to her, because she slapped him for it," John murmured in concern. "I trust you will get to the bottom of this?"

"Most certainly," Prospero promised.

"Good. Now, I believe I hear Elise on the stairs." John nodded toward the door of the drawing room. "Shall we?"

Prospero followed Elise's father into the entryway by the foot of the stairs. Elise and Mary were dressed and ready to leave, but his wife's face was a bit pale. She'd been under too much strain today. He would find out what was the matter and fix it, whatever it was. His new valet, Conley, was also ready and had a travel case gripped in each hand. The valet carried the cases out to the waiting coach, while Elise hugged her father goodbye.

Prospero's heart stilled as he saw how much this moment pained both father and daughter, just as it had in the church. John stroked his child's hair and murmured something that made Elise tear up, nod, and whisper something in return. Then John let go of her and held out a hand to Prospero.

"Have a good journey, my boy."

At that moment, Prospero no longer felt like a man standing outside in the cold. John's two words, *my boy*, had brought him into the warmth of his new family, claiming him as his son where his own father had abandoned him.

"I will write to you every day," Elise promised her father.

"I rather hope you won't," her father said with a grin. "There ought to be other things to help keep you busy. Now off you go, before you miss your train."

Elise was quiet for most of the train ride to Southampton as well as the boat ride to the Isle of Wight. But it wouldn't be kind to press her on the matter until they were truly alone. Prospero had rented a small house by the sea rather than stay at one of the expensive hotels. It would give his wife easier access to the beach and cliffs.

The house came with its own cook, an upstairs maid, and a footman, and there were spare rooms for Mary and Conley to stay in. He and Elise would share the largest bedchamber.

He stood behind Elise now, hands on her waist as she took in the cozy bedroom where he hoped they would spend at least half their time. He couldn't deny his hunger for her, and he knew she desired him just as much. They had already shared a bed, had already been intimate, though not fully. Still, it was perfectly understandable for a woman who'd never been with a man before to be anxious.

"Would you like to dine before we settle in for the night?" he asked as he rubbed her waist.

"Y–yes, let's dine first." She turned in his arms, ready to flee the bedroom, but he caught her before she could slide past.

"Elise, what did you and Mr. Holmes speak about at the breakfast this morning?" He figured he would press his advantage to get the truth out of her while she was unsettled.

She blinked. "Mr. Holmes?"

"Yes, you slapped him at the wedding breakfast, and then a violin was delivered to your house before we left, along with a note saying you'd won. Won what, might I ask?"

"I . . ." She tried to hide a flash of guilt, but he had gotten very used to reading his new wife.

"The truth, please, *wife*." He spoke the word with affection rather than in reprimand. He needed her to believe that truth and sharing between them would work. He pulled her closer to him, holding her as comfortingly as he could.

Her face reddened. "I'm afraid you'll be upset with me when you hear the entire tale. But to be fair, you and I didn't know each other when this all began . . ."

"Why don't you start at the beginning?" He led her deeper into the bedchamber and closed the door. He sat on one of the large armchairs and pulled her to sit on his lap. He like the weight of her there, and he liked how he was able to wrap his arms around her hips and hold her, and she seemed to find as much comfort in it as he did.

"It began a few days before we met. Mr. Holmes was driving me mad with his violin playing. It was disrupting our meetings at the society, and he knew what he was doing because I had specifically asked him before not to play on certain days and times. I went next door to confront him, and, well, we ended up making a wager instead."

"What sort of wager?" He didn't like the sound of that at all, but he waited to pass judgment until he'd heard the entire story.

She explained the terms of her wager to study him and how she had sent Cinna to his club to lure him into the interview that day with the advert she'd had printed.

"Why did you choose me?"

"I didn't. Mr. Holmes did. He thought you would prove the most interesting because you lived your life in the gray, as he called it. You weren't a perfect gentleman, given your scandalous past, but neither did he think you a villain."

Prospero hummed softly, not quite sure what to make of the detective's assessment. "And the gentleman who was reading the paper was Cinna?"

Elise nodded. "She'd snuck into the club once before,

and we thought she'd be best. If it had been me, you might have recognized me at the interview."

"I thought I recognized her, when you first introduced us."

A hint of mischief came back into Elise's eyes. "That you did."

"And these other men who were present the day I interviewed with you? Were they part of your plan?"

"Not exactly. I hadn't anticipated how many people would show up in response to the advertisement. I had to do something to drive them all away. Most of them bolted when they realized a woman would be in charge of the study, but others were more difficult to dissuade."

Prospero thought over all that she had said. "So what did you and Holmes speak about at the breakfast?"

"I spoke to him about collecting my prize, the violin, and he made a distasteful comment about me . . . about me marrying you to win the wager." She shuddered. "I lost my temper, slapped him, and said—"

She halted suddenly.

"Said what?"

She swallowed nervously. "I told him that I could not understand you unless I loved you, or rather, that to *understand* you was to love you, or something about knowing—" She began to ramble, but he caught her chin.

"Do you love me?" he asked, trying to hold in the hope and excitement that love could come so swiftly for them.

"I suppose I do . . . ," she mused. "Having never been in love before, I cannot say I know what it truly feels like," she admitted. "Do you?"

"Do I love you, or do I know what it feels like to be in love?" he asked.

She placed her hands on his chest, and she stroked her fingers over his ascot. "Both, I suppose?"

"I think I must be falling, in answer to your first question, and not until this moment, in answer to the second."

That was the first moment he and Elise spoke words of love, albeit in a roundabout way that oddly seemed to suit them. She lifted her gaze from his ascot to his eyes, then down to his lips, and they both realized that dinner could wait.

ADAM JACKSON GLARED AT THE NEWSPAPER THAT discussed the wedding breakfast of one Prospero Harrington, the new Earl of March, to Elise Hamblin. So, it was done and done quickly. But his plans were already in place. His revenge was close—he could almost feel the release of that pressure that had been building for weeks in his head.

"Celine!" The townhouse shook as he bellowed his sister's name. She came at once, head bowed, eyes still black from where he'd struck her earlier.

"Yes?" Her voice was a whisper.

"You will find out if the newly wedded couple are at home this evening. Pay whatever servant you must and then come straight back."

She was quiet a long moment. "What will you do to avenge our brother?"

He eyed her with suspicion. "You now finally agree that March must suffer?"

She nodded. "I do. I see that now. What will you do to him? Kill him?"

Adam smirked. "Too simple. I'll make him *wish* he was dead. I will kill that pretty new bride of his and leave him to hang for it. I might do it tonight, once they are asleep." He waved a hand at her. "Now go find out what you can and return at once."

His sister ducked out of the room. He waved for a footman to pour him a fresh glass of brandy. If he was going to strangle a woman tonight, he wished to enjoy it fully. The drifting feeling of brandy flowing through his veins always made violence more fun. And he did so love to have fun.

❧ 17 ❧

Elise stood very still as Prospero closed the door and slid the latch to seal them in. The message was clear: he did not want them to be disturbed. Her heart began to pound and throb against her eardrums as he came toward her. They were alone, as they had been many times before, but everything was different now. She was not here to explore his world—she was here as a part of his world. As his *wife*. It all felt too surreal.

I am married . . . and this is my wedding night.

Prospero gently raised her chin up to face him. His eyes were like the sea at night, with faint glimmers of moonlight. If she plunged beneath the surface of that gaze, she might never want to surface again.

"This is no different than any other night." His breath was warm upon her skin as he stroked her bottom lip. "Only this time, we finish what we started, and it will be even better than before."

She nodded, but damned if her body didn't betray her with a sudden shiver.

"Undress me." He clasped her hands, raising them up to his chest, then continued to stroke her hands with his fingers in reassurance.

That active movement somehow helped calm her. Removing his clothes gave her some control over the situation. She tugged the fold of his ascot and pulled it free of his neck, letting it drop to the ground. Then she unbuttoned his gray woolen waistcoat, taking care with each button as she slid it free.

"You're doing very well," he said.

Perhaps the old Elise would have scoffed at his praise, but this new Elise, the woman who had given herself over to this new life, felt like a newborn foal struggling to stand on shaky legs for the first time. She handled his shirt next, taking care to remove it, enjoying a secret thrill that made her blood hum in the most wonderful way. He had a light undershirt beneath that, and Prospero raised his arms so that she could remove that as well.

With his chest now bare, he placed her hands on his skin again. She moved in close, nuzzled the hollow of his throat, and ran her palms over his chest, marveling at his strength and the trail of dark hair that went from his naval down to below his waist. He held still, but she could feel the excitement upon his breath whenever she put her hands on him.

"I am *yours*, Elise. Yours in *all* ways. Touch me, whenever you wish, however you wish. It is your right now, as my wife." He held her hands to him for a long moment, letting her feel the beat of his heart. It was steady, calm, so unlike her own. And even that soothed her, that he was so calm, so at ease, that it made her start to feel the same.

"How are you so calm?" she breathed. "I feel like my heart is about to burst in my chest," she confessed.

Prospero's lips curved in a smile that held such affection, such sweet indulgence that something inside her changed forever in that moment as he replied.

"I am calm only by my force of will to be gentle with you, to be the man you deserve this night . . . and every night after. I am yours, my darling wife."

This man was hers. He belonged to her. How strange. She'd been quite happy alone. Quite satisfied. She'd felt no emptiness, nor any longing to have anyone in her life other than her father. But now that she had this beautiful, kind, compassionate, and attractive man to call her own, she would never give him up. In that moment, her life divided into two eras. The era before she loved Prospero and the era after. This realization calmed her own racing heart, and suddenly she was filled with not only excitement but an endless sense of peace.

She explored the light thatch of hair on the upper part of his chest with her fingertips and then traced his flat male nipples until they hardened slightly beneath her touch. He held his breath as she explored him, until she ran her fingers over the line of his waist where his trousers still hung on his hips. His breath hitched as she began to unfasten them.

She nibbled her bottom lip as his trousers dropped to the floor. He stepped out of them before he removed his shoes, stockings, and smallclothes. Though he was now completely naked, she remained fully clothed. His cock was an admirable size compared to what she'd seen carved in museums and her own scientific explorations.

"You may touch it," Prospero encouraged in a low, slightly rough voice.

She moved one hand along his lean, hard hip down to the V-shaped muscles that pointed down toward the most male part of him.

He nodded, and when she hesitantly touched his shaft, he let out a pent-up breath.

"Does it hurt when you are aroused?" she asked as his cock stiffened sharply at her touch. She'd always wondered about whether such a rush of blood to one area could be uncomfortable when touched.

"No, darling. You simply feel too good." He caught her wrist and gently guided her hand back to his shaft, showing her how best to stroke him.

Elise leaned against his chest as she touched him, curling her fingers around his shaft and holding him. His eyes closed and his lips curved up as she moved her hand up and down.

"That is one of the many ways you will conquer me, wife," he whispered huskily. "Touch me like this and I will do *anything* you ask."

Excitement heated her blood, and she leaned her body ever closer to his as she continued to stroke him. A deep, aching pulse started within her own body, one that she knew on an instinctive level could only be satisfied by this man. Feelings, sensations she'd never felt, never imagined, started to pour into her from all sides.

A cool breeze came in from the open windows that smelled of the sea and sky. She felt the warmth breath of her husband upon her neck as he leaned down to feather kisses along her jaw, the tickle of his hair upon her cheek and the feel of his satiny hardness in her hand as she continued to stroke him.

"Now it's your turn." He gently turned her to face away from him. She had to relinquish her hold on his cock and held still as he unfastened the laces of her dress and bustle. The elaborate day gown was removed quickly, and she gasped as he cupped her bottom through her petticoats. Then he gave her bottom a light smack.

She spun around. "Prospero!"

He caught her waist, laughing as he stole a kiss. It then turned into something slow and wonderfully languid as he cupped her bottom and held it, squeezing lightly. It drew a long sigh from her. His tongue teased her, making her moan. She was barely aware of his hands unfastening the ties of her petticoats and the laces of her corset. Chilling air kissed her skin as the last of her undergarments dropped to her feet.

"I finally get to see these beautiful breasts," Prospero said as he broke the kiss. His large hand cupped her left breast, gently kneading it and rubbing the nipple with the pad of his thumb. It peaked into a hard point at his touch, and she gasped at the heavy fullness that now made her breasts ache.

He slowly bent in front of her. Once he was level with her breasts, he sucked one nipple into his mouth while gently cupping the other.

Heat shot straight through to her core and her knees buckled. "Oh God . . . ," she whimpered and dug her hands into his hair, holding on to him as he drew her breast deeper into his mouth, sucking harder.

The bond between them only grew stronger as his mouth and hands explored her in ways she'd never imagined. She was trembling as he moved to suck her other breast. The content look upon his face as he closed his eyes and flicked his tongue over the sensitive peak made her dizzy.

"Prospero, I . . ." She wasn't sure what she meant to say next, but she couldn't finish her sentence because he slid one hand between her legs and penetrated her with two of his fingers. Something exploded inside her so fast that she let out a shriek, only to silence herself by slapping a hand over her own mouth. Her fiendish husband only smiled as he continued to play with her and suckle at her breasts as she wavered on her feet while dizzying waves of pleasure moved through her in the wake of that first exciting rush.

Prospero released her nipple and stood so that he could catch her by the waist. She tried to speak again, but once more, words failed her.

He scooped her up and laid her on the edge of the bed, spreading her legs wide. She tried to close them out of instinct rather than intent, and her body flushed with heat at the vulnerable feeling of being left so open. She was still weak from the explosive pleasure she'd just experienced and couldn't resist him when he pressed her legs wide again.

"Lie back, darling." She did so, and he raised her legs up a little and tucked them around his hips.

Her breasts moved up and down as she breathed and gazed down the length of her body to where Prospero stood, right between her thighs. He stroked one hand down her belly while his other guided his cock toward her. She had the sudden panicked thought that he wouldn't fit, but logically, if his member could grow in such a way, then surely her—

She gasped as he surged into her. There was a pinch of pain and a discomforting pressure. She didn't like that at all.

"Breathe," he said, but it was hard to do when she was so uncomfortable.

He leaned forward and pinched one of her nipples. The sharp pain made her both tense and then relax. The pressure in her womb began to ease as she drew in another calming breath.

"You *pinched* me."

Her husband grinned wickedly. "I had to distract you so your muscles would relax." She had to admit, his trick worked.

"What happens now?" she asked. "Are we done?" She stared at the place of their joining. She had seen animals mate: birds mostly, and a pair of cats once. She wasn't quite sure what to expect next.

He chuckled. "Not even close." He moved his hand to her mound and brushed his thumb over the small bud of her clitoris, and she clenched her inner muscles down around him in response. The action was instinctive, but she couldn't help but analyze it even in the midst of her rising passion. Her body was responding more on instinct to him than she'd ever imagined, given how little the illustrious men of science had claimed it would. Perhaps the society should pen a secret pamphlet and share it with the women of England, letting them know that there was so much to gain by asserting themselves in the act of love making and embracing their instincts. Before she could think further on this, her husband distracted her with his deep voice.

"That feels good," he growled. "Do it again, love."

She clenched her muscles down on him, and he continued to rub and tease her clit.

After a long moment, a heavy ache built down in her lower belly, and Prospero finally began to move. And when he did . . . It was like nothing she'd ever experienced in her life. The pulling out, leaving her empty, and the thrust in, making her gasp and rise on the bed. The sensations that sparked to life inside her now were wonderful and exciting. She wanted it to never stop, but at the same time she wanted to reach that pinnacle of *something* she could feel was so close.

"Fuck, you are beautiful, Elise." Prospero drove deep into her again, his pace quickening. His hair had fallen over his eyes, making him look younger, more boyish, as his face displayed a mix of determination and rapture.

She clawed at the bedding. "You're beautiful too . . ." And it was true. He was the most beautiful thing she'd ever seen. She couldn't tear her gaze away from him as the lamplight played across her husband's chest as his muscles moved. He gripped her thighs harder, his fingers digging in as he moved deeper, faster, each harsh pump of his hips sending him deeper into the well of her very body and soul.

He leaned over her, their gazes locked as he thrust over and over, lust illuminating his face, and yet something softer, deeper shone in his eyes. He captured her wrists with his hands and laced his fingers through hers.

"That's it, love," he whispered. "Take me, all of me, as deep as you can." He drove into her, leaving her only a bundle of feminine instincts as she frantically tried to lift her hips to meet each jerk of his.

"Prospero—" She'd once had a dream of flying, of racing toward a cliff and throwing her arms wide as she felt the air catch her, lifting her up high into the sky. The moment she breathed his name, she *flew*.

Glorious. Blinding. Breathtaking. The ground dropped out beneath her as the world shrank to just this moment, this bed, this man. Blissful heat rippled over the surface of her skin and her eyes closed as she surrendered to the feeling of truly being herself with Prospero.

When she finally came down, she was spinning wildly inside, until she landed gently back upon the bed, just as a seed from a great sycamore tree would land and nestle into the soil. She wondered what she would grow into over time. Would this feeling of belonging make her grow deep roots and yet still reach for the sun? She dearly hoped so. Tears blurred her eyes as she felt Prospero's lips upon her cheeks. Somehow he'd withdrawn from her body while she'd drifted down from the clouds. She hadn't wanted that sense of connection to him to end, not when she felt so adrift, so vulnerable and raw.

"Shhh . . ."

She realized she was weeping softly. She reached for him, curling her arms around him as he lifted her up, moved her deeper onto the bed, and then lay down with her still wrapped in his arms.

"Don't cry, darling." Prospero tightened his hold on her.

How could she explain how she felt? New, raw, vulnerable, different down to her very bones? Were there words strong enough, clear enough to describe all that? She doubted it. Nothing would ever be able to explain what she was feeling.

"I'm not crying," she lied, and buried her face against his neck.

"Did I hurt you?" he asked.

She shook her head as she nuzzled against his chest.

He brushed the backs of his knuckles over her cheeks. "Then tell me, what's the matter?"

"I didn't know . . ."

"Know what?"

"That being with you could feel so . . ." Again, the words that had always been her allies deserted her.

"Wonderful?" Prospero offered. "Wonderful was how it felt for me."

At this, she lifted her face to look up at him. "Truly?"

"*Truly*. I've been with many women, but nothing has ever felt like it did with you." A warm, lazy pleasure moved through her entire body. She could have stayed here forever, just as she would have lain upon a blanket beneath a brilliant summer sky and listened to the comforting drone of bees among the wildflowers.

"I rather think it's because we care for each other deeply, don't you?" The hesitancy in his tone suggested he was analyzing this change himself.

"You mean love?" she asked.

"I think so. Would you mind terribly if I fall madly in love with you?"

He'd said it as a tease, but she couldn't deny the serious look in his eyes.

"No. Would you mind if I fell madly in love with you as well?" She was so terrified to even speak the words, to put her deep desires and deeper fears in the same sentence.

"I wouldn't mind at all," Prospero replied, and he pulled her head toward his for a long kiss.

PROSPERO HELD HIS WIFE IN HIS ARMS, LETTING HER drift to sleep while his own thoughts wandered in his brain, preventing him from doing the same. If he hadn't been in love with his wife before, he certainly was now. And it wasn't because he had taken her to his bed. No, it was because she'd put her trust in him in a way no one ever had before. She'd bound her life and her freedom to his own, and with that, she had unknowingly given him her heart. How could he not offer her his own in return?

His wife was a brilliant, wonderful, compassionate person, and she was falling in love with him. Prospero held her close, feeling like it would never be close enough. His world orbited around a single brilliant star named Elise.

Today had been difficult for them both. He'd removed her from her father's care, taken her name away from her, taken half her fortune, her future as she'd once envisioned it, and all he could do was love her and swear that he would make her happy. His throat tightened as he imagined what might have been different about today if he'd never gone to that duel all those years ago. Would his parents have stood in attendance at his wedding? Would his mother have still had the March family jewels to gift to Elise? Would he have honeymooned at Marchlands and shown her his childhood haunts?

But no, it was foolish to imagine what might have been. The young Prospero had died at the moment Aaron

Jackson perished. It was no use wishing things were different. That Prospero never would have met Elise.

"We are both so different, aren't we?" He stroked his fingers through Elise's golden hair and replayed the love he'd seen shining in her beautiful brown eyes tonight. He didn't deserve this woman, or a second chance, but he'd be damned if he turned away from her now that he held her in his arms.

I will be worthy of you, he vowed. *No matter what.*

CELINE PERKINS KNOCKED ON THE DOOR TO THE Hamblin townhouse. Her heart was caught in her throat and her hands were trembling. She felt as though she would toss her accounts at any moment, the way her stomach twisted inside her. She didn't want to be here.

The butler answered the door. "Yes?"

"I'm Mrs. Celine Perkins. I'm here to see Lord and Lady March. Are they at home?" She almost whispered the words. Adam wasn't here, but she swore she felt his eyes upon her. Her brother had that way about him. His dark, malignant presence seemed to follow her wherever she went.

Adam isn't here, she reminded herself. It was silly because she knew he was at home drinking himself into a violent temper. If only her husband hadn't died, she could have stayed free of her older brother, but fate hadn't been so kind.

Perhaps she deserved it, after what she'd done to Prospero, dragging him into a fight that was never his. This might be her only chance to save innocent lives, and she had to try.

"I am sorry, madam, but Lord and Lady March left for their honeymoon," the butler replied.

"Honeymoon? Thank God," she murmured to herself. But as the butler started to close the door, she held her gloved hand out, pressing it to keep it open. "Please, is Mr. Hamblin at home, then?"

"He is, but it's too late for visitors, madam."

"*Please*," Celine begged him. "It's a matter of life and death."

The butler stared at her a long moment, and whatever he saw in her face convinced him to listen.

"Just a minute. Please step inside while I inquire if the master will see you." The butler ushered her in and closed the door, then vanished down a corridor. When he returned, he indicated for her to follow him. "The master will see you."

He ushered her inside a study and closed the door behind her. Mr. Hamblin sat in his chair at his desk. He stood and waved for her to sit in one of the chairs facing him. He was a tall, broad-shouldered man with gray streaking the temples of his dark hair.

"Mrs. Perkins, my butler informed me that it was a matter of life and death? I pray that is an exaggeration."

Her throat was suddenly dry. "I fear not. My brother was Aaron Jackson, the man who died in a duel with Lord March."

"I recognize the name. What is this about, Mrs. Perkins?"

"It's my older brother, Adam. He is . . ." She swallowed

as she knew only the truth would work. "He is mad. He still wants revenge against Prospero, even after all these years. My brother means to kill your daughter and frame Prospero for it."

"What?" Hamblin growled the word dangerously. "He wants to kill my child?"

"He sent me here tonight to see if they were home. He expects me to return and tell him what I've discovered. He doesn't know that I planned to warn you instead. He is dangerous, and he means to do what he says. I knew I had to warn you."

"Why didn't you go to the authorities with this information?" Hamblin demanded.

"Mr. Hamblin, my brother is a brutal but powerful man. If he thought for a moment I would go to the authorities, I would be dead already. I—"

Crash! Something hard hit the closed door of the study, causing them both to gasp.

"You said your brother sent you here?" Mr. Hamblin whispered.

She gave a jerky nod, her body frozen in terror. Adam was *here*. He hadn't waited for her to return, but instead he'd followed her. *Oh God!*

"Get behind me!" John whispered as he opened the drawer to his desk, drawing out a revolver. He'd started to load the cylinder with bullets when the door crashed open. Celine flung herself behind the protective shield of Mr. Hamblin.

Adam stood in the doorway, a sick smile twisting his handsome face into a terrifying mask. At his feet was the footman, unconscious or dead, she could not tell. Adam's eyes were bright with madness, drink, and a lust for death.

"Celine, you've disappointed me," Adam said coolly, but his gaze was on Mr. Hamblin, whose hands shook as he tried to get the bullets into the gun.

"You won't be fast enough, old man," Adam said. He lunged toward them.

Hamblin tossed the gun aside and raised his fists, ready to fight. Celine screamed. The two men collided in an explosion of punching and bellowing. Furniture smashed, papers fluttered through the air, and bookshelves crumpled against the impact of the bodies of the men as they fought. Celine scrambled to grab the gun on the floor, but it was kicked under a shelf, out of her reach. For a moment it looked like her brother was losing, but after Hamblin connected with a hard right hook, the older man's face suddenly drained of color. He staggered back, one hand clutching his chest. He crashed into his chair and crumpled to the ground.

Her brother advanced on the fallen man, as if preparing to finish the job.

Celine did the only thing she could think to do and threw herself in front of Mr. Hamblin.

Adam moved to push her aside. "You traitorous little—"

She stabbed him with a letter opener she found on the desk, but he batted it aside and backhanded her so hard that her head struck the edge of the desk. Everything vanished in an instant.

Adam panted like a wild animal as he stared at the two lifeless bodies on the floor of the study. They weren't the two he had planned for, but it didn't matter. The liquor in his veins made everything seem wonderfully possible. His bitch of a sister was dead, as was March's father-in-law. All Adam had to do now was find March and his bride. Then he would have the vengeance he so craved.

He kicked the old man's body, satisfied when the limp figure didn't react. He left the ruined study to get back into the corridor. One of the servants he'd attacked lay on the floor, slowly regaining consciousness. He grabbed the footman by the lapels and pulled him to his feet.

"Where did March go?"

The servant's face was swollen with the blows he'd taken, but he shook his head defiantly. Adam slammed the man's skull against the wall.

"Where!" he bellowed again.

"W—Wight . . . Isle . . . of Wight . . ." The footman's eyes closed and he slumped.

The Isle of Wight. Adam smiled and licked away a smear of blood on his lips.

"I'm coming for you, March."

"Really, Sherlock, this is highly unusual. You made enough of a mess at the wedding breakfast this morning. I don't think we should—" Watson tugged on Sherlock's arm. "Are you even listening to me?"

"Hmm? What?" Sherlock had just reached the front

door of the Hamblin home and hadn't been listening to Watson. He had the same focus he always had right before he solved a case, to the exclusion of all else. There was something he didn't see yet, some detail that was missing that would make everything become clear. He ran his gaze over the exterior of the house. It was quiet, but the front door was open . . . barely.

Holmes placed a hand on Watson's shoulder, halting his friend when the doctor reached for the door knocker.

"Watson, ready your pistol, if you please," Sherlock said as he unsheathed the short sword from his cane. Watson removed his pistol and gave a subtle nod.

Holmes pushed the door open and stepped inside, sword ready. The townhouse was silent . . . No . . . it wasn't. He heard a faint sobbing from nearby. He tracked the sound and found a young maid clutching an elderly man in her arms. They lay half-hidden behind a partially fallen tapestry. The butler was unconscious. The maid lifted a tearstained face up to Sherlock and cried out in alarm.

"It's all right, miss," Sherlock said, crouching close to the girl. "Tell me what happened."

In halting sobs, the girl relayed a story of a man bursting into the house, attacking the butler and one of the footmen. The other female servants and one of the younger footmen had fled, hoping to find help. But she had stayed behind to care for the butler.

Watson knelt and took charge of the butler, measuring his pulse and examining his condition.

"Where are Lord and Lady March?" Sherlock demanded.

"They left for the Isle of Wight for their honeymoon

several hours ago." The maid wiped her eyes and looked at Watson. "Will he live?"

Watson nodded. He'd have a mighty sore head, but he should recover.

Sherlock's hand was still tensed on his sword. "And what of Mr. Hamblin?"

The maid raised a pale, trembling finger to point down the corridor across the entryway. "In there . . . I was too afraid to look. I'm sorry!" She burst into quiet sobs, and Watson patted her hand, reassuring her she'd been very brave to stay.

"Watson, behind me." Sherlock straightened and headed for the corridor. They found the injured footman the maid had mentioned lying near an open door. The fellow was still bleeding from the back of his skull.

"Christ, we need to take this man to the hospital at once," Watson muttered gravely.

Sherlock held a finger to his lips as he approached the open door of the study, where light still shone from the lamps inside. Watson joined him.

"My God," said Watson when he saw the destruction of the room.

Sherlock catalogued the damaged furniture, upended chairs, the ink from broken bottles that splattered in wild patterns over the room, showing quite clearly that someone had fought for their life. No, *lives*, he corrected as he noticed two bodies that lay behind the desk. One was a woman in her late twenties or early thirties, and the other was John Hamblin.

"Watson!" Holmes motioned his friend forward. Watson knelt and measured the pulse on the wrist of the girl.

"Barely alive," he said darkly. "Another ghastly head wound." He moved to Hamblin, and his face filled with the sorrow of a man who carried the lives of others upon his shoulders.

"Sherlock, who did all this?" Watson growled.

"I believe I know, but there's no time. You stay here and see that these people reach the hospital. I must go to the Isle of Wight at once. I can only pray I won't be too late. Watch for my telegram."

"But, Sherlock, the man who did this is a *monster*. You cannot go alone," Watson argued.

Sherlock gave a slight smile at his affection for the doctor with a soldier's heart who'd become one of his dearest friends. Watson was needed here. "I must, old friend. I set Miss Hamblin upon the path of this beast when I sent her to study Lord March. This is no one's fault but mine. If I can save two more lives, it still won't wash the blood off my hands, but I have to try."

❧ 18 ❧

The act of mating can be enjoyable for both sexes. There is far more stimulation of the body for both male and females than has ever been discussed in scientific investigations previously. The actions of the female need not remain passive during mating, nor does she function solely as a vessel to perpetuate the male's bloodline. The art and act of mating can be a deeply satisfying encounter for both partners involved . . .

Elise paused to pull the loose bedsheet up around her body. She sat at the small writing desk in the bedchamber of the cottage Prospero had rented for them. Squinting in the dim candlelight, she analyzed the hastily scribbled notes she'd made the night before. It was a little after four in the morning, but she couldn't wait to put her thoughts down after what she'd experienced on her wedding night.

Prospero lay sleeping, naked save for a blanket half draped over his lower back, buttocks, and upper thighs. He was so warm that he needed few blankets to sleep in at night, something that also fascinated Elise. She always seemed colder at night, and sharing his heat was very satisfying, among other things. Perhaps this natural difference in temperature between males and females was meant to encourage females to get close to males? He had roused her twice throughout the night with coaxing touches and exploring fingers before he slid into her and rode her until they both cried out in pleasure.

With a grin at how her body heated at the mere memory, she turned back to her paper.

A fair-to-excellent-performing male will find the tender and sensitive places with his mouth or hands and use those places to quicken the female's desire. Such dedication to the act of lovemaking and to the female's enjoyment of the act has a lasting effect on how the female feels toward the male. It's natural to presume it creates a preference for this male above others. This further deepens the bond between the male and female and can emphasize the desire to remain loyal to each other, and thus increases the chances that the female will desire to bear offspring with a male who can be relied upon for support and affection. These observations are limited to the author's specific and at the moment limited experiences, but with further investigation via herself and through discussions and research with other females on the matter, this author will refine her observations and conclusions.

Elise bit her bottom lip as she thought over the multitude of changes she had gone through in the last week. She had done two things she'd never planned on: having sex and getting married. She found that both were pleasing to her and prayed that would not change. She felt wonderful, but the idea that Prospero might lose interest in her left a bleak hollow feeling inside her chest. He had vowed to be true to her, but only time would prove if that was true. She had to be brave and face her future with him with a positive outlook.

Prospero's sleep-roughened voice came from the bed. "You're up early, darling. Are you all right?"

Elise turned in her chair. "Yes, I woke up with some observations rumbling around my mind and had to put them down on paper."

"Care to share them?" He rolled onto his back and folded his arms behind his head as he watched her in an attractive, leonine way that made her nipples pebble, especially when she noticed that he was already aroused.

Her gaze trailed down his body. "Not yet. But I would like you to tell me how I can reciprocate what you did to me when you kissed me between my legs. You mentioned that a woman could do something similar to a man? I assume that I have some way to engage your cock so that . . . well . . . so that you will be as excited as I become when you . . ." Lord, it was embarrassing talking so honestly to him. She'd never been that shy about sex, but it had never been so personal before because she'd never been speaking to a lover before.

"When I taste your honeypot?" he teased. A gleam lit his blue eyes. "Well come over here, little naturalist, and I will show you." He patted the bed, and Elise abandoned her notes and came to him, her body already humming. She crawled onto the bed, the bedsheet still wrapped around her.

"Let the tutoring begin," he said in a teasing tone as he pulled the sheet away, forcing her to let go of it. It pooled around her waist and bared her breasts to him.

"Now the first thing you should know is that all men can be driven speechless at the sight of a woman's breasts. Any shape, any size, it matters little. We love them all. A woman's breasts are powerful tools to use against us." As he spoke, he reached out to cup one of her breasts, then rolled a nipple between his thumb and forefinger. She shifted restlessly, and a soft sigh escaped her as she watched his eyes dilate. When he dropped his hand, there was a flash of disappointment in her. But she processed his words. Men could be driven speechless?

Elise snorted. "I find them to be quite frustrating. They are heavy, and when they are put in a corset, they can be shoved up into one's face. And when I sleep on my side, they press together in the most irritating way."

Her husband winked at her. "To you they must be irksome. But men are endlessly fascinated and obsessed with them. When you want my attention, wife, you have but to reveal these beauties"—he gestured at her breasts— "and I will fall at your feet, waiting for your next command."

"Is that so?" Elise glanced down at her breasts, frowning. What on earth could he find so desirable about them?

As if sensing her puzzlement, he nodded at his lap. "Come here and straddle me," he said with a sly grin. She abandoned the bedsheet around her body and crawled over, settling her knees on either side of his hips, her bare mound rubbing against his cock through the thin counterpane of the bed that separated their bodies.

"Now offer your breasts to me," Prospero said.

"Offer my . . . ?"

"*Yes*." The word was spoken so wickedly that the wanton creature inside of her purred in response. Her breasts felt suddenly heavy in a way that only seemed to happen when Prospero was focused on them.

She leaned forward, cupping her breasts with her palms from beneath so that they were raised like offerings to him. Her nipples were hard peaks, eager to feel his lips.

He leaned forward, hands cradling her back as he bent and took one nipple between his lips and sucked. The explosion of sensations made her gasp, and she clenched her thighs around him as she rocked forward, eager to get closer. She pressed her breast against his mouth, moaning as he kneaded it with his hand while continuing to suck. An intense pang of pleasure at the entrance of her body was followed by an embarrassing flood of wet heat between her legs.

Prospero moved his mouth to the other breast, nuzzling the second peak before nipping it with his teeth, making her shriek. She had discovered that a hint of pain, such as a love bite or a light spank on her bottom, made her explode that much harder when a climax roared through her. And her new husband was well aware of this fact. He nibbled on her breasts before licking them and sucking again until she could stand no more.

"Now, ready to torture me, minx?" he asked.

It took her a moment to comprehend his words through the hazy fog of her own need.

"What?"

He laughed. "Ah, what an innocent little creature you are. Scoot down a bit." He urged her back and tossed the counterpane aside to reveal his lower body and his impressive erection. He gripped his shaft, curling his fingers around it and moving his hand up and down.

"You can do this with your hand, but it's even better with your *mouth*."

"My mouth?" Elise stared at his cock. "It won't fit. You would choke me."

Again, her husband laughed. "Not all the way, love, just as much as you can take comfortably. You can use your hand to hold the rest of me."

She moved back down his body, bending over him as she knelt on her hands and knees. Her breasts dangled down, and Prospero reached out and cupped one, pinching a nipple lightly and sending a fresh zing through her.

"Now, open your mouth and explore me," Prospero encouraged. Heat scorched her as their gazes met. She opened her lips and flicked her tongue against the head of his cock.

His hand on her breast tightened and his teeth sank into his lower lip as he nodded for her to continue. She licked again, then hesitantly gripped the base of his shaft with one hand. She opened her mouth wide as she lowered her head over his cock and sucked.

He hissed out a breath and gave a gravelly growl. "God, yes, darling, like that."

She eagerly bobbed her head up and down. She was quick to see why he must like this, because it simulated the carnal act far more exactly than merely using her hand. And the degree of control she had opened up many new possibilities for arousing him and herself.

Interesting . . .

"You amaze me, wife. You can drive me mad even while lost in thought," Prospero said.

Elise giggled, her mouth still around his cock. He started to laugh until she sucked again, and his laugh dissolved into another groan. He abandoned his hold on her breast and threaded his fingers into her hair.

This form of sensual torture was going to be her favorite way of teasing him. She moved slower, faster, used her tongue more, and even tried to take more of him once she felt confident enough. Then she sucked harder, moving at a steady rhythm, and suddenly he was trying to warn her.

"Love, please, I'm going to—"

She tasted something salty, and she swallowed in surprise as he released his seed into her mouth.

"Tell me I didn't frighten you," he groaned. "I didn't mean to do that."

She took a moment to slide her lips off him and swallowed again, then grinned.

"You always stay between my legs when I come apart with pleasure. Why can't I do the same to you?"

"Well . . . I suppose you have me there. I feel bloody primeval for enjoying it so much." He looked somewhat troubled, but she wasn't. She'd liked what she'd done, liked that he'd been out of control.

She moved up to straddle him, her body still seeking its own release, but she had learned that a man needed time to recover between acts of coitus. She settled on his lap, his cock rubbing against her wet center as he pulled her head down toward his for a kiss.

Their mouths met in a slow, lingering caress, tongues exploring with heavy need. She squirmed on his lap, and he lightly swatted her backside. She whimpered, and he cupped her bottom, his large, strong hands holding her in an almost bruising grip. She wasn't sure how long they kissed, their bodies fused together, before, without warning, he toppled her back on the bed and she found herself flipped over onto her hands and knees.

"Ready for a hard ride, love?" he asked in a dark growl that sent wild shivers through her. She nodded.

He knelt behind her, his cock nudging at her entrance, and he gripped her left hip and rammed in almost brutally. This sudden invasion, when she was so wet, so ready, was glorious. She cried out, clutching the bedsheets in her fists as he began to hammer into her. His hips smacked against her backside again and again, his cock stretching her and filling her until she couldn't think, but could only feel him everywhere around her. She pushed back against him and lowered her head onto her hands against the bed.

"Yes," Prospero grunted harshly. "That's it." He dug his hands into her hips, smacking against her so hard the bed creaked in protest. He fisted a hand in her hair, pulling on the strands to make her arch her body, and her entire being simply came apart.

Waves of color crashed across her half-closed eyes. A tremor rolled through her, so violent that her legs quaked. Her inner walls spasmed and desperately tried to hold his cock inside her, but he continued to pound her relentlessly, driving her mad because her sensitive flesh couldn't take any more.

Elise screamed Prospero's name as he drove in three more times, and then his own shout of pleasure joined hers. She collapsed beneath him on the bed, her body no longer able to hold her up, and he followed her down. He lay atop her prone body, bracing himself on his forearms. He thrust into her more gently now, his hips twitching. She reached behind her to touch him, needing to feel the way his body trembled as it matched her own. She dug her fingers into his hip, holding on to him, and he shuddered and let out a ragged breath against her neck. The weight of his body, his cock still inside her, the wet heat filling her in such a sinful way as they both caught their breath was . . . it was simply beyond imagining. She'd never thought she would want or need this—or *him*—so much. But she did.

"My God," he breathed before he planted soft kisses on her shoulder. "I think you nearly killed me."

She felt like she was drunk on whiskey and couldn't stop smiling. A frisson of faint fear still trilled inside her, warning her that this, the connection between her and Prospero, would fade someday. But she pushed that fear away, not wanting to miss a single moment with him.

"You are incredible, wife." The word *wife* had become an endearment he used for her, rather than a term for her place beneath him. When he said *wife*, it meant she was his partner, his woman, his lover, his everything. This man was as fascinated by her as she was by him. She could feel it in every kiss, every touch, every lingering look.

And she felt the same. How could she not? Prospero allowed her to be herself, allowed her to explore and learn this new world of physical pleasure on her terms. Most of society told women that such pleasures were only for men and that a lady's wifely duty was to suffer a man's touch while receiving none of her own. What a lie they'd been told all these years. The thought broke her heart. She had to find a way to change that perception.

"Well, was your experience of mating everything you hoped it would be?" Prospero asked as he withdrew from her and then rolled their bodies so they lay beside each other in the bed. He pulled the sheets up over them, tucking his arm around her waist, holding her cocooned against him.

"I had so little hopes, given what other women over the last few years had told me in whispers about how this would feel. I was told to lie back and do nothing and that there was to be no true enjoyment from the act, not if I was to remain a lady."

Prospero rolled his eyes and chuckled. "What nonsense. Women should lie back and be worshiped by men. But few men seem to realize what wonderful creatures women are. That they are bright, empathetic, brave, and far stronger than most men in all the ways that matter."

The honest truth in his words had her heart fluttering wildly. Perhaps all those years in Paris as a companion to women had given him insight into the true nature of women. For that, she was infinitely grateful, because he would always see her as a real creature, not a shadow meant to stand behind him.

"Could you ever imagine a world where women have all the same rights as men?" she asked. She'd tried to envision that future so often, but it always seemed out of reach. For her, there was only the struggle.

He brushed the back of his hand over her cheeks. "I can, but it will take a hard fight for women to achieve it. The only value most men believe in is power. The last thing most of them will desire is to relinquish any of it. 'Tis a pity. After meeting women like you and your friends, I suspect the world is far dimmer because you are prevented from shining. If you were to have the same education, the same ability to apply yourselves to the world, wouldn't it be far better for everyone? I believe by treating you mentally and physically the same as a man would children, men have in fact limited their own successes." Prospero frowned, deeply troubled by his own words. "Nothing was ever gained for humanity by holding others back or enslaving them to a half-life."

"You truly believe that women are capable of doing all that men can do? I once had a man tell me that when my menstrual flow begins, I become useless because no blood flows to my brain; therefore, I cannot be expected to think rationally."

Anger flashed in his eyes. "I damned well hope you gave him a good retort, or at the least a good kick between the legs. The blackguard deserves nothing less." She wanted to cuddle closer and kiss his face all over for his beautiful rage on her behalf.

Elise chuckled. "I explained to him that if such was the case, men's minds must be worse off because their penises require a steady flow of blood in order to become erect, and given how often men sleep with women, men must be *constantly* useless, instead of simply few days a month." She peeped up at him, grinning wickedly.

Her husband's laugh shook the room, and he wiped tears from his eyes as he reigned in his control. "My God, I adore you."

He rolled on top of her again and kissed her until they were both blissfully *useless*.

PROSPERO SLIPPED OUT OF BED AND PULLED ON HIS trousers, then leaned over to kiss his wife's cheek. She slept soundly on, unaware of his study of her beautiful form. Her curves were on full display, with the sheet barely covering her hip and one adorable leg. Her blonde hair was in wild tumbles around her face, and her long lashes fanned out over her cheeks. He wanted to stare at her forever, but his stomach grumbled, demanding a different sort of satisfaction. Smiling, he slipped downstairs to the kitchen and startled the cook, who was rolling some dough on a flat wooden surface.

"My lord!" the woman gasped.

"Pardon me, Mrs. Godwin. Could I trouble you for a tray of cold cuts and perhaps some fruit?" It was half past four in the morning, but he was hungry. He had developed an appetite from all the bedroom activity with Elise, and that only made him grin again.

"Of course." Mrs. Godwin abandoned the bread dough, set her rolling pin aside, and filled a tray with an assortment of meats, cheeses, and fruits. She also found him a bottle of wine and two glasses.

"Thank you kindly." He bussed a kiss on the woman's cheek and then carried the tray back upstairs. He met Mary outside the door to the bedchamber. She'd risen early to see to the washing, given the cloth bundled up in her arms.

Mary's eyes lit with amusement to see him only half-dressed. "You're up early, my lord."

He greeted her with a bashful grin. "Mary." He would have to get used to his wife's maid seeing him in a state of undress.

"How is she? My child?" the lady's maid asked with a

hint of concern. "She never knew about men before you. Not in a romantic way, I mean."

He gave her a soft smile. "Do not worry, she is well. And she has mastered me like she has everything else in her life. That woman owns my soul, Mary. Rest assured I am hers to command, and I worship her."

Mary's eyes widened at his words. "I knew you would be good for her. I said that the moment I saw her fluttering about to get dressed for that first dinner. She was finally excited about something besides beetles and fossils."

Prospero chuckled. "Well, I hope she never loses her excitement for those things, or anything else she enjoys. She has a remarkable mind, and I won't allow it to go to waste."

Mary patted his cheek as though he were a young lad and then shooed him back into the bedchamber before closing the door behind him.

He approached the bed and gave Elise's shoulder a gentle nudge. She raised her head and blinked owlishly in the candlelight.

"Have a bit of food before going back to sleep, darling." He set the tray down and then joined her on the bed.

She brushed the hair out of her face and pushed it over one shoulder. "What time is it?"

"I'd say close to half past four. We have a few hours yet before we should rise." He plucked a grape from the stem and offered it to her. She took it from him with her lips, seeming not to notice as she let him feed her.

She nestled closer to him. "I was thinking we could go to Culver Down. There's a lovely beach there, and we could scout the cliffs for a chance to find some fossils," she suggested as accepted another grape from him. He listened to her between adorable mouthfuls of fruit, about what she knew of the cliffs and their hidden mysteries. Prospero continued to feed her as he listened to her, and when she glanced down at the empty plate, she blushed.

"I ate too much."

"Nonsense," he said. "You need food to keep up with me in bed." He winked and won a blushing grin from her.

"Well, there is a certain sense to that. A female in the midst of frenzied mating should eat to sustain her energy levels."

He growled playfully as he pushed the tray out of the way. "Frenzied mating, hmm? I do like the sound of that."

She giggled as he pounced on her and tickled her stomach, then pinned her beneath him on the bed.

MARY CARRIED HER LOAD OF LINENS DOWN THE HALL and paused as she heard low voices coming from the bedchamber of the little cottage. It was an even mix of male chuckling and Elise's giggling laugh. A laugh Mary had not heard since her mistress was a young girl.

Yes, Lord March was the right man for her darling charge. He had shown Elise that being a woman and embracing the feminine side of herself didn't mean she had to leave her studies behind or give up her scientific pursuits. Mary's throat tightened as she continued down the stairs.

It reminded her of the old days, when Mrs. Hamblin was a young bride and Mr. Hamblin was a strapping young man. They had been such a wonderful couple with a wonderful marriage. And now it seemed through luck and fate that Elise would have the same thing in her own life. For that, Mary whispered a prayer of thanks.

She nearly tripped walking toward the washroom when a rhythmic thudding above her head started, just as the cook passed by Mary on the way to the kitchen.

"Randy devil," Mrs. Godwin muttered. But there was amusement in the cook's tone rather than disgust.

Mary bit her lip. Yes, March would keep Elise in bed quite a bit, but that was one of the pleasures of being newly married, and the young couple had every right to enjoy it. It wouldn't be long before a child would be on the way, and mayhap a wee grandchild would keep Mr. Hamblin in good health.

Yes, a child would be just the thing for their house. Mary hummed a nursery rhyme to herself as she started on the washing, already thinking about which room would be best for a nursery when they returned from the honeymoon.

❧ 19 ❧

Sunlight warmed Prospero as he stood watching Elise, his hands on his hips and a smile curving his mouth. His wife wore her men's trousers, a shirt, and a dark-blue waistcoat, but thankfully, she had forgone the binding of her breasts, her wig, and her mustache. She wasn't trying to hide who she was today, and for that Prospero was glad.

She'd pulled her hair back into a queue at the nape of her neck and secured it with a ribbon to keep her locks out of the way. Prospero stood beside her at the base of Culver Down. The cliffs that abutted the low-lying beach were chalk-white and topped with grass. The cottage they had been staying at was only a short way up the nearby sloping hill.

Cattle dotted the slopes of the northern side of the isle, nibbling on grass while seabirds whirling above the beach, hunting for fish. Earlier, Elise had pointed out both peregrine falcons and wood pigeons among the seabirds when they'd first come down to the shore. It seemed fitting that

337

the word *Culver* was supposedly derived from the Old English word *culfre* for "dove." Elise had shared that fact with him when they'd first walked down to the beach. The chalk-white cliffs reminded him of the white wings of doves.

The Atlantic was deep and rich in a thousand shades of blue, from the pale frothing seafoam to a darker sapphire that would turn obsidian in the evening. It was a starkly beautiful contrast against the white of the cliffsides.

During the day, there had been many visitors to this part of the isle, many of them frolicking along the shore and even a few men dashing into the sea in their swimsuits. The ladies stayed on the beach, umbrellas shielding their skin against the sun as they gossiped or watched the birds and the sea. Children had rushed to build castles from wet sand and play games under the watchful eyes of their mothers.

Elise hadn't worried about the sunlight. She'd simply gone about her digging, not caring that she would turn pink by nightfall. Prospero had delighted in watching the small crowd that had stopped to watch her work throughout the day.

More than a few children had gathered around her, curious to see the shells she'd freed from the stone with her tools. She crouched down to speak to them, showing them the ammonites she'd discovered and explaining the long history of the earth and the great creatures that had once roamed this land.

"You mean the great and terrible creatures from the British Museum?" one Scottish girl asked. Her little pinafore had been embroidered with flowers by some loving mother's hands, and yet it was stained with seawater and sand. She gazed up at Elise in wonder, and a lump formed in Prospero's throat as he watched Elise with the child. She was warm and welcoming with the girl's interest.

"Yes, exactly! Have you visited the museum?"

The girl's dark curly hair bounced as she nodded. "We saw the wee beasties and the . . . the *vast* beasties." She opened her arms wide to show just how big, and Elise chuckled.

"And did you enjoy seeing those creatures?"

The girl grinned shyly. "What did they eat?"

"Plankton, sea vegetation, possibly even small crustaceans."

"And are they still in the ocean? Or are they gone?"

"They aren't alive anymore, but the nautilus is perhaps a descendant that is still alive today," Elise said. "Why don't you take this to your mama and papa and show them? Tell them what it is and explain what you learned." Elise put one of the ammonites into the girl's palm and closed her fingers around it.

"Thank you!" The child rushed away to show her parents her new treasure.

Prospero had a feeling that today had lit a spark in the girl's heart to reach for knowledge, no matter how hard it might be or how many men might try to stop her.

"Be free," Elise had whispered as she watched the child run off with her new find.

Now as he stood an hour later watching Elise work, Prospero let out a breath as a sense of peace filled him. Elise's father had been right—time away from London had done them both good. His wife—oh how he found such a delight in those two words—was digging on a spot on the cliffs with a set of tools that she used for her fossils.

He recalled her excited discussion about a woman named Mary Anning, who had been a working-class woman whose fossil discoveries would change the course of both history and science. But because she was a woman, and one of the laboring class at that, she was prevented from joining the Geological Society and her discoveries were never taken seriously during her lifetime. It hurt Prospero's soul to know that she'd been so mistreated by the supposedly illustrious men of science.

"Would you fetch my trowel?" Elise asked. "I left it in my bag."

"Yes, darling." He kissed her cheek and then left the cliffside to walk back up the path toward where they'd left her bag of tools.

"Bloody hell, that's a woman!" he heard a man exclaim.

Prospero turned to see a pair of gentlemen who'd paused in their stroll along the pedestrian path that paralleled the beach. They now stared at Elise as she bent to chip away at a spot on the base of the cliffs.

"Who the devil let her out of the house? It is a disgrace, that is," the second man added.

Prospero tensed as he stared at the two men who were glaring at Elise. "I will thank you not to speak ill of my wife like that."

"God's blood, you let your wife run about dressed like *that*? You should take better command of your woman, sir. It's unnatural to let a woman wear trousers. You, sir, are letting her develop an unnatural sense of freedom that is directly against a woman's natural purpose, which is to be silent and bear children for the benefit of her husband."

Prospero strode up to the two men, fists clenched, and gripped the man by the collar, lifting him up onto his toes.

"My wife is free to do as she bloody well pleases, and if you remove your head from your arse and take a look about you, you might realize the world would be better if women were given the freedom to think and exist outside the whims of men."

The man's eyes flashed with both fear and rage as he tried to free himself.

"You're bloody mad! Let go of me!" he demanded.

"Gladly!" Prospero shot back, and shoved the man so hard he fell onto his backside on the walkway.

"Just who the devil do you think you are?" the other man shouted as he helped his friend stand up.

A cold smile slid across Prospero's face as he realized that the black mark upon his name would finally become useful. "Who am I? I am Prospero Harrington, the Earl of March."

"March? Isn't that the fellow who—" The man stuttered to a stop. He and his friend began to back away.

"Yes, I am the man who will shoot a man on a field of honor for what I believe in." His voice was quiet but cutting, the threat in it sharp and dangerous. "So speak of my wife again or any woman like that in my hearing and you will face the barrel of my gun."

The two men turned tail and ran back up the hill, losing what little dignity they still possessed. It took him a second to let go of the rage drumming inside him. Prospero turned around, a grim scowl on his face, and nearly ran straight into Elise. She'd abandoned her digging and had come up behind him. Her face was pale.

"I'm sorry, love, I didn't mean to threaten them in front of you." It must've been terrifying for her to hear her husband speak so casually about shooting a man. God, he was a thoughtless fool.

She blinked. Her soft brown eyes were so innocent of the dark ways of the world, and he never wanted that innocence of her heart to vanish.

"You . . . ," she began, then halted, then drew in a deep breath and began again. "You defended me," she said. "I heard what they said. Sea breezes carry sound to the cliffs, you know . . ." She paused, shook her head, and tried to focus on her words again. "You truly meant what you said." It was a statement rather than a question.

He nodded, his throat constricting as he saw that she finally believed in him. He would never clip her wings, or cage her into a life she didn't want. She was capable of great and wonderful things, and he wanted her to live her dreams and make her discoveries, knowing that he stood beside her, ready to defend her against any man who would dare try to stop her from living a full life of her own making.

She threw herself against him so hard that he grunted as he caught her in his arms. He smiled against her lips as she kissed him. This kiss was better than all the others that had come before because he tasted her love and now fully, finally, her trust.

He tightened his grip around her, holding her close as he kissed her back, letting her feel his joy, his love. When she finally pulled back, the late-afternoon sun was hanging low in the sky, haloing her with a golden glow.

She was his warrior wife, his Joan of Arc.

"I would go to war for you, for the right for you to have a *full* life," he whispered. Every creature on this earth deserved that, but especially women. Women had so much taken from them, so much of their own autonomy, power, and value stripped away and given over to men. It broke his heart to think of all the women who had no chance to escape the cages that were slammed down around them the moment they first drew breath in this world. But Elise . . . his beautiful, brave, wonderful wife—she'd escaped her cage, and he be damned if he'd ever let her return to it.

Tears clung to her dark-gold lashes as he brushed his thumb over her cheek to catch a few stray tears. She closed her eyes and leaned into his hand. An immense fullness in Prospero's chest made it hard to breathe. He would gladly die for this woman.

"Would . . . you like to see what I found?" she asked, changing the subject. She nodded toward the cliffs, her adorable hesitancy making his heart skip a beat. Someday he hoped that she would lose that hesitancy entirely.

"I will *always* want to see what you found." He would never forget the sight of the brilliant smile she gave him for the rest of his days.

She grasped his hand and pulled him back along the winding path.

LATER THAT EVENING, THEY SHARED DINNER MEAL BACK at the cottage. Elise finished her wine and abandoned her seat at the intimate little dinner table. She walked around toward Prospero, who had pushed back his chair, preparing to stand. She gently placed a hand on his chest and pushed him back down. Startled, he grinned as she lifted her skirts to straddle him.

They were quite alone now, at least in the small dining room. Mary and Conley, Prospero's valet had taken their supper an hour ago in the kitchen with the cook and the maid. It seemed they were all quite happy to stay away from the newly married couple, who made use of any surface to get acquainted on the sensual level.

Elise would've been embarrassed at the servants knowing their bedroom activities, but Prospero was simply too irresistible to her. So she'd abandoned her sense of propriety and embraced her passion instead.

She reached between their bodies to slowly unfasten his trousers. His cock was already hard and straining against his clothing when she palmed it. "I was thinking . . ."

"Oh? I do so love your thoughts," Prospero said, his voice low and husky as he slid his palms up under her skirts to caress her outer thighs. God, she loved the feel of his powerful hands on her body. Because those hands had always treated her with care, even during the more intense moments of their bedplay.

She freed his cock from his trousers and gripped it firmly, making him groan. "We should have a walk. Perhaps a midnight dip in the sea. The moon is so bright we can practically see everything." She slowly guided his cock toward her entrance and started to ease onto him. This was a new position for her, but she liked how she felt as she took him this way. She rocked upward a little and paused with the tip of him barely inside her. He groaned, his hands on her thighs tightening.

"Swim . . . walk . . . whatever you want, darling, just don't stop."

She giggled, but his eyes turned hard with the dangerous lust she'd created in him. He gripped her hips beneath her skirts and yanked her down on him, impaling her fully in one swift thrust. She cried out in startled pleasure, her hands clutching his shoulders to hold herself steady. Her fingers curled into the fine cloth of his waistcoat, scoring the silk fabric with her nails. Yet she didn't care—she'd buy him as many new ones as he pleased.

"You . . . are wonderfully wicked," Prospero murmured as he buried his face in the valley of her breasts, which pressed tight against her bodice. He kissed the heaving swells as he moved his mouth up to her neck and nipped in just the right spot to make her body seize with desire. Her womb spasmed and she clenched her inner walls around his shaft.

"And you are torturing your wife," she whispered, breathless.

He chuckled against her ear before he flicked his tongue inside the delicate shell, which only made the pangs of desire stronger. Elise whimpered.

"Please . . . Prospero."

"I do so love to hear you beg me, wife." He bit down on the lobe of her ear. "I love it because you lose your control with me. One should never hold on to one's control with one's lover," he teased.

"Take me now," she demanded.

He laughed. "And that I love even better. Demand all of your wifely rights, and I am yours to command, darling."

She didn't have to ask again. He took her, using her body deliciously as he lifted her up and down, pounding into her, letting wave after wave of desire build inside her.

Even after the first orgasm, he continued to move her

up and down, taking her hard . . . and it was glorious. He always knew just what to do to her body to push her beyond her limits.

"That's it, love," he breathed against her neck. "Come for me."

"I . . . can't," she whimpered. Her clitoris was so sensitive now, her body exhausted from the first two times she'd melted with pleasure.

"You can, darling, for me," he growled, and his hold turned almost rough as he pumped deeper into her.

Their eyes met, and her body exploded like a primed canon. Blissful sensations ripped through her with such strength that her hoarse scream ricocheted off the walls of the house. It felt so good it *almost* hurt. Her vision turned white, and she nearly blacked out with ecstasy. For a second she thought she was dying. And then air rushed into her lungs and she was gasping, crying, and clutching at Prospero.

"It's all right, darling," he murmured, pressing soft kisses to her cheeks. "I've got you . . . I've got you."

Elise couldn't speak. She just held on to him, grateful for the stability of his body as she slowly came down from the moment. He patted her back and stroked a hand down her hair, whispering soft, sweet, wonderful things that her mind couldn't process as she regained her breath. Her thighs shook so hard that if she had dared to stand, she would have collapsed at once. She no longer had the strength left to move.

It should have embarrassed her, to be straddling her husband in a dining room, their bodies still bound intimately together. But he didn't seem to mind, so she couldn't find it in her to care.

She murmured his name and nuzzled her face against his neck, grateful that she could be vulnerable like this with him and yet not feel weak. How very wrong she had been, thinking those two things were one and the same.

He threaded his fingers through her hair, breathing against her temple.

"Elise."

"Hmm?"

He kissed the crown of her hair. "There is an ache inside me that shall never be soothed, never eased, lest you are in my arms. If I could but spend the rest of my life setting my very heartbeat to match your own, I would die a happy man." His words grew gruff as emotion choked him. "I love you."

Elise lifted her head and stared into his eyes. When he said it, her heart went very still and she felt an unbelievable sense of peace, as though she'd stepped through a portal where time was still and she was safe. There were no storms in the depths of his eyes, but she saw an endless spiral of blue hues, so like the sea. She trusted this man with her whole heart.

"I thought no man would ever see me, see the *true* me," she confessed in a whisper. "To every man before, I was some silly creature in skirts, just waiting to be married off, bedded, and bred for children. I wasn't a person, with a heart or a mind, with dreams and desires that lay beyond the domestic sphere. But to you . . . I . . ."

"To me, you are everything." He brushed the back of his hand along her cheek. "You are everything you could ever dream. Let no one tell you otherwise."

She traced his lips with a fingertip, and he caught her

hand, kissing her fingertips, making her smile through fresh tears.

"I love you too," she whispered. "So much that it frightens me."

"Don't be afraid of love, darling. We are experiencing it together." He held her close, offering her the soothing comfort she so desperately needed.

A short while later, Elise regained her composure, and as she started to think about what had occurred between them, she giggles.

Prospero held her still, their bodies still joined. "What is it?"

"I was thinking I should write a pamphlet for women about sex. About how orgasms can feel different. It seems no experience is quite the same."

"An interesting hypothesis, little naturalist. But I believe vigorous testing will be required in order to support your theory." He gave her bottom a light pinch. She clenched around his cock instinctively, making him moan. "Lord, I love it when you do that."

She leaned forward, twining her arms around his neck. She brushed her lips over his, teasing him.

"Well, what do you think?" she asked, her mind returning to the question she'd first asked him when they'd begun to make love.

"About different orgasms and researching them? Yes, I say. *Emphatically* yes, and I shall be your partner in this matter of research."

She chuckled and shook her head.

"I'm sorry, my mind was wandering. I meant about the moonlight walk and swim. No one goes to the beach in the evenings, and the currents aren't very strong. It would be romantic."

"Are you turning romantic on me?" he teased. "If so, I shan't complain."

"Perhaps I am. Would you care to come with me and find out?" She pressed another kiss to his lips and then slid off his lap. "I will have Mary change me out of this dress and meet you at the beach in, say, fifteen minutes?"

"I will have the cook prepare a basket for us with some wine and a few of those delicious blackberry tarts she made today. We can eat them after we've had enough swimming." He gave her such a heated look she knew he wasn't talking about swimming.

"Don't forget to bring a blanket or two," she said before she rushed upstairs to change.

With Mary's help, she changed out of her gown and into her trousers and blouse. She bid good night to her maid and told Mary not to wait up. Mary simply chuckled, blew out the lamps, and retired for the night.

The full moon was so bright, Elise had no difficulty in following the gravel path that led to the beach next to the cliffs of Culver Down. She watched Prospero standing near the shore, facing the sea, a basket and rolled up blanket at his feet. He could be so quiet, so contemplative, and she sometimes wondered how much he dwelled on the past, of what might have been had it not been for that duel. She wanted to show him that the only way through the darkness he felt from his past was to push forward into the future. Someday, when her father was gone, Prospero was all she would have, and she wanted to be there for him the way he was for her in her darkest moments.

Smiling, she continued down the hill toward him. A

flash of movement caught her eye. She turned to see a man strolling in the dark, swinging a cane as he whistled softly. His gray beard was almost silver in the moonlight, and his spectacles winked in white reflected flashes. He nodded politely at her as he took care to make his way along the gravel path that ran parallel to the shore.

She wasn't surprised to see someone walking here, but she had hoped the night would turn away even the most determined walkers so she and Prospero could enjoy some privacy, but alas, that was not to be.

"Lovely evening, isn't it?" she said to the older gentleman as he drew near on the path. She would wait for him to pass by and out of sight before she and Prospero started removing any clothing.

"It is indeed," the man replied with a smile.

She turned back toward Prospero, taking a moment to enjoy the sight of him. He cut a handsome figure, silhouetted by the pale light and the shining, twilight sea.

And he's mine. The thought filled her stomach with butterflies.

A moment later, that feeling changed to one of warning, one that came an instant too late as something swung toward her head.

THE SOUND OF A SCREAM. UP THE HILL FROM THE BEACH, Prospero caught sight of two men struggling . . . no, a man and *Elise.* They broke apart. The man swung something—a cane—and Elise fell to the ground.

Prospero's heart leapt into his throat as he sprinted up the sandy slope toward the gravel path. But he'd already lost precious seconds as the man who had struck Elise now lifted her up in his arms and carried her over his shoulder toward the cliffs. The man had a head start on him and was much closer to the cliffs than the beach. Terror dug its claws into Prospero's chest.

He was going to throw Elise off the cliffs...but why? There was no time to ask that question, only the urgent need to stop him. What if he couldn't reach them in time? What if he couldn't stop the man from throwing her over the edge?

"Stop!" Prospero bellowed as he raced to close the distance between them. The man threw Elise's body to the ground twenty feet from the edge of the cliffs. Prospero lunged for Elise, but the man swung a cane at him, one that had a sharp-edged silver hooked handle.

Prospero lurched back a step, dodging what would have been a shattering blow, then lunged forward at the opening now provided. Prospero reached up to claw at the man's face, peeling away the false beard that had been stuck to his skin, and the spectacles he wore slipped free of his face. The figure, which had seemed oddly familiar, was now instantly recognizable.

"You!" Prospero growled as he was pushed back.

Adam Jackson smacked the cane's handle into his palm, ready for another attack. Prospero held himself back, disturbed at the unsettling look of satisfaction upon the man's face.

"We meet again, March," he said smugly. "It was almost too easy to find you."

"We weren't trying to hide." Prospero's tone was

entirely ice. "We didn't think a madman would follow us here."

He glanced at Elise, but she still lay unmoving. A killing rage he'd never felt in his life now surged through every fiber of his being. Jackson had hurt Elise. Prospero would tear this man into pieces and cast him into the sea.

Adam laughed. "Madness? You call justice *madness*? You seduced my sister, killed my brother, and left my name in ruins. This is just the beginning of your suffering, March."

Adam sneered. It was the only warning Prospero had before Adam tossed his cane aside and pulled a revolver that had been hidden in his waistcoat. He aimed it square at Prospero's chest.

Prospero held still, afraid to make any movement that would force Adam to fire. Christ, he'd never imagined this would be the consequence of protecting his damnable pride all those years ago. If only he'd walked away when Aaron had thrown his glove down and demanded satisfaction . . .

Prospero stared at the gun, feeling that primal fear of knowing that he could die in a single instant. But he had so much more to lose this time.

His gaze turned to Elise. She lay unmoving upon the ground, a trickle of blood at her temple, but he was sure that she was breathing.

Focus, he reminded himself. *The man is a viper, and you cannot afford to be bitten.*

Distract and delay. That was what he needed to do until he could find a position that would give him the upper hand, if one even existed.

"You're mad, Jackson. You just attacked my wife and me. Do you think the law will take your side?"

"They won't have to, not when they discover the grisly scene of your deaths. How will the papers report it, I wonder? Lord March kills his new bride on their honeymoon in a fit of rage, then ends his own life in shame? Yes, that has a lovely sound to it." The wild gleam in Jackson's eyes made Prospero's stomach clench in dread.

So that was Jackson's plan? Kill them both? This man was beyond mad. Prospero had never imagined someone could be filled with such a black heart.

"You think anyone will believe that I would kill my wife?" he challenged, still hoping to buy some time. "I've proven myself to be a man of control since the day your brother died. No one would think I would do such a thing. Besides, killing her so quickly after our wedding wouldn't make any sense. Too many witnesses have seen us affectionately enjoying our honeymoon to believe your lies."

He hoped that might set the cogs and wheels in the man's mind turning, if only for a moment, to give Prospero a chance to lunge for him.

"Oh, they will believe me," Adam said with the confidence of a lunatic. "Everyone knows that a woman like *that* would drive any man to murder." Jackson waved his free hand toward Elise. "Bloody bitch acts as if she has a brain, but she's nothing more than a tart in a skirt, like all the rest."

Prospero's fists clenched, but he had to keep the man talking. "What about me? Your sister chose me as a safe harbor to push her wiles upon, but I never seduced her. Your family began this pack of lies that has driven us to this moment. I'm offering you one last chance. Walk away from here. Leave now, and tonight's events will be forgotten."

"The only lies here have come from your mouth, dog," Adam snarled and raised the revolver, a bright look in his wild eyes.

Prospero dove at the other man just as he fired the gun. A desperate move, but the only one left to him. A blinding pain tore through Prospero's shoulder. Under any other circumstance he would have stumbled, but the rage inside him kept him on his feet.

Stop Jackson. Save Elise. The words repeated over and over in his mind. He dove for Adam just as the man pulled back the hammer on his revolver.

They collided, hitting the ground hard, causing his next shot to go wild. Prospero landed on top of Jackson and struck him hard in the jaw. Jackson grunted and countered with a blow to Prospero's ribs. Jackson snarled like a wild animal. The cold fire of bloodlust burned deep in the pits of the man's eyes.

Prospero landed another blow on Jackson's temple, but the man didn't go down. Jackson kicked, knocking Prospero back. Both of them scrambled back to their feet.

Blood ran down Prospero's arm, but he gritted his teeth and raised his hands, ready to continue the fight. With a brutal grin, Jackson lunged at him, attacking with a flurry of hard blows. Prospero grasped Adam's neck and kneed him hard in the stomach, knocking the wind from him, but the pain in his shoulder prevented him from keeping his grip. Prospero felt the breeze at his back growing stronger, and he realized that his foe was inching him toward the Culver Down cliffs.

"This is the end, March." Jackson's face split in a triumphant grin as he shoved Prospero's wounded shoulder hard. Prospero retreated a step to avoid being struck again.

His back foot slid off the grassy edge and fell into empty air. A sudden pitch formed in his belly as he lost his balance. He clawed at Jackson's shirt, but the other man was just out of reach.

Prospero fell, seeing only the pale gleam of moonlight in the other man's dark eyes, the way his lips curled up in a snarl. In the distance was Elise's prone body, so far out of his reach.

His life had become something worth fighting for because of Elise, and now he wouldn't be there to save her. The vow he'd made to her, to protect her, would be broken.

This was the end.

"Prospero!"

Elise's cry sounded so far off as he stared up at the cloudless sky filled with stars. He had but one image in his mind and his heart as he fell: Elise, smiling up at him after having given him the kiss that had changed his life.

Then his body collided with the rocks below, bringing an end to his pain . . . to everything.

❧ 20 ❧

Elise woke up with a throbbing pain, and she gently touched her temple. Her fingers came back sticky with blood, which looked black in the moonlight. Lord, she was bleeding. Why was she bleeding? She couldn't remember how she'd gotten here or why she was hurt. Had she fallen?

Her questions were answered by the sounds of two men fighting at the edge of the nearby cliff. She turned. It was Prospero and the man she'd met at the ball a few nights ago . . . Adam Jackson. It was hard to gather her thoughts together as her head throbbed. Adam was trying to kill them.

She scrambled to her feet as Prospero began to lose ground, forced back toward the edge of the cliff.

"No!" Adam had boxed Prospero in, with no way of getting past him to safety. Jackson thew a punch, and Prospero stumbled back over the cliff. One terrifying second later, he vanished from view.

"*Prospero!*"

A raspy laugh escaped Jackson as he turned and came down the slope after her. He didn't bother to run at her—he took his time, his evil grin widening as though he was imagining how he would take his time with her.

Well, she wasn't going to go down without a fight. Elise bent and tugged a small digging knife free of her boot. She'd kept it with her just by habit when she wore her digging clothes, but now she prayed it would save her life. She raised the knife, the blade flashing white in the moonlight as she prepared herself for his attack. When he was within a few feet of her, he looked down at her tiny weapon and laughed.

"What a pretty little blade. All the better to slice you to ribbons with." He lunged and she dove to the side, slicing at his chest. She scored a hit, and he howled and whirled. She lost the advantage in an instant, though, because his arms were too long and she was still in reach.

He backhanded her across the face so hard she went sprawling down the hillside, tumbling over and over before she came to a stop, her knife lost in the darkness of the night. Stars dotted her vision, and her ears rang so loudly she couldn't hear her own panting breaths.

Elise tried to stand, but her knees buckled and she had to brace her hands on her thighs until she could move again. Her first few steps were more like stumbles, but she had to get to the cliff. There was a chance Prospero had fallen into the sea. Perhaps he'd survived the fall. That feeble hope was the only thing that kept her moving.

Then hands, cold and hard, latched onto her from behind, jerking her to a stop.

Jackson spun her around to face him. "I'm going to take

my time with you, little bitch." He gripped her throat, squeezing.

No air moved in or out of her lungs as he slowly crushed her windpipe. She was going to die. The thought sent her mind spiraling. Each time she blinked, the world seemed to move slower and the sounds grew fainter. Her mind, deprived of oxygen, began to pull up memories for her to see, perhaps to comfort her in her final moments.

Prospero standing in the doorway of her office at the society's headquarters, a dashing figure with eyes that shone with surprise and curiosity . . . bent over the display of beetles at the British Museum, marveling at their shiny iridescent wings . . . whispering words of love on their wedding night . . .

Darkness closed around her vision, tunneling toward a distant glimmer of some yet-unnamed star. Whatever her body and his became after death, at least she would be with Prospero, as all things on this earth would be and had always been. *Stardust to stardust . . .*

A deep voice rang out sharply across the hill. "Jackson!"

Elise opened her eyes just as she heard a gun fire.

Jackson's grip on her throat eased and air trickled into her damaged airway, making her wheeze as she tried to breathe despite the pain. The cold grin on Jackson's face faltered, and he glanced down at his chest. Blood swelled around a spot close to his heart. To Elise's air-deprived mind, it looked like a blooming rose.

Though his grip had loosened, he still held on to her throat as he stumbled toward the cliff's edge, taking her with him. Despite his mortal wound, he carried her as though she were nothing more than a child's doll.

"Elise!" The voice was closer now, but whoever was

coming to her rescue had come too late. She couldn't free herself of Jackson's hand as he toppled over the cliff, taking her down with him. She screamed as the wind whipped around her body and the ground spiraled beneath her.

Something caught her arm. Pain ricocheted through her as she heard a sickening pop from her shoulder, and she passed out from the sudden shock of pain.

When her eyes fluttered open, she lifted her head to stare at the steep white cliff face of Culver Down.

She was nearly fifteen feet down from the top of the cliff. There was a ledge that jutted out, and she was hanging suspended by her arm from that ledge. How was it possible that she'd managed to stop her own fall partway down the cliffside? She tried to see what had caught her. Had her hand become caught in a jutting rock, or . . . ?

No. Another hand, a large, strong male hand, had hold of her wrist. Through the fog of pain, she saw a face staring down at her over the ledge just above her.

"Got you!" Prospero grunted.

Dear God, he was alive! Bleeding, in bad shape, but *beautifully* alive. Tears from pain, joy, and sweet relief blurred her vision. Blood dripped onto her face from his other arm, which he braced on the ledge.

"Hang on," he grunted. "I'll haul you up."

She clawed at the rock in front of her, trying to help as he pulled her up to the ledge that protruded from the side of the cliff. A shriek of agony escaped her as he grabbed her bad shoulder to haul her up. The second she was up on the ledge, he tucked her against his side. They both lay on their backs, panting and staring up at the cliff and sky above them. For a long time, neither of them spoke.

"I love you." Prospero's ragged voice was edged with pain.

Too short of breath and in too much pain to speak, she merely lifted his hand up to her lips and pressed a kiss to his bloodied knuckles. A distant shout from above then came down to them.

"Lady March!" The voice was familiar, but her thoughts were too murky to recognize it.

"Is . . . is that Sherlock Holmes?" Prospero asked, his voice shaking.

It took her a moment for the name to make sense. She hurt so badly, and her body was still quaking.

"Lady March!" the voice called again, and finally her memory connected it to her irritating neighbor.

"Here!" Prospero called out. "We're here, Holmes." It sounded like those words cost him everything, but he had managed to cry out, and for that she was glad. She still had no ability to talk.

Holmes's head appeared over the top of the cliff as he searched for and spotted them. He had a pistol in one hand, but he put it away when he saw it was only the pair of them. So he must have been the one to shoot Jackson, Elise realized.

"Lord March! Thank Christ. I thought I was too late for either of you. Stay there."

"We await you at your leisure, Mr. Holmes," Prospero replied with a pained chuckle.

A while later, or at least that's how it seemed, something thick and snakelike tumbled down over the cliff and landed next to them with a thump.

"It's a rope," Prospero murmured. He lifted the rope, his brows drawing together. "Surely he can't expect us to climb?"

Elise, finally able to gather her wits, forced herself to sit up and examine the rope. Pain, dull and leaden in her dislocated shoulder, still made her thoughts terribly foggy.

"Lady March," Sherlock called down to her. "Do you perchance know how to tie a figure-eight knot?"

"Y—yes," she called up to him as her teeth started to chatter. She was going into shock, but she was still able to focus on what she needed to do.

"You do?" Prospero asked in surprise.

"Yes, I learned from a naval officer who came to the society last year. He instructed us on various styles of knots. The figure-eight is the best knot to lift something heavy, such as a body. But I'm afraid I shall need you to do it for me. I cannot move my left arm."

"Of course. Tell me what to do." Prospero grasped the rope, and she carefully instructed him.

"Now put the rope around you, and Mr. Holmes will be able to pull you up."

Prospero gave her a hard look. Then, without a word, he dropped the rope around her and tightened it.

"But—"

"Hush, wife. You and I can have a long discussion about whose safety matters more once we are safely off this ledge." He checked the strength of his work and then gave a small tug on the rope to test the strength of whatever weighted it on the other end.

"But what about you? You're bleeding! You've been hurt!" Elise protested and reached out, grasping his hand. He leaned forward, still kneeling on the rock ledge, and pressed his forehead against hers and closed his eyes.

"It isn't a deep wound. I'll be up right after you, darling."

"You promise?" A level of hysteria entered her voice that she couldn't help. The pain and fear of the last several minutes was taking its toll. And she knew he was lying about it not being a deep wound in his shoulder—he was so pale, it terrified her.

"I haven't let you down yet, and I have no plans to." He kissed her softly, and for a wild, panicked moment, she was terrified of leaving him alone on the ledge. What if it collapsed and—

Prospero called up the cliff face. "She's ready, Mr. Holmes!"

The rope suddenly tightened, and she was jerked up into the air. She kept her gaze locked on his face as she climbed higher, leaving him behind.

When she reached the top, she saw that Sherlock, Mary, Conley, Mrs. Godwin, and even the young house-maid had all helped pull her to safety. Sherlock leaned forward and grabbed her bad arm to pull her the rest of the way up. She cried out, and he grasped her right instead, pulling her fully up over the side.

"It's . . . dislocated," she told him.

"Ah, I see . . . give me a moment." He removed the rope from her body and then took her bad arm, lifting it and moving it until the shoulder shifted back into place. She whimpered, but the pain suddenly lessened and breathing became easier.

"Better?" Holmes asked as he crouched beside her. His face was lined with weariness, made him look far more human than she'd ever seen him before.

She nodded. "Thank you."

"'Twas a simple technique Watson once showed me."

"Please, help Prospero. I fear that ledge won't hold him forever."

Holmes left her to rejoin the others as they began hauling up her husband. Soon, Prospero's bloody arm appeared over the ledge as he tried to pull himself up over the top, but ultimately he required Holmes to hoist him to safety. Only then did Mary drop her part of the rope and rush over to Elise.

"My poor dear," she cooed, as though Elise were a child who had fallen and scraped her knee. Mary wrapped her arms around Elise, holding her until Prospero was helped to his feet and was able to join them.

His shoulder was bloody, as was his head, but he was walking, moving, and that meant he might be all right. Elise scrambled to her feet with Mary's help, and he took her into his arms.

Prospero held her, stroking his hand down her back. He kissed the top of her head before he let out a slow sigh, and the muscles of his body seemed to lose some of their tension.

"It's over," he said.

She nuzzled his throat with a sense of relief, losing herself in the moment of just being alive with him.

"Lady March . . . ," Sherlock began uncertainly.

His voice made her mind start to work again. She turned to the detective.

"How did you find us? Did you know that Jackson would come after us?"

Holmes's face paled. "A few days ago, I saw him examining an entry in the betting book in Berkeley's. That's when I realized there might be an issue with him."

"Bet? What bet?" Prospero asked.

"Your friend Lord De Courcy placed a wager that the two of you would be married by Christmas. Mr. Jackson read the wager after De Courcy left the room, and his expression warned me that he still held a great resentment toward you, March." Sherlock cleared his throat. "Once I received your wedding invitation, I took it upon myself to tail the man on and off the last few days. Lady March, I'm terribly sorry . . ." Sherlock was uncharacteristically sympathetic in his tone.

She felt a pit of dread forming in her stomach. "Mr. Holmes, what is it?"

"Jackson came searching for you and March the other night. He broke into your home and attacked your servants. Your father fought him off, but he suffered an attack of angina pectoris—an attack of the heart . . . I'm sorry. He's gone."

The rest of Sherlock's words faded as Elise's knees gave out and she sank to the ground.

PROSPERO CAUGHT ELISE AS SHE COLLAPSED AND TRIED to lift her up, but he could barely manage it.

"Let me take her," Conley said. "You've been wounded, my lord. It would only injure you further to carry her back to the cottage. Please."

Prospero reluctantly passed his wife over to the valet. As they began the long walk back to the cottage, he listened to Sherlock explain what had happened, but his focus was still on Elise. She stared straight ahead, unaware of her surroundings. She'd gone into shock.

"Celine Perkins, Jackson's sister, was also at John Hamblin's home and was injured in the fight as well."

That caught Prospero's attention. "Celine was at Hamblin's townhouse?"

Sherlock patted his pockets as if searching for something, possibly his pipe, which Elise had told Prospero he always carried with him; not finding it, Sherlock frowned and continued. "From what I understand, she had hoped to warn you and your wife, but Jackson followed her, suspecting betrayal. Watson stayed behind to see to her and the injured servants. I came straight here. Thank God Jackson did not hide his trail well. The man was more of a Brutus than a Caesar in his thinking. I can only assume he had some silly intention of making your wife's death a murder and yours a suicide."

"He said as much while we fought," Prospero said, his tone grim. "He's mad."

"I agree. In my many years of study, I have come across some men who possess a thirst for pain and violence. Oftentimes, those who are prone to violence or the abuse of others had childhoods or environments that cause them to express themselves with violence, foul as it is. But men like Jackson are born without souls, without the desire to feel anything but the excitement of causing pain to others. It is my belief that such men are not meant to be a part of society. They are dangerous and destructive."

Prospero was relieved when they finally stepped inside the cottage. He wasn't sure he could have walked much farther. He'd lost too much blood and his head felt damned light.

"I shall have a hot bath drawn for you and Elise, my lord," Mary said, then ushered Conley, who still held Elise in his arms, into the master bedchamber.

"I shall be there in a moment, Mary," Prospero said before he turned back to Sherlock. "I trust that you will inform the authorities of what has happened tonight?"

Sherlock nodded. "I will indeed. They may require statements from both you and your wife, but I imagine that can wait until morning. Until then, you need your shoulder examined. I am no doctor, but I am quite familiar with human anatomy and have observed Watson's work on a number of occasions."

Prospero stared at his blood-soaked sleeve. He'd practically forgotten about it in the fight, and afterward his only worries had been for Elise. He pulled his waistcoat and shirt off, wincing at the waves of pain the movement caused. Sherlock called for the housemaid to fetch a bottle of scotch and some cleaning cloths. Prospero held still as the sting of alcohol was placed on his wound and the blood was wiped away. Then Holmes examined the back of Prospero's shoulder.

"Well, the good news is that it went through your shoulder and exited the other side," said Holmes as he applied a bandage. "But it will still take a damned long time to heal. We should have you see a proper doctor as soon as one can be sent for."

Prospero wasn't really listening. His mind kept going back to when he saw Elise falling over the cliff, coming straight toward him, and knowing he had but one chance to save her. The moment played over and over in his mind. What if he hadn't caught her? His hands shook.

"March, you must pull yourself together, for your wife's

sake. You both nearly died tonight, and she's just lost her father. Women are fragile creatures. They—"

"Women are the *farthest* thing from fragile," Prospero growled, though his tone was quiet. "You spend an inordinate amount of time ignoring women because they do not interest you, Mr. Holmes, but I dare you to take a closer look at them. They live beneath our feet, trampled under men's callous desires and baser needs. They are denied autonomy of their bodies and their minds. They carry children within them, and often perish when their bodies break apart by bringing those children into the world. They are told they are weak, that they are foolish, that they are ignorant and do not require education. But it is men who have kept them thus. Still they do not give up. Women take blow after blow and yet they rise. Hope still shines in their eyes as they dream for better lives. I know that I have you to thank for meeting my wife in the first place. A wager regarding whether or not she could come to understand the inner workings of the human male? Perhaps you should take that same wager and take a closer look at the fairer sex you so quickly dismiss.

"So I ask you, Mr. Holmes, what have these events taught you about women and their strength? My wife had a dislocated shoulder. Yet while blinded by that pain, she taught me how to make a figure-eight knot and then insisted that *I* go up the rope before her. These are not the signs of a weak creature, wouldn't you agree?"

Sherlock was quiet, but his stiff shoulders loosened after a moment.

"I suppose you are right, and it is most certainly my fault that this danger came to your door. I should have warned you, but I wasn't certain that what I feared would come to pass. I should have trusted my instincts." He collected his coat and hat. "I will go to the authorities at once to report what has happened and will be present with you tomorrow when you speak to them."

Homes took his leave, and both Conley and Mrs. Godwin came in to fuss over Prospero. It took him a while to reassure them that he was all right. Then he stepped into the master bedchamber to find his wife already in a tub of hot water. Steam rose from the large copper bathing tub. When Mary noticed he'd entered the chamber, she came over to him and, after a quiet discussion, left him to tend to Elise.

Elise sat with her knees pulled up, her injured arm wrapped around herself. Her bare shoulder was dark with the beginnings of bruising, and her hair lay in thick dark-gold ropes down her back. She stared into the distance, lips slightly parted.

He stripped out of his clothes and climbed into the tub behind her. He was tall enough that the water only came up to the middle of his chest, leaving his bandaged shoulder dry. He curled his good arm around her waist, and she flinched at his touch.

"Easy, my love," he said as soothingly as he could.

It was breaking his heart to see her so hurt, inside and out. He examined her swollen left shoulder, as well as the cuts and scrapes over her arms and hands. A bruise was forming on her right cheek, and blood was matted on her temple, even though she'd washed her hair. He wet a cloth and wiped the remaining blood away. She didn't flinch this time, but instead angled her face toward him to let him clean her more easily. As she did so, he saw the fresh tracks of her tears gleaming in the lamplight on her cheeks.

Seeing this beautiful, intelligent, caring woman cry without making a sound . . . Lord, it was killing him. Sherlock was so wrong about women, so very wrong.

So many unsaid words hung on Prospero's lips as he tended her because none held the depth or breadth of what he felt in that moment. To love this woman was to be caught in the twisting winds of a hurricane before he was pulled safely into the eye of the storm, where all was calm with a pure, mysterious peace. She was a force of nature, a thing to love and worship with all his heart. To live without her was to live no life at all.

So he said the only thing that could come close to what he felt, even though it lacked any poetry to it. All that mattered was that it was true.

"I love you."

Only the fire in the hearth with its popping and cracking of logs disturbed the stillness of the room. Then she leaned back against him, her soft breath a reassurance he desperately needed.

"I know." She took one of his hands and pressed a kiss to his bruised knuckles as she had done when they lay side by side on that tiny ledge. "If you hadn't caught me . . ." Her voice wavered.

"But I did." He curled his other arm around her waist. "I will *always* catch you. I know you don't want to think about what will happen once we leave this cottage, but whatever does happen, we will be all right, because we will be together."

Perhaps if he kept saying it, it would come true through sheer will. But the truth was, everything had changed.

John was gone. Certainly, John had believed that he didn't have much time, but to learn that his death had come under such brutal circumstances, and because of Prospero's past . . .

The truth was, Prospero wasn't sure if Elise would ever forgive him for that. He certainly would never be able to forgive himself.

The water began to lose its heat, and it was time to put his wife to bed. He got out of the tub and dried off before he helped her out and wrapped her in a large white cloth, rubbing the water from her skin. She allowed him to drop her nightgown over her head, and then she walked over to their bed, quiet as a lamb, and almost as meek.

He tucked her beneath the sheets, mindful of her injured shoulder, before he joined her. She was asleep even before he settled in beside her. So he held her close as he lay awake, trapped in his own thoughts. He was afraid to sleep, lest he face whatever troubled dreams were waiting for him.

❧ 21 ❧

The world held a gray cast as Elise went through the motions the following morning. A doctor put her arm in a sling, and she was told to keep her movements restricted. The authorities arrived and she gave her statement, along with Prospero, before their return journey to London. She'd stood on the deck of the ship, looking out on the water, her gaze unable to penetrate the layers of blue to see into its depths. All of this had happened, and yet she'd barely been aware of it.

Her father was gone.

Seabirds followed them as they reached the coast and disembarked. Prospero stayed by her side every step of the way to the train station. He spoke little, yet she was relieved. She needed quiet, and he seemed to sense that. He always seemed to know just what she needed.

When the train arrived in London that evening, Mary and Conley were sent on to the townhouse ahead of them. Prospero assisted Elise into a waiting coach, but he didn't give the driver the townhouse address straightaway.

"Do you wish to visit with Cinna and Edwina?" he asked. "Or we could go to the society's headquarters and stay there for a little while . . . until you are ready." His gaze was so full of compassion that tears pricked her eyes. He knew that being in the company of her friends or within the walls of her society would give her comfort.

"Could we go to the headquarters? I don't feel up to explaining to my friends what has happened." She would have to tell them tomorrow, but she couldn't face that situation just yet. It would make her father's death too real, too final.

Prospero gave the driver the society's address on Baker Street, then joined her inside the coach. Elise burrowed against him, resting her head on Prospero's shoulder and taking in his scent as she closed her eyes. He kept his good arm around her shoulders, tucking her into him, making her feel protected and cherished.

The coach stopped at Baker Street, and they climbed out to face the society's headquarters. It seemed fitting to be here now, the place where they'd first met. They walked up the steps together, hand in hand. The butler greeted them and informed them it had been quiet today and they had the house to themselves.

Elise went straight to her study and found the room much the same as when she'd interviewed Prospero. He followed behind her like a silent shadow as she checked on her plants, which had been watered in her absence. The frogs and turtles in their glass aquariums had likewise been fed and were doing well. She moved past the towering bookshelves, her fingers tracing the spines of all the books that had given her so much joy over the years. It was like shaking hands with old friends.

She removed her sling for a moment and picked up the large jar that held the privet hawk moth. It was sitting on top of a flower, its white antennae quivering as it stared up at her. She stared back, marveling at its beautiful wings with two spots that looked like bright blue eyes. It was time for her little friend to be set free. She let out a sigh and walked over to the bay window of her study. Prospero, sensing what she was about to do, opened it for her.

With a wince of pain, she removed the lid from the jar and stood at the window's edge, tilting the jar toward the back garden where a lush world of flowers awaited the moth, but it didn't move. After a moment, Elise reached into the jar and gently cupped the moth in her palm before she lifted it out. Then she opened her palm and leaned in to whisper to the insect.

"There is a wide, wonderful world out there for you. All you must do is spread your wings and fly."

The moth's wings fluttered hesitantly, and then, with one shivering wave of its antennae, it took flight and fluttered its way through the garden until she lost sight of it.

A sob rose in Elise's throat. She turned and pressed herself into Prospero's chest. He wrapped his arms around her, and she cried until she had no strength to move. She was left bone-weary and empty inside.

Her husband tilted her face up to his and brushed away the stray tears still shining upon her cheeks with gentle fingertips.

"Feeling better?"

"It's all rather silly, but yes. I despise crying."

"Why?" he asked.

"Because it makes me feel weak."

"Yes, we are told it is a sign of weakness, aren't we? But

I rather think it's the opposite. You cry because of the wealth of love you had to give to your father and now have no one to receive it. But it takes courage to love and courage to give love to others. Such tears to me are a sign of that strength."

"How do you understand women so well?" It was a question she'd asked him before, yet each time he provided some new answer.

"In France, my livelihood depended on understanding women and what made them happy. But to understand their joys, you must also understand their sorrows. I believe the problem with most men is that they spend so little time with their wives, mothers, or sisters that they never come to understand them or the lives they lead."

She sighed and tucked her face back against his chest. "Well, I am glad you did."

Prospero ushered her to the settee and seated himself with her on his lap. Something furry suddenly jumped up beside them. It was Pallas, the society's resident Pallas cat. His wide, striped face stared at her before he raised a fluffy paw and kneaded her arm and purred. Pallas's green-gold eyes were wide and innocent as he continued to purr.

Prospero chuckled. "Someone is glad to see you."

Elise lifted the hefty ball of fur and settled Pallas upon her. The cat kneaded her lap before settling down and half closing his eyes. The three of them sat for a long time until the lamps burned low. Eventually, Prospero removed the cat, setting him gently on the floor.

"Sorry, old boy, but it's time we head for home." He gave the cat an affectionate stroke on the head.

"Must we leave? Perhaps we could move in here," Elise suggested.

Prospero cupped her cheek and gazed down at her. She saw the hint of laugh lines at the corners of his mouth and eyes. Strange, she'd never noticed that before. How was it that he could find joy in the world when he'd lost so much and been so hurt?

Prospero stroked his thumb along her cheek, his blue eyes burning bright. "Life is full of things that will hurt you. And while many will tell you otherwise, there is but one real cure."

"What cure?" she breathed, unable to tear her gaze away from his.

"Love, my heart—*love*. It pierces every veil of darkness, chases every storm cloud away. It warms those who would perish from the cold. Love keeps our lives moving forward. We may stop upon the path and look back, aching in our hearts for what we once had, but love gives you the strength to face the future. We all lose people we cannot replace, but love gives us the strength to grow around our grief."

Her heart beat faster as he traced her lips with his thumb. "How do you know this?"

A soft smile curved his mouth. "Because loving you kept me moving forward. You cured me of my grief, darling wife. *You*."

"I love you." Worlds could be built upon those three words, perhaps the most powerful words in the vast expanse of time and space.

Prospero winked at her. "I know." Somehow, he always knew what to say, even when he was teasing her to raise her spirits.

He helped her stand, and they left the society's head-quarters. Elise felt sick at the thought of returning home to a world without her father, but Prospero was right. One could stop and look back, but one could never *go* back.

She clutched her husband's arm tight as they climbed the steps to her—no, *their* home. Beyond those doors would be pain and grief, but she could survive it. When the front door opened, Roberts's solemn face met them.

"My lady." He stepped back to let them enter, then bowed to Prospero. "My lord."

Elise saw the dark bruises on the butler's throat. "Roberts! Are you all right?"

"I'm fine, my lady, quite fine. Just a bit bruised." He offered her and Prospero a rare smile. She examined the two footmen in the hall next, both of whom looked as bruised and beaten on the outside as she felt. Adam Jackson had truly been a monster to harm so many people.

"And you? My lady? I was told you and his lordship were attacked."

She nodded at her arm, which was back in its sling.

"And you, my lord?" Roberts asked.

Prospero chuckled. "Just a small wound. It will heal." He patted his bad shoulder gently, but still winced. The dressing was hidden beneath his clothes.

Something niggled at the back of Elise's mind until it clicked into place.

"Roberts, why is the staff not dressed for mourning? They ought to be in black or wearing black armbands. Papa should have—"

"It's all right, darling. Your father left instructions that he did not want anyone to dress for mourning, not even you. No matter how scandalous it might be," Prospero said.

Roberts cleared his throat. "There's something you

THE CARE AND FEEDING OF ROGUES

must both see at once." He turned away without a word and headed upstairs.

Elise followed. Most likely, she was being led to see her father's body lying in repose. It was customary to have people dressed in their burial clothes at their home. Her fingers dug into Prospero's sleeve as Roberts opened the bedchamber door.

"You are not alone," Prospero reassured her, and they stepped into the room together.

She had prepared herself for this moment, but she was not ready for the sight that actually greeted her.

Her father lay on the bed, alive, and the sight made her burst into tears.

"Elise, sweetheart, I cannot possibly look *that* dreadful," her father said, his voice rough. Dr. Watson stood beside the bed, measuring her father's pulse. He lay back in bed, propped on a few pillows, his face pale.

Her heart slammed to a sudden stop as she stared at her father. He was alive. Relief swept through her like a powerful wave, and behind that came a flash of anger that Mr. Holmes had misinformed her. But that fury quickly faded as she saw her father give her a weary smile. That feeling that she couldn't breathe, that she was slowly suffocating, began to ease.

"Good God," Prospero gasped, clutching Elise tight. "John, you're all right!"

Her father gave a raspy chuckle. "Far from it, but I am alive. Welcome back, my boy. I'm sure this is quite a shock for you both."

"Indeed, but a welcome one," Prospero replied.

"Mr. Holmes said you perished." Elise rushed to the bed and threw her arms around her father, uncaring how much pain it caused her shoulder. She just had to touch him, to feel his heartbeat and know he wasn't some dream.

"For a moment, I believed I was," her father said as he held her. "But Dr. Watson worked a miracle." Her father let go of her and then studied her face. "What happened? Mr. Holmes spun some fantastical tale about you being thrown off a cliff by that bastard Jackson." He examined her arm in her sling, and his gaze shifted to Prospero. "And you, lad? Holmes said you'd been shot."

Prospero joined Elise beside the bed and held out a hand to her father.

"Apparently, we are all quite hard to kill. That's two brushes with death I've thankfully walked away from."

Her father shook Prospero's hand. "Well, let's not have a third, eh?" He turned his focus back to Elise. "Did you really fall off the cliff, my child?"

She nodded. "Prospero had already fallen, and I thought that he was dead. But he landed on a ledge about fifteen feet down. When Jackson took me over the cliff with him, Prospero reached out and caught me. That's how I injured my shoulder."

John's gaze turned back to Prospero. "You kept your promise, my boy." His words shook a little.

"He did," Elise said, holding back a sob.

Prospero leaned down to kiss her temple. "And I will keep it every day for the rest of our lives."

"Well now, this is all happy news! Let's have no more crying. Not when—"

John was interrupted by the bedchamber door opening. A woman close to Prospero's age stepped inside the room. Her face was marred by bruises and her lip was cut. She turned bright red when she saw the crowd gathered at Elise's father's bedside.

"Celine?" Prospero said the name with surprise.

"Oh, Prospero!" the woman gasped, her face now ash white.

Prospero's surprise quickly turned to anger. "What the devil are you doing here?"

"Easy, my boy. She saved my life. And yours too."

Celine's gaze dropped to the floor, and Elise had a moment to study her. She was lovely, her elegance understated in a blue-and-white striped bustle gown that had no extra frills or embellishments. So this was Celine Jackson, the woman who'd told her older brothers that Prospero had seduced her. The woman who had set all the events that followed into motion.

"Can I speak to you?" Celine asked Prospero, then glanced at Elise. "Actually, may I speak to both of you?" She stepped outside of the room and waited for them to join her.

Elise exchanged a look with Prospero, whose lips had formed a hard line, but he nodded in silent agreement that they should hear what she had to say.

PROSPERO CLENCHED HIS FISTS AS HE FACED THE WOMAN who had featured in so many of his worst nightmares as the puppet master behind his ruin.

"There will never be enough apologies I can make to you," Celine said. "I was trapped in a terrible situation with my eldest brother and saw no other way to escape him. I thought you could save me if we were married, and telling them you seduced me was the only way I could force you to. I see now how foolish and selfish that decision was. I never thought . . ."

Celine's brown eyes filled with tears, and he couldn't fail to notice how pale she was beneath the bruises on her skin. This was not the woman he'd imagined all these years who had so callously hurt him with her lies. She'd simply been a young woman, desperate to break free of a horrible and dangerous life. He might have done the same had he been in her position.

"After you left for France, I managed to marry, but when my husband died unexpectedly, I was forced to return to Adam's house. Only this time, Aaron wasn't there to step in and protect me from Adam . . ." She began to tremble.

Elise reached out and caught Celine's hand, giving it a gentle squeeze.

"We don't blame you," Elise said. "We know your brother was a monster, but he is gone now. You never have to worry about him again."

If Prospero had not already been madly in love with his wife, he would have been now. To show such compassion and empathy for Celine after all that had happened . . . Elise's heart was even bigger than he had imagined.

"Does your brother's death leave you in a decent financial state?" Prospero asked.

Fear colored Celine's face. "I honestly don't know. I was never allowed to know about such things."

"Never mind that. We will help you," Elise said. "I will send you home with the address of my society's headquarters. We can meet with you and analyze the account books once you find them. I would check your brother's study first. That is where most account books and ledgers are usually kept."

"Your . . . society?" Celine asked in confusion.

"The Society of Rebellious Ladies."

Celine mouthed the words in confusion. "You rebel? Against what?"

Elise grinned. "Against anything and everything that dares to hold women back. We can help you find employment if you need it. We hold weekly meetings where society members instruct others in newly learned skills or topics. Everything from engineering to musical composition to understanding the stock markets."

Celine's eyes grew wide. "Heavens. I've always wanted to learn such things, but Adam said I was nothing but a . . ." She didn't finish. Prospero held in a breath of relief. If she'd dared to say what her brother had called her, he'd want to bring the man back from the dead just to kill him again.

"Good. We will be glad to help you," Elise promised.

Celine turned back to Prospero with a bittersweet smile. "It seems you found her, after all. The woman who is your perfect match."

"It seems I have." He hadn't forgotten that long-ago night in the gardens where he and Celine had spoken of love matches and perfect partners. That had been another life, but she was right. In this new life, he'd been given the gift of that perfect partner in Elise.

"Do you need us to hire a hackney to take you home?" Prospero asked.

"Oh yes, but I came to see Mr. Hamblin first. He was

so brave when he saved me. I wanted to make certain that he's been healing well."

"Of course," Elise said, and Celine hurried back into the bedchamber.

Now alone in the corridor, Prospero pulled Elise into his arms. He swept his gaze over her features, an image he would carry in his soul for the rest of his life.

"Am I truly your perfect match?" Elise asked. Hope burned in her warm brown eyes, and all the years of loneliness and quiet desperation he'd felt for the last several years had faded away the moment he'd met her.

There was only Elise, the woman he loved so much it hurt.

When a person truly gave their heart to another, it was possible not only to catch a glimpse of heaven but to dwell there forevermore. He tucked his fingers under Elise's chin and tilted her head up.

"You are so much more than just a perfect match," he said. "You are my gift from the heavens, the beginning of everything." He lowered his head and covered her lips with his, relishing her soft gasp.

She curled an arm around his neck, and he deepened the kiss, thinking of how marvelous and bright the future would be for the women Elise would inspire in the years to come, and how being husband to a rebel was perhaps the best experience of his life.

She blinked as their lips parted, her soft bedroom eyes giving him wild ideas even though he knew neither of them was quite up yet for anything so vigorous, but he could manage gentle lovemaking easily enough.

A mischievous glint filled her eyes, one that sent a

shiver of desire through his entire body. "I was thinking . . ."

"You know I adore it when you start thinking," he teased.

"Well, once my papers are ready, I was thinking of paying a visit to the Geological Society of London to present my findings on my latest fossils. That means I shall need to sneak into their meeting in disguise. Would you help me?"

He chuckled. "Help you sneak into a male-only meeting of a bunch of grumpy old scientists and have you shock them out of their top hats? I can think of nothing I'd rather do." He tucked her arm in his. "But right now, we have something else to study first, and we must conduct that research thoroughly . . . until we are both quite *useless.*"

EPILOGUE

Elise sat on a blanket at the edge of the back gardens of Marchlands, admiring the wilderness beyond the carefully trimmed hedgerows and neatly tended flower beds. Just then, a pair of deer, a mother and her fawn, wandered out of the nearby glen not twenty feet from where she sat.

Elise tucked her light-blue-and-pink striped gown around her knees as she watched the scene unfold before her. A sketchpad lay on her lap as she drew the mother and fawn from various angles, trying to capture their musculature just right. She would never quite have the skill that Cinna and Edwina possessed. They had far greater talent when it came to replicating what their eyes could see.

Once the deer had vanished back into the trees, blending with the dappled and emerald shadows, she became aware of a presence behind her. She turned to see Prospero approaching. He'd left his coat at the house and wore only his tan trousers, a shirt, and a dark-blue waistcoat. His shirtsleeves were rolled up, exposing his tanned forearms. Her belly quivered in excitement at the sight. She had yet to understand the phenomenon of how a man's bare arms could excite a woman. Perhaps it was because muscled arms promised a strong, able-bodied mate, and the baring of those arms showed that the male was not afraid to do hard work. That would explain part of the attraction, she supposed. She made a mental note for further study on this.

"Your pamphlet has been published, and it's already sold more than a thousand copies!" He reached behind himself to pull out a folded bit of paper. Prospero joined her on the blanket. "I hope you don't mind, but I sent a confirmation to approve the second and third printing should the demand continue, which I believe shall happen." He sat down and leaned back on his elbows and stretched his legs out, crossing them at the ankles.

Elise kissed him on the cheek. "Thank you." She'd grown so accustomed to touching him, to kissing him, to showing her affection in ways she'd never easily managed before. But Prospero was made for a woman's love. He was far too beautiful, too irresistible, not to want to reach out and touch him.

"I'm always happy to assist you, my little naturalist." He winked at her.

She had hoped her instructive pamphlet regarding the nature of men would be somewhat welcome in the secret circles of women in society, but it was beyond all her hopes that it would be selling as well as Prospero had just reported.

"You've done something remarkable," he said to her. "Be proud of it."

"I am. It's just not quite real to me yet."

That was the truth. She'd half expected the publisher to refuse to print the pamphlet, but he had agreed. That had been two months ago. She'd been so busy she'd almost forgotten she was on track to be published in the past month. She'd been working with the society to have lectures on more than just Mondays, and she'd been helping Celine manage her brother's investments so she could take control of her future.

As for Prospero, he'd been busy on something else entirely. Her father had purchased Prospero's ancestral country estate, Marchlands, back from its new owner and gave it to Prospero and Elise as a wedding gift. They had left London for the estate as soon as her father was well enough to travel again.

The heart attack had affected the strength in the left side of her father's body, leaving him with a weakness in his arm and leg, but he'd been improving daily. Dr. Watson had taken a personal interest in the matter and had given him a list of exercises to complete each day to rebuild his strength and coordination. Now he walked with only a slight reliance on a cane.

She'd been so worried about him, but more than once, her father had gotten a strange look in his eyes as he'd stared at the glowing sunbeams coming in from a nearby window. He'd just smile softly and say he'd been told it wasn't time yet. She'd asked who had said that, and he'd merely chuckled and said she wouldn't believe him if he told her. But deep down, Elise somehow knew what her father wouldn't say. She'd been studying science a good portion of her life, but she knew there were things that still could not be explained, things that came from a person's very soul. So she'd asked no more questions, and instead found a strange peace in knowing that when the time did come for her father to leave, he wouldn't be going to that next place alone. Her mother was waiting for him.

Prospero and her father had taken charge of restoring the ancestral estate of Marchlands back to its former glory, a task that had exhausted both men at the end of each day. But Elise had no complaints when her husband collapsed into bed beside her. He would fall asleep instantly each night, but with a smile on his lips. She understood why, of course. He was earning his place in the world just as he'd longed to do. He was proving himself worthy through hard work, and it had given him an immense sense of satisfaction.

In addition to this success, Prospero had impressed her father's business contacts and was now investing, with Elise's agreement, some of their own money into trains and the latest locomotive technology, and the investments were paying them back tenfold in profit. Her husband was a natural businessman, just like her father, which made them quite a pair when they put their heads together and worked on deals. She was proud of him and all that he had accomplished.

Prospero now stared into the woods after the recently departed deer, lost in his own thoughts.

"Where's my father?" Elise asked.

"Pardon? Oh, he's working on the accounts. I've been asked to fetch you for luncheon."

Rather than stand up, he lay flat on his back and folded his arms behind his head, staring up at the sky. Elise set aside her sketches and lay beside him, propping her head in one hand and laying her other palm on his chest. She traced the line of his profile with her eyes, and a deep longing stirred within her. Was it possible to love another person so much that it left an ache so sweet it was hard to breathe?

"Are you happy?" she asked after a moment.

He reached up to thread his fingers through hers, then held her hand against his chest.

"Am I happy?" he asked himself in a philosophical tone. "For a long time, I believed my name to be a curse. Rather than good luck and prosperity, I was doomed to suffer and lose all I held dear. I was wrong. I believe the question, rather, is how could I *not* be happy? Even if I had nothing else, so long as I had you, that would be the only thing that truly mattered to me. I never imagined another being could become one's world, but you are, darling wife." He lifted her hand to his lips and kissed her knuckles. "Now lie here with me and let's find shapes among the clouds."

"What?" She chuckled as he pulled her to lie back down beside him.

"All those who dream must look heavenward," he said, but his face was no longer looking toward the sky but rather toward her.

"You're not looking at the clouds," she said as she looked back at him.

"I am already looking heavenward," he said. He curled an arm around her waist and pulled her a few inches closer until their shoulders touched.

She gazed back into his eyes, seeing the sky reflected in their depths, and that sweet ache in her breast grew only stronger.

"As am I."

Sʜᴇʀʟᴏᴄᴋ Hᴏʟᴍᴇs ᴇɴᴛᴇʀᴇᴅ ʜɪs ғʟᴀᴛ ᴏɴ Bᴀᴋᴇʀ Sᴛʀᴇᴇᴛ and smiled at the sight of Watson resting in his favorite armchair, papers spread out before him as he read.

"A parcel came for you." Watson, who was hidden behind his paper, freed one hand to point at the desk in the corner, which was covered with newspaper clippings and notes. On top of it was a large oblong package.

Under other circumstances, Holmes would have delighted in telling Watson exactly what was inside and who had sent it. The size of the package told him the former, while the penmanship on the address informed the latter.

However, there was one thing he was not certain of, and his own interest in the matter dictated that he open the package immediately. Using a knife to cut away the twine, he removed the brown butcher paper.

As expected, the box contained a violin case, but that was not the question pressing at his mind. He opened the box, and a cursory examination indicated it was indeed *his* violin based on the few scuffs and scrapes he'd given the case over the years. He undid the clasp and opened the case. His instrument rested safely inside with a piece of folded paper tucked between the strings. He slid the paper out and opened it to read.

Mr. Holmes,

I believe this is yours. Seeing as how you were kind enough to introduce me to my wife, albeit through very unconventional means, I thought it only right to return your beloved instrument. I have but one condition. I ask that you do not play it during any hours in which the Society of Rebellious Ladies has its meetings. I understand you play in order to help your mind solve a case, and I respect that. But I expect you to respect my wife and the ladies next door because they also require focus if they are to push the boundaries for ladies everywhere.

Sincerely,

March

HOLMES PLUCKED THE VIOLIN OUT OF THE CASE AND then removed the bow. He checked the tuning and then ran the bow over the strings, feeling the melancholy notes sink into his blood in the most wonderful way. His mind began to work on his current case.

Watson set his paper down. "Oh, they gave it back to you?"

Sherlock set the violin back in its case. "Yes, they have."

It was Monday, and sadly, the society was in session today. At least he would not have to be involved with any more schemes or wagers. He had learned his lesson. Stay well away from intelligent women. His lips twitched. Well, perhaps he would not stay *entirely* away. They were his neighbors, after all.

"I have a meeting with a client in half an hour, Watson. Care to join me?"

"I suppose I should. If I don't come along, I dread to think what mischief you will get up to."

"My dear Watson, I would never seek out mischief. It simply has an irksome tendency to find me," Sherlock said as he fetched Watson's cloak for him, and they left Baker Street.

GUY DE COURCY LOUNGED IN THE DEEP LEATHER armchair of a little pub whose name he'd quite forgotten after his fifth scotch. He had come here tonight hoping to silence the voices in his head, the ones that told him he wasn't good enough.

Faint white scars lined his knuckles and stood out on his skin in the lamplight of the dingy taproom—grotesque reminders of when his father had locked him in the basement cellar for three days without food or water.

He'd only been ten years old then. Christ, he wished he could banish those bleak memories from his mind forever.

Flexing one hand, he studied the marks in the firelight with a cold, emotionless view. They weren't terribly visible, not unless his skin became tan from the sun. But other marks, ones left by a hard rod, had left permanent patterns on his back and upper thighs.

The once noble house of De Courcy had, in his lifetime, become nothing more than a den of vipers. Even his mother hadn't tried to intercede to save him or his little sister. Alyssa had died the same night that he had been locked in the cellar.

Today would've been Alyssa's birthday. She would've been thirty-one years old.

"Another drink, love?" a passing barmaid asked as she held up a bottle of scotch.

"Yes . . . and leave the bottle." He pulled the bottle out of her hand and placed several coins in her palm. The girl's eyes widened, and she quietly pocketed the coins. *Smart girl,* he thought.

Rather than pour himself another glass, he simply drank from the bottle. The lamplight began to glow brighter, the haze of light around each lamp spreading into diamond bursts that stretched across his vision. That was a good sign. He was halfway to his blackout point.

He never should have returned to England, but damned if he'd let Prospero face London society alone. But everything had turned out well for his friend, and he was glad.

Now Guy wondered if perhaps he should just return to France. It would be easy to get lost in that city. And he wanted to be lost.

A man's voice drifted across the room. "Belmont, yes put Cinna Belmont down."

Belmont.

Guy knew that name. *Cinna Belmont.* Stunning eyes filled his head, and he drunkenly smiled. Ah yes, the fine dancer who possessed a tongue sharper than a rapier. He'd enjoyed verbally fencing with her, and he'd enjoyed dancing with her.

"So that's five," another man said. "We should draw lots to see who gets Belmont. Remind me of the stakes?"

"We have a month to seduce our chosen bride. The lucky man who marries first shall be entitled to five thousand pounds from each of the other men once they marry."

"Hold on now—I don't have a damned shilling to my name," another man argued.

"That doesn't matter. Once you marry, the money from your new wife's inheritance will be yours. You can spend it on horses and whores, but first you must pay your due to the winning man."

Grumbling came from the table behind Guy's armchair. His interest had been piqued at Cinna's name, but his mood had soured when he realized in what context these men had been discussing her. Wagering over ruination and seduction? Even he wouldn't stoop so low.

"Any other rules?" a man asked. "Are we to observe the behaviors of *gentlemen*?"

The others burst into laughter at that.

"If you must forcibly bed your chit, then do it. The only rule is that the first man to marry wins."

"But this is unfair. That Belmont bitch is coldhearted. She never attends balls or dinners. How the devil can anyone even get her alone enough to compromise her?"

Guy set the scotch bottle down on the table. So these men had intentions to force women into marriage, possibly rape them? Not while he still had some of his wits left about him.

Guy stood, thankfully still able to walk, and approached the table of men.

"Excuse me," he said dryly as he cut in on their conversation. A piece of paper lay in the middle of the table with five ladies' names in one column, and a second column had been drawn and labeled "Gentlemen."

Ha, these are no gentlemen.

But he noted only four at the table.

"Do you need a fifth man?" he asked with a low chuckle.

The other men, faces he recognized from social engagements, all stared back at him in surprise.

"You want to join us, De Courcy? We were about to throw dice to see who would be stuck with which woman."

"Then allow me to help you at least settle one of them." Guy picked up the pen that lay next to the paper, and he leaned over on the table as he wrote *Guy De Courcy* beside *Cinna Belmont.*

At seeing his name next to Lady Cinna's, a strange flutter rippled through his chest. It would have shocked him more had he been sober, but he was far from that.

"There. Done. So as I understand it, we have a month to seduce and marry them?" he asked. He had every intention of spoiling the plans the men had for the other young ladies involved.

The other men all shared smiles, as if they had tricked him. The fools. He knew Cinna was a prickly pear, but he knew her better than these men ever could.

"The last man to marry or any who fail to marry must pay double to the winner," the leader of these fools said to him.

Ten thousand pounds . . . Lord, that was a bloody queen's ransom.

"Very well," Guy replied with the confidence only a bottle and bad decisions could give a man.

Lady Cinna, I will see you at the altar.

THANK YOU SO MUCH FOR READING *THE CARE AND Feeding of Rogues*! Don't worry, Cinna and Guy will get a story someday soon as will Edwina and Nicholas.

Be sure to follow me on the links below to never miss a new release by following me through all of my social media profiles, my newsletter, private reader group and more by visiting www.laurensmithbook s.com where you can find all of my links!

Or join my Patreon to receive exclusive advance full chapter previews each month, new ebook releases, new print book releases, new audiobook releases and special exclusive merchandise!

If you loved this book! Please leave a star rating or a review on whatever app or device on! It helps other readers find my books!

ABOUT THE AUTHOR

Lauren Smith is an Oklahoma attorney by day, author by night who pens adventurous and edgy romance stories by the light of her smart phone flashlight app. She knew she was destined to be a romance writer when she attempted to re-write the entire *Titanic* movie just to save Jack from drowning. Connecting with readers by writing emotionally moving, realistic and sexy romances no matter what time period is her passion. She's won multiple awards in several romance subgenres including: New England Reader's Choice Awards, Greater Detroit BookSeller's Best Awards, and a Semi-Finalist award for the Mary Wollstonecraft Shelley Award.

To connect with Lauren visit her at:
www.laurensmithbooks.com
lauren@laurensmithbooks.com

facebook.com/LaurenDianaSmith

x.com/LSmithAuthor

instagram.com/laurensmithbooks

bookbub.com/authors/lauren-smith

patreon.com/LSandECBooks

tiktok.com/@laurenandemmabooks

Made in the USA
Middletown, DE
18 September 2024

60557109R00241